Mistletoe and Mofongo

The Saucy Chef Series Book One

Lyra Blake

Blake Publishing

This novel's story and characters are fictitious. Certain long-standing institutions and agencies are mentioned, but the characters involved are wholly figments of the author's sometimes questionable imagination.

Contents

To all my kindred spirits who secretly (or unashamedly) binge sappy holiday romance and believe food is love.

Content Information

This novel contains mentions of parental loss and the loss of loved ones.
It also includes divorce.
Some people with certain convictions may consider it to contain cheating,
but I did not intend that in my writing, as spousal abandonment happened before any subsequent relationship.

Chapter One

Home is wherever your family is.

Family is whatever you make it.

For me, it was a coffee shop in Portland, shooting the shit with the three Rivera brothers. I leaned back against the brown leather couch, resting my cup of spiced coffee on my knee as I basked in the antics of the closest thing I had to my brothers.

"You don't understand," Gabriel was saying, nearly spilling the hot drink he held as he used his hands for emphasis. His dark brows raised, giving his sharp features a comical look. "She managed to disassemble the tablet and put it back together. She's a genius."

Xander chuckled. "I thought you said she shattered the screen."

"That's beside the point." Gabriel waved it off.

"I think that might very much *be* the point," Julian added with a laugh. All the brothers had similar features, dark hair, and strong bone structure. They were taller than me, but I'd fit right in between

Gabriel and Xander with their varying skin tones. We were all Puerto Rican, friends since we were younger. They'd known my *Abuelita* and adopted me into their large family after she passed. Julian had been integral in the success of my business. His marketing strategy was gold.

Gabriel scowled at his brothers. "If it were your kids, you'd think the same as me. She's a genius for a toddler."

"I think they're all geniuses," I said with a smile. "But I do love how much little Adrian takes after me in the kitchen."

Julian choked on his coffee at the mention of his toddler son. "He cracked a dozen eggs behind the couch."

"Budding talent at its best," I said with a straight face. "Let them learn to love food at a young age. Carry on the family traditions."

Xander smoothed a hand over his perfectly styled, nearly black hair. "And here I thought the family tradition was marketing."

The rest of us chuckled when he realized he'd left out his profession as a corporate lawyer. He didn't try to correct himself, just shook his head and took another sip of his coffee, then smoothly changed the subject. "I heard your sous chef left."

"Yes." I nodded, bouncing my foot. I wouldn't say I liked staff turnover, but it was inevitable in the restaurant industry. Few made their careers at one establishment. "His wife wanted to move back to her hometown before their baby was born, and he landed a job as head chef at a restaurant there. I'm happy for them. It just leaves me in the lurch for our holiday season."

I liked celebrating major holidays at my restaurant, *El Corazón Boriкén*. I'd take any excuse to spread joy and merriment. That meant planning activities that benefited the community. It was much easier to do with a partner. Typically, my sous chef would play that role and act as head chef when I traveled to my other restaurant locations. That happened less now that I felt more settled in Portland near those I considered family.

"Are you doing interviews?" Gabriel asked. "I could see if any of my contacts would be interested."

The youngest Rivera brother was an ace at negotiating and securing acquisitions. I had no doubt that he'd find me the best, but I tried not to burn bridges in the industry if I could avoid it.

I nodded. "Yes, but I'm not looking to poach from another restaurant. I have a few interviews lined up in the next couple of weeks. Manuel doesn't leave town until the end of the month, and he's willing to help train his replacement."

"Fair enough," Gabriel conceded. "If you change your mind, just let me know."

"Will do." I looked around at my friends, thankful to have men like them in my life.

We were an odd group, with Julian and Xander dressed in expensive suits and Gabriel and me in running clothes. The elder Riveras were heading to the office after coffee, but Gabriel and I had gone for a run before our weekly meeting. I knew they only did it for my benefit because they were together every day at the office. They didn't need to meet in a coffee shop every Monday morning. They knew it was my day off and made time to see me.

Wednesday through Sunday, I was dedicated to my restaurant, working most of the days either cooking or giving attention to things that needed to be done at my other locations. My managers usually handled business, but as the owner, I was inevitably tapped to put out fires when necessary. It helped that I was careful about my selection process for employees. There were rarely issues with how the restaurants were run. I tried to spend as much time as possible in the kitchen doing what I loved.

I also had a healthy social media following with verified accounts and people who loved the positivity I tried to spread in my videos. Back when I had only one restaurant location in Miami, I started making little videos around the kitchen. Nothing fancy, just me cooking and talking. It was still sometimes surreal to think that millions of people wanted to watch me, but after the first videos went viral, I realized I'd been blessed with a platform to reach more people than I'd ever imagined. I started using it to uplift others and raise money for charities. Now it was part of my day, a way to connect with others worldwide.

"Everybody smile and wave," I said as I pulled out my phone and took a quick video of our little group sitting on the couches drinking our morning coffee. The brothers indulged me, hamming it up for the camera. They were used to the spotlight as billionaire moguls at their company, Atabey Industries. I looked into the camera and spoke. "Remember, family isn't always blood. It's the people who stick with you through all the shit life throws at you. Pick yours wisely, and love them with everything you have."

It didn't take long to edit the clip and post it to my social media accounts. The brothers continued chatting, and I was content to listen to their banter. I'd always wanted a large family. Someday, I hoped to create my own, but so far, I hadn't met anybody who made me want to put my mother's ring on their finger.

"Are you done using us for clout?" Julian smirked when I looked up at him.

"Yeah, because I need you for followers," I volleyed back. "When's the last time you cooked something? If I remember correctly, you called me to cook for your wife when your charm didn't work."

Gabriel smacked Julian on the shoulder and laughed. "You're never going to hear the end of that one."

"I feel no shame." Julian rotated the ring on his left hand. "It got me the girl, didn't it? Worth it."

"Can't argue with that," I admitted. I brought my coffee cup to my lips, only to realize it was empty. I frowned and glanced at my friends, holding my cup up. "I'm going to get a refill."

I made my way through the Monday morning crowd to the front counter and waited patiently while a curvy blonde tapped her chin, contemplating her order. It wasn't a hardship, given the view from behind, with her light blue jeans hugging her hips. She wore a pink sweater that screamed money, but I could see the darker blonde roots of her hair like she hadn't been to a salon in a while, and her white sneakers were worn.

"It's not life or death. It's just coffee," the businesswoman behind me muttered loud enough for the blonde to hear. Her shoulders stiffened, but she didn't turn around at the jab.

"Ma'am?" the barista implored, raising her brows.

"Sorry," the blonde muttered in a soft, melodic voice. "I'll just have the spiced coffee. As big as you can make it."

The barista gave the blonde the total, and the blonde reluctantly handed over a credit card. I saw her shoot a look at where another barista was adding whipped cream, caramel, and nutmeg to the top of somebody's coffee. Could she not afford the drink she wanted?

I didn't have time to ask because she moved off to the side, and it was my turn. "Another spiced coffee. The works."

"Coming right up, sir." The barista smiled.

"Is she a regular?" I asked quietly, tipping my head toward the blonde as I pulled my wallet from my pocket.

"Yeah," the barista confirmed as she took my card.

"I take it that wasn't her usual order," I surmised, receiving a nod in return. "Put her regular order on my card, then."

The barista nodded and told me my new total. I signed the receipt and slid my card back into my wallet as I moved to wait for my order. The blonde stood with her arms wrapped protectively around her middle, her rosy lips pursed slightly, making her face look drawn. Something about her countenance made me want to cheer her up.

"Mondays, huh?" I said lightly, rocking on the soles of my running shoes.

"What?" The blonde whipped her head in my direction, and I raised my eyebrows as I waited for her to answer. Color bloomed across her cheeks as her lashes lowered over stunning blue eyes. "Uh, yeah. Sure."

"Don't worry. Coffee makes everything better," I offered.

She gave me the side eye, and I caught her muttering under her breath, "Not everything."

It was a shame such a beautiful woman was so disagreeable. She was no less deserving of happiness than the rest of us.

I decided to try to talk to her again. It couldn't hurt. "Headed to work?"

The look she shot me told me she thought I was an idiot or a creeper. She lifted her chin slightly. "No."

"Coffee for Macy!" the barista called out, setting the spiced hot brew on the counter. The blonde swiped it up.

"Wait a minute. Macy?" I stepped to the side so she wouldn't leave, and her eyes widened in alarm. Behind her, the barista placed an iced drink on the counter next to the coffee I ordered. "I think you're forgetting something."

"I don't think so," Macy snapped, absently pressing the cup's lid to her lips. In that split second, I realized she was distracted and usually drank iced coffee. She wasn't thinking about the blazing hot brew in her cup.

"I wouldn't do that," I warned. "It's hot."

Too late.

With a glare, Macy sucked the coffee into her mouth, and I saw the moment she registered the temperature. Her face reddened, and a spray of hot caffeinated mist spewed from her lips and all over my white t-shirt, marring the pristine fabric with tan splotches.

"Oh, shit!" She fanned her mouth and looked mortified as she took in my shirt. "I'm so sorry!"

"It's okay," I reassured her, holding the bottom of my shirt away from my body to survey the damage. "I needed a shower. I hear caffeinated spa treatments are all the rage, anyway."

She snorted adorably before pressing her lips firmly together. "I'm sorry, I shouldn't laugh. This isn't funny."

"No, it's not." I reached around her and grabbed my order, handing her the iced coffee. "I was trying to tell you I'd ordered your usual. Now, I guess you can use it to soothe that burned tongue."

The thought of her tongue did something to me, and I felt my cock twitch slightly at how she might be able to use it in a more pleasurable way. No. Not okay to fantasize about random coffee shop women.

"Um, thanks." She took the cup and sighed as she sipped on the chilled brew. "I'll pay for your shirt if it's ruined."

I held my free hand up. "No need. I'm sure it'll be fine after a little stain remover."

"I insist." Macy turned to reach for her purse that hung at her side, but she didn't see the businesswoman behind her.

"Watch it!" I warned.

I couldn't say for sure, but I was pretty sure the dark-haired woman in the suit pushed Macy away before they could collide. I watched in what seemed like slow motion as the hot coffee dropped from Macy's hand as she cried out, keeping her footing.

I jumped back but wasn't fast enough to avoid the coffee staining my grey joggers. The businesswoman huffed and pushed her way past us and out of the store, seemingly indifferent to the havoc she'd wreaked.

Macy stood there like a statue, her hand covering her mouth as she took in my soiled appearance.

I offered her a little grin and shrugged. "It's a Monday."

I thought I heard another sound, but she hid it well behind her palm. Finally, she took a deep breath and dropped her hand, frowning. "You have to let me give you something to replace the clothes. I feel awful."

"Don't feel bad." I took a sip of my coffee and nodded at the barista, who approached us with a couple of wet rags. "That could have happened to anybody. I've had worse stains on my clothes. Blood is more difficult to get out."

Both the barista and Macy looked at me strangely, and I realized how it had sounded. "I'm a chef. Blood from animals."

That seemed to pacify them. The barista tossed one of the rags on the floor, and Macy bent to help clean up her coffee, ignoring the barista's insistence that she didn't need to do that. Her blonde hair covered her face like a curtain as she cleaned my sneakers. It was odd to have her on her knees before me, but those thoughts about her mouth flared to life again.

Then she lifted her head, and there was no mistaking her noticing the bulge in my joggers. Her mouth opened in a little O, and my breath caught in my chest. My cock twitched, and she jumped, breaking out of whatever thoughts she was having and quickly backing away after making sure nobody was behind her. The barista took the rags and told us to watch out for the damp floor.

Macy kept her eyes squarely on my face and cleared her throat. "I—"

"Don't try to give me money again," I admonished. There were no rings on the fingers of her left hand as she gripped the iced coffee. Maybe I was insane, but it seemed like a good time as any to shoot my shot. "I'd take your number, though. Social media?"

Her eyes narrowed, and those plump lips pursed, bringing back the slightly sad look on her face. "I–I don't think so. I'm sorry about your clothes."

I turned as Macy brushed past me and rushed out the door before I could say anything else, keeping her head straight ahead.

"Smooth," Gabriel said from my left. The brothers had approached from behind and had caught our little exchange.

"You can't win them all." I sighed, disappointed that she'd run off. I couldn't blame her. Imagine telling grandkids you'd met their grandfather when you covered him in your coffee.

I looked at my damp clothes and chuckled to myself.

Chapter Two

I HATED MONDAYS.

And people.

To be fair, I hated most days. And most people.

Others went out of their way to avoid me as I trudged back to the condo I shared with my best friend, Leo. I knew I gave off a negative vibe with my perpetual resting bitch face, but I didn't care anymore.

I'd once been a relatively happy person—perhaps even cheerful. I had plenty of friends, was happily married to my high school sweetheart Ethan, and I'd been looking forward to starting a family.

That all changed a little over a year ago when I came home from the spa to find the house I shared with my husband empty and a hastily scrawled note on my bedside table explaining that he wasn't interested in being married to me any longer, and he was leaving. He didn't offer any insight regarding his sudden decision.

I did what any woman in my position would do—I called his phone repeatedly, only to discover he'd disconnected the number later that day. Then I curled up in my empty bed and cried for two days. After not hearing from me, Leo used her spare key and broke into my house, finding me at what I thought was my all-time low.

Funny how things can get even worse than you think. Leo dragged me out to a bar, and when I went to pay my tab, all of my cards were declined. She covered the drinks and followed me home, where I logged into the bank accounts I shared with my husband, only to find them empty. Not only had he left me, but he'd left me penniless, canceling my credit cards and taking all of our money.

Ungrateful asshole. I'd worked my ass off to help put him through college, working at two different diners as a server, then moving up to a nicer restaurant as a line cook. It didn't bother me at the time; I wanted my husband to reach his full potential, and I was happy in the kitchen. Part of me felt immense pressure from my mother to succeed where she'd failed at marriage. Though, now, I didn't believe she'd failed. My father had been faithless, and my mother took the blame that was his to bear.

Just like me.

For a year, I'd waited and hoped Ethan would return on his own. I'd been too ashamed and afraid to let people know I'd been such a poor wife that my husband left me. My background in the service industry came in handy, and I was able to get a job as a server downtown. I moved out of the house when I received the foreclosure notice, and Leo and I moved in together.

Finally, Leo managed to break through my belief that I was responsible for Ethan's actions, and she convinced me to file for divorce, if only to avoid being held responsible for Ethan's debts. I'd reluctantly filed, but it was taking some time because nobody could find Ethan. The judge said he would finalize the divorce before the new year, regardless of whether my estranged husband could be located.

I opened the little picket fence that blocked the path to the condo Leo and I rented after Ethan left and found the door unlocked. It was a cute little row of condos, all smushed together and painted to fit in with the historic homes in the neighborhood.

"Leo! I'm back!" I called out as I toed my sneakers off in the entry.

I heard her steps before she came barreling around the corner, a spatula in hand. Leo was petite to my curvy and had black hair to my blonde. Her green eyes glimmered with mischief. "Come on. I'm making pancakes!"

"I should just marry you," I joked as I followed her into the small kitchen and leaned against the white quartz countertop. The condo was simple, everything in shades of white and grey that was nearly white. It made the tight space seem bigger than it was.

She laughed and shimmied her hips. "Baby, you can't handle all this."

She flipped a pancake, and I burst into a fit of giggles. "Leo, those are penis pancakes."

"I know!" she said slyly. "And we're going to enjoy decimating each and every one of these dicks. Pretend they're Ethan."

I raised a brow at her.

"Or not," she amended, her face twisting in disgust. "I don't want to think of putting his pathetic dick in my mouth. No specific dicks. Just generalized representation of the oppressive patriarchy."

"I can get behind that," I agreed, pulling plates out of the cupboard and setting them on the counter next to the stove. Leo piled pancakes onto our plates while I found forks and napkins. We weren't picky about using the dining table, so we stood at the counter to eat.

"Oh, I almost forgot!" Leo bounced away and brought back a bottle, pouring the contents over our breakfast. "Marionberry syrup."

"Makes it look a little graphic, don't you think?" I asked drolly, watching the reddish-purple syrup drip down the side of the stack.

Leo nodded and shoved a bite of pancake in her mouth, moaning in approval. "The best kind. If dicks tasted like this, I might not hate all men so much."

I rolled my eyes and dug in, making quick work of the phallic breakfast. "I'm sure there's a fanfic with pancake penises and syrup fluids somewhere."

"No thanks." Leo's nose scrunched up. "I'm good with the inanimate breakfast. How was the coffee shop?"

I sighed and shook my head, remembering the debacle. "Well, a handsome man tried to be nice, and I spit coffee all over him."

"What?" Leo held her fork suspended, mouth hanging open. "I'm guessing it wasn't something consensual and kinky."

"Definitely not," I confirmed, focusing on cutting my next bite. "Then somebody bumped into me, and I dropped the coffee, getting his pants. It wasn't my finest moment."

Leo covered her laugh with her palm. "I'm sorry. But it's kind of funny. What did he do?"

"Told me he wouldn't let me compensate him for it," I said, remembering how his dark brown eyes had shone with humor. "He bought me a coffee and asked for my number."

"Oh shit! You got a date after that?" She held her hand up to high five, but I shook my head until she dropped it back to the counter.

"Not exactly." I looked away, dropping my fork to my empty plate and running my hand through my hair before turning back to her. "I panicked and ran out of there."

"You just left the attractive man who was interested in you?"

"Yeah. What kind of guy even does that?" I waved my hands in the air. "How would I ever live that down? I never want to hear the phrase 'spit on me like the first time we met' in bed, so it wouldn't have worked, anyway."

"Okay, you have a point, I guess." Leo took our empty plates, rinsed them off, and then loaded the dishwasher. "Look at the bright side—it means we can still create chaos at the bar together."

"I don't think I've ever been accused of creating chaos anywhere." I'd always been the good girl, the good student, the good wife. Reliable. *Boring*.

"That's okay. You're not a dog, even if you're a bitch sometimes." Leo snickered. "You can still learn new tricks."

"I love it when you get romantic," I said drily.

"You're going to love me even more when I tell you the news," she said, crossing her hands over her heart in an exaggerated beating motion.

"I'm not sure that's possible."

A wide grin spread across Leo's face. "I got you an interview at the restaurant."

"I was wrong," I admitted, hugging her tightly. She worked as a server at a popular restaurant downtown and made more than I ever had. "I do love you more. Thank you!"

She planted a kiss on my cheek and squeezed me back. It was the most action I'd gotten in a year. "You deserve it. I have a good feeling about this. Imagine it; you as a chef at an exclusive restaurant!"

My chest tightened with nerves. Things that seemed too good to be true often were. Like my marriage. "We'll see. When is the interview?"

"Wednesday morning." She popped a pod into the coffee maker and set her mug underneath, pressing the start button. "That gives you two whole days to panic and pull yourself together. You got this."

Her faith in me was more than I could offer myself.

***

My palms were damp, and my heart nearly beat out of my chest as I reached for the handle on the front door of *El Corazón Borikén*. I stepped into the colorful restaurant that reflected the owner's homeland. The dining room looked typical for a fine restaurant with the black cloth-covered tables and perfect place settings, but it was somehow more alive with the bright, primary colors splashed across the walls in paint and art.

I didn't see anybody, so I called, "Hello?"

No response. I wondered if I'd somehow gotten the time wrong. My chest tightened with anxiety—another fun result of my husband abandoning me. I was petrified of doing the wrong thing and the embarrassment that followed.

I'd just turned to leave when a familiar, cheerful, accented voice called out behind me, "Good morning!"

I closed my eyes and pressed my lips into a thin line, cursing the universe for my luck. Slowly, I turned to face the same man from the coffee shop on Monday. Only, this time, instead of running gear, he wore black slacks and a pristine white chef's coat, the white cravat artfully ringing his neck. It was striking against his tanned skin and black hair. His dark brown eyes exuded warmth and mischief. *Matteo Gonzalez* was scrawled in white across the right side of the coat. I'd spat all over the head chef of a Michelin-starred restaurant.

He grinned at me knowingly, and I tried desperately to keep a straight face instead of breaking down at my bad luck.

"Macy, right?" he asked, stopping in front of me and holding his hand out. I rubbed my sweaty palm down my black pants and placed it in his, feeling a tingling sensation spread out from where his warm skin met mine. "How's your tongue feel?"

Without thinking, I ran my tongue across my lips as I stared at his mouth and wondered what his tongue would feel like against mine. Wait, he'd asked me something. "My tongue?"

"Yeah, the burn," he clarified, that annoying grin still plastered on his face.

"Oh, it's fine. Feels good." I blinked slowly, realizing how inappropriate our conversation sounded.

Matteo cleared his throat and dropped my hand, seemingly reaching the same conclusion. "Well, that's good."

"How are your clothes?" I asked in return. "Were they salvageable?"

He chuckled, and I relaxed a fraction. "They're fine. Let me introduce myself now that we've got that out of the way. I'm Matteo, and this is my restaurant. It's nice to officially meet you, Macy."

"Likewise," I lied. Could I turn around and walk away? What if he asked Leo about me? My friend would probably throw me under the bus if she thought it would be for my own good. *Shit.*

"Leo told my manager, Araceli, good things about you," he said congenially. "Why don't you follow me back to my office? The others will be here soon, and things are quieter back there."

I trailed behind Matteo, absolutely not glancing down at his muscular ass when his chef's coat shifted as we walked to his office. It was styled like the dining room—no stark white walls. The furniture and the walls were black, with colorful artwork and photographs of Matteo in his restaurants and in locations worldwide. He was smiling in every photo and always surrounded by people.

"Have a seat." Matteo pointed to the chair across from his desk as he sat behind his desk and leaned his forearms on his desk. "Why don't you tell me a little about your industry experience."

I pulled my neatly folded resume from my purse and slid it across the desk. "Here's my resume. I've worked in various capacities at several restaurants over the years, most recently as a line cook."

"I see." He glanced down at the papers, but his face didn't betray what he was thinking. "And why do you want to work at *El Corazón Boriken?*"

My face heated as I drew a blank. I was used to showing up and handing my resume over without much thought. How much of my story was I supposed to give him? "I—"

"You can admit it's because of the money." Matteo chuckled and folded his hands, tapping his first fingers on the desk. "That's a driving factor for most people."

"Well, yes, of course, that's a big part of it," I agreed. My thoughts became jumbled, and I spewed words at my prospective employer, much like I had the coffee. "I don't know what the right answer is here. I love food. I love cooking. Talking isn't one of my strengths."

"Don't worry about saying what's right." Matteo's voice was kind, like somebody talking to a wounded animal. I cringed internally at my reference. "I'd rather know how you feel."

I choked on my saliva, my mind instantly slipping off the sidewalk of sanity and straight into the gutter. What was wrong with me?

"Do you need some water?" Matteo broke through my thoughts. "You look a little flushed."

"N−no, I'm okay, thanks." I recovered and smoothed my hands down the front of my cream blouse. Matteo's eyes followed, then snapped back to my face.

"Let's tour the kitchen," he suggested, standing suddenly and walking to the door, holding it open from me. It was more of a demand, and I pushed myself out of the chair and closed my purse as I walked through the doorway, pausing to let Matteo lead the way to the kitchen.

When he pushed through the doors, my mouth dropped open. It was like a cook's wet dream, everything pristine in white and brushed chrome. The organization was impeccable. I forced myself to focus on Matteo's explanation of the various areas of the kitchen, answering the occasional question about my experience with certain things.

I'd never leave a job if I got to work at a place like *El Corazón Borikén*. I turned back, getting one last look at the kitchen I'd probably never set foot in after the disaster that was my interview.

"Thanks for coming in today, Macy," Matteo said professionally. He didn't offer his hand this time but wore that same smile. I wasn't sure whether I wanted to wipe it off his face or let it reassure me.

"Thank you for your time," I replied automatically.

"Somebody will contact you within a week," he explained, holding the door open for me. I could take a hint. "Have a nice day."

"You, too," I said over my shoulder as I left. My heart dropped as I turned and walked down the street to catch the MAX, Portland's light rail. I fought back the tears of disappointment, telling myself it was doomed from the start. I'd survived worse letdowns.

Chapter Three

I MADE MY USUAL trip to meet the Rivera brothers at the coffee shop on Monday morning. They could tell I was quieter than usual, but I couldn't bring myself to tell them about Macy's second interview later in the day. Instead, I'd shifted the conversation to their wives and children, taking the heat off me. I felt a little guilty, but they'd no doubt find out about Macy soon enough if she passed the practical part of the upcoming interview.

I jogged from the coffee shop back to my apartment in the building Julian owned and hopped in the shower to wash the workout from my body. Macy's interview was in a little over an hour, leaving me enough time to get dressed and drive to *El Corazón Borikén*.

The hot water poured down on me, and I sighed, leaning against the white tile wall. I wasn't typically plagued by thoughts of the people I wanted to help, but the curvy blonde was firmly ingrained in my brain.

I'd interviewed five candidates for the position of my sous chef, three of whom were qualified. So why had I stared at Macy's resume as I sat in my office after closing on Saturday night? She wasn't the most experienced and had no formal culinary schooling. Her name should have been off my list immediately, but I couldn't let her go.

She'd managed to look so effortlessly beautiful, yet at the same time, her eyes betrayed a deep sadness. I wanted to see those baby blues shine like the sea off the coast of Puerto Rico. She'd been in awe of my kitchen, the first sign of life she'd shown since the interview started.

I wanted to put that look back on her face. My friends would say I had a bad habit of picking people and making them into projects, but I couldn't help it. A part of me felt a responsibility to make the rest of humanity see the positives in life. Everybody deserved to smile again.

So, as much as logic told me to choose the man who went to a prestigious culinary school and had worked in another Michelin-starred restaurant, my heart overrode reason. I'd roughly tugged the knot on my cravat, slipped the black cotton fabric from my throat, and tossed it to my desk before typing out a quick email to Araceli and asking her to call Macy in for another interview.

Only time would tell if that was a mistake.

***

I arrived at El Corazón Borikén just before ten and took my time dressing and getting the kitchen set up. There was something about being the first person in the restaurant; it was a privilege I never took for granted. The quiet, just me and the equipment, everything cold and clean, just waiting for me to create.

Food is art, a consumable bit of beauty, more fleeting than the great works hanging on walls in museums but no less important. After all, food was a necessity for survival. Since the beginning of time, people have eaten and found ways to improve what they put in their mouths.

To be able to share what I created with others was special. I lived for that moment when somebody took their first bite of something I'd made, that breath of silence as they experienced the explosion of flavor, felt the texture, the love that went into the preparation.

It was popular to be a foodie. There was no shortage of budding critics who lived to give their opinions. I supported people doing whatever they wanted, but I much preferred the average person who had no idea what they were doing with food. Their discovery of something new was always a joy for me. I looked for staff who appreciated experiencing food—they were the best at connecting with the customers.

I had no problem admitting that I was sentimental regarding my profession, and I did my damndest to spread my passion wherever I went. Having four restaurant locations was more than I'd ever dreamed for myself, and if my parents and *Abuelita* could see my accomplishments, they would no doubt smile with pride.

The tune I whistled as I began pulling out ingredients echoed through the empty space. I contemplated making Macy find everything on the list, but I didn't want to push her too far and scare her away. It showed mettle that she stayed for the interview even after realizing who I was.

By the time I'd finished, three bowls filled with fresh ingredients sat in a row on the metal prep table, with the recipe neatly placed before them. I nodded my approval and washed my hands. A light knock on the kitchen door signaled Macy's arrival, and I turned just as she entered.

"Good morning," I greeted her with a smile and open arms. I wouldn't actually hug her. That wouldn't be appropriate for her culturally. Most of my employees were used to the more affectionate nature of those of us who grew up in Latinx families.

"Morning," she replied cautiously, looking around. She was adorable in her black slacks and white collared button-up; no doubt her uniform when she was a server. Her blonde hair was pulled back in a bun, and she wore sensible clogs on her feet. "Is it just us?"

"The restaurant is closed today," I confirmed. "I thought it would be easier if there weren't a bunch of the typical kitchen racket. I'm going to test your chops."

Her eyes widened slightly in surprise, but she quickly schooled her features and nodded. "Makes sense. Where do you want me to start?"

I motioned toward the prep table. "I've set everything out for you. Go ahead and look over the recipe while I grab you an apron."

Macy hastily approached the prep area, leaning over and bracing her left forearm on the table while using her finger to trace the recipe as she read. Her hip cocked out to the side, drawing my attention to her perfect, heart-shaped ass and thick thighs. I swore I would remain professional, so I spun away from the temptation and took deep, centering breaths as I found a spare black apron.

Fuck me; she was biting her lip when I returned. My heart raced in response. A single woman shouldn't be able to have that kind of effect on me.

"Here." I offered Macy the apron, but instead of handing it over like an average person, I moved behind her and slipped it around her waist. She drew a quick breath but said nothing. While she centered the apron, I tugged the strings at the waist and folded the material so it fit properly before tying a bow in the back. I momentarily let my fingers linger there, savoring the body heat radiating through her white shirt. Her scent was floral and subtle, likely expensive.

"Th–thanks," Macy mumbled, pulling away from me.

She didn't glance back as she surveyed the kitchen and found cutting boards, knives, and bowls. I demanded meticulous organization in the kitchen; it made for a more productive working environment when nobody was searching aimlessly for things. I crossed my arms and leaned against the end of the table, watching as Macy worked.

"Have you made *sofrito* before?" I asked, making small talk. I could have sworn Macy side-eyed me disapprovingly before setting her knife down.

"No," she answered shortly. "At least not like this. The one on the menu at the Mediterranean restaurant was tomato-based."

I nodded and opened my mouth to respond when my phone rang in my pocket. Macy's lips pursed as she resumed finely mincing the peppers. "Give me just a minute. I need to take this."

Gabriel's name flashed across the screen when I pulled my phone out. I pushed through the kitchen doors and swiped to answer. "What's up?"

"Olivia and I are stopping by," he said cheerfully. "I saw your car out back, and you know how she loves any excuse to see her uncle."

"This isn't the best time." I froze, looking toward the front door and seeing Gabriel's figure beyond the glass. He was still in a suit, so he must have come from work. His wife, Jane, sometimes worked from home with their younger daughter Luciana. Little Olivia was perched on his shoulders, waving her hands in the air.

Gabriel chuckled and rapped his knuckles on the glass. "Don't worry; we won't take much of your time."

"It's unlocked." I wasn't sure I wanted to unleash Gabriel on Macy. He would no doubt remember her from the coffee shop incident. If I kept him in the entry or back in my office, he might not even know she was in the kitchen. That would have to do.

Gabriel pushed the door open, setting Olivia down so she could toddle her way to me as I walked to greet them. "*Tio* 'Teo!"

I swooped the toddler into my arms, smiling at the dark-haired cherub. She was the perfect combination of her mother and father, but her more delicate features and hazel eyes were all Jane. "*Pequeña mirlo!*"

"Make me fly!" She flapped her arms and squealed when I turned her in a circle, making her fly like a blackbird—her nickname. Her father and I chuckled at the squawking noises she made before I set her back on her feet. "Kitchen! Sweets!"

21

Before I could stop her, Olivia was off like a shot, heading straight toward the doors. Her tiny stature didn't stop the door from swinging when she hit it full-force and disappeared from view. That's what I got for keeping treats on hand for my adopted nieces and nephew.

Gabriel loosened his tie as he strode past me and called over his shoulder, "Don't worry, I'll get her."

So much for keeping him from seeing Macy. I hurried after him, stopping just inside the door next to Gabriel, watching as Macy knelt before Olivia, smiling and talking on the little girl's level.

As Olivia pointed to Macy's apron and asked question after question, Gabriel tilted his head thoughtfully. His eyes widened with recognition before he turned to me with a grin, brows raised. "Hey, isn't that the girl from—"

"Say anything, and I'll eighty-six you from all of my restaurants," I threatened low enough that Macy wouldn't hear.

"It's like that, huh?" Gabriel ran his thumb across his jaw and tried to keep a straight face.

I shook my head. "I don't know what you're talking about."

"I could elaborate if you'd like," he teased.

"I'd rather you didn't." I shot him a warning look. "She's interviewing for Manuel's position."

"Ah, I see," he said knowingly. "And she just happened to show up for an interview?"

I rolled my eyes at his prying question. "Her friend works here and scheduled the interview with Araceli. This has nothing to do with the coffee shop."

Gabriel seemed disappointed at that, but it didn't take him long to recover. "You know, it could be like one of Viola's books. An unfortunate meeting, but then you touch, and there's that spark. Has there been a spark?"

"I'm not discussing this with you."

"There was!" he chuckled, and Macy looked up, noticing us standing there.

"Daddy!" Olivia rushed to her father. "Macy is chef, like *Tio* 'Teo!"

"Is she now?" Gabriel shot me one last look.

Olivia nodded seriously. "I be chef, too! Like Macy. She's nice."

Macy blushed as she smiled at the little girl. I wondered if she had children of her own.

"Well, that's the most important thing," Gabriel said. He stepped forward and held out his hand, flashing the smile that had brought plenty of women to their knees before he married Jane. "Gabriel Rivera. And this little pest is Olivia, my daughter."

I was secretly relieved when Macy didn't recognize his name. The billionaire brothers had plenty of groupies around town. She shook his hand briefly. "Macy Hart. And Olivia isn't a pest. She's brilliant."

"I like you," Gabriel said with a laugh as he looked at me pointedly. "I was just telling my brothers that she's a genius."

"Oh, I didn't realize you were Matteo's brother," Macy responded, looking between us.

"Only by choice," Gabriel confirmed. "He's stuck with us now, though. Isn't that right, Olivia?"

The little girl clapped her hands gleefully, then pointed to the freezer. "Sweets!"

"Patience, *pequeña mirlo*," Gabriel admonished. "Remember your manners."

"Tio 'Teo, please?" Olivia asked with puppy dog eyes.

"Of course." I brushed past Macy on my way to the freezer. It only took a moment to get one of the fruit popsicles I kept on hand for the little kids, but that was long enough for Gabriel to start gabbing.

"Do you have kids of your own?" he asked, watching as his daughter high-fived Macy over and over. "You're great with Olivia."

"Oh, no," Macy answered. "I never had the chance with my ex."

"I'm sorry," Gabriel said sympathetically.

"Don't be." She deftly showed Olivia how to have a thumb war, intentionally letting my niece win. "You didn't run out on me."

That was more information than she'd given me. I was tempted to let Gabriel keep talking, but I had a practical interview to conduct.

Gabriel's face darkened. He valued family over everything. "The man must have been an asshole."

"Your words," Macy agreed with a small smile. She stood and smoothed her hands down her apron.

"Here, *amore*." I offered the popsicle to Olivia, and she giggled her thanks before popping the frozen treat in her mouth.

She paused by Macy. "Want to watch. Please."

"Here, Olivia." Gabriel picked his daughter up and walked around the prep area, so they were across from Macy. "You can watch from here. That is, if you don't mind, Macy."

"Not at all," she said with a wave of her hand. I caught her biting her lip when she looked away. They were making her nervous, but I couldn't exactly kick them out without seeming rude. If Macy ended up with the position, she'd see the Riveras around occasionally.

She resumed mincing the onions and peppers, and I focused on her knife skills, which were more than adequate. Unlike when I'd asked her questions, she kept on mincing when Olivia asked questions, answering them kindly and seamlessly. It made me hope I provided the best kind of distraction.

"Where's the chicken?" Olivia asked, looking around. Of course, she'd think an entire meal should be prepared with *arroz con gandules*. She'd seen plenty of family members make it in her short lifetime.

"I'm not making chicken today," Macy answered with a smile. "At least, not that I've been told."

"We'll start simple," I offered. "I figured you knew how to sauté chicken."

Macy grinned, and my heart seemed to float for a second. "I hope so."

"It's wrong," Olivia declared as she finished the last of her popsicle. Drops of red juice dotted her pink dress.

"Okay, my little food critic," Gabriel chastised lovingly. "I think that's enough from you for today. Time to go home and see *Mamá*."

"*Mamá!*" Olivia echoed, blowing me kisses as Gabriel walked toward the door. "Love you, *Tio* 'Teo!"

I pretended to catch her kiss and sent one back. "Love you too, Livvy. Be good for your *Mamá*."

"Thanks, Matteo." Gabriel patted my shoulder as he passed me. "Nice to meet you, Macy. Best of luck with this guy."

I glared at him, but he just grinned wider.

Macy paused and offered them a short wave. "You, too. Bye, Olivia!"

"Bye, Macy!" Olivia called out as she disappeared through the door.

Silence descended on the kitchen, and I looked at the cutting board full of onions, peppers, garlic, and cilantro.

"How is it?" Macy asked as I wiped down the opposite side of the prep area to make sure there weren't any sticky spots where Olivia had enjoyed her treat.

I hadn't given her any instructions on preparation for the *sofrito*, and it showed, but only in the method. She'd done well.

"It looks good." I grinned when Macy's eyes danced with pride, but I couldn't help but joke with her, pointing to the food processor at the edge of the table. Her smile dropped as she followed the direction of my finger. "We usually use the Robo Coupe, though."

Chapter Four

ALL THE TRIUMPH I'D felt at Matteo's praise melted away as I realized a food processor was sitting at the end of the prep area. Of course, I should have thought to use it. I was basically making salsa.

He just stood there grinning like he didn't have a care in the world. Maybe he didn't. After all, he was a celebrity chef and could probably close all of his restaurants tomorrow on a whim and still have enough money to live off of for the rest of his life. I'd once been what people would consider well-off. My husband made good money, and I'd wanted for nothing. Destination vacations, luxury vehicles, designer clothing, expensive perfume—I'd had everything but the love of the only man I'd ever loved.

Discontent and jealousy swirled in my chest, threatening to drown my rational thought. I shoved the emotions down. Matteo didn't deserve my disdain. He'd worked for everything he had and deserved to enjoy that success. I just had to focus on making something out of myself instead of relying on a man to supply my worth. The kitchen was like home; I could do this.

Taking a deep breath, I directed my attention back to the task at hand. I'd made a bowl of *sofrito*, and now I had to make a rice dish. *Arroz con gandules*. It looked like a form of rice and beans, but the *gandules* were little greenish things.

"I need to go grab some more containers," Matteo said as he looked at an empty spot on a shelf with various plastic storage containers. "I'll be right back. You good for now?"

"Yeah." I nodded, trying to look confident.

He headed out of the kitchen, and I practically dove for my purse, reaching in and clutching my phone as I quickly looked up recipes for the food I needed to make. If I'd known Matteo wouldn't include prep instructions, I would have researched beforehand. I liked to come prepared, and I wasn't used to recipes with only ingredients listed.

Having things thrown at me suddenly was nightmarish and induced a panic that I knew was illogical, but my brain didn't like to cooperate. I could feel my breathing regulating and my pounding heart slowing as I read through the preparation instructions on a recipe similar to Matteo's. It was simple, really.

"Cheating already, are we?"

I jumped at Matteo's voice next to my right ear, my instincts from self-defense kicking in at the worst possible moment as I slammed my phone backward—right into his nose.

"Shit!" Matteo hissed as he recoiled, grabbing his face. "That's quite a backhand you've got there."

I cringed and tossed my phone onto the table. "I'm sorry! You were just so close!"

"Don't be." His voice was muffled behind his palm as he grabbed a paper towel. It came away with a drop of red, making my stomach twist. "You've got good instincts. Any potential attacker would think twice about accosting you after that."

"Maybe, but I'm guessing that isn't on the list of requirements you have for a sous chef."

"I don't know," Matteo mused, tossing the paper towel in the trash and washing his hands. "If we ever had a kitchen rumble, I'd want you on my side, *ariete*."

I was afraid to ask for a translation. "Does your kitchen often devolve into chaos?"

"Only recently," he said drolly, quirking an eyebrow. "But what is life without the unexpected?"

"Predictable," I said flatly. The unexpected in life hadn't gone well for me.

Matteo pinched the bridge of his nose. "I find I like the unpredictable."

I didn't believe that for a second. The man was trying to make me feel less embarrassed. "If you want me to go now, I can."

"You no longer want the job?"

"Of course, I want the job still," I said before pointing to his face, where his nose was already swelling. "Why would you want me to work for you after I broke your nose?"

"It's not broken," Matteo explained. "Might be a bit bruised and hurt like a bitch for a day or two. Lucky for you, I judge prospective employees by their culinary skills, not their uppercuts."

I snorted and slapped my palm over my mouth. Matteo chuckled and motioned to the food. "Please, finish. I shouldn't have joked about cheating. I appreciate your ingenuity. I'd rather you do it right than have too much pride to seek assistance."

Rather than protest any further, I quickly washed my hands and got back to work, pulling out a pot and setting it over medium heat on the stove. I added *sofrito* and bacon, and soon the fragrance floated through the air. Tomatoes were next.

"See, much better use for those hands. Make food, not war." Matteo waved his hand over the pot and inhaled. "Not sure I'll be able to judge this properly with my nose out of commission."

He walked over to the soda machine and dispensed ice into a cloth before placing it over his nose and resuming his position, leaning against the prep table behind me. My face burned hotter than the gas stove in front of me as I added the bright orange *sazon* spice, tomato paste, and chicken broth.

I pointed the long-handled spatula at him. "You know, it wouldn't hurt to warn a person before you get that close."

"I think I've learned a valuable lesson today," Matteo chuckled. "I can't say a woman has ever complained about my proximity before."

"I'm sure your ego will recover," I replied drily. Inwardly, I wondered what it would feel like to have him close.

It wasn't long before I'd finished adding ingredients, and it was time to cover the pot to let it slowly simmer and come together. I began cleaning up after myself, throwing out food scraps, and taking the dishes to the sink. I rinsed them, and then Matteo was by my side, loading them into the tray and sliding it all into the dishwasher.

"Thanks," I muttered. I couldn't remember the last time a head chef had helped me with menial tasks. Usually, they were screaming out orders to the staff while we worked frantically to keep up with demand.

Matteo shrugged. "We're a team at *El Corazón Boriken.*"

After taking one for himself, he tossed me a cloth and sprayed down the surfaces I'd worked on. I kept my face on my task, but watched his muscles flex under his chef's coat out of the corner of my eye as we wiped the prep tables down. He was so... nice. I wondered if it was a façade or who he really was. Men lied, as evidenced by Ethan pretending everything was fine for ten years before leaving me without warning. It was hard to believe there were good men in the world.

"Did you set a timer?" Matteo asked, pulling me from my thoughts. I hadn't, and I spun and lifted the lid on the pot. It looked cooked but not overdone. He'd just saved my ass.

"I think it's done," I said, reaching for the pot holders hanging on the wall and pulling the pot from the flame. "You'll have to tell me because I've never made rice like this. It smells good, though."

Matteo set two bowls and spoons on the table and motioned for me to serve us. "Go ahead and do the honors."

I bit my lip and spooned a bit into each bowl. Enough to taste, but not so much that it would be a chore to finish if I'd bombed the dish. I held my breath as Matteo blew on his bite and popped it into his mouth. His eyes closed, and the corners of his lips tipped up in a smile as he took his time chewing and swallowing.

"You sure you're not Puerto Rican, *ariete*?" he mused, opening his eyes. "It's not quite like my *Abuelita's*, but it's good."

I exhaled and grabbed my bowl, spooning up some of the rice dish and carefully tasting it, so I didn't burn my tongue. The flavors exploded on my tongue, and I heard myself moan in pleasure. I'd never had anything quite like it, but I knew I wanted to make it again. It was like a warm hug on a rainy Oregon night.

"See?" Matteo pointed his spoon at me. "You were worried about nothing. Have more faith in your abilities."

"I wasn't—"

Matteo lifted a brow, and I snapped my mouth shut, letting the rest of my white lie trail off. He was right. It had been a long time since somebody besides Leo had encouraged me.

"Thank you," I said instead. "I'm glad you like it."

He nodded, placed several plastic containers on the counter, and then slid lids next to them like he was dealing cards. "You live with Leo, right?"

"Yeah," I confirmed, finishing the last of my *arroz con gandules*.

Matteo began scooping the rice into the containers. "You take this home with you and share it with her. Tell her I want to know her thoughts when she comes to work on Wednesday."

"I can't take all of this," I protested, looking at the three full containers.

He glanced at me and separated one from the group. "Fine. I'll take one. Feel better?"

I opened my mouth, but no words came out. Rather than make more of a fool of myself, I snapped my jaw shut and nodded.

"Now, we'll all enjoy your skills later."

I pressed my lips together, trying to convince myself his words were innocuous. He hadn't intended to sound suggestive, but a part of me that had been dormant for many months sparked to life at the thought of Matteo enjoying my *skills*. I had to get out of there.

"I appreciate you giving me a chance today," I said hastily, reaching for the containers and setting them with my purse before reaching for the large pot. "I'll just wash these dishes and get out of your hair."

"Don't worry about that." Matteo took the pot from me, effortlessly lifting it with one of his large hands and gathering the bowls and spoons with his other hand. He strode toward the sink and began spraying the pot. "I can wash a dish as well as you, I promise."

"O–okay." I looked around, realizing there was nothing else to be done. "I'm going to go then. Have a nice day. Thanks again."

"You too, Macy."

I spun and hurried out of the restaurant, eager to avoid any more awkward moments with Matteo. I only hoped he liked my food enough to overlook the assault.

***

Days passed with no word from anybody at Matteo's restaurant, and Leo didn't have any inside information about employment decisions. All she could tell me was that they hadn't hired anybody for the position, to her knowledge. Then, in true Leo fashion, she'd said Matteo would be a fucking idiot not to hire me after tasting the food I'd made. It should have been reassuring, but I was stressed because no news wasn't good news to me. I contemplated whether I needed to schedule more virtual therapy visits to help cope with my insecurity.

My anxiety had been a menace since Ethan left. That fear of abandonment presented in many surprising ways—like assuming rejection when I had no information in either direction. It didn't help that I didn't have a current job to go to after the last restaurant I'd worked for let part of the staff go after the summer season. Their business relied heavily on tourists, so the fall and winter seasons were slow. It hadn't been personal; I was just one of the newer employees, and those with seniority were prioritized.

I just needed to stop drawing the short stick in life. *El Corazón Borikén* was a prime opportunity, and I'd do just about anything to work there, even if it meant having heart palpitations every time I was near Matteo Gonzalez.

"Macy," Leo called out from the kitchen. "Staring at the rain on the window won't make him call."

I turned from where I'd been staring blankly into the dark for the past half hour. Leo had worked the early shift at the restaurant and found me like that when she came home. "What? Who said I was waiting for Matteo to call?"

"Not me." She smirked and tossed her black hair over her shoulder. "I didn't mention him at all, but it's telling that his name was first on your mind."

"Oh, fuck off." I shook my head and didn't bother hiding my smile. She had me.

"Come on, let's order food and open a bottle of wine." Leo held up two bottles. "Red or white?"

"It's fall," I replied. "Red."

Leo giggled and put the white wine away before stabbing the red with a corkscrew. "You know there's no hard and fast rule. The wine police won't break down the door and storm in yelling, *put the pinot gris down!*"

I covered my snorting laughter with my palm. "The fact that you've thought about that is mildly disturbing."

"Oh, I have contingency plans for everything," she assured me. "I'd toss the wine at them, and they'd fall to the floor to keep the bottles from breaking. Meanwhile, we'd rush out the back."

"Sometimes you concern me." I laughed again and poured the wine into glasses Leo set on the counter.

"Sometimes I concern myself," she admitted. "But then I remember there are worse things than eccentricity."

"So true." I held up my wine glass. "To eccentricity."

"To doing whatever the hell you want," Leo added. We clinked glasses and sipped on the pinot noir while she pulled up a takeout menu on her phone. "See anything you want?"

"Not really." I shrugged and took another sip of wine. "I'm not sure how hungry I am."

"We could make cookies and watch cheesy movies for the rest of the night," she suggested. It wasn't a bad idea.

"I'll get the chocolate chips," I offered, setting my glass down and sifting through the baking ingredients in the cupboard. I put all the dry ingredients on the counter while Leo found the things we needed in the fridge. We'd baked cookies together so often over the years that we didn't need the recipe.

"So if you get the job, are you going to be able to work with Matteo?" Leo asked as she unwrapped sticks of butter and tossed them in the bottom of the mixing bowl while I measured the sugars.

"I don't see why I wouldn't be able to. He's kind of a big part of the restaurant."

"He hasn't said anything about you punching him to the others," she said, adding the paddle attachment and raising the bowl.

I flipped the mixer on and raised my voice over the sound of the motor. "Small favors. I can't take that back."

"The rumor floating through the staff is that he's secretly cage fighting on his days off."

I scoffed and turned the mixer off so Leo could add the eggs. "That's ridiculous. I'd bet money that man is a pacifist."

"Why? Because he didn't defend himself against your savage attack?" she shot back, dancing away as I flicked flour at her.

"You're never going to let me forget that, are you?"

"Not a chance," she confirmed, keeping a safe distance as I added the last of the ingredients. "I'm so proud of you."

I side-eyed her. "For hitting somebody?"

"For being a badass." Leo threw an arm over my shoulder. "I always knew you had it in you. Just let it out more... maybe in a way that won't get you arrested."

I laughed and waited for her to put parchment paper on a sheet pan before portioning the cookie dough.

"I'll try, but no guarantees about staying out of jail."

Chapter Five

I HAD AMPLE TIME to make a decision on my new hire. I'd even tried to pick up the phone and call one of my most qualified applicants, but my fingers refused to dial any number but Macy's. It would have worked to pawn the responsibility off on Araceli, but again, I couldn't do it. So I sat in my office on Monday morning after coffee, trying to talk myself out of what I was about to do.

Gabriel had thrown me right under the bus earlier, bringing up Macy when I couldn't get out of talking about her. I calmly explained that she was a prospective employee—nothing more—but those sentimental assholes had us walking down the aisle in less than five minutes. Though I laughed along with the joke, the thought of Macy in white, smiling at me like she had when she was cooking, stuck with me. I didn't even know the woman, but my romantic heart had pined, anyway.

My *Abuelita* always said my parents were soulmates, and that's why they left the world together. It was a lofty, if macabre notion, but I'd clung to it all these years and always hoped I'd feel the same for my wife one day. Was my interest in the sad woman who'd come into my life with the chaos of a winter storm something that I forced because of my desire for connection, or did soulmates truly exist? And if so, could she be mine?

I couldn't dwell on that. Macy deserved more than a man who thought her ass was hot and her scarred soul was something to be healed. My penchant for helping people was taking a strange turn, and there had to be boundaries. I was offering her the job because she'd shown herself to be capable and hungry for it.

Settled on my course of action, I picked up my phone and dialed the number I'd already memorized.

"Hello?" Macy's soft voice trailed down the line.

"Good morning, Macy," I greeted her. "This is Matteo. Gonzalez. From *El Corazón Borikén*."

Oh, that was good. I could hear Gabriel's phantom voice echoing in my head, "Smooth."

"Oh, yeah, hi." I could hear the tentative question in her voice, a slight waver of trepidation.

"What are your plans for this week?" Had I just asked that? It sounded more like I was asking her out than preparing to offer her a job.

"My plans?" There was a long pause, and I feared she'd hang up and block my number. "I guess I don't have any."

"How about we change that?" Fuck me. This wasn't what I'd practiced in my head. I quickly tacked on, "That is if you're still interested in working for me."

I'd never suffered from a lack of confidence until that moment, waiting for her to answer like my next breath depended on it.

"You're serious?" she questioned.

"Of course."

"Then, yes!" she answered breathlessly. "When do you want me?"

All the time, ariete. I kept that thought in my head and said, "Wednesday morning at ten. Manuel and I will train you for the next two weeks and get a feel for how you work with the rest of the staff."

I could hear squealing in the background—probably Leo—before Macy shushed her roommate. "Yeah, that works. I'll be there Wednesday at ten."

"Great, see you then. Have a good day, Macy." There, I'd sounded perfectly normal.

"You too. Bye."

She hung up, and I breathed a sigh of relief. What was I, a teenager calling a girl for the first time? My body was practically vibrating with the rush of excitement running through me. She'd said yes. I'd see her again. Regularly—for the foreseeable future.

I rested my forehead against my desk. Had I completely lost my mind? I was about to torture myself every time she was in my sight.

***

"She's here," Manuel announced as he breezed through the kitchen doors and grabbed an apron off the hook, slipping it around his waist and tying it around his rotund center. The man was a teddy bear, and his patient nature was perfect for instructing Macy. "You ready to roll?"

"Yep." I adjusted my cravat, feeling suddenly confined by the cotton fabric.

"Bring on the fresh meat!" Diego called from the line where he was prepping cilantro for *sofrito.*

"You two be nice," I warned Diego and Carlos. They were a bit indelicate in the kitchen. My evening line cook, Amaia, could give as good as she got, but I hoped they'd keep it toned down when Macy was present.

This was like any other training. I'd done it so many times that it should be like riding a bike. Only, as Macy walked through the

37

swinging kitchen doors in her white chef's coat, the only thing I wanted to ride was those ample hips.

I cleared my throat and smiled. "Good morning, Macy!"

"Morning," she replied with a slight frown. So we were starting out like that today.

"Macy, I'm Manuel," my sous chef said as he approached with an outstretched hand. "I've heard a lot about you."

"I don't know whether that's a good or bad thing." She shot me an accusatory look, and I shook my head to tell her I wasn't responsible.

"Leo has been singing your praises for weeks now," he explained, and Macy visibly relaxed. "We get a few hours with you before she arrives."

"Yeah, she's got the evening shift," Macy confirmed. Manuel pulled an apron from the hook by the door and handed it to our new co-worker. She pulled it taut around her waist and tied it deftly, smoothing her hands down the front of the white material and clasping them in front of her. "Where are we starting?"

Manuel answered before I could take the lead. "I want to see how you handle yourself on the line. Matteo says you have enough experience to cook, but you'll need to learn the specs for our recipes here."

"I can do that." Macy nodded and followed Manuel to the opposite side of the kitchen.

"These stooges are Carlos and Diego. Watch what they do, but don't let them haze you." The men in question glared at their superior for ruining their fun, and Manuel chuckled. "Boys, this is Macy. She'll be me in a few weeks."

"She's a fucking sight better than you," Carlos joked.

Macy's face flushed red, but she politely said, "It's nice to meet you both."

They nodded, not missing a beat of their prep. Diego pulled a knife off the wall and reached for a cutting board, setting it down conveniently between him and Carlos. I'd have to watch those two.

"Here," he motioned to Macy and pointed his shoulder to a bag of onions. "Grab the onions and start mincing. We need to make more *sofrito.*"

Macy reached for the onions and started breaking them down, but instead of mincing them, she roughly chopped them to the same size as Carlos was making the green bell peppers. I grabbed my knives and began laying out what I'd need for the lunch rush as I watched them out of the corner of my eye.

Diego narrowed his eyes. "What are you doing?"

"Breaking down the onions," she explained mildly, grabbing another and chopping it up.

Diego shook his head and asked, "Do you know how to mince onions?"

She set her knife down and turned to face him. "I do. I also know how to use the Robo Coupe. Do you?"

Both line cooks froze as she called them on the shit they were pulling. Her lips quirked up in a smile, and Diego laughed and tapped the side of his head with the back of his wrist. "Smart."

"You're going to fit in just fine." Carlos slapped Macy on the back hard enough that she jolted, and a surge of protectiveness made my fist clench around the handle of my knife. I quickly set it down before I did something stupid.

What the hell was that about?

I turned away, determined not to let the little blonde distract me from my job. Manuel was grinning and giving me a subtle thumbs-up just below the edge of the prep table. "Nice job, boss. I think you've got a winner."

That's what had my pulse racing, and a tiny part of my mind warned me that I was already digging myself a hole I wouldn't easily climb out of.

***

"Behind you!" Macy called out as she passed behind me with a sauté pan full of perfectly browned chicken thighs. She'd caught on quickly to the routine in my kitchen, moving as fluidly as the rest of the staff in only a few days.

A spark inside her came to life when she was in her element. I felt a smug sense of pride that my kitchen did that for her. While she was generally quiet, she could keep up with the antics of the line cooks and had no sense of superiority over the rest of the staff. That, combined with her obviously understated skill, made her damn near perfect.

I'd never felt the kind of tension that I was constantly aware of between Macy and me. When her chef's coat brushed against mine as she moved past, it was like a live wire between us, sending electricity shooting up my spine. She smiled a bit wider when it was directed at me, and twice I'd caught her watching me when she didn't think I was aware. I wondered how I could get closer to her without interfering with our work relationship.

The last of the dinner rush kept my staff occupied, and I spent my time focused on the guests who had paid for the chef's table in the corner of the kitchen. They received my dedicated service and a customized menu paired with some of my favorite wines for the price per head. Though I preferred to serve family-style meals, there was a demand for small, beautifully plated bites.

Tonight, I started with an assortment of fried appetizers before moving on to *asopao de pollo*, a traditional chicken and rice soup sure to set the mood for the evening by warming the belly and the heart. One bite of my *Abuelita's* recipe, and you'd never settle for chicken noodle again.

The main course consisted of *pernil* and *arroz con gandules*—topped with a bit of the crisped pork skin for each diner and paired with a mid-bodied Grenache. I took time to explain each dish and share stories from my childhood when my *Abuelita* taught me how to cook with her. It was always a pleasant bit of nostalgia as I gave them a taste of a place they usually hadn't been to.

When their conversation grew louder, and they'd finished another bottle of wine, they leaned back and relaxed in their chairs. That was my cue to get dessert to the table. I'd prepared *tembleque* in molds, then plated them as I created a sauce out of pineapple, sugar, and dark spiced Puerto Rican rum. Leo helped me take the dessert plates to the table while I brought the sauce and a lighter. As my guests watched, I poured the spiced sauce over the coconut custard and held the flame close, making a performance out of the flambe.

I relished the predictable *oohs* and *ahhs* as they waited for the alcohol to burn off. Then there was that moment I lived for—the seconds of silence as they savored their first bites of the sweet dish. Smiling, I told them to enjoy their meal, and made sure Leo took *coquito* to them when they'd finished their dessert.

By the time the guests left and the staff cleared the table, it was nearly closing time. The kitchen was done for the night, and the last customers settled their bills in the dining room. I glanced over and watched Macy finish putting food from the line away. She pitched in wherever something needed to be done without others asking. She might act standoffish, but underneath she was thoughtful.

"So, how did you like your first week?" I asked her as I approached.

The smile on her face faded slightly, and she bit her lip. "I felt like it went well."

"I didn't ask you for a self-evaluation, Macy," I teased. "I asked how you liked it. Or didn't like it, I suppose, but I think it would be impossible for anybody to dislike a place with so much heart."

"I liked it," Macy acknowledged quietly. "It might be the best kitchen I've worked in."

It felt like she held my heart in her small palm as she offered me the compliment. I tried for levity. "Good. I'd accept nothing less."

Macy shifted nervously but said nothing else. Strands of her blonde hair had escaped her low bun, framing her face. Desire coursed through me when she bit that bottom lip again, and I saw a hint of her pink tongue. On a thoughtless whim, I reached for the still-warm pot on my workspace and snagged a spiced pineapple out of the

41

brown sugar sauce. Macy's eyes widened as I approached, but she didn't turn away. I'd take it.

"Open for me." My voice came out gravelly with the command, but Macy's jaw dropped obediently with the prettiest gasp, and I placed the fruit between her lips, feeling her tongue brush my finger as she took the morsel from me. All of my blood rushed south.

"*Oh.*" The sound was orgasmic, and I stood transfixed on Macy's look of pleasure, imagining how she would look, making that face as she lay under me, surrounding me. Her following words were nearly a moan. "This is amazing."

Somebody made a sound, and I broke free of my inappropriate daydream to find Manuel and the line cooks staring. I realized then how unusual it must have looked that I fed Macy. I had no doubt that they'd noticed my reaction to her sounds.

Macy slapped her palm over her face to muffle the sounds and turned red like a tomato. Desperate to save her from embarrassment, I snatched up the small saucepan and found another pineapple, then approached my shocked sous chef and practically shoved the pineapple into his mouth, smearing sauce across his cheek in the process.

"What the—"

I didn't give him a chance to say more as I moved on to Diego. The man recoiled and plucked the pineapple from my fingers. "I think I can manage on my own, chef."

Carlos waved me off when I turned in his direction. "No thanks, I'm good, chef."

I shrugged it off like nothing was abnormal about suddenly hand-feeding my staff members. "Okay, then. Let's wrap it up and get out of here. The bar is still open, and the first round is on me."

That got them moving again. Sunday nights, we often found a bar that stayed open until midnight and had a couple of drinks to unwind after the workweek. I would need it after the little show I just put on for everybody.

"You coming?" I asked Macy as she removed her apron. "The invitation is open to the entire staff."

"Thanks," she said, then paused, looking behind me. "Leo and I are going to head home, I think. I need a solid twelve hours of sleep."

She laughed in that melodic way, making it seem less like rejection, even though her blush told me she was probably avoiding further interaction with me.

"Yeah, totally," I replied. "I guess I won't see you at the coffee shop in the morning, then."

"Probably not," she confirmed, and looked toward the door. "Leo's waving through the window. I'm going to get going. Thanks again, Matteo."

Her genuine smile of gratitude filled my chest with warmth, and my body hummed with interest when her shoulder brushed my arm as she passed. I turned, watching the subtle sway of her hips as she walked out the door. The kitchen seemed to cool a few degrees, as if Macy had taken some of the warmth with her.

Chapter Six

THE TREES IN DOWNTOWN Portland were brilliant shades of orange and red, at least for now. It seemed we always ended up with a fall windstorm that snatched the color away before the leaves fell on their own. It was Tuesday morning, and Leo had convinced me to go out for coffee. I was nervous that we might run into Matteo, but that was ridiculous, given that I would see him five days weekly at work. What was one more morning?

The misty autumn breeze gave way to the warmth of the coffee shop as we entered. The smell of roasted coffee permeated the air, and the familiar sounds of the baristas at work and customers chatting made me feel at home. I looked around as Leo and I took our place in line, a tiny thread of disappointment weaving through my heart when I didn't see a familiar, tall, tan, and fit chef anywhere.

"The usual, for both of us," Leo chirped when we reached the counter. There was no point in objecting; even if I paid, Leo would slip the money back into my pocket later. It was heartwarmingly obnoxious, but I love her for it.

She took our spiced coffee from the pickup counter and found a couple of empty plush chairs in the back of the coffee shop. I took the coffee she offered me and settled into the cushions, content to relax for a while.

"What do you want to do today?" Leo asked as she slurped at her coffee.

"We probably need to go grocery shopping since the only food in the fridge is a couple of heels of bread, cheese, and some chicken stock," I said blandly. We were frugal about food since our rent ate up most of our income. So much for the myth of housing being more affordable with a roommate.

Leo tapped her chin. "I don't know. I feel like you're creative enough to come up with something using those ingredients. Oh! I've got it. You could cook noodles in the broth for chicken soup and make grilled cheese."

"We can have that for lunch," I said with a smile. "Right after we get back with our groceries."

"Fair enough." Mischief flashed across her delicate features. Her black hair was pulled up into a high ponytail, making her cheekbones appear sharper. She wore a black hoodie and black jeans with her black combat boots. I practically looked like a schoolteacher next to her with my jeans, blue sweater, and practical windbreaker. "I suppose you'll need sustenance for all the long, hot nights in the kitchen."

I paused my coffee cup on the way to my lips, narrowly avoiding another coffee incident as I choked and Leo laughed. "You make me wish I hadn't said anything."

"Oh, don't be like that." She patted my thigh playfully. "I can't blame you for thinking Matteo is hot. He totally is. And the way he looks at you when you're not looking—I wish somebody would look at me like that."

"He doesn't look at me like anything except the clumsy new cook," I muttered, taking a sip of my coffee. I didn't have anything to offer a man like Matteo. Hell, I couldn't keep my own husband happy, and I'd known him since we were teens.

Leo shook her head at me. "You have to stop putting yourself down. I'm not afraid to tell everybody here every amazing trait you have."

"Please don't," I begged, knowing she was completely serious. She'd done the same thing in a bar when she'd convinced me to file for divorce from Ethan. My face heated with the memory of my embarrassment. "I'm good at my job. Happy?"

"It'll do for now," she nodded.

"I'd be better if I wasn't always so distracted by my boss."

"You could fuck him," she suggested flippantly. "Have you watched his fingers as he rolls *mallorcas*? It's like he's touching a lover."

I rolled my eyes. "Yeah, that'll help. It wouldn't be awkward coming to work and seeing his face every day after that."

"I'm so proud of you for thinking of it as an eventuality instead of shooting the idea down altogether," she giggled and twisted a lock of her hair around a finger.

"Why do I put up with you again?" I asked ruefully and tested my coffee again, and sighed as the creamy, sweet, spiced iced drink slid down my throat.

"Because I'm amazing, and you can't help but love me," she answered without pause. "I'm your platonic life partner. Maybe you should tell Matteo that before you sleep with him. He should know we're a package deal. It might be awkward when he finds me wandering around his place."

"*Leo*." I dragged her name out and sighed dramatically. "I don't need to tell our *boss* anything because I'm not going to sleep with him."

"Famous last words," she shot back with a grin.

"What about you?" I turned the topic back on my friend. "Who's your work crush?"

"Are you asking which of the foul-mouthed line cooks I'd bang?" She thought about it for a minute, giving me enough time to savor the spice in my coffee. "If I have to pick, it would be Amaia. She's hot. Or Hector."

"The bartender?" There were so many employees at *El Corazón Borikén* that it was hard to keep them all straight.

"Yeah, the hotter twin."

"How can you even tell the difference?" I asked incredulously. "They're *identical*."

Leo shrugged. "He handles the shaker so authoritatively. I'd love to see how he'd use that firm hand on me."

"You're ridiculous."

"You asked." Leo drummed her fingers on the armrest of her chair.

This conversation wasn't going any better than the last. I set my coffee cup on the little table between our chairs and fished around in my purse, finding a small notepad and a pen. "Let's make a grocery list. Last time we ended up with three containers of chocolate milk and no eggs."

"I don't see the problem," she said with a straight face. "I guess we can add another half gallon of chocolate milk if you need it."

"You're a child," I chastised playfully. I added two half gallons of chocolate milk to the list. And eggs.

"Acting your age is overrated," she said flippantly. "I'd rather be fun."

"Leo, we're only twenty-seven. We can still be fun."

She arched a brow at me, silently telling me that we both knew I was not a fun person by nature, and I pursed my lips. Sometimes I wish Leo's personality could rub off on me just a little. I longed to feel carefree. When was the last time I didn't worry? Probably before I married Ethan. That was perhaps telling of my relationship with my estranged husband, but the knowledge didn't fix my broken social skills.

I tapped my pen on the paper pad until Leo began rattling off a list for me to write down. It didn't take long to plan the week's meals.

"And condoms," Leo added.

"You're having sex with a guy?" I asked, surprised she hadn't mentioned it. Leo's tastes ran with whatever whim overtook her, but usually, I was the first to know about anybody who caught her eye. Contrary to what many believed about her sexual freedom, she was monogamous in a relationship.

"No," she answered. "It's just good to be prepared for any eventuality."

"Leo."

She held her hands up. "I'm not saying you have to bang Matteo. But I'm going to make you go bar hopping with me, and you haven't been on birth control for at least six months."

"I've never in my life slept with a guy I met at a bar," I protested. She wasn't wrong about the birth control. I hadn't even thought of it. After my last prescription ran out, I didn't bother to refill it because I couldn't afford it, and I couldn't see myself as anything but celibate for the rest of my lonely life.

"Maybe that's the problem," Leo suggested with a wave of her hand. "You need to pick up a guy. Or a girl."

"I prefer penises," I said drolly. "And silicone is less likely to ruin my life than flesh and blood."

"I'm not telling you to get hitched. Just be open to a little rendezvous and a few orgasms." She waggled her eyebrows at me, and I giggled at her antics.

"I won't rule it out," I conceded to pacify her temporarily.

"I'll take it." Leo clapped her hands, realizing I might not have gotten off so easily. "I've got just the place to take you tonight."

Shit. When I groaned, and Leo laughed gleefully, placing my coffee back in my hand. I gulped it down greedily. I was going to need it if I had any hope of getting through the day.

***

For the first time in as long as I could remember, I was looking forward to something. It was an unfamiliar feeling, but I counted it as progress even though it was work. Baby steps, my therapist would say. She used to tell me that anything that wasn't moving backward was progress.

I'd worked at *El Corazón Borikén* for two weeks, and I loved it more every day. I dared to allow myself to feel happy, but I was cautious. My position wasn't permanent until Matteo and Manuel thought I'd learned enough.

I stood in the staff bathroom in the back of the restaurant, washing my hands and using the damp paper towel to dab at the shiny spots on my face. Working in a kitchen might sound glamorous, but the reality was a lot sweatier. Chef's coats were thick, and the air was always hot and humid between the ovens and the grill. I'd started bringing a change of clothes for the end of the night, so I could feel human and not go home smelling like cilantro and lime. It helped a little, but the only way to get rid of the permeating scent was to shower, and I was often too tired by the time Leo and I got back to the condo to bother.

I pulled the elastic bands from my hair and ran my fingers through my blonde locks, gathering the stray strands and twisting it back into a low bun. A little water on my palms helped tame the flyaways that wanted to rebel.

Satisfied that it would hold for the rest of the evening, I headed back to the kitchen, where the rest of my co-workers were already closing things down. I looked around while I washed my hands, but Matteo was nowhere in sight. Maybe he'd left early. Most of the head chefs I'd worked for in the past didn't stay through closing, but every night I'd worked so far, Matteo stayed with his staff and was the last one out the door. I respected that, even if I found his cheerful attitude grating late at night when I was exhausted.

"Need help?" I asked Amaia. She was packing up the things on the line that could be stored in the refrigerator overnight.

"Yeah, sure." She waved a colorfully tattooed arm toward the food she hadn't stored. Amaia was tall enough that I had to look up, and her bleached blonde and pink hair curled in a close-cropped cut around her face.

I got to work emptying the other containers of the last bits of veggies and grabbed a container for the *sofrito*, pouring it in after labeling the top with the erasable marker I kept in my apron pocket.

"Is Leo picking you up?" Matteo's voice at my right startled me, and I watched in horror as the *sofrito* seemed to slosh out of the container in slow-motion, flying through the air and covering the front of his chef's coat.

"Shit!" I quickly set the container on the prep table and surveyed the mess. It hadn't gotten on the floor, but I'd have to clean the table again. "I'm so sorry."

"I guess my reflexes haven't improved enough, *ariete*," he said with a laugh. The others joined in, snickering, but I was too mortified to find the humor in it.

I pulled the towel from my apron strings, but Matteo held up his hands to stop me. "Don't worry about it. I just came to ask if you had a ride tonight."

"No, I'm taking the MAX," I answered, cringing at the green covering his black coat. I suppose it could be worse—his jacket could be white. I wiped the rim of the container of *sofrito* and ensured it was closed tightly, just in case. I couldn't be trusted not to launch items at other people.

"We're heading out, chef!" Ian, the other line chef, called out as he and Amaia left the kitchen.

"Goodnight!" Matteo called out with a wave. When we were alone, he turned back to me. "I'm not going to let you walk to the MAX station at this time of night. I'll take you home, but I need to get cleaned up. Come find me when you're ready to leave."

He turned and headed toward his office before I could object, leaving me standing there with my jaw hanging open. I wasn't sure I could handle sitting in a car with Matteo without other people around as a buffer. What if something startled me, and I hit him, knocking him out and making us crash? It was unlikely, but my anxiety decided it was an excellent time to fixate.

I breathed deeply and looked around, finding things to see, touch, hear, smell, and taste. My racing heart slowed, and my mind cleared. I concentrated on cleaning the *sofrito* off the prep table and disinfecting it again before putting the container in the walk-in. It didn't take long for me to change in the employee locker room down the hall from Matteo's office.

I shoved my uniform in my bag and slipped into my coat, pulling a black knit beanie onto my head. Slinging the bag over my shoulder, I made my way toward Matteo's office. The door was open a crack, and I reached to knock but froze when I saw the man in question standing shirtless behind his desk.

My breath caught as I took in his tanned, muscular torso. He had tattoos covering his right arm and over his chest. I had no idea he'd been hiding them under his clothing all this time. It wasn't odd, but it was fucking hot, and I pressed my thighs together as he stroked a palm down his chest and stomach. My eyes followed hungrily until he reached his black pants, and I realized he was about to take them off.

I gasped, then panicked and spun, plastering myself against the wall as Matteo turned his head. I held my breath and counted to ten, hoping he wouldn't come to investigate the noise. When I only heard the rustling of clothing, I let out my breath silently and crept down the hall to the bathroom. I leaned over the sink, panting. Holy fuck, the man was like a dark svelte god with lean muscles carved from stone.

I could feel the wetness between my legs and stared at my red face in the mirror. There was no denying it; Matteo Gonzalez was the first man who had turned me on since my husband. And he was my boss.

I needed the job; I couldn't afford to jeopardize my best income in the past year. I ran my hands under cold water until my fingers were numb, then dried them and pressed my palms to my face, trying to calm my heated cheeks.

When I was confident any lingering color could be attributed to wearing extra layers inside, I emerged from the bathroom. I stomped down the hall so there could be no mistaking my approach. I rapped on the door and stepped back as it swung open, revealing a fully dressed Matteo.

"Ready to go?" he asked with an easy smile.

"Yeah." I nodded.

"Come on. I'm parked out back."

I followed as he led us to a black truck. It was just high enough off the ground that I struggled to pull myself up when he opened the door. Strong hands wrapped around my waist as I slipped, launching me into the front passenger seat.

"There you go, I've got you," Matteo said. "Buckle up now."

He closed the door, and I quickly put my seatbelt on, thankful for the darkness that hid my furious blush. I wasn't sure my embarrassment could get much worse at this point.

"Where am I headed?" Matteo asked as he climbed into the driver's seat effortlessly. I gave him the directions, and he pulled out of the parking lot and drove down the nearly deserted streets of downtown Portland.

I shivered from nerves, and Matteo glanced at me, his brows furrowed. "Cold?"

"A little," I lied. I was burning up from our proximity, and I swear if he touched me again, I'd combust completely.

He cranked up the heat and flipped the radio on when I didn't say anything else. Folk-pop broke the silence, and I watched from the corner of my eye as he moved his head to the music and his lips silently recited the lyrics. He had beautiful lips.

Stop. I needed to focus on anything else but how his full lips glistened in the street lights when he licked them. My traitorous mind flashed visions of him using that tongue on me, and I shifted in my seat, drawing his attention.

"Everything okay?" he asked, looking at where I had my thighs tightly together and my white-knuckled hands clasped in my lap.

"Perfect," I forced out, breathing a sigh of relief when he turned onto my street. "You can just pull up there."

He pulled to the side of the street where I'd indicated. The condo was a little further down the road, but there wouldn't be parking.

"Thanks for the ride," I said as I flung the door open and hopped out, nearly falling from the distance to the ground. I closed the door behind me and nearly screamed when I saw Matteo standing there. "What are you doing?"

My words were accusatory, but he just gave me that lopsided grin. "Making sure you get safely to your door."

"I'm capable of walking down the block," I griped, turning and stalking toward my home without waiting for Matteo. It only took him a moment to catch up with his longer strides. Our arms brushed as he kept pace on the narrow sidewalk.

"It's not about capability," he explained. "Call it chivalry if you'd like."

"Haven't you heard?" I asked like I was about to bestow a great secret upon him. "Chivalry is dead."

He chuckled and stopped when I opened the little white picket fence in our small yard, holding it with a flourish as I passed through. "I promise you I'm very much alive."

"You're the embodiment of the definition now, huh?" I couldn't help the caustic remark. It was a defense mechanism.

"My *Abuelita* would have never tolerated anything less," he said congenially.

I stopped at the front step and turned to face him. He raised a hand, and I held my breath as he brushed a blonde strand from my face, tucking it under my beanie. The walls closely guarding my emotions came tumbling down in an instant.

"Safely home, *ariete*," he said. "Goodnight."

"Thank you," I whispered as he walked away. I couldn't feel the cold with how he'd heated my blood with a single touch.

Chapter Seven

I WAS A PATIENT man, one not prone to emotional outbursts. It rarely paid off to get angry, and the world was better when people spread positivity. That's why I redoubled my efforts with Macy. I'd seen the vulnerability she tried to hide beneath her prickly surface.

She thought she'd gotten away with her little voyeur moment outside my office, and the memory of how flustered she'd been after running away when I decided to see how far she'd go made me chuckle. I'd tested her when I'd reached down to remove my pants, and she'd done exactly what I predicted. Macy was undoubtedly as attracted to me as I was to her, but she also had the sense not to take things too far.

It had taken all of my self-control to resist kissing her lush lips when I walked her to her doorstep. My dreams had been filling in that missing moment for days now. This morning, I was launching an all-out assault of happiness on the woman I wanted.

I whistled as I walked into *El Corazón Borikén*, carrying an extra coffee. I was a few minutes late, which meant Macy had already unlocked the doors. Today I'd get to give her the good news about her future at my restaurant. I couldn't wait to watch her smile.

After changing in my office, I gathered what I needed and waltzed into the kitchen to find Macy already setting things up for the day. She turned and acknowledged me with a slight nod, her arms full of fresh produce.

"Good morning," I said, holding up the second cup of coffee. "I thought you might want some fuel that didn't come out of the pot in the corner."

"You brought me coffee?" she asked, her voice heavy with suspicion. "Why?"

"Mostly because it's too early for champagne," I answered with a shrug, putting the coffee down within her reach. "I figured we'd celebrate with caffeine."

She set her items on the worktable and propped her hands on her hips. "Celebrate what?"

"Your permanent position as my sous chef." I held out a new white embroidered chef's coat and grinned as her mouth dropped open.

"Are you serious?"

"I wouldn't joke about this, Macy," I assured her, slowly taking a step forward, much like you might deal with a skittish animal. "Your own talent is responsible."

"I don't know what to say," she whispered, her bottom lip trembling with emotion as she removed her plain jacket, and I helped her into the coat emblazoned with the restaurant logo. Her blue eyes were watery when she looked into my face. "Thank you."

"You're welcome," I answered. "But it's all on you. I wouldn't have let Manuel go if he and I weren't both confident in your abilities. You're a good fit here, Macy."

She looked away, blinking furiously. I wanted to reach out and hold her face, tell her she didn't have to fear emotion when she was with me. Her tears of joy were a welcome sight, and I'd kiss them if she'd let me. I needed to rein myself in.

"Better drink the coffee while it's hot," I joked, shaking the cup so she could hear the ice.

Macy nodded and cleared her throat before reaching for the coffee and taking a tentative sip. She'd learned her lesson from the day we met. "You got my favorite."

"It wouldn't have made much sense to buy something you hated." I grinned to lighten the mood since it felt like we'd come dangerously close to sharing a moment. I couldn't tell Macy. She'd reinforce those steel walls around her heart if I even hinted at her softness.

I was saved from figuring out the direction of the conversation when Carlos breezed through the double kitchen doors and nodded at me, offering his fist for me to bump. "Morning, Chef. Macy."

"You can call her chef now, too," I tossed out.

Carlos laughed and whacked Macy on the back. "Congrats, Chef!"

"Thanks." Macy smiled, and I savored the moment. I'd done that. She'd made it possible, however. I hoped one day she would see her worth as I did.

***

"Okay, everybody, gather around!" I called out at the end of the night. "Somebody grab glasses. I've got the booze."

Leo ran off to get the cups as I produced a pitcher of *coquito*, a spiked coconut drink. When she returned, I poured the staff glasses of the sweet, creamy treat and handed it out. When everybody had a glass, I found Macy where she was lingering in the back and pulled her up front next to me. She blushed, embarrassed to be the center of attention.

"By now, all of you have heard that Macy will be my new sous chef." A few people cheered and clapped. I lifted my glass, and the others did the same. "Let's celebrate in style. To Macy!"

"To Macy!" the staff echoed, and we all drank *coquito*.

"You didn't have to do that," Macy muttered under her breath when the others walked away to finish closing up.

"Of course I did." I reached out and patted her shoulder, unable to stop myself from trailing my fingers down her arm. "You're on my turf. I get to be as nice as I want to be here."

"I didn't mean to sound ungrateful," she said, frowning.

I clenched my fist at my side, resisting the urge to smooth the furrow between her brows. "You didn't. You thanked me this morning."

"I just—I like staying under the radar," she admitted. "I don't need recognition. They don't need to use a title."

"Macy, stop." I tugged on the sleeve of her jacket, ensuring nobody watched as I pulled her out the kitchen door and down the hall to my office.

As soon as we were inside, I shut the door behind Macy. She took a step back, anchoring against the wall. I leaned forward, bracing a hand next to her head and tipping her chin up, so she had to look me in the eye with those wide blue eyes.

"You have to stop undervaluing yourself," I said firmly. Her skin was warm under my touch, and I found my thumb gently stroking beneath her plump lower lip. "You aren't *just* anything. You are talented and beautiful and deserve everything you've earned."

"I—"

I cut her off. "I'm not finished. The staff will call you Chef, and you'll stand tall and fill that leadership role for them because that's your damn job, and I wouldn't have given it to you if I didn't think you were perfect for it."

I pushed off the wall and spun away, running a hand through my hair. I was so frustrated with Macy but so fucking aroused. I couldn't let her see what she did to me, and I couldn't take advantage of her apparent vulnerability. I needed her to listen to my words.

"Matteo," she rasped behind me. When I turned, I nearly forgot myself. She looked so lost, and I wanted to tell her she didn't have to search anymore, that I'd found her. "Thank you. I know I'm awful at accepting compliments. I don't often believe that I deserve them. There's a lot of baggage involved that I don't want to talk about, but I want you to know that it means something to me."

It wasn't often that I found myself speechless, but there I stood, unable to say a word in response because I was so surprised by her openness. I knew a wrong move would result in her closing up again, so I simply nodded.

Macy pivoted, pulled the door open, and then glanced back over her shoulder. "But Matteo?"

"Yeah?" I forced out.

"If you ever put me on the spot in front of everybody again, I'll sneak out the back."

I grinned as she swept out of the room, happy to see that spirit. It only made me more determined to put her on the spot.

**

Macy locked those emotions down tight after her first official day as sous chef. She was all business and did her best to maintain at least three feet of space between us at all times. I took that as a sign that she was aware of whatever attraction pulsed between us when we were close. What she didn't understand was how much her stern, almost off-putting attitude appealed to me. It was like a challenge to get her shell to crack, to see her eyes light up with a smile.

I'd been overcoming challenges all my life. Eventually, Macy would see that and, hopefully, gracefully bow to my desire to make her happy. So many people in my life loved me, and it pained me to see how blatantly different her experience must have been. I still didn't understand how her former husband could have let her go. Even as a pessimist, she had a heart for others. It was clear in how she spoke to others and never refused to do her part in the kitchen.

So there I stood in my office, getting dressed for work, when I saw Macy walking by. I grinned to myself and called out her name. "Macy!"

I watched as she stopped, sighed, and straightened her shoulders before turning and entering my office. "Morning, Chef."

It was her typical response, an attempt to remind herself or me that I was her boss. "Good morning, Macy."

"Did you need something?" she asked, placing her hands on those gorgeous hips.

I pointed to the cup of coffee on my desk. "You need your coffee."

"You brought coffee again?" She sounded almost resigned as she stepped forward to take the cup, lifting it to her nose and inhaling the spiced scent through the tiny opening in the lid. Her eyes closed for a moment as she breathed deeply. There was a little more life in the blue when she looked at me again. "Thank you."

"You're welcome," I replied. I swiped my cravat from my desk and wrapped it around my neck before knotting it. Macy's eyes followed, her pupils dilating as she watched my fingers work. They transfixed her until I tucked the ends of the cravat under my white chef's coat and finished buttoning it.

It took a moment for her to realize she was still staring at my neck. She cleared her throat and stepped back, narrowly missing the chair behind her. "I'll see you in the kitchen."

She didn't return my smile and nod, nearly fleeing from my office in her haste to get away from me. Again, I told myself she was overwhelmed by whatever sparked between us when we were close.

I returned a few emails and touched base with Araceli before donning my chef's hat, gathering my things, and making my way to the kitchen, where my staff already had prep for the day well underway. A glance at the clock on the wall told me we still had some time before the lunch rush.

"Hats on, everyone!" I called out as I set up my filming equipment. I was relatively informal about my kitchen unless we were going to be in the public eye. Then I wanted us all to look put together. My line cooks and dishwasher quickly pulled on their black ball caps with the monogrammed restaurant logo.

Macy looked around, realizing she didn't have a hat. At least I hadn't seen her wear one yet. She always pulled her blonde hair back into that low bun. My favorite part of the night was when she changed after work and let those blonde locks down to sway freely against her back.

I took the two toque styles and offered them to Macy. "Here, you can pick from these."

Her shoulders slumped in relief, and she reached for the hats, her fingers briefly brushing against mine and sending the familiar zing of electricity up my hand. She examined the styles, then looked at the beret style I wore. "I can't have the same hat as you. I'll take the skullcap."

"You can wear either; I'm giving you the option," I clarified. While it was traditional for the tallest hat to be worn by the head chef, I didn't stand on tradition.

"I'm good with this," she said, slipping the skullcap over her hair and adjusting the back to perfect the fit.

"Good." I addressed the entire kitchen staff. "I'm going to take some video of the kitchen activity, then move on to a cooking demonstration. Just act natural."

Macy turned back to her workstation, but my plan involved her. "Macy, come help me, please."

She shot me a wary glance but nodded, shuffling over to my workspace. I placed my phone in the ring light and adjusted the angle for the video before removing it and shooting B-role of the line. Everybody looked a perfect combination of busy and happy.

I slid the cutting board toward her. "Go ahead and start slicing the plantains."

Satisfied, I put my phone back in the ring light holder and began gathering ingredients for *mofongo*. My viewers had seen me make it before, but today's tutorial wasn't only for their benefit; it was the start of my plan. I nodded at my *mise en place* and hit the button to switch to a live video on social media.

"Good morning!" I spoke animatedly into the camera. "If you're slacking off at work, congratulations—you made it just in time for *Mofongo Musings*, where I make *mofongo* and share ridiculous little stories. You may even get a bit of wisdom here and there."

I caught the corners of Macy's mouth lifting as she listened to me ad-lib my way through prep, and I told a funny tale about mistaking salt for sugar as a child. My *Abuelita* took it all in stride and started labeling her containers, and I was personally invested in not eating a salt lick again.

"Now that the oil is hot, we carefully place the plantains in the pan and fry them for about five minutes. I'll show you the golden color you want to look for as soon as they're finished." I watched as Macy did her best to avoid the camera. Instead of allowing her to fade into the background, I threw her into the spotlight. "You haven't met my new sous chef yet. Macy, come closer and let everybody see you."

Her eyes widened, and she gave me a subtle shake of her head. "Oh, I couldn't."

"Nonsense." I tugged on her coat and pulled her in front of the camera, where she froze. "Everybody welcome Macy. She's caught on quickly, and I can confidently say that she'd get *Abuelita's* stamp of approval on the dishes she prepares."

Macy blushed furiously and managed an awkward smile, then waved at the camera before stepping back and turning the plantain pieces to brown the other side. So she wasn't about the public image. Comments poured in from my viewers, greeting Macy and asking questions.

"They want to know if you're single," I tossed over my shoulder, grinning as I waited for her to answer.

"I'm single," she replied quietly, tapping a rhythm on her thigh with her nervous fingers. Warmth suffused my chest when she smiled and added, "But I don't do online dating."

"Breaking hearts already, I see." I chuckled and lifted my shoulders at the camera. "Sorry, friends, you'll have to make reservations if you want to taste what she's cooking. Right now, she will grab the mortar and pestle and break down the plantains as soon as they're drained. See that gorgeous golden color? The plantains, not Macy's hair, folks."

She giggled at that, and I lost my train of thought as she wrapped her fist around the pestle and mashed the plantains with garlic. All my thoughts turned inappropriate, and I spun away for a moment to get myself under control. The rest of the live exhibition felt like the sweetest torture, watching as Macy smiled more and gripped my heart with her dry humor.

There was no denying the desire I felt for her.

Chapter Eight

MY BOSS WAS A sadist. I could have sworn he got off on embarrassing me publicly with the way he kept pulling me in to help him with his live videos. I looked around the empty kitchen, silently running through my anxiety-coping exercises as I tied my apron and found a cutting board to help with food prep. Being one of the first people at the restaurant gave me a chance to breathe and think in peace.

"Good morning, Chef!" Amaia called out as she and Ian filtered through the kitchen door. She came already caffeinated, and her energy was endless. Ian offered a nod as he passed, heading straight for the coffeemaker to brew the potent sludge he preferred to guzzle for the first two hours of his shift.

I acknowledged them with a wave and started on the daily rundown. "We've got a fully booked lunch schedule. No VIPs, but there are two chef's tables booked this evening."

"Any menu changes?" Ian asked as he washed his hands behind the line cook station. He poured himself a cup of coffee and leaned against the counter as he sipped from his mug.

"Not today," I answered, grabbing a bag of onions to break down for *sofrito*.

"Got it." Amaia nodded as they got to work.

Over the next half hour, the servers trickled in, and I flitted around to different areas as lunch orders came through. It wasn't until there was a lull that Matteo strode through the kitchen doors, looking as hot as ever in his jacket and hat.

"Hats on, everybody!" he announced, waving his phone in the air. "Time for some musings!"

I groaned inwardly and closed my eyes, willing my expression to remain neutral. There would never be a time when I was in the mood for a social media display. I barely even maintained my own presence online. Ever since Ethan left, I'd pulled away from my accounts where mutual friends from school might ask questions I didn't want to answer.

"You ready, *ariete?*" Matteo's voice behind me made me startle, but I was getting used to him sneaking up behind me, and I managed not to toss the plate of *mofongo* I was garnishing.

I nodded brusquely and wiped around the edge of the plate. "Whatever you need, chef."

"Let's knock it out." He grinned and added, "Just don't take me out."

I rolled my eyes, and he chuckled at my response, squeezing my arm reassuringly before walking away to set up his camera. He glanced around the room to ensure everybody had proper attire before going live and holding the selfie stick out.

"I hope I caught you at a great time," he greeted his viewers, ad-libbing as more joined. "I'm going to do something new for *Mofongo Musings* this week. Sometimes it's a story; sometimes, it's an affirmation. Today at *El Corazón Borikén*, we're kicking off a season of thankfulness early, and what better way to get in a more festive mood than to find out what everybody in my home away from home is thankful for!"

He turned and waved his hands at the rest of the staff, and I gripped the edge of the prep table. My brows furrowed as I tried to figure out his game.

"I'll go first and tell you how thankful I am for every person in this building. I may have made my dreams a reality, but they could never have come true if it weren't for all the other people who work tirelessly alongside me." Matteo looked every staff member in the eye as silence filled the room. "Thank you, every one of you. I'm so grateful for what we've made here."

I couldn't help but smile with the rest of the kitchen staff, even though I hadn't done anything groundbreaking in the grand scheme. Matteo was the visionary among us.

The dishwasher, Chance, was thankful for a second job that helped his family. Amaia gave a shout-out to Portland's inclusiveness since she'd come from the Midwest and a decidedly different way of life. Ian turned and grabbed his cup of caffeinated sludge and held it up, giving a joking ode to the brew for helping him through each day.

Matteo turned toward me, and his smile made me freeze in place for a moment. He was next to me before I could put a cohesive thought together. "How about you, Macy? What are you thankful for?"

My heart raced as I silently panicked, trying to think of anything to be thankful for. I didn't think Matteo wanted me to mention my estranged husband leaving me penniless sarcastically. Quickly surveying the area, I zeroed in on the bag of onions.

I snatched two from the bag and held one in each hand with what had to be a near maniacal grin on my face as I said with more enthusiasm than anybody had ever shown for the bulbous vegetable, "I love onions!"

Matteo's eyes widened slightly, and his jaw ticked as he tried to hide a smile. The silence stretched between us, and my face heated. I felt lightheaded. Was I about to pass out? He cleared his throat and plucked the onion from my right hand, tossing it into the air and catching it without letting the selfie stick wobble.

"Ah, the onion," he mused in a voice reminiscent of old science films in school. "One of the oldest foods used by cultures across the world. This amazing Allium might not be nutritionally dense, but it packs a punch of flavor vital for so many dishes."

My jaw dropped when Matteo winked at me and continued his impromptu culinary lesson. "Onions are foundational for cooking things such as the French *mirepoix*, where onion leads the pack in a two-to-one-to-one ratio with celery and carrots. You may notice it in something as simple and timeless as chicken soup."

What in the hell was happening? I snapped my mouth shut and braced myself against the prep table. I was trapped in the public eye because Matteo wasn't finished.

"Have you ever heard of the holy trinity in Cajun and Creole cooking? I'm not talking about religion, friends. Onions, bell peppers, and celery make up the base for popular favorites such as gumbo and jambalaya."

Matteo pointed to the *sofrito*, and I quickly poured some into a small white bowl, then handed it to him like a good assistant. He made a show of smelling the veggies and sighed happily, the smile on his face widening.

"Finally, we have the life of Puerto Rican cooking—sofrito. Apologies to all my French culinarians who like to claim the origin of nearly every food, but *sofrito* predates *mirepoix*. It goes all the way back to medieval Spain in one form or another, even before the colonizers came to Puerto Rico. The kind I make consists of onions, peppers, garlic, and cilantro, just like *Abuelita* taught me."

He spoke with such passion that I couldn't tear my eyes away. Chef uniforms weren't known for their sex appeal, but on Matteo, it had my blood heating, and not with embarrassment for once. My mouth watered as I imagined what it would be like to taste his lips against mine.

"You might say it's *El Corazón Borikén*," Matteo said with a grin. I knew he didn't mean that he was the heart of it all, but there was a twinge in my chest that longed for somebody to love me with as much passion and dedication as he dedicated to his craft. After a year without Ethan, I realized the love I felt for him was that of a naïve girl who believed in fairy tales and happy endings. No man who loved me as much as I thought could leave me without a trace.

A nudge to my shoulder drew me out of my thoughts, and I lifted my eyes to see Matteo tipping his head curiously. "You okay, *ariete?*"

"Yeah," my voice cracked, and I cleared my throat, unable to keep eye contact. "Fine."

"Thanks for dropping that right into my lap." He set the onion back at my workstation with a nod.

"Just using my social ineptitude for the greater good," I replied drily. Maybe I could cry tears of frustration and blame it on the onions.

Matteo shook his head. "You're not inept, Macy. You're endearing. Stop being so hard on yourself."

I felt the brush of his fingertips across my lower back send electricity pulsing along my spine as he left me standing there, considering what he'd just said.

***

Leo dragged me out to a bar after work because I told her there was no way I was recounting my onion debacle without her buying me enough drinks that I wouldn't care about my feelings anymore. We piled into a booth at the back, and she set two shots of whiskey in front of me.

"Here you go." She motioned for me to drink up.

I took the first glass and knocked it back, counting the burn at the back of my throat as deserved punishment for my asinine behavior at work. I'd never been great around people. Leo and Ethan were the two people who seemed to accept me as I was. Matteo brought out the worst of my awkwardness, but he never mocked me when I tripped over my words. Ethan used to poke fun at it, laughing it off as a joke. I wondered what it meant that I feared Matteo hurting me with mocking words more than it had ever mattered with my ex.

"Do you need the second shot, or are you going to spill now?" Leo asked, sipping on her beer. She wore ripped black jeans and her white button-up shirt from work, but she'd added a vest over the top and rolled her sleeves. Paired with her boots, she rocked the daddy look better than most men. When we were waiting for our drinks, a petite blonde had slipped her a piece of paper with a number and held her hand up, mimicking a phone. Leo took it in stride, shooting her a suave smirk and nodding her thanks.

I looked down at my oversized white sweater and black fleece-lined leggings. Men were not clamoring to get my number, but I probably wouldn't give it to them, anyway.

I grabbed the second shot glass and finished it before reaching for a fry in the basket between us. "I don't suppose there's any getting out of this?"

"Not a chance," she said, lifting a brow.

"Fine." I took a deep breath and let myself recall the day's earlier events. "Matteo asked us what we were thankful for, and the others all had great ideas. My mind blanked, and I don't know why, but I said the first thing that came to mind."

"Onions," Leo finished for me, struggling to keep a straight face.

"I developed an immediate affinity for them, I guess." I shrugged.

Leo pointed a fry at me. "It's like you've got Stockholm syndrome from that time your chef made you cut onions until you ran out of tears."

"Must be."

"Did the garlic feel left out? I feel like they're good bedfellows," she teased lightly.

Matteo had listed it as an ingredient in *sofrito*. "It got an honorable mention."

"I hope you oiled them up well." Leo was heading straight for the gutter, but once she got started, it was hard to curtail the behavior.

"No oil."

"Ah, raw-doggin' it, huh?" She giggled when she saw the look on my face. "I like your style."

"You're so gross sometimes." I shook my head and laughed at her suggestive banter. Instead of getting another drink, I poured myself water from the pitcher on the table and gulped half the glass down.

"Think positive, babes," she said with a mouthful of fries. "It could have been worse. Sounds like Matteo saved your ass."

I couldn't argue with her there. "Yeah, I guess he did. It would have been better if he'd never put me on the spot to begin with, though."

"You're working for a celebrity chef." She used her hands to emphasize her words. "It comes with the territory. You're lucky he doesn't just set up a live video to film for hours on end."

"I'd quit."

"No, the fuck you wouldn't." Leo rolled her eyes at me. "You need the job too much, and I think you like Matteo enough that you won't walk away. You want to see where it goes."

"There's nothing to *go* anywhere." I lied—kind of. I didn't know for sure whether Matteo was interested in me as more than his sous chef. He was nice to everybody. I wasn't good at hiding my attraction to him with all the blushing and brain-farting.

Leo wasn't ready to let it go at that. "We should find out. We could see if the others are still at the usual bar. Sometimes Matteo goes with them. I could conveniently forget to wait for you, so he has to give you another ride home."

"I am not manipulating the man into spending time with me." Sometimes I questioned Leo's sanity, because that was a little much. We weren't in a high school drama where the entire plot revolved around lies. I would never want a relationship built on anything but the truth. I'd already been there, done that, and was painfully aware of how much of an abysmal failure it had been.

"Are you planning to stay single and celibate for the rest of your life?" she asked, signaling to the server and ordering another basket of fries. I was going to be bloated from the carbs in the morning.

"Probably not," I offered. "But it's only been a year since Ethan left. The divorce isn't even finalized. I'm not ready to get out Cupid's bow and start hunting for another husband."

"Maybe you just start by being open to the possibility of somebody else in the future," Leo suggested, leaning forward and resting her forearms on the table. "Maybe somebody tall, dark, and Puerto Rican."

"Stop it," I groaned, covering my face with my palm. "Being open to our boss would be a disaster in itself. So many things could go wrong with it."

"But that's not a guarantee. Things could go right instead. Allow yourself to live again, Macy," Leo said, her eyes filled with compassion. "Reach for the life you want. Nobody is going to hand you a happy ending."

Her words hit home, but along with them came another realization—one person seemed determined to show me what happiness was like.

Chapter Nine

THE OCTOBER WIND RATTLED the door of the coffee shop, but it was warm and cozy where I sat with the Rivera brothers for our Monday coffee meeting. They were chaotic as usual, debating who made the best pancakes for their Sunday brunch, and had immediately disqualified me from the running because I had an unfair advantage as a professional chef.

"Olivia ate two of my blueberry pancakes yesterday," Gabriel bragged, crossing his ankle over his knee. He'd worked out early and came dressed for the office in a dark green suit with an orange tie and orange socks peeking out between his pants and brown dress shoes.

Xander rolled his eyes at his youngest brother. "Of course, she ate them—you're her father. She'd eat liver and onions if you made it for her."

"At least I cook." Gabriel lifted a brow at Xander, who had a personal chef prepare meals for his family every week.

"Jean ensures every meal has the correct nutrients," Xander said smugly. "Tell me, what's the nutritional value of chocolate chips?"

Gabriel took a long drink of his coffee before responding. "Some things are about feeding the heart, not the body."

They both had valid points, but the best solution was somewhere in the middle. "I always say it's best to feed the body and soul."

"And that's why people love you," Julian said with a smile. "You bring something good to a world that often lacks love."

"I've been blessed by those I love. It's only right that I share it with others." My *Abuelita* spent her life loving me as she thought my parents would have, and as a result, I never questioned where I belonged or my self-worth. It bothered me that people couldn't see that it was simple humanity to love and support others.

Julian patted me on the shoulder in a brotherly way. "Nobody will ever doubt your sincerity."

"How are things going with the grumpy chef?" Gabriel asked. Xander gave him a subtle kick in the shin as he crossed his legs. "Come on. You know you're curious."

"Be nice," the oldest Rivera admonished.

"I'm not being mean. I'm being straightforward." Gabriel turned back to me. "It seems like the perfect opportunity for you to turn on that charm and turn her frowns upside down."

There was no keeping anything in my life from the three of them. They had a sixth sense about anything to do with a woman, and when I told them the little blonde from the coffee shop showed up at my restaurant to interview for the position of my sous chef, they had a field day with it. Julian acted casual, but I'd been getting texts and calls from his wife, Luna, who always brought up Macy. I couldn't turn her down, so I spilled everything. If anything ever came of whatever it was between Macy and me, she'd need the fortitude to face my found family.

"So?" Julian nodded in my direction.

"There's not much to tell," I admitted, wishing it weren't true. "We work together, but I don't think she's ready for anything else. From what I've gathered, she's going through a divorce."

Gabriel puffed out a breath. "But she's not with her husband now?"

"No, he's not around."

"She's fair game, then," he concluded. "You should get on that before somebody else moves in on her."

"For fuck's sake." Xander ran a hand down his face. "She's not a football—she's a person."

Gabriel shrugged. "Love is a game. I just want to see Matteo win."

"I'm not sure you're the one who should give him relationship advice." Xander finished the last of his coffee and set the mug down, focusing on his youngest brother. "Jane literally left the state when you fucked up."

"How is that any different from Viola moving back to Florida because she didn't think you had feelings for her?" Gabriel shot back.

I let them exchange brotherly barbs because it meant they weren't focusing on me. Finally, Julian cleared his throat. "All I hear is that neither of you is qualified. And before you come for me, I'm not saying I'm any better."

"I appreciate that," I finally spoke up.

Julian continued, "You should talk to our wives. They can tell you how to avoid acting like an ass."

"Oh, I like this idea." Gabriel grinned and rubbed the artful stubble on his chin. "Fuck knows if Jane can put up with me, she can give you some pointers."

"I don't think I need any help," I protested. "As I've said, there's nothing between Macy and me, regardless of my wishes. Not all of us go and claim women like neanderthals."

"Yeah, but it worked," Xander mumbled as he checked his phone. "Speaking of women, my wife is craving chocolate peanut butter ice cream, so I need to run to the store."

"At eight in the morning?" I questioned.

They all looked at me like it was obvious, and Xander shook his head, his dark, styled hair not moving an inch under his gel. The man could make disapproval an art form. "You don't question a pregnant woman."

His brothers nodded in agreement, and I shrugged. They would know better than me on that front. I didn't have any experience with pregnant women or babies. Though, now I wondered if I should pay more attention as my friends grew their families. I wanted kids of my own one day.

Xander stood and hooked a finger through the handle of his mug. "I'm going to get going. Her list will grow if I don't get the ice cream soon."

We all chuckled. He inclined his head toward me. "I'll have Viola call you if she has any useful advice."

"Sure thing." I smiled, but inwardly I cringed. There was no way I could tell a pregnant woman her opinion wasn't welcome. If I upset Viola, Xander would be up my ass about it. I didn't have a death wish.

"You know that when Luna and Jane catch wind of this, there's no stopping them," Julian stated.

"Yeah, I know." I would need more coffee if I were fielding calls from all the women.

Julian's phone chimed, and he swiped his finger across the screen, smiling at whatever he found. "I need to head into the office."

I doubted that whatever put a grin on his face was work-related, but I knew better than to question it because he'd probably tell me things I didn't want to know.

"I should get going, anyway." I had some things to organize for an upcoming charity event I held every few months, and there wasn't enough time to focus on it when the restaurant was open. I was confident I could pull Macy into working with me.

We moved to the exit, dropping our mugs in the dish bin on the way out. I thanked the baristas and gave them a friendly wave before stepping out into the misty breeze. I'd be soaked when I ran home, but the cold made me feel more alive.

Gabriel gave me a firm pat on the shoulder. "See you soon."

"Bring your family to the restaurant soon." I couldn't resist teasing him a little in return for putting me on the spot. "I'll let Olivia help make your dinner and show her who the real pancake champion is."

He laughed as he walked away, calling behind him, "You can try."

***

Our customer demographic leaned heavily toward families during weekend brunch, and I loved watching as they spent time together enjoying food and conversation. I had the opportunity to make all my favorite pastries from childhood and see others creating memories linked to those flavors.

The kitchen staff stood behind a long row of tables, making fresh *crema* and *revoltillo* to order. I ran to the back to get more eggs and returned with the bowl to find Macy focused on a little blonde girl asking a slew of questions about the food. Macy's smile made the corners of her eyes crinkle as she explained scrambling the eggs and adding veggies to the mix.

As the little girl watched, her blue eyes widened at the way Macy effortlessly tossed peppers and onions in the pan with our house-made *chorizo* and sprinkled cilantro over the top. The fire flared as she set the pan down again, and the little girl breathed, "*Wow.*"

My skin tingled with the need to be closer to Macy, to breathe in the joy she exuded whenever she cooked. I grabbed a few eggs and stood next to her, cracking them into a metal bowl and quickly whisking them into a fluffy froth before handing the bowl over.

"Thanks, Chef." Macy directed one of those smiles my way, and I fucking melted inside.

"You're welcome, Chef," I answered with a wink. The little girl giggled, and Macy turned her attention back to the customers as she finished preparing their Puerto Rican-style scrambled eggs and plated them artfully.

The girl's father took the plates from Macy and nodded his thanks, nudging the little girl to move forward so the next customer could have food. She called back in a lilting voice, "Thank you, Chef!"

"You're very welcome," Macy said with a smile and wave before clearing the pan and beginning the process again.

Reluctant to leave her side so soon, I helped with the mise en place at the station. Macy shot me a sidelong glance but didn't miss a beat greeting and conversing with the customers. She was a natural at it when she relaxed. I wondered how often she'd been able to let her guard down and just *be* in her life. It seemed she spent much of her time wound tight, like she was waiting for the worst to happen.

At the next lull, Macy stepped back and dug her thumbs into her lower back, stretching and letting out a soft moan that had me crossing my legs to hide my immediate reaction. I wondered whether she would moan like that with me between her thighs.

"You're good with kids," I said to distract myself. "First Olivia, now the little girl this morning."

She twirled the end of her blonde ponytail around her finger nervously. "Thanks."

"Do you have kids of your own?" I asked, realizing she never spoke of her family other than a few bitter words about her ex.

"Oh, no." Macy shook her head sadly. "Ethan never seemed to be ready."

Ethan. I hated him for putting that regret on her gorgeous face. "But you want a family?"

"I did," she murmured, smoothing her apron and straightening her white skullcap. "It's hard to find a man who would make both a good husband and father."

"Do you think your experience is coloring how you view the rest of the male population?" I asked cautiously. It felt like I was treading toward dangerous waters, but I couldn't stop. I wanted to wrap my fingers around every tidbit of information Macy had surrendered.

She smiled ruefully. "I know it is. Looking back, it's clear that Ethan never wanted a family. He enjoyed showing me off. He was charming from the moment we met in high school, but always a little distant. I'm not sure he ever really loved me—at least not like I loved him. I was a fool to fall in love."

"I don't think it's ever foolish to share your heart."

Macy's face twisted, and I glimpsed the deep wound underneath. "You might change your mind when it's broken and bleeding out inside you."

"I lost both of my parents when I was a toddler," I revealed, unsure how much she knew about my past. Her eyes snapped to mine, and I saw regret there. "There was a hurricane, and a tree fell on the part of the house where their room was. It killed them instantly as they slept, and a neighbor found me screaming in my crib the next morning."

Macy's hand flew to her cheek. "I'm so sorry. I didn't know."

"My *Abuelita* raised me after that," I explained. "She gave me her passion for cooking and showed me all the love my parents would have if they had lived. She wanted nothing more than to see my success, but she passed before I opened *El Corazón Borikén*."

Macy's mouth hung open, and her eyes filled with tears, but she said nothing, so I continued. "All of that made me even more convinced how important it is to share my love, regardless of whatever heartaches may come, because life is short, and I never want anyone to doubt how much I care."

"I don't know how you do it," she whispered, blinking rapidly. "You must be so strong because I can't figure it out."

I glanced around to ensure nobody was watching, then reached out and wiped a tear from where it trailed slowly down her cheek. "I'm not stronger than you, *ariete*. I refused to let my heart join those I love in the grave. They wouldn't have wanted that. I *live* for them, for myself."

"He didn't die, though." Her voice broke. "He didn't love me. And it makes me afraid that nobody else will, either."

I motioned to the line. "Look around you. Everybody here sees your value, and they care about you. I don't say that we're a family lightly. I mean it. Please, don't let one asshole douse that flame inside you. I can see it flickering every time you're here."

Macy nodded, swiping another tear from her face and clearing her throat. "Right. I know."

"Speaking of caring," I segued, sensing that her moment of vulnerability had passed. "I have a class coming up, and I need a sous chef."

She looked surprised. "You teach classes? Like, for cooking?"

"Those who do should teach," I responded with a shrug. "What good is it to have a passion if you don't pass it on to others?"

"You've got a point." Macy glanced down to the end of the line, and I saw her fingers tap against her thigh, counting the customers making their way toward us. "When do you need me?"

Now. Forever.

My thoughts startled me, and I grabbed an onion, slicing it in half and letting the gas burn my eyes to bring me back to rational thoughts. Macy didn't want to be possessed. She wanted to love and be loved in return.

"Monday evening," I supplied. "It's just a community cooking class here at the restaurant. Nothing fancy, just the basics. It's off the clock, but for a good cause. You think you can handle it?"

"Yeah, I think I can manage." Macy gave me a hint of that smile I loved, and my heart swelled.

Every moment I was around Macy made me more of a liar to my found family. She would never be *just* a sous chef. I only hoped that she wouldn't be one of the people in my life who left scars on my heart.

Chapter Ten

"WHAT ARE YOU GOING to wear?" Leo asked as I stood in front of my closet in my black bra and underwear.

I rolled my eyes at her. "My chef's uniform. It's a cooking class."

"Oh, come on, it's as good as a date. At least wear that hot little tank top that makes your boobs look fabulous." She yanked the red top from where it was buried among the rest of my clothes.

"This is absolutely *not* a date. It's more like community service." I reached for my black pants and stepped into them, hopping as I pulled the waist over my hips and ass. "Besides, nobody is even going to see what I've got on under my coat."

"Then you have no reason not to wear it," Leo said smugly as she thrust the red fabric into my hands.

I reluctantly tugged it over my head. "You're awful; do you know that?"

"Think of it as my form of community service." She grinned and tightened her ponytail. "Both you and Matteo deserve a little happiness."

"I think he's happy all the time," I grumbled. A twinge of regret made my chest tighten as I remembered him sharing the past tragedy in his life. I couldn't begrudge Matteo's happiness when he clung to every positive moment after losing his parents and grandmother.

It hit me that the feeling I counted as resentment was jealousy. I envied his ability to process grief and move past it. Meanwhile, I was stuck in a rut that Ethan had dug, unable to pull myself out of the ditch and get back to living my life. Sure, I went through the motions, but the moments I felt truly happy were few and far between.

"Nobody is happy all the time," Leo pointed out. "Not even me, and I'm amazing."

"You are amazing," I agreed.

"Awfully amazing," she shot back with a laugh. "What time do you have to be at the restaurant?"

I looked down at my watch and was startled by the time. "In half an hour! I've got to go if I don't want to be late."

Leo moved out of my way as I slipped into my chef's coat while I moved through the living room, finding my jacket and pulling it on before grabbing my bag. She handed me a hat and gloves, and I nodded gratefully as I donned them.

"I think I've got everything." I hugged my friend briefly. "I'll text you when I'm on the way home."

"Sounds good." Leo opened the door for me, and I rushed past. "And Macy?"

I stopped on the walkway and turned to look at her. "Yeah?"

"When Matteo offers to drive you home, let him."

"Fine." I didn't have time to argue. She gave me a triumphant smile and wiggled her fingers at me before she shut the door.

I hurried through the neighborhood to the nearest MAX station. Thankfully, I only had to wait a few minutes to catch the next train, and it was only a few blocks from where I got off to the restaurant. I arrived two minutes before Matteo instructed, allowing me to catch my breath at the corner of the building before walking calmly inside.

"Macy!" Matteo spread his arms wide and greeted me from where he stood in his uniform by a row of dining tables that had been moved together. "I'm glad you could make it."

"Hey." I pulled my gloves off and shoved them in my pockets. "I'm going to put my stuff away, and I'll be right back."

Matteo inclined his head, and I skirted around him, dashing to the back room to store my things and take one more look in the mirror. The hat had mussed my hair, so I pulled the elastic from it and ran my fingers through the blonde strands, restoring order enough to twist them back into a low bun. Since Matteo was wearing his chef's hat, I grabbed mine and tied it snugly in the back.

While I knew Matteo only asked me to help him as a professional courtesy, my heart fluttered against my will when he was near. I wanted him to like me, to be attracted to me, even though I wasn't sure I wanted to accept my attraction to him. It was probably something I should talk to my therapist about, but that was something to think about later.

I swiped some tinted gloss across my lips and cleaned up a smudge of mascara under my eye. My vanity might have driven me to wear makeup, but I stopped short of trying to impress, opting for neutral shadows and liner. It was subtle, but classy. Satisfied with my appearance, I tied my cravat and headed back to the dining room.

"Looking good," Matteo called out with a grin, making me blush. He pointed to a stack of mixing bowls on the metal prep table in front of the makeshift classroom. "Can you put one of those on each of the tables? Everybody gets a bowl, a spatula, and the ingredients."

"Yeah, got it." We began distributing items across the tables. It seemed odd to have such low prep areas, but I wasn't going to question my boss. I figured he knew what he was doing.

Soon, we completed the mise en place for each table. I stepped back and admired our handiwork.

"They should be here soon," Matteo said, as he looked toward the door.

He was proved right when a moment later, a mother stepped through the door with a little boy who couldn't have been over eight. His curly hair flopped over one eye, and he pushed it back, looking around the room. When he spotted Matteo, his entire face lit up. *Same, kid. Same.*

"Chef!" The boy waved as he scampered across the floor.

"Hey, Alex!" Matteo gave him a high five in greeting. "It's great to see you again. I hope you thanked Lori for bringing you back."

"I did," the boy said proudly, glancing back at the blonde woman who had taken one of the seats arranged further back. She gave him an approving nod.

"Good." Matteo gave him a light pat on the shoulder. "Go ahead and pick a workspace. We'll wait until the others arrive to get started."

It didn't take long to realize that Matteo's community cooking class was for kids. In the next ten minutes, eleven more eager students arrived with their adults, and soon we had a full house. I did my best to smile and shake hands, but the kids flocked to Matteo with laughter and smiles. Most seemed to know who he was, and in more than a celebrity chef online kind of way. Matteo knew their names and talked to them with ease.

One small girl with black hair covering her face hung back from the others, her shoulders hunched and arms crossed over her chest protectively. I recognized her reticence and walked over, bracing my hands on my knees, closer to her level.

"What's your name?" I asked gently.

She flinched at my voice and her hair parted enough for me to see one deep brown assessing eye staring back. I held my breath until she finally answered, "Sam."

"It's nice to meet you, Sam. I'm Macy." I held a hand out, but she shrunk back, so I fiddled with the buttons on my coat instead. She was skittish, so I tried to act chill. "Have you ever been to a cooking class here before?"

Sam nodded but kept her eyes on the table in front of her, her frail-looking fingers brushing over the red-handled spatula.

"Well," I said enthusiastically. "I hope you have a great time tonight. I'm going to stand by Chef Matteo, but I can't wait to cook with you."

Again, Sam nodded, but said nothing. I hadn't been a timid child, but sometimes crowds of strangers put me on edge. I felt for the little girl.

Matteo clapped his hands rhythmically, and the kids rushed to find their tables. When they had quieted down, he began his spiel. "Welcome to the *El Corazón Borikén* Halloween cookie decorating extravaganza!"

The kids cheered, and I realized I was in for a very different cooking class. Matteo shushed them with a downward motion of his hands. "You each have tools and ingredients at your stations. If you listen closely to instructions and follow them, your cookies will be just like my *Abuelita's*. Now, let me introduce you to my sous chef, Macy. Everybody welcome her—it's her first cooking class."

A chorus of greetings bombarded me, and I smiled and waved at the excited little faces. It didn't take long to fall into the groove as Matteo taught the kids how to cream butter and sugar, then add the rest of the ingredients in order. We walked among the students, lending a hand where needed and cleaning up rogue flour.

The kids put their finished, wrapped cookie dough in the walk-in while they took turns washing and putting away their bowls and utensils. Matteo didn't leave out any step in the process, making them take responsibility for their hard work.

When it was time to roll out the dough and use cookie cutters to cut out leaves, ghosts, pumpkins, and other Halloween shapes, impulse control flew out the window, and quite a few students sampled the raw sugar cookie dough. Matteo just laughed and told the kids to pace themselves, so they didn't get stomach aches before they ate the finished product.

We had plenty of room in the ovens for all the half-sheet pans, and I loaded everything up so we didn't have any unintentional injuries. When I saw Sam hanging at the back of the crowd again, I approached and offered to help her put the pan in the oven.

"You can walk over with me," I explained when she didn't respond.

"Hey, Sam!" Matteo gave a warning of his approach before standing next to the little girl. "How about I take that for you? Macy will stand with you, and you can watch, okay?"

She nodded and allowed Matteo to take the cookie sheet. As she watched him place it in the oven, her hair shifted away from her face, and I smothered a gasp with my palm. The side of Sam's face was a mottled mass of angry scars. She quickly covered her cheek, glancing around to see if anybody had noticed the slip.

"We can wait in the dining room with the others," I offered, trying to act like nothing had happened. Sam nodded and followed the other kids to where everybody chatted with the adults while they waited for the cookie timer to go off. I mentally shook off the shock, knowing it wasn't my place to ask what had happened.

After we had pulled the cookie sheets from the oven, Matteo rolled the sheet pan cart to the dining room to cool while he went over the decorating instructions.

"Now, the fun part—frosting!" Matteo whisked a white cloth off of tubs of colored frosting. The kids cheered again, and Matteo motioned me over to help portion out the frosting to each aspiring baker.

More frosting ended up coloring tables and tongues than on the cookies, but both children and adults devoured the finished treats. The class drew to a close, and I offered to wash the remaining dishes while Matteo saw the guests out.

I'd just finished putting the last of the sheet pans away when I heard him push through the kitchen doors.

"Coffee?" he asked as he grabbed himself a mug.

I shook my head and dried my hands. "No, I'm good, thanks. I want to go home, fall into my bed, and sleep for twelve hours."

"Same," he chuckled, putting the mug away. "What did you think about the class?"

"You're an amazing instructor," I said truthfully. "Those kids all love you. I think your *Abuelita* would be very proud of you."

"Thank you," Matteo said quietly. "I'm sure she would be. You were great with them, too."

Now was my best chance to ask the question burning at the back of my mind. "The little girl. Sam? Do you know her story?"

"All the kids at my classes are either in foster care or were adopted out of foster care," Matteo explained somberly. "Sam's mother died when she was a baby, and her father was a monster. She was removed from his custody after he pressed her face against an open oven door because she dropped a cup of milk. She was five."

I couldn't stop the cry of distress that escaped when my heart seized with sympathy. "Oh, poor Sam."

"Many of them have tragic stories. I wanted to give them something that allowed them to be kids and enjoy something, free of all the shit in their lives."

I walked over to where Matteo stood and reached my hand out to touch his arm reassuringly. "You did. I could see how much all of them loved cooking with you. It was amazing."

"It will never be enough," he said sadly. My heart ached for the man standing before me, who had experienced tragedy but was so selfless that all he cared about was making sure others were happy.

"Do you have a sixth toe on one foot?" I asked abruptly, unwilling to let the threatening tears take hold. I needed to change the subject.

"Come again?" Matteo looked perplexed.

I pointed at his black clogs. "An extra toe? You know, because there's no way you can be this damn perfect. You must have a hidden flaw."

"I'm far from perfect," he laughed, tapping the toe of one shoe against the other. "But I'm sorry to disappoint you. Ten fingers and ten toes. Only the standard number of appendages."

My eyes were immediately drawn to the location of one appendage that I thought of too often for my own good. Matteo cleared his throat, and I looked away quickly.

"My eyes are up here, Macy." Was it just me, or had his tone deepened, those accented words flowing smoothly from his tongue?

I couldn't tear my eyes away from the heat I found in those dark pools, from how he ran his tongue across his bottom lip suggestively before pulling it between his teeth briefly. Was it wrong that my eyelids closed, that I leaned in, feeling the heat of Matteo's body so close to mine? My lips parted, and I breathed him in, feeling a tug low in my abdomen.

"Macy," he whispered against my mouth before his lips brushed against mine, just the barest touch.

I let out a sigh of quiet desperation when he pulled back, opening my eyes long enough to see the moment he threw caution to the wind. Matteo's hands framed my face, and his lips crashed down on mine, his tongue probing for entrance that I granted. He tasted of sugar and spices, of longing and lust. I was lost in him, in the glide of his tongue against mine and the feel of his stubble against my lips.

It was over too soon, and I felt the loss of Matteo's touch poignantly when he took a step back. My entire body shook with the intensity of it all. My chest heaved as I tried to catch my breath, as I looked at him questioningly. Maybe I had done something wrong.

"Stop whatever thoughts you're having right now, Macy," Matteo admonished, stroking his fingertips down my arm. "You were perfect. Addictingly so."

"Then why—"

He motioned around us. "We're standing in the kitchen, and that is not how I want to start things with you."

"I don't know if I can." I let the meaning hang in the absence of spoken words, but Matteo nodded his understanding.

"I'm not going to force you," he assured me. "But if you're interested—if we start—I won't be able to stop."

It was unfathomable that he could desire me so much, but I'd never felt the kind of electricity that pulsed through my body with his kiss. Maybe he meant what he said.

"Okay," I answered. "Can I think about it?"

"Absolutely." Matteo began unbuttoning his chef's jacket. "Why don't you get changed, and I'll drive you home."

I nodded and walked to the lockers in a daze, my fingers brushing against my kiss-swollen lips, trying to make the sensation last as long as possible.

88

Chapter Eleven

I KISSED *MACY*.

I was still fixated on it a week later. That single minute of my life brought more joy than almost all of my accomplishments. I was ready to whisk her from the kitchen and take her back to my place and never stop, but I knew she wasn't there yet. There were too many invisible scars on Macy's heart for her to give in so easily.

Rather than make her stop us, I decided to pull back and give her the time and space she needed to accept where things were headed. I wasn't going to let her go. Everything about how our lips fit together told me she was meant to be mine. I just had to wait until she realized it, too.

"Corner!" Macy's voice rang out as she brought a tray of sweet dessert *empanadas* from the rack to the prep area. The smell of guava and spices filled the air.

"Need a hand?" I offered as she grabbed a stack of plates.

"Sure. Thanks, Chef." She gave me one of her smiles, and I grinned as we worked shoulder-to-shoulder to get the desserts ready for service. I took every opportunity to brush my body against hers when there was no danger of ruining the presentation on a plate.

"I think we're done," Macy said as she plated the final *empanada*. "Thanks again, Chef."

"You're very welcome, *Chef.*" I loved the way she blushed when I used the title. I did it as often as possible, and she finally stopped protesting.

"Chef!" Leo bounded through the kitchen doors. "Table six wants to know if you've got a minute to spare."

"Yeah, I can pop out there real quick." I took my apron off and washed my hands before donning my chef's hat and following Leo. I tried to talk to my guests whenever possible, but the kitchen was a chaotic environment without much downtime, given that the restaurant was almost always fully booked.

I greeted Leo's customers, who had traveled from Washington to eat at *El Corazón Borikén*, and told my server to send them *empanadas* on the house as I walked away. It didn't take me long to stop by the other tables and greet my guests before returning to the kitchen. The renewed aroma of *sazon* and cilantro hit my nose and made me smile.

The rest of the night passed quickly, filled with the sounds of the grill and plates clinking as the servers whisked them from kitchen to customer. We finished cleaning up, and Macy leaned against the prep table, sighing and clearly exhausted. I wiped my brow on my sleeve and looked around the kitchen, satisfied with a job well done.

"Let's get everybody in here real quick," I called out. One of the servers ran out the doors to spread the word, and I poured myself a cup of coffee while I waited for everybody to gather around. "It's October, and you all know what that means. It's time for our pumpkin carving contest!"

Tired cheers echoed through the kitchen. Every year we held the contest, and the winner received five hundred dollars. The winning pumpkins were always impressive.

"When do we need to have them in?" Leo asked.

"Bring them on Wednesday," I told her. "That gives everybody their days off to work on the pumpkins. I'll take Wednesday and Thursday to judge and announce the winner on Friday. That's all for tonight. Get home safe."

I nudged Macy in greeting. "Are you ready to put those carving skills to use?"

"I've actually never carved a pumpkin," she admitted, biting her lip. "At least not for art. I've cut them up to roast them."

"How is that even possible?" I asked, astonished. Pumpkin carving was a staple childhood experience.

"My mother wasn't really into the DIY decorating," Macy explained. "Our house always looked magazine perfect, but I don't remember my mom ever making decorations. She always hired a company or bought things from the store. The pumpkins on our front porch were plastic."

"A travesty," I said dramatically. It gave me an idea. "I'm a veteran pumpkin carver. We can work on them together."

"Oh, you don't have to do that," she protested, working on a knot in her low ponytail.

"Nonsense." I wasn't going to let her out of this one. "I'll pick you up Monday afternoon and give you the whole pumpkin carving experience. Block it off on your schedule."

"I—" Macy stopped and took a deep breath, blowing it out slowly between those plump rosy lips. "Fine, we can do that. Monday afternoon."

"Awesome." I beamed at her, already looking forward to our informal date. I wouldn't use that word with her, though. "Do you need a ride home?"

She waved me off. "Thanks, but no. Leo and I can catch the MAX."

"Let the man with the heated truck take us home, Macy," Leo pouted as she approached, already wearing her coat. "We'd love to accept, Matteo."

"Let me get changed, and I'll meet you by the back door." I silently celebrated that small win, happy to have Leo on my side when it came to Macy. I'd break down those walls eventually.

***

"Where are we?" Macy asked as I pulled into the gravel parking lot of the farm.

"A real-life pumpkin patch." I chuckled when she did a double-take. "You didn't think I'd take you to the store to pick out a pumpkin?"

"I did, yes."

"I figured you'd never been to a pumpkin patch if you'd never carved a pumpkin." I hopped down from the truck, circled the vehicle to open Macy's door, and offered my hand to help her. "Was I wrong?"

"You were right," she admitted, taking my hand and sliding to the ground. "So, what do we do here?"

I led her to the little stand where they were selling apple cider donuts. "We eat sugary fried foods and find the perfect pumpkins to carve. My treat."

"Oh, you don't have to do that," she protested, her blonde hair framing her face as she shook her head. I rarely saw her with her hair down, and it looked so soft that my fingers itched to touch it.

I raised a brow at her. "I don't want to hear you say that again. I don't do anything I don't want to do. Watching you experience a pumpkin patch for the first time brings me joy."

"I guess I can't take that away from you." She took the little brown bag of donuts I offered her and followed me out to the field. The smell of rain and vegetation replaced the sugar and spice of the food stand.

"Your kingdom, m'lady." I waved an arm in a broad arc, and Macy giggled. Heat shot straight to my groin, and I clenched as many muscles as possible to stop myself from being the weird dude sporting an erection in public.

Macy walked down the rows of pumpkins, looking at the various sizes, shapes, and colors. I admired her round ass and swaying hips, covered in jeans that looked like they were painted on. She wore little brown boots and an oversized brown sweater that hid those delicious curves. It made me want to wrap my hands around her waist and pull that fabric tight to reveal her figure beneath.

"So, how do I pick one? Is there some kind of trick to choosing the best carving pumpkin?"

"Pick whichever pumpkin you like best." I popped a sugar-coated donut in my mouth and closed my eyes as I savored the sweet, spiced flavor. Macy was staring at me when I looked at her. "Don't make it more complicated than it needs to be."

She bit her lip and leaned down, her fingertips grazing over a white and orange speckled pumpkin. I was not going to rush her along with that view. Instead, I contentedly followed as I munched on donuts, answering questions here and there. I knew next to nothing about pumpkins, but I loved carving them, and I made a mean pumpkin soup—the thought had me contemplating getting a few sugar pumpkins for dinner.

"Oh, I like this one!" Macy exclaimed from further up the row. She'd found a modestly sized, perfectly proportioned orange pumpkin. Of course.

"Looks great!" I called to her. "I can carry that for you."

"No need!" She traipsed back toward me, trying to see over the bulk of the gourd. "I've got it!"

Only she didn't. She tripped on a rogue vine a few feet away, and the pumpkin flew straight for my head. I dodged the projectile—a feat I attributed to my experience avoiding Macy's unpredictable hits—and thrust my arms out, catching Macy and rolling us before she could hit the dirt.

She landed on my chest, her lips a hair's breadth from mine. I inhaled in her minty breath and felt my cock harden in my jeans and press against her thigh. It was not the time or place for him to get involved. I was trying to woo Macy slowly until she was too in love to protest. "Are you okay?"

"Yeah, I'm good," she panted, fingers curling into my white jacket—the same jacket she'd showered with coffee at our first meeting. "Thanks for catching me."

"No problem."

She wiggled her hips as she pushed herself to a sitting position and then to her feet, offering me a hand so I could stand. I savored the feel of her palm against mine and the soft smile on her face when I rubbed my thumb across her knuckles.

"Oh, no," Macy moaned when I moved. I turned to see what she was looking at. The perfect pumpkin lay scattered across the dirt in pieces. "Now I have to find another."

"We'll figure it out," I assured her as I kicked the broken pumpkin to the side. "Come on. And maybe let me carry the pumpkin this time."

Macy's laughter warmed me, and I admired her willingness to brush off her mishap and renew her search for the perfect pumpkin. It gave me hope she would one day set her past aside so she could embrace her future—preferably a future that included me.

"This one is close." She pointed to another perfectly portioned pumpkin. "I'll take it."

I leaned down and picked it up, carrying it back toward the farmhouse and snagging another for myself. Since we'd come in the early afternoon, there wasn't much of a line, and it didn't take long for me to pay for the pumpkins despite Macy's protests.

"I'll tell you what," I murmured low, leaning close to Macy's ear before opening her door so she could climb in. "I'll let you cook me dinner sometime if you're set on repayment."

She huffed out a laugh and waited for me to sit in the driver's seat. "I doubt I could make anything that would impress you. You're the celebrity chef."

"Don't underestimate yourself. I will taste whatever you give me," I said, coming up with a few ideas of things she could let me taste. It had been too long since I'd tasted the flavor of her lips. I navigated back into Portland and my apartment building.

"Wow, this place is nice," Macy breathed as I pulled into the underground parking and found my assigned spot. I held the door and gathered the pumpkins before leading her to the elevator bank and hitting the button.

"You remember meeting Gabriel Rivera?" I asked. She nodded as she stepped into the elevator, and I pressed the button for my floor. There was only one other apartment on the same floor. "His brother Julian owns the building and lives a floor above me."

"Oh, that must be nice to be close to your family."

I loved that she'd accepted the Riveras as my family without question. "Most of the time. It also means getting calls for missing ingredients and cooking tips."

"That's just the worst," Macy giggled as she exited the elevator and waited for me to open my front door.

"The first time I was in this apartment was to cook for Julian's wife, Luna," I explained, holding the door for her. We stepped into the spacious, neutral-toned space, which wasn't my preferred aesthetic. Julian kept the apartment furnished for family visits, so I didn't make a fuss about it. The kitchen was to our left with its pristine white cabinets and light countertops, and the living room was to the right with tan couches and a coffee table. "He'd royally screwed things up, and she wouldn't speak to him. So I showed up and softened her with my amazing food. She ended up taking him back and marrying him. Now they have a kid."

"Wow, that's some powerful culinary talent," Macy teased. I liked her playful side and wondered if she hid it at work to remain professional. "Where are we going to carve the pumpkins?"

"Right here." I deposited them onto the dining table next to the wall of windows framing the downtown Portland view. I pointed to the stack of newspapers on the edge of the table. "Go ahead and spread those out to contain the mess. I'll grab the carving accessories."

While I retrieved the carving knives and a bowl for the pumpkin guts, Macy got busy prepping the table. I pulled out my phone and used the universal remote to put a Halloween movie on the tv that hung opposite the couches.

"Is that a specialty pumpkin carving set?" Macy asked when I unrolled my small carving knives.

"Maybe."

"And Hocus Pocus?" She inclined her head toward the tv.

I nodded. "It helps to set the festive mood."

"If you say so," she mumbled, selecting a small, wickedly sharp blade.

"Aren't you going to outline your design first?" I held up a washable marker and tapped it on the top of her pumpkin.

Macy's brows furrowed as she took the marker from my fingers. "I have no idea what I'm going to do. What design are you making?"

Usually, I tried to outdo everybody at the restaurant, but with Macy over, I didn't want to waste time on an intricate motif. "I figured I'd keep it classic and simple with a silly face. Pick a shape for the eyes and nose, then decide what kind of teeth—if any—you want in the smile. Just draw it on so you can follow the lines."

I grabbed the other marker and showed her what I meant, sketching triangle eyes and a matching nose, then a mouth with little fangs. I turned the pumpkin so she could see it better, and she silently began drawing, biting her bottom lip as she worked.

"Perfect," I praised when she stepped back, and I looked at her cheery jack-o'-lantern face with its half-moon eyes and a wide smile. "Now we carve. Do I need to give you the safety spiel about using sharp knives?"

"I think I can manage," Macy said with a playful edge to her voice. "But can you keep up?"

"Ooh, a challenge. I like it." I leaned close enough to smell Macy's perfume. "Should we make a wager?"

"I'm game," she said immediately. A determined look crossed her features. "What did you have in mind?"

"I'll post a picture of each pumpkin online. Whichever gets more votes wins," I proposed. "The loser makes dinner."

Macy stuck her hand out toward me, and I clasped it in mine. "Deal."

Chapter Twelve

MATTEO COULD CARVE STRAIGHTER lines than me. Damnit. I looked at the design carved into his pumpkin, which had taken him less than ten minutes—and I could tell he'd slowed down to make me feel better about my snail's pace—and grimaced when my eyes shifted to my pumpkin. It looked like I'd down ten cups of coffee before wielding the carving knife. My semi-circles were wobbly, and my jack-o'-lantern's smile simultaneously looked sad and maniacal.

I crossed my arms and tapped my fingers against my elbow, contemplating whether there was anything else to be done about the situation. Probably not. I wouldn't be in the running for the cash prize, but at least I wouldn't be the only person at *El Corazón Borikén* without an entry.

"It's not that bad," Matteo said as he approached. He'd learned to make himself known more than a few feet away to avoid my killer startle reflex.

"It's not polite to lie," I retorted. "I'm okay with not being the best in the bunch. Really."

"You still have a shot at winning the popular public opinion," he mused, snapping photos of our finished pumpkins. "People might take pity on you."

"Your trash talk game is strong."

"I only speak the truth."

"Ah, but your ego is born of beating an amateur." I tapped the top of my pumpkin. "Is that really any kind of victory if it's handed to you without effort?"

Matteo chuckled and picked his pumpkin up, stroking it in a way that made me wish he would do the same to me. "Yes. I spent a whole ten minutes on this work of art, and I will savor any victory."

"You have no shame," I admonished playfully, wrapping up the newspaper and tossing it in the trash can in Matteo's kitchen.

"I'm sure I've got plenty of it somewhere," he answered. "Just not when it comes to the pumpkin carving competition. If you think this is tough, you should see all the pumpkins people will bring to work this week. The prize money is nothing to scoff at."

"Yeah, definitely." I washed the newspaper ink from my hands as Matteo separated the pumpkin seeds from the guts. He was probably the only person I knew who still had physical copies of newspapers. I read all of my news online. "I don't think I have the artistic talent to be in the running for that kind of cash."

He paused, holding up a pumpkin pulp-covered hand. "Don't worry. More people lose than win. You'll have another chance in December, anyway. We have an ugly sweater competition with the same prize. Start thrifting now and make it epic."

"Let me guess." I tapped my pointer finger against my chin. "You have an epic ugly sweater."

"You know it," he said with a grin. "Hand me that sheet pan, will you? There's parchment in the second drawer down."

I reached for the metal pan, set it on the counter where he'd placed all the pumpkin seeds in a bowl, and found the roll of parchment paper, ripping off a piece big enough to cover the bottom. Matteo rinsed the seeds and patted them dry before arranging them in a thin layer on the tray.

"Do you like spice?" he asked, holding up a jar of red spice. I couldn't see the label, but I assumed it was something like chili powder.

I had a horrifying image of myself stuck in his bathroom with my ass on fire and decided not to chance it. "Let's go with mild but flavorful, if that's okay with you."

"Sure thing." He put the spice away and pulled out others. "Salt, pepper, garlic, curry powder, cumin. Give me a hand?"

I nodded and grabbed a couple of spices, our arms brushing as we seasoned the pumpkin seeds together. Matteo nodded when satisfied and popped the pan into the oven he'd already preheated. I washed my hands and helped wipe down the surfaces we'd used. It was like muscle memory for those who worked in a kitchen.

"Now for the fun stuff," Matteo declared with a clap.

I looked around. "Decorating pumpkins wasn't fun?"

"Did you love it?" he asked in return.

"It was fine," I said. It hadn't been my kind of fun, but after so many years of doing everything my ex wanted to do, I wasn't sure what *my* type of fun was, anyway.

Matteo clicked his tongue at me. "*Fine* is not what I'm looking for. I want you to smile like you do when Leo says inappropriate shit as she passes you in the kitchen."

I choked on my saliva and coughed, feeling my face turn red as I remembered some other things my best friend had said about our boss. The man who was smirking at me. "You can hear her?"

"She's not the most subtle," he said with a lifted brow. "But it's nice to know I'm hotter than a freshly fried plantain."

I covered my face, mortified. "*Ohh*, let the earth just swallow me right now."

Matteo laughed and patted me on the back gently. "Don't be embarrassed. It was flattering."

"You should stop eavesdropping on your staff," I retorted, trying to decide whether I should send a text to Leo with our emergency code. Whenever we went out, we knew we could always text *this is the best ever*, and the other would immediately call with an emergency to bail us out. It was like a safeword for dates. But I was still telling myself this wasn't a date, and Leo was so set on seeing Matteo and me hook up that she probably wouldn't help me out.

Matteo shook his head. "Not a chance. The kitchen is the best place to hear all the good gossip."

I didn't know what to say to that. He left me wondering exactly how much of what Leo and I spoke about he'd overheard. What he'd repeated was relatively tame. She'd compared a particular appendage of his to a fat plantain once.

Matteo rummaged around in his cupboard, gathering more ingredients for something. "Do you want boozy or virgin?"

"Clearly not a virgin," I said drily, earning a laugh from him. "I think I need booze after your revelations."

"Perfect. I'm going to make the best spiced—not spicy—hot chocolate you've ever had." He held up a bar of chocolate.

I propped my hip against the counter. "You're setting the bar high."

"I know I'm good for it," he replied, pulling a small saucepan from the cabinet. "You can reward me with your moans of pleasure."

My eyes widened, and he froze for a moment before turning to me with an apologetic expression. "I mean, yummy sounds. Because you'll love the hot chocolate."

"Right." I nodded like I'd understood him from the start. I shoved thoughts of the ways he could make me moan out of my head.

Matteo launched into a story from childhood where his *Abuelita* taught him to make the non-alcoholic version of the hot chocolate. He was using her recipe, with a few modifications he'd come up with over the years. It didn't take long for him to whisk the boozy chocolate to a froth as it heated.

"Can you get a couple of mugs out of that cupboard?" he asked, pointing to his right. I found a couple of white coffee cups and set them on the counter, stepping back to give him space. He reached into the refrigerator and pulled out a bag, placing the contents at the bottom of each cup.

"Is that cheese?" I asked, incredulous.

"Of course." He chuckled when he saw my expression. "I promise, it's amazing. You'll see."

He poured the chocolate concoction over the cheese in each mug, used a planer to grate thin bits of dark chocolate over the foam, then handed me one of the mugs before rinsing his dishes and loading the dishwasher. It struck me how clean he was, not leaving anything to sit when it could be taken care of immediately. It was admirable.

I inhaled the spicy chocolate aroma, catching a hint of the alcohol but none of the cheese. Out of habit—learned from my coffee mishap—I blew on the brew before taking a tentative sip. Flavor exploded on my tongue, and the warmth filled me with a feeling of *home* that I wasn't sure I'd ever experienced.

"*Oh*," I breathed, surprised by my emotional reaction. Was I tearing up over a drink?

Matteo's understanding smile only made it worse. "I told you it was that good."

"It's witchcraft," I said, choked up.

"My *Abuelita* would roll in her grave if she heard that," he said teasingly. He reached out and brushed his thumb across my cheek, where one of those traitorous tears had spilled over. "It's *heart, ariete.*"

I couldn't disagree, because whatever he'd put into that drink was more than words could define. It was almost addicting, and before long, I realized Matteo had stood silently watching me drink the entire cup of cocoa. He handed me a spoon, and I watched him scoop up the cheese from the bottom before following suit. Impossible. It shouldn't taste that good, but it did.

"More?"

"Yes, please." I handed him my mug and watched him prepare seconds. The movie credits rolled, and I felt a sinking feeling that our afternoon was already over. While pumpkin carving might not have been my brand of fun, I enjoyed every minute I spent with Matteo.

"Why don't you pick another movie?" Matteo suggested, handing me his phone. I felt a flutter in my stomach as I walked over to the TV, realizing that he didn't want me to leave yet.

"I'm not a big fan of scary movies," I said, tapping the phone screen to look through the Halloween-themed movies. "I hope you don't mind if I pick a family movie."

"Pick whatever you want, Macy," Matteo called out. "It's not the movie I care about."

Well, then. He couldn't get much clearer than that. I didn't know what I thought about his intent, but I didn't hate it. There was a real possibility that I was catching feelings for Matteo. For my boss. It should be wrong, but it felt right.

I chose a family Halloween movie from the nineties and settled in the center of the couch. So I wasn't being exactly subtle. Matteo brought the mugs over and handed mine to me, the spoon already inside so I could scoop out the melted cheese. He sat close enough that his thigh touched mine when he relaxed, and little shocks of electricity shot to my center from where our bodies made contact. I never thought I'd feel those sensations again. It made me feel alive.

"How hungry are you after the donuts and hot chocolate?" Matteo asked, turning to focus on me instead of the movie. "I could make us dinner, we could order out, or we can just have snack food."

"I'm not terribly hungry," I admitted, feeling full and a little warm from the spiked drink. "We can do whatever you want, as long as it's not Indian food."

"Not big on spicy anything, hmm?"

"My stomach isn't," I explained, keeping it vague. I was pretty sure it was against first-date etiquette to discuss explosive diarrhea.

"Gotcha." Matteo nodded his understanding. "How about non-spicy Thai food, then?"

My mouth watered at the thought. "Sounds good to me."

We settled down and watched the movie, and when the food finally arrived, Matteo brought it to the coffee table so we could eat as we watched. He wasn't a big talker, but occasionally exchanged comments with me. It was the perfect combination of being attentive without being obnoxious.

One movie turned into two, and Matteo brought out the seasoned roasted pumpkin seeds, then told me I had to try his homemade caramel corn, so I helped make the sweet treat. Then he brought out the spiced rum, and I was in heaven. If I could have picked the perfect day, that would have been it.

During the third movie of the evening, my eyelids grew heavy, and I leaned to one side. Matteo's muscular arm wrapped around my shoulder, drawing me to his warm chest, and I gave in to my exhaustion.

***

Ethan was home. I could feel him lying underneath me. It was odd because he never liked to be close. Maybe being away for so long had changed his mind. I breathed him in slowly, but something didn't smell right. He'd changed his cologne to something more subtle. His chest rumbled as I stroked my fingers down his shirt, lifting the hem to feel his bare torso.

He'd developed abs in the last year. That probably meant he would demand I go to the gym more. He'd always hated that I was curvy. I allowed my hand to trail down, down to where I found the bulge beneath the waistband of his pants. He was hot and hard and very large compared to what I remembered. I stroked that firm ridge, wanting nothing more than to be filled and loved.

"Macy." The gravelly voice broke into my dream state. It didn't belong to Ethan. "Macy, what are you doing?"

"Matteo?" My eyelids fluttered, and I blinked against the light. Was it morning?

"Not that I object." His laughter rumbled beneath my cheek, and I realized I must have fallen asleep on him. How embarrassing.

I shifted, but my hand was stuck. I squeezed my fist and finally popped my eyes open to see that my hand was down Matteo's pants, wrapped around his—

"I'm so sorry!" I yanked my hand free, mortified that I'd been touching his dick. What must he think of me? "I swear, I didn't mean to touch you... there."

"It's fine." He chuckled and adjusted the prominent bulge in his pants. "It was certainly not the worst way to wake up."

I realized I was staring and tore my gaze away from that sizeable appendage. "I don't think I've ever been so embarrassed in my life."

"Is it as big as the plantains?"

Shit, he *had* heard that. My stomach twisted with regret. I was going to have to move. I didn't know where I'd go, but I could never show my face at the restaurant again.

"I have to leave," I said, standing abruptly and wobbling.

Matteo followed, but all I could see was the outline of his cock in his jeans. I couldn't look him in the eye.

"Macy." His hand wrapped around my wrist gently. "I can't let you go yet."

"What do you mean?" My mind raced with every horrible possibility. Was my boss a serial killer, and I'd just walked eagerly into his clutches?

"Breakfast," Matteo answered, tilting his head toward the kitchen. "You're probably hungry."

As if in agreement, my stomach chose that moment to growl loudly. I cursed my innards for their poor timing.

"See," he said almost triumphantly. "Waffles are the answer. I'll start as soon as I brush my teeth. Nobody likes morning breath."

I contemplated sneaking out while he was in the bathroom, but my brain was so jumbled that I could only find one shoe. He returned as I was bent over, searching under the couch, but said nothing. He just walked to the kitchen and started pulling out ingredients. I stood up and tried to fix my hair.

"Leo!" I blurted, drawing an odd look from Matteo. "She's going to wonder where I am. I didn't come home last night. I need to call her."

I fished around the couch until I found my phone. I pressed the button on the side, but the screen remained black. "Shit, it's dead. She's going to be so worried."

"She was maybe mildly concerned when she texted me half an hour ago," Matteo said mildly. "I told her you were sleeping."

"You talked to her?" I groaned, rubbing a hand down my face. "I'm never going to hear the end of this."

"You can worry later," he said dismissively. "For now, go to the bathroom and do the girl shit. I think I've got an extra toothbrush in the drawer on the right. Then come and have coffee with me. It will be like we're real adults having breakfast together."

I couldn't argue with that, so I did as he suggested. I'd save the breakdown for when I was alone at home.

Chapter Thirteen

"CHEF!" I CALLED OUT to Macy, who was finishing up a plate that needed to go out. "I need three *mofongo*."

"Yes, Chef!" she yelled back over the din of the kitchen. I could trust that she'd get the job done right, even without my supervision. The restaurant was busy enough that I was rushing to man the grill.

I didn't have time to get distracted by her presence, even though she was on my mind for most of my waking moments. After our accidental sleepover, she'd been distant and skittish around me. I couldn't convince her that the sleep-groping hadn't bothered me, but I didn't think she'd appreciate hearing how much I liked it. I woke up hard every morning, imagining her small hand on my cock.

At the restaurant, I kept trying to come up with excuses to work next to Macy. Eventually, she'd have to move past her embarrassment and figure out how to work with me again. It wouldn't do to have a sous chef who literally ran the other direction if I came near.

As soon as I completed orders for the lunch rush, I dragged myself to the coffeemaker and made another pot—first caffeine, then alcohol after we finished for the night. I saw Macy eying the coffee, and I lifted my cup and raised my brows in question. She jerked her head from side to side, turning me down needlessly.

I'd say she was only hurting herself, but that slight rejection ate at my insides. It had been a long time since I'd had deeper feelings for a woman, and I'd never met somebody who made me feel quite like Macy. Her smile lit up my day, and her frowns made me want to fight whatever invisible foe made her brows pull together.

I looked around the kitchen and realized Macy had taken her break. Fuck, if I didn't miss her presence. It was irrational. I cleaned my prep area and waited for her to return. When she waltzed through the kitchen door, I realized she'd have to wash her hands before donning her apron again.

Seeing my opportunity, I snagged the apron from the hook and snuck behind Macy as she reached for a paper towel to dry her hands, knowing it would be harder for her to hit me. I slipped the apron around her waist and pulled her back into me as I tugged on the strings.

"What are you doing?" she hissed at me, keeping her eyes straight ahead and face neutral.

"You're avoiding me," I murmured against her ear, crossing the apron strings in the back and bringing them back to the front.

"I'm glad you noticed." She snatched the strings from my grasp and whirled to face me as she took her aggression out on the bow she was trying to tie. "Maybe take a hint."

"I don't think you mean that."

Her eyes narrowed. "Are you saying I don't know my own mind?"

"Something like that, I guess." I shrugged. "I think you're afraid of what you feel for me, and something in your past is stopping you from taking the leap and seeing what we could be."

"You can be my boss," she snapped. "I feel your authority."

"Oh, really?" I asked suggestively, taking a step closer. "Is it my *authority* you'd like to feel? You liked it last time?"

That got the reaction I was hoping for. Macy's face reddened as she no doubt remembered how my cock felt in her hand.

"Ugh," she grumbled, exasperated. "That's not what I meant, and you know it."

"So you did like it," I teased. Macy turned a deeper shade of tomato.

"I have no opinion one way or another," she said diplomatically. "It was a mistake, and I'd rather not dwell on it. Now, if you'll let me get back to work."

"Of course." I moved out of her way and held my hand out as I gave a little bow. "Ladies first."

"Thank you." She marched past and checked the incoming orders.

That wouldn't do. She couldn't escape me that easily in *my* kitchen, though I had to admire her boldness.

I grabbed a food scale and bowl before returning to my station. "Diego, you're on the grill."

"Yes, Chef," he replied. We were between busy times, and the orders would be slower, so the boys could handle them. I had plans for Macy.

"Chef," I called over the tables.

"Yes, Chef?" Macy's aggravation permeated her words, and the look she gave me would have killed lesser men.

"We need to make *empanadas*. Go ahead and pull out the ingredients. We'll whip up the dough and fill them together."

And I thought she was angry before. I could see her bite her cheek as she contemplated her answer. To egg her on a bit further, I smirked and mouthed *authority*.

"*Yes, Chef*," she said through gritted teeth. Things banged as she gathered the ingredients we needed, and I braced my hands on the edge of the table, bowing my head to hide my smile of amusement.

"Here you go." Macy set everything on the table and snatched the scale and bowl from me, measuring things on her own.

"Remember, it must be filled with heart," I admonished, tapping my fingers against my chest. "Take a few deep breaths. Maybe count to ten. *Chef.*"

She probably would have thrown me into traffic if she could have hauled me out the door.

"Don't worry," she said with false levity. "Thanks to men, women learn to *fake it* early on."

"That's a shame." I leaned closer and lowered my voice. "I promise you'll never have to fake *anything* with me. You're not very good at it. I can see right through your act right now."

"And what act is that?" she ventured.

"The one where you pretend not to like me." I lifted a brow. "I'll never forget how you felt in my arms, how you relaxed and even snored a little."

"I do *not* snore!" she exclaimed in a hushed tone.

"Fine, you purr," I conceded playfully. "My point was that you relaxed enough to sleep on me and seemed to enjoy yourself just fine during our time together. I'm not sure if the morning freaked you out or what."

"Maybe I just realized what a horrible idea it would be to canoodle with my boss."

"*Canoodle?*" I chuckled. "Is that what we did in the morning?"

"We didn't *do* anything," she insisted. "I can't be held responsible for what my hands do while I'm unconscious."

"I seem to remember it took you a minute to let go after you woke up," I pressed. "I think you liked it."

"You want to know what I was thinking?" she asked, slamming a spatula on the worktable.

"Tell me," I replied, nudging her hip with mine.

She leaned close, and I lowered my head to hear her soft words. "I thought you were my ex. Happy? I dreamed of the only man I should never think of again."

Well, that put a damper on things. "Your ex."

"Yep." She nodded her head once. "So forgive me if I'm a little reticent to be around a man who makes me dream of the one who left me."

"Macy," I said, shocked at her words. "I'm not him."

"Yeah, well." She wiped her hands on her apron. "I thought he was a good guy for a long time. That sure bit me on the ass in the end."

I rubbed my palm over my chest. Her words hurt. "It's not fair to judge me based on what he did."

"I can't help it," she admitted quietly. "So please, don't push me."

"I won't accept that." I grabbed her hand in a way the others wouldn't see. She didn't immediately pull away. That was better than nothing. "I think you're stronger than you give yourself credit for. You can overcome whatever is telling you that there's no hope with men."

Macy shook her head, her gorgeous blue eyes glistening with tears that made my heart ache.

"Look," I said with resolve. "You can push me away as many times as you want. That won't make me stop waiting for you. I'll be right here when you're ready, and I'll show you that I'm different."

"Matteo." Macy's lip quivered.

"Don't." I pressed a finger to her lips briefly when I really wanted to touch my lips to hers. "I don't need your words right now. You have nothing to prove to me."

I walked away, needing a moment to regroup as much as Macy needed time away from me. I wasn't sure how patient I could be, but she was worth it.

***

It didn't take long to realize I wasn't willing to allow Macy to recede into her shell again. I gave her space for a couple of days but started assigning her minor tasks where she'd have to interact with others. I kept up my *Mofongo Musings* and tried to slip her into them when possible. My social media content output had doubled, and people started asking about Macy's social media. She didn't have a presence I knew of, but her awkward, dry humor endeared her to my viewers.

That morning I'd decided to do another live tutorial, and I roped Macy into joining. To justify it, I explained how to make guava filling for *empanadas* while she stirred the pot on the stove. It was like second nature to walk viewers through *Abuelita's* recipes. I didn't believe in gatekeeping knowledge, so most of my recipes were available free to the public on my website.

My mouth was moving, but my focus was really on Macy and how beautiful she looked, her skin pink and shiny from the heat of the burner in front of her. I could never tell her I thought sweat was sexy on her. It made me think of how she might look underneath me, with me moving inside her, making a sweat break out across her body as we shared our passion. I could practically feel the heat against my skin as I envisioned holding her close to me, her legs wrapping around my waist as I thrust deep inside her soft body.

"Chef!" Macy's alarmed voice broke through my thoughts, and I gave her a puzzled look. She pointed to my sleeve. "You're on fire!"

My eyes shot down, seeing the flame quickly eating through the rolled sleeve. "Shit!"

The heat from my daydream had been very real, and it was blackening my chef's coat and licking at my flesh. I was about to be a live version of *pernil*. Others in the kitchen exclaimed over my situation, rushing around and trying to find something to put the creeping flames out.

"Here!" Macy reached for a pitcher of water I used while filming and tossed it on me, dousing my entire front and putting the flames out.

"Thanks." I raised my voice to be heard over the noise. Cold water chilled me, and I suspected Macy's help had been a bit of revenge as well. "I see your aim is still true."

She smirked and offered an innocent shrug. "Comes in handy sometimes."

"Not the kind of hot celebrity chef I was going for," I said to benefit my viewers, who were blowing up the comments with their concern and offering to call an ambulance for me. "I'm fine, everybody. Just a little added char for the blackened chef dish."

Macy rolled her eyes, unamused by my attempt at humor. "If you could not add the stench of burned flesh to dinner, that'd be great."

"I'll do my best." I gave her a brief salute. "But you might check the guava filling."

Macy's eyes widened, and she rushed back to the stove, letting out a cry of distress. "Now look what you've done!"

"Me?" I pressed my hand to my chest and tried for my most innocent look, hamming it up for the camera.

"Yes, you!" Macy switched the burner off. "If you hadn't gone and caught yourself on fire and made me play firefighter, the filling wouldn't be a black lump at the bottom of the pot."

"Well, it looks like we're aiming for rustic pioneer campfire cooking in the kitchen today." I chuckled and pulled the pot from the stove, handing it to one of our dishwashers.

"I think the folks on the Oregon trail burned things less than we did today," she said ruefully and waved toward the camera. "Maybe we should just show them something that doesn't require heat."

"It would probably be better for my insurance," I joked. Regrouping, I addressed the viewers. "Okay, what do you think? Do you want to learn how to make *coquito*?"

I watched the affirmative messages scroll on the screen and laughed. "Okay, the majority wins."

Macy began gathering the things we'd need for the drink, and I ad-libbed until we were ready.

"Who can tell me what *coquito* is?" I waited until somebody had the right idea. "Right, *prinpdx*, you got it. Are you from Puerto Rico? I thought so. We're going to blend coconut cream, canned milk, sweetened condensed milk, spices, and rum. These are things you either have in your pantry or can easily pick up at your local grocery store. Now, I cannot stress enough how important it is to use a good Puerto Rican rum. *Abuelita* wouldn't have it any other way."

I grabbed the bottle of spiced rum I kept in the kitchen and poured two shots, offering one to Macy as she returned. "For luck, because clearly, we need it!"

We tipped the cups back, and I felt the smooth burn as it traveled down my throat. Macy's eyes sparkled with humor when I glanced at her, and I offered her my best smile. She turned predictably pink, and that familiar heat in my heart joined the feel of the rum. She was every bit as affected by me now as she had been on our unofficial pumpkin carving date. I could practically feel her acquiescence approaching.

Macy would be mine soon. I just had to hold on to that hope.

Chapter Fourteen

"**I**'M GOING TO QUIT," I said as I stood behind *El Corazón Borikén* and leaned my head against the side of the building.

"You're not going to quit," Leo said with a roll of her eyes.

"What kind of best friend are you?" I asked accusingly. "You're supposed to be unconditionally supportive of whatever I want to do."

"I am," she said with a smirk. "I'm unconditionally supportive of you *doing* Matteo."

I slapped a palm to my face. "*Stop*. We are not *doing it*."

"You stayed the night at his house, Macy," she reminded me. "You fondled him."

"I wish I'd never told you that." I'd regretted it every day since because I'd been right. She would never let me live it down.

"You could never keep anything from me," she pointed out, burrowing deeper into her coat until all I could see were her eyes peering over the collar. "I've watched you in that kitchen with him every day. You don't hate him. You want to jump his bones. And from what you said, it's the size of a femur."

"I can't with you," I said as I shook my head. "I never said it was the size of a femur."

"Just a large plantain, then."

"I swear, if you ever say anything like that in the kitchen again, I'll walk out and ruin your hopes of me ever sleeping with our boss." I rubbed my hands together, trying to get feeling back in my frigid digits.

Leo tipped her head to the side, which made her look like an owl. "I'm not sure I understand why you're still denying yourself six feet-something of that tan demigod inside. He wants you, and judging by how he looks at you when you're trying to pretend he doesn't exist, he doesn't just want a quick fuck. That man has eyes that say, 'here's a key to my place; let's grow old together.' You don't see that every day."

"He just thinks he wants me." I flung my hands out. "He doesn't even really know me."

"Maybe that's because you haven't let him." Leo pointed a finger at me. "Is this really about him not knowing you or your fear that if he knows you, he'll reject you like Ethan did?"

She was going to dig that dagger right into my gut. No last requests. "Probably both."

"As your best friend who loves you more than my own life, I cannot let you live like this," she said confidently, drawing me into a hug. "You deserve so much more. If you won't reach for it, I'll start meddling."

"Leo," I said in warning.

"Too late. I'm the meddler now." She grinned and took a bow. "Now you'll have to watch out for the demigod dick and me. I should get myself a cape. What do you think?"

"I think I've tasted regret enough for a lifetime," I said ruefully.

"Perfect." Leo bounced excitedly. "Let's get you a taste of that gorgeous Puerto Rican instead. Do you ever wonder if he tastes like cilantro?"

She took me by surprise. "I didn't until now."

"I'll need you to report back on that one, then," she said thoughtfully.

"I don't taste like cilantro. Why would he?"

"Are you sure?" Leo raised a brow, and before I could stop her, she snatched my wrist and ran her tongue across the back of my hand.

"*Leo!*" I yanked my hand away and wiped it on my pants. "What the hell do you think you're doing?"

She shrugged. "Just checking. You taste like soap."

"I think our break is over," I said without checking my phone. "And I think you need to lay off whatever the hell you're taking."

Leo cackled and opened the door for me. "Maybe you need to start taking it. It's called optimism."

"Whatever." I pushed past her and hung my coat in the back room with my other things before trudging back to the kitchen and washing my hands.

"We've got a chef's table in ten," Matteo said as he breezed past.

I wracked my brain, trying to remember whether I'd seen that. "Was that on the schedule?"

"Nope," he popped the end of the word. "It's a VIP."

"Okay, I got it." I tied my apron on. "I can handle the grill while you work on it."

"Sounds good." He grinned, and there was something about the glint in his eye that I didn't trust, but I brushed it off as my own paranoia. I always waited for his antics, even though he'd backed off a bit since he'd set himself on fire.

I busied myself with the orders coming in, but there was no mistaking when Matteo's guests arrived. The entire kitchen staff greeted the tall, dark-haired man who looked like he could be a model and his shorter, blonde companion.

"Macy, come on over here," Matteo called out, and that same suspicious feeling returned.

Still, I could tell him no. "Yes, Chef."

Diego stepped up to take over the plating of a dish, and I wiped my hands on my apron as I approached the chef's table.

"Julian, Luna, this is my sous chef, Macy." Matteo made the introductions, but I recognized the names from our conversations. "Macy, this is my brother Julian and his wife, Luna."

"It's so nice to meet you finally," Luna gushed, taking my hand and shaking it gently. "We've heard so much about you."

It always made me nervous when people said that. I side-eyed Matteo, but he just sucked his lips in his mouth and widened his eyes. "It's nice to meet you, too."

"Likewise," Julian said, standing and giving me an air kiss next to my cheek.

I stood there, frozen by the familiar greeting. "Do you come here often?"

"When we can get away for a date night," Julian responded. "Our son is spending the night with his cousins tonight. I think you've met my brother, Gabriel."

"Oh, yes." He was the one who had the adorable little girl. "His daughter is Olivia, right?"

Julian nodded. "That's her. I'm the better-looking brother, though. Just ask Matteo."

"No chance in hell am I taking a side there," Matteo said with a laugh. "I'm here to cook for you; though, I thought you might like to try Macy's cooking tonight if that's okay."

"Oh, that sounds delightful!" Luna exclaimed, looking expectantly at her husband.

Julian nodded indulgently. "That sounds great. Are you ready to wow us, Macy?"

"Absolutely." I was sure the smile I plastered on my face was frightening, but it was either smile or burst into tears. "I'll get right on that."

I spun and shook my hands nervously, having a tiny panic attack at the prospect of making the chef's menu on my own. I ran through my coping technique as quickly as possible until Matteo's palm landed on my shoulder, making me jump.

"Hey, you didn't hit me that time," he observed lightly. "We're making progress, *ariete*."

"Why did you do that?" I hissed at him when I was certain his guests wouldn't overhear us.

"I thought it would be a good opportunity for you," he said, his expression concerned. "Is that not okay?"

"No. Yes. I don't know." All my thoughts were jumbled, and I could feel my breaths coming rapidly as my heart pounded in my ears. I felt lightheaded and wavered.

"Woah." Matteo steadied me with his hands on my upper arms. "You're okay. I won't force you to do it if it makes you this uncomfortable."

"I don't do well with change," I admitted thinly. "I've never made the chef's menu on my own."

"Then we'll do it together," Matteo said decidedly. "The restaurant is winding down. I have time to help you. Will that make it better?"

"Yeah, actually." It was like the weight threatening to crush my head lifted. "That would be great."

"Okay, great. This is the current chef's menu." Matteo guided me to his prep area and pulled out his chef's recipe notebook, flipping through the pages and pointing to one. Then he turned to another page. "But *this* is the meal you're going to make. Julian has very specific tastes. You know how to make all of this, so it's nothing new or weird. And I guarantee that Julian and Luna will love whatever you make."

I looked up at him. "Are you sure? Isn't he a millionaire or something? He's probably used to way better than I can make."

"Billionaire, actually," Matteo said like it was nothing.

"Oh, that's better." I could feel my throat closing up. My body was trying to off me, so I didn't have to suffer more humiliation.

"That's what he's built for himself," he explained. "But he grew up in San Juan. You're making him the comfort food of his childhood. He brings Luna here when he wants a taste of home, to escape the pressures of life. They're here for the *heart*, and I'm confident they'll taste it in your cooking. I wouldn't have asked you to serve them if I wasn't."

I offered him a small smile. "You're the best at pep talks. Do you know that?"

"I'll add it to my resume," Matteo joked. "You ready to start?"

"Yeah, I'm good." I took a deep breath and got to work, pulling out chicken thighs and finding a pan. We kept a pot of *arroz con gandules* on the back burner, but we cooked everything fresh for the chef's table, so Matteo started a new pot. I put together small salads as an appetizer for Julian and Luna. It was decidedly off-brand for the restaurant, but Matteo told me it was Luna's preference. A part of me desperately wanted to impress the man who was a brother to Matteo and the woman he spoke so highly of.

"Here you go," I said as I set the salads in front of them.

"Looks delicious," Luna said, picking up her fork and stabbing the lettuce.

I nodded and got to work on the main dish, browning the chicken thighs in a pan while the rice cooked on another burner. Matteo gave me my space, but stayed near enough that I could ask him questions if necessary.

It turned out he'd been right. Once I got started, everything came naturally and seemed a lot less daunting. My smile was genuine when I set the main dish in front of our guests.

"Why don't you sit for a moment?" Julian suggested, motioning across from them. "I'm sure we could get an extra chair."

I tried to decline politely. "Oh, I'm fine standing, thanks."

"How long have you lived in Portland?" Luna asked between bites. "Matteo said you were an Oregon native."

"Yeah, I grew up in a small town and moved to Portland years ago with my ex-husband," I explained. I didn't get the familiar twinge of pain in my chest when I mentioned him. *Interesting.*

"And you've worked in the restaurant industry before?" Julian asked. I wondered if I was attending some kind of informal interview.

"Off and on, yes." I didn't want to explain my work history. "I love working here, though."

"That's so great." If possible, Luna's smile got even brighter. "I bet Matteo's a great boss."

"He's undoubtedly the best chef I've ever worked under," I said, not caring that it probably came across like I was sucking up.

"Are you trying to drive my sous chef away?" Matteo asked as he approached my side.

"Of course not." Luna crossed a finger over her heart. "We just want to get to know the woman you talk about so much."

Matteo blushed at her words, and I could feel the heat creeping up my neck. He talked to his family about me. I didn't know what to do with that information, but I knew there was a good possibility I was already over my head because I didn't hate the notion. It made me feel warm inside.

***

"I swear, if you make me watch another episode of this barbecue show, I'm throwing the remote at the tv," I called out to Leo, who was in the kitchen pouring wine.

I heard her laugh. "I just want to watch something that looks delicious while we eat Cheetos."

After grocery shopping, we'd spent all of Monday vegged out on the couches, eating crap and sipping wine. I'd even slipped into a clean pair of pajamas because I wasn't putting any effort into looking human for twenty-four hours.

"Oh, fuck!" I heard Leo swear and the sound of a wine glass slamming down on the counter.

"What's going on?" I asked, trying to see her. "Is everything okay?"

"Yeah, no. I'm fine," she answered.

I started looking for other food-themed shows to watch, finally settling on one with Anthony Bourdain, my all-time favorite chef. It still saddened me to think of his passing, so I focused on his dry commentary.

It wasn't long before Leo dropped to the couch next to me, making me bounce and nearly spilling the glasses of wine. I snatched my glass from her hands. "Careful! It's a crime to spill good wine."

"I'm not sure you could consider this good wine," she said, holding the glass up to the wine as if she were examining it. She sighed heavily.

Leo didn't do sad sighs. "Are you sure nothing is wrong?"

"I have to tell you something," she said somberly. "Show you something, actually. It's a picture."

"A picture of something awful?"

"I mean, yeah," she said, swiping her thumb across her phone screen. "I just need you to sit where you are and maybe down that glass of wine real quick."

I shot her an incredulous look. "I'm not chugging wine."

"Half the glass then," she negotiated. "I'll show you after you drink half the glass."

"Fine." I took a couple of big gulps of the pinot noir.

Leo nodded her approval and held out the phone. "I saw a post from Aaron today."

"Aaron from high school?" Maybe something happened to him.

Leo nodded slowly. "He's on vacation."

"Well, that's nice, I guess," I said. "But I don't know why that would be upsetting."

She sighed again, and I started getting nervous. "It's more about the picture he posted."

"Well, if you want me to see it, just show it to me," I said impatiently.

"Fine." Leo swiped across the screen and handed me her phone. "Just know I'm here for you."

"Okay, right," I blew her off and looked down. My jaw dropped, and ice ran through my veins as I saw the picture on the screen. "Ethan."

"Yeah." Leo nodded and gnawed on her bottom lip.

I shivered. There, on a beach in an exotic locale, stood my estranged husband with a model-worthy, leggy blonde plastered to his side, his hand wrapped around her tiny waist. "I don't understand."

"Aaron ran into Ethan and that chick on his vacation," Leo explained. "He calls her Ethan's *assistant*. There's no way with how he's all over her. I'm guessing Aaron doesn't know what Ethan did to you."

I chugged the rest of my wine. My stomach lurched, threatening to expel its contents. "I feel sick. How could he do this?"

"He's an asshole. We knew that when he walked out on you," Leo replied without hesitation. "I'm so sorry, Macy. I'd help you bury the body if I could."

"Thanks," I said through the tears that had fallen. The pain I thought I'd gotten over returned with a vengeance, holding my heart in a vice grip. I didn't realize a heart could break twice for the same person. *Fuck you, Ethan.*

"What I can offer you is more wine and screenshots to hand to your lawyer." Leo shrugged and handed me her wine glass so I could finish it. "And lots of hugs. And maybe penis pancakes we can tear into tiny little pieces and feed to the birds."

"Yeah, that sounds good," I hiccoughed. "Maybe we start with the hugs."

She spread her arms and drew me to her, nestling my head under her chin and stroking my head as I soaked her purple plaid flannel pajamas with my tears. "You're in luck. That's my specialty."

Chapter Fifteen

"**Y**OU HAVE TO BUY marshmallows," Macy said, pointing to the shelves of the fluffy treats in front of her at the store.

"Oh, yes, for spiders!" Leo added, clapping her hands gleefully and making her fingers into spider legs. Macy shuddered when she walked the finger spider the arm of her coat.

When I asked Macy to accompany me on a store run before the restaurant opened, I hadn't expected her to drag her best friend along, but it worked out. I allocated half my budget to snack foods for the upcoming Halloween party at *El Corazón Borikén*. Every year I closed the restaurant and transformed the dining room into a trick-or-treat haven, where kids could walk to different stations, play games, and get candy. It was an easy place for parents to rely on for a safe environment for their kids.

As much as I loved cooking the food of my childhood, non-Boricua children were less enthusiastic about eating it on Halloween. They were more interested in candy and prizes, but I liked to serve a little buffet of treats for both parents and children.

"Do I want to know how you make spiders out of marshmallows?" I asked, unfamiliar with the treat.

Leo grabbed a bag of stick pretzels from the cart and held it next to a pack of large marshmallows. She lowered her voice ominously. "You stab the pretzels into the marshmallows."

She smashed the bags together for effect before tossing them back into the cart and humming Itsy Bitsy Spider. "You have to do it. It's a Halloween staple."

"If you say so." I wasn't about to argue with her. She scared me a little, but I could see why she was so good for Macy. They were opposites but had the same caring heart underneath their differences.

"We need white chocolate for the bloody fingers," Macy said, looking down at her list. She'd come prepared with a notebook of treats she'd looked up online and the ingredients to make each one. I followed her down the baking aisle. "Here we are. This and a little fake blood will do nicely."

I had difficulty imagining how dipping pretzels in white chocolate made them resemble fingers, but if the kids liked it, I didn't care how ridiculous it sounded. I liked a good chocolate-dipped pretzel but usually ate them without the blood.

Macy tapped her notebook with a pen, then pointed toward the cereal aisle. "Rice Krispies are next."

That was easy enough. I led the way and grabbed several boxes of cereal. Rice Krispy treats were a staple at all of my family events. Adults and children loved them, and they were versatile and easily adapted to whatever holiday we celebrated. Chocolate spider webs for Halloween, leaves for Thanksgiving, and trees for Christmas. I didn't like to add candy and sprinkles because it took away from the classic crunch of the rice cereal. Call me a purist, but I couldn't do it any other way.

"What about drinks?" Leo asked as Macy checked things off her list.

"Usually, I just make some red punch and throw some ice cube eyes in for effect," I explained. "It's always a hit."

Leo nodded her approval. "I like it. Bloodthirsty."

"Not exactly." I shrugged. The glint in her eye made me slightly nervous. "How about we move on to the candy?"

"My favorite!" Leo declared, skipping down the aisle while Macy and I followed at a more sedate pace. The woman had endless energy, and she might even have me worn out by the time we finished at the store. "I hope you're not planning to get that crappy cheap stuff, chef. Splurge for the name-brand chocolate bars. And do *not* hand out toothbrushes with your prizes."

"What's wrong with toothbrushes?" I had an order of kids' toothbrushes back in my office, waiting to be handed out at the fishing game. She must have seen them at some point.

Leo looked at me like it was obvious. "That's what you get when you're trick-or-treating, and a dentist lives in your neighborhood. It's so not cool."

"I think I'll do it anyway," I concluded, grabbing bags of candy as we reached the aisle filled with sugary treats. "I'll tell kids it's a little something for their parents."

"You can apologize for making them all hyper and remind them you still prioritize dental health," Macy offered, cutting off whatever Leo was about to say.

A thought entered my mind as I watched my sous chef carefully examine the candy selection before choosing her favorites. "I know you hadn't carved pumpkins before last week. Have you ever gone trick-or-treating?"

Leo snorted out a laugh, and Macy shot her a quelling look. "Of course, I've been trick-or-treating. My mother didn't love holiday traditions, but she didn't keep me locked away."

"Just checking." I realized Leo might be my best ally when asking questions about Macy's past since they'd grown up together. "What things did you go as?"

Macy bit her lip and looked away, a sure sign I'd made her uncomfortable. I'd also learned that the information she hid at those times was usually something I wanted to know. "Oh, just the usual stuff. Ghosts, witches."

"Don't let her fool you," Leo interrupted. "Macy might be quiet, but she could put together a mean costume. One year, she made mermaid tails and coconut bras for us to wear. She even cut out felt shells and hot glued them to clips for hair accessories."

"That's pretty incredible," I said with a smile. "What else?"

"We really don't have to talk about this," Macy said nervously. "It's not that interesting."

"I find it fascinating." I reached past her shoulder to pluck a bag of candy from a higher shelf and added in a whisper, "Everything about you fascinates me."

She blushed like ripe strawberries and pretended the label on the bag in her hands was the most interesting thing she'd ever read.

Leo rattled off their costumes through the years. "Let's see; we definitely did ghosts and witches, the mermaids, chefs—big surprise, lawyers, old ladies. Oh, and the last year we did costumes, Macy was really into astrology and made us two halves of a bull because she's a Taurus."

"Why did you stop?" I knew it had been the wrong thing to ask when Leo's face fell, and she went completely silent.

Macy paled. "I started dating Ethan."

The ex. Fuck.

"Yeah, that asshole." Leo flipped off the ceiling. "May he get sand where the sun don't shine and the unsavory kind of crabs."

"Leo," Macy implored, cutting her hand through the air.

Leo narrowed her eyes at Macy and put her hands on her hips. "Don't you even think of defending him after everything he's done. He deserves some of the bitchiest karma."

"Not now. Please." Macy sounded almost desperate.

Leo took the hint, reaching out to squeeze her friend's hand. "Yeah. I'll make us more penis pancakes when we get home."

"Sorry, what?" I couldn't help my curiosity.

Macy covered her face with her hands and glared at Leo from between her fingers. "I'm disowning you after this."

"You love me, and you'll never be rid of me," Leo shot back. "I'm like that little piece of gum you can't get out of the tread of your shoes. It's futile to try."

I covered my laugh with a cough and cleared my throat while patting my chest. Macy wasn't fooled and directed one of those caustic eyes in my direction.

"Don't encourage her."

"Oh, please do," Leo countered. "I've been dying to make penis pancakes national."

"It's a product?" I asked, confused.

"It should be. It's the most cathartic way to get over men," she said. "You can make any size and shape of dick you want, then tear them up into tiny pieces. Kind of like burning somebody in effigy."

I cringed at the mental picture and cupped myself. "That sounds horrible."

"Plenty of men are horrible," Leo supplied. "Not you, of course. You're one of the good ones."

"Thanks, I think." My dick hurt at the image I got of the women in front of me tearing penis replicas to bits in their anger. Probably best not to piss them off. They would likely get along well with Bella, the youngest Rivera, and the only sister. She had that same brash streak, though life experiences had made her more cautious over the years.

"Is that everything?" Macy ran her pen down the list in her notebook and glanced at the items in our cart.

"Yeah, I had the décor delivered directly to the restaurant, so we just needed the food items," I answered, ready to escape the odd mood that had overtaken our group. "We can head to the checkout."

Macy fished around in her purse and produced a small white envelope. "Great. I brought coupons."

It didn't take long to purchase and load the bags of treats into the back of my truck. At least it wasn't raining, just cold and windy, typical for the end of October in Portland. When we arrived at *El Corazón Borikén*, the others helped take everything inside and got lunch service underway while Macy and I focused on the Halloween menu.

"Chef, where do you want all the pumpkins?" Araceli asked as she stepped into the kitchen.

"You can set them in my office for now," I answered. "There should be room next to the prize wheel."

"Will do."

I nodded my thanks and returned to my food list for the occasion. Absently, I opened a bag of tiny chocolate peanut butter pumpkins and unwrapped one, popping it into my mouth. It would be rude not to offer one to Macy, so I unwrapped another.

I held it up in my fingers. "Want one?"

"Sure." Macy leaned forward and took the candy from my hand, her soft lips brushing against my fingertips before she pulled away and made a soft sound of pleasure. "So good."

"Yeah," I breathed.

My cock was rigid in my pants, and I longed to draw Macy to my chest and share the taste with her. I held myself in check and settled for licking the residual chocolate from my fingers as she watched. Her chest rose and fell with her heaving breaths, and I hoped her nipples were hard under her chef's jacket. The familiar flush colored her face and neck above her cravat.

She was just as affected as me and wasn't running from it. My heart demanded that I take her hand and whisk her to my office, where I could feed her sweets while I tasted her sweet center. Maybe that was my cock. It was getting harder to tell the difference between feelings of lust and something more.

I turned to my laptop and the recipes we were writing out for various treats. With only a few days until Halloween, we had time to pre-make some items to save time on the day. I still paid my staff their regular wages and set a tip pumpkin by the door for guests to contribute if they chose. I didn't charge admission for our Halloween event because I wanted all families to have the opportunity to participate if they wanted.

"Why don't we get started on the Rice Krispy treats?" I suggested, pulling the cereal boxes to the front. "Those should hold well."

"Sure." Macy nodded, and we washed our hands before gathering the necessary supplies.

"Let's do enough for all the cereal." After moving the candy out of the way, I set a couple of large metal bowls on the prep table. "The recipe multiplies well. Let's quadruple it."

Macy's brows raised. "How many guests are you expecting?"

"I think last year we had nearly three hundred people come through," I shared. "But I've been plugging it on each live this year, so I expect up to five hundred."

"That's a lot," she said, shocked. "We might need double that amount of treats."

"There will be enough variety to cover the numbers by the time we're done," I assured her. "How much catering and large event work have you done?"

"Not anything this large," she admitted. "The restaurants I worked at didn't cater like that. Usually, the biggest events were large business meetings, but we had a rehearsal dinner one night with about fifty people."

"This will be educational then." I chuckled and unwrapped sticks of butter, tossing them into the large pot on the stove.

Macy sent me a confident smirk and waved a long-handled spatula in my direction. "I think I can handle Halloween treats."

It didn't take long for the aroma of butter, sugar, and vanilla to fill the air, giving the kitchen a decidedly unique scent since our lunch menu was being made simultaneously. I wondered if I could get away with integrating cilantro into something sweet. Portland might be one of the few places that would embrace it.

We tag-teamed the large bowls of cereal, evenly distributing the melted orange marshmallow goo over the tops, laughing as we tried to avoid bumping into each other in the tight space. Finally, we wrestled the cereal into submission and poured it out onto buttered, parchment-lined sheet pans to cool and set. The decorating would wait for later.

When I returned from sliding the sheet pans onto a rack, I found Macy frowning and peering down at her phone, marshmallow fluff smudged across one cheek. I approached and swiped the sweet stuff from her face, popping my finger into my mouth as she startled.

"What are you doing?" she asked sharply.

I held up my hands in surrender. "Just cleaning you up. No harm meant."

"Sorry." Macy sighed and sank back against the wall, dropping her phone to her side. "I didn't mean to snap at you. I'm just stressed."

"What's got you so upset?" I ventured, longing to fix whatever it was.

"Nothing."

"It's *not* nothing." I tapped the toe of my black clog against hers. "Come on, spill."

Macy shook her head slowly. "I don't think you want to know."

"I wouldn't ask if I didn't want to know."

"I found my ex," she blurted.

"I didn't realize he was missing," I replied, realizing she was about to share more than she had in the two months we'd worked together.

"Just over a year ago, Ethan left me with only a letter telling me he'd never really loved me and that I shouldn't bother looking for him because he didn't want further contact."

"Wow, what an asshole," I said, disgusted with the sad excuse for a man. Who did that to their wife?

"Yeah, he is, but it took me a long time to see it," she said regretfully. "Leo finally convinced me he wasn't worth giving up my entire life. I lost our home and vehicles because he emptied our bank accounts to fund his future."

"What?" I asked, incredulous. "There was nothing you could do?"

"Not unless I could find him. And I didn't have enough money to hire a private investigator. Every penny I make goes to my lawyer, who is helping push the divorce through," she explained, pulling out her phone and turning the screen toward me so I could see the picture of two couples on a beach. "But last week, Leo found him. Or rather, one of our former classmates ran into Ethan in the Caribbean. My husband and his *assistant*."

She spat the last word with such anger that her hand shook. I looked at the blonde man with the perfect smile and the thin, busty blonde at his side.

"He's an idiot for letting you go." Macy's eyes glistened with tears, and I searched for the right words. I only came up with the truth. "If you were mine, I'd never make the same mistake."

Chapter Sixteen

THE RESTAURANT DIDN'T SMELL like Puerto Rican food for the first time since I began working at El Corazón Borikén. Instead, it smelled sweet, of the candy and treats we'd prepared for our Halloween guests. Matteo and I spent two days cooking to prepare for the event, and it was satisfying to watch it all finally come together.

Aside from a small seating area, the tables and chairs were stored behind large swaths of black fabric draped around the edges of the dining room. We set the games up at intervals around the room, and all the staff members showed up to help. Most of it looked like something you would see at a school carnival: a prize wheel, blind fishing, ring toss, and the like.

The food table boasted a massive spread of spooky, sweet charcuterie with all the things we'd made, a red punch with eyeballs floating inside at either end, and an elevated cauldron centerpiece filled with dry ice bubbling in the water. It was child-friendly, but there might be some sticky fingers by the night's end.

Fog crept across the floor from a machine toward the back, creating a festively spooky atmosphere. It wasn't anything too scary, just the perfect amount of fanciful. Some of the staff was already in costume, but I'd been working on a few last-minute things, so I wore black leggings and a long-sleeved black shirt I'd cover with my costume.

"Half an hour, folks!" Matteo called as he emerged from the kitchen with another platter of sweets. "Let's get in position."

"Macy, you need to get dressed," Leo said as she grabbed my arm, dragging me to the back room. She already sported her costume that matched the staff theme of changing weather. She was a gust of wind, artfully drawn on large pieces of cardboard attached by zip-ties. It was simple but effective.

"I thought I might just work on restocking food and prizes." I wasn't eager to don the costume Matteo assigned me.

"Nobody escapes this." Leo rolled her eyes and shoved me into the back room, picking up my cardboard sandwich board-style costume and slipping it over my head. When I tried to look in the mirror, she grabbed my hand and led me back to the front of the house. "You'll be fine. Nobody is going to stare at you. Just remember, this is supposed to be fun. Smile once in a while."

"Ah, there's my sunshine!" Matteo exclaimed, arms spread wide in the dark storm cloud costume he wore over his chef's uniform.

"Very funny," I muttered, adjusting the giant cardboard cutout sun. I felt like I was in a grade school play waiting for my mom to wave from the front row. Only my mother never showed up to those. It was Leo's parents who cheered us on.

"Come on, put on that sunny smile, and get ready to greet our guests!" Matteo patted me on the head, and I glared at him before whirling around and nearly taking out Leo in my haste to get away.

"I know that look," Leo whispered from my side, as close as her costume would allow. "You're not quitting. It's one night."

"If the pay wasn't so good—"

"You'd stay for the storm cloud," Leo finished for me.

I sighed. "I hate it when you're right."

"There's a thin line between love and hate," she said jovially. "But right now, try to look like you love all this. Here come the kids!"

I watched as the first guests filtered through the gauzy, sparkly black fabric covering the doorway. Araceli, dressed as a fortune teller, complete with a crystal ball, greeted the families and gave out basic instructions to direct them through the event. Soon enough, the restaurant was filled with children laughing happily.

It didn't take long for me to get caught up in the celebration, and I operated the prize wheel for a time. It didn't matter what the wheel landed on; I gave out a generous amount of extra candy in addition to their prizes. What was trick-or-treating without all the treats a plastic pumpkin could hold?

Amaia came to relieve me so I could take a quick break, but I didn't make it far before Matteo found me. "Wait a moment. Let's do the song!"

"Really? Right now?" I looked around, seeing how crowded the dining room was.

"Ian, come here!" Matteo called out. I guess there was no getting out of it now.

The men stood before me, and I closed my eyes, praying for the earth to swallow me whole before Matteo went through with his little skit. No such luck.

"Okay, one, two, three," Matteo began before breaking into song, his voice an unmistakable, mesmerizing baritone. "Rain, rain, go away."

I reluctantly joined in, forcing myself to smile because it seemed to entertain the children. At the song's end, Matteo and Ian danced away, leaving me in the spotlight. I don't know if my movements looked like dancing or convulsing, but I made it to the end.

As soon as I finished, I hurried away. I should have had a shot of Matteo's spiced rum beforehand.

"That was great," Matteo said as he caught up to me at the back of the room.

"I'm sweating," I groaned at my admission. "It was humiliating."

"I guarantee the kids didn't see it that way." He tapped the sun in front of me. "They were all dancing with us. I think a little part of you enjoyed it, too."

I scoffed, and he smiled indulgently. "Maybe a teeny, tiny part of me liked making them happy."

"That's my girl."

The words of praise made my entire body tingle with warmth. I leaned toward him, my eyelids lowering and mouth parting. I thought he would meet me in the middle for a kiss I'd longed for ever since the night I helped him with the cookie class. Only, he didn't lean in. He pulled away with something akin to regret in his eyes.

"Only a couple more hours left now," he said, shoving his hands in his pockets. "Think you can survive?"

"Uh, yeah," I said, confused. "I'll be fine."

"Good."

I turned and wandered off in a daze, unsure of where I stood with Matteo. He'd flirted with me nearly every day, and I'd finally decided that maybe it wouldn't be so bad to reciprocate. I'd told him about Ethan. Had it all been a colossal mistake? Perhaps he didn't want me anymore because of the baggage from my past. I wouldn't blame him.

"What's wrong?" Leo asked when I returned to the game area.

I looked around. Matteo hadn't returned to the dining room with me. "Nothing. Just ridiculous expectations?"

"Did Matteo ask you to do something you can't do?" she prodded. "Was it about the song and dance number? That wasn't personal. They do it every year."

I held up a hand to stop her. "No, nothing like that. It was *my* unreasonable expectation. I tried to kiss him, and he backed away."

"Do I need to open a can of whoop-ass on him?" Leo balled her fists and bounced back and forth on the balls of her feet.

"No." I shook my head. "Let's not resort to violence in front of the children."

"Later, then?" She looked a little too eager for violence. "I could jump him as he leaves. He'd never see me coming. I'm like a shadow. Silent and deadly."

"Shadows are deadly?" I couldn't help but smile.

"Absolutely," she said assuredly. "If you're afraid of them, you might have a heart attack and die. Or things could lurk in them. Like me."

"Have you already started drinking?"

"Of course not. That's what we do after the event." She waved her arm around. "We tear everything down in an hour, then Matteo buys a round for everybody down at the bar."

"Is that why you made me bring extra clothes?" I questioned. "You weren't concerned that I'd get stains on them."

Leo giggled and shook her head. "I knew if I told you I wanted you to look hot for Matteo later, you'd never agree to take an extra outfit. So I offered to throw the extra clothes in your bag for you."

I was suddenly concerned since she'd been plotting. Leo was unpredictable at best when she got an idea into her head and tried to make it a reality. "What exactly did you pack for me?"

"That's for me to know and you to find out later," she said cryptically.

I rubbed my temples with my fingertips. "I think I'm getting a migraine."

"No, you're not." She handed me a piece of candy. "You're just hungry because you skipped dinner. Have some calories and maybe a bottle of water. You need to hydrate before you drink, anyway."

"How much do you think we're going to drink later?" I asked warily.

"I'm going to have a couple," she said with a shrug. "I'm going to make sure you have enough to loosen up and stop hiding from Matteo."

"I'm not hiding," I protested. "I just tried to kiss him, remember?"

"He probably didn't know what to do with your sudden personality change," she offered. "Maybe he thought an evil sex spirit possessed you since it's Halloween."

"Do you ever run out of ridiculous ideas?"

She laughed and unwrapped a lollipop, giving it a lick and settling it on the inside of her cheek. "I haven't yet."

***

"I swear, my nipples are going to freeze off," I griped, pulling my coat tighter around my body as we walked the two blocks to the bar.

"Look at the bright side," Leo quipped. "They'll be perfect headlights to entice Matteo."

"They'll be visible to every person in the bar!"

She shrugged. "Ignore the others. If it'll help, I'll pinch mine, and we can be twinsies."

"Twinning nipples with you has been a lifelong dream of mine," I said drily.

"You know, if you think you'd be into it, we could present as a pair to Matteo." I could just make out her waggling eyebrows in the dark. I scowled in response. "Or not."

"I think sex with you might ruin our friendship."

"Well, shit." Leo snapped her fingers. "There goes my plan to get you into a marriage pact if we're not married by thirty-five."

"Sorry to disappoint." The bar came into view, and Hector held the door for the others. I hurried inside, eager to find respite from the freezing air. The warm wood accents did little to warm up my fingers, which had lost feeling on the short walk.

Leo shrugged out of her coat and hung it on a hook under the bar counter. "See, that wasn't so bad."

"That's relative," I responded, blowing hot air into my hands. "I can't believe I forgot my hat and gloves. I can't believe you packed a fucking tank top with my jeans."

"You look hot," she said with a wink. "And I packed a sweater, too."

I looked down at the thin, open-weave black sweater so big the wide neck was halfway down my arms. "This hardly counts as clothing. My shoulders are bare."

"Don't worry; your nipples look fabulous." Leo scurried away when I shot her a death glare, ordering tequila shots for us. She gave me an apologetic grin when she returned and held a shot glass out to me. "Peace offering?"

"Why can't I stay mad at you?" I asked, tossing the shot back and grunting as it burned my throat. With the rest of my body so cold, it felt like straight fire.

"I'm your lobster," Leo trilled, making her hands into lobster claws and clicking them like castanets. I felt a warm presence at my back as I giggled at my friend's antics.

"Who's having lobster?" Matteo's voice had a tinge of gruffness to it after talking over all the noise at the restaurant for hours.

"Nobody," I blurted. "Leo's just being Leo."

"Ah." Matteo nodded like that explained everything. I wondered which of her eccentricities he'd witnessed since she'd worked for him. He'd seemed taken aback by some of our conversation at the store earlier in the week.

"I told Hector he could buy me a drink." Leo hopped down from her stool and sauntered to the other end of the bar, where the bartender was lining up shots for the restaurant staff. Diego offered us shots, but Matteo took one for me and declined the other.

Everybody lifted their shot glasses in the air. Diego yelled out, "To Matteo!"

The rest of us echoed the sentiment, and Matteo nodded graciously, the color in his cheeks heightening. When everybody finished their whiskey shots, people broke up into groups and wander to other areas of the bar.

"Do you want another?" Matteo asked, nodding at my empty shot glass.

I thought about what Leo said and nodded. "Yeah, thanks."

He waved the bartender down and looked imploringly at me when she asked what he wanted. "Lady's choice."

"Rum and coke, please," I answered. That should be safe enough. The bartender set my drink down, and I took a sip, feeling chilled again.

"Do you want my jacket?" Matteo offered when I shivered involuntarily.

I shook my head. "No, thanks. I'm good. Just a cold drink. Why don't bars serve hot drinks on freezing nights?"

He chuckled. "I make a mean hot buttered rum."

"See, that sounds perfect," I responded with a smile.

Matteo tapped his long fingers against his thigh. The jeans he wore fit him perfectly, showing off his toned physique. He'd exchanged his usual jacket for black leather, and I could have breathed his scent all night.

He cleared his throat. "If you'd like, we could go back to my place, and I could make you one."

"But earlier–"

"I was an ass," he finished, leaning close enough that I could smell mint on his breath. "I handled it all wrong. You offered yourself, and I wanted nothing more than to bite that bottom lip and suck it into my mouth, but I didn't want to pressure you. I wasn't sure a quick kiss in the back would be enough."

"Oh," I breathed. My lips felt hot with the promise of the kiss he'd described. Did I want to go home with him? I knew he wouldn't push me further than I was willing to go, but I also didn't want to lead him on. Sex wasn't something I'd be comfortable with yet, and I didn't want to stay the night again without an established relationship. That just wasn't who I was.

"Should we get out of here?" Matteo asked, hope in his voice.

My brows furrowed. "I'm sorry. I can't."

"That's okay." He smiled gently and straightened to put more distance between us.

"Not that I'm not attracted to you," I tried to explain, keeping a vice grip on my drink. "I'm not ready for all that."

"You don't have to explain yourself to me, Macy. I understand, and I respect that."

Why did this man have to be so fucking perfect? I wanted to touch and taste him, wanted to be close to him. It made me think twice about accepting his offer.

Only, I had to be true to myself. "I think I should probably head home, anyway. I rarely stay out late. Have you seen Leo?"

"Yeah." Matteo pointed to the corner booth in the back, where I could barely see Leo's form underneath Hector's. It was clear they were on their way to a good night. There went my exit strategy.

I forced a laugh. "Well, I guess she's not leaving anytime soon."

"I can give you a lift," he offered. "I'm sure Hector will make sure Leo gets home safe."

"Maybe." I pulled out my phone and texted Leo rather than interrupting whatever was happening in that booth.

"Or I can just hang out here with you."

I saw Leo's hand reach into her purse on the table, then she peered around Hector and found me. I wiggled my fingers at her and shot her a thumbs-up. She grinned, then focused on her phone for a moment before tossing it on the table, saluting me, and disappearing behind Hector again.

My phone buzzed, and I looked down to read it before glancing back at Matteo. "Let's get out of here. Leo's occupied for the night."

He chuckled, waved the bartender over to close his tab, and then offered his hand as I slid down from the bar stool. His truck was parked at the curb outside, and Matteo cranked the heat without me asking. I sat quietly, leaning my head back and closing my eyes as I listened to him sing along with the songs on the radio as he took me home.

When we reached my block, he found a spot closer to my place, and I waited for him to open my door and help me down. He was a true gentleman in action and thought. I tried to think whether Ethan would have been as patient, then I silently chastised myself. Matteo didn't deserve to be compared to him. They were night and day.

"Did you have fun tonight?" Matteo asked, entwining his fingers with mine as we walked to the little white picket fence.

"Surprisingly, yes," I answered, smiling. "It was a little unhinged, but enjoyable. You've created something really cool for the community."

"You already know how I feel about giving back, so I won't bore you with it again." He opened the gate, and I passed through first, waiting for him on the other side so we could walk together the last few feet to my doorstep.

"I'm never bored listening to you," I said softly as we stopped in front of my door. I found my key and unlocked the deadbolt, but I couldn't bring myself to go inside yet.

I turned, and Matteo pulled me to him with one imploring look, his fingers spearing through my hair as our lips met in a kiss that tasted like whiskey and want. I heard him growl low before he deepened the kiss and slipped his tongue between my lips, exploring my mouth as his hands stroked down my back and settled on my ass.

He drew a moan from me as he massaged my ass, pressing my hips to his so I could feel the evidence of his desire. I ran my hands up his arms and grasped the back of his neck, wishing his hair was long enough to run my fingers through. Matteo was warm, despite the chilly temperatures. He set me on fire with each touch, each stroke of his tongue against mine.

I gasped when he dragged his lips from mine and nipped my jaw, kissing his way to my neck, where he sucked gently beneath my ear. I didn't know how long we stood there, steam rising from our bodies in the cold, but finally, Matteo pulled away from me with an almost painful groan.

He kissed me chastely on the lips one last time. "Goodnight, Macy."

"Goodnight." It was all I could manage as he turned and walked into the night, his breath lingering in white puffs behind him.

Chapter Seventeen

I HAULED BAGS OF tiny gourds and greenery into *El Corazón Boríken* on Thursday morning. Now that it was November, it was time to get the restaurant appropriately decked out for the month of fall leaves and pumpkin everything.

"Woah, what've you got there?" Macy asked as she stood on tiptoe, then ran ahead to open the kitchen door for me, even though they would have swung on their own.

"It's the season of thankfulness," I responded cheerily. "Time to decorate again."

"Do you decorate for every month?"

I nodded and set my things down on a prep table off to the side. "Most of them."

"That seems like a lot of work," she observed, reaching for her apron.

I shrugged and started pulling items out of the bag. "Sometimes, but I enjoy it. I think it helps everything feel more personal when people walk in."

"I'd have to agree there, I think."

"You up for a video this morning?" I pulled out my phone and set it on the prep table while I grabbed my video setup.

Macy nodded and smoothed her hands down her chef's coat. "Yeah, I can help if you need it."

"Thanks."

She was so much more relaxed around me now that we'd established that our attraction was mutual, and she wasn't fighting it anymore. It was still damn near impossible to find time alone unless we got together outside of work, and Macy wasn't quite ready for that yet. I couldn't wait until she let me take her out on a date. I thirsted for more knowledge about her and devoured every bit of information she revealed.

"What are we doing today?" Macy interrupted my thoughts. I was only distracted again as I watched her pull the white skullcap onto her head and tie it under her low ponytail.

I motioned to the décor on the table. "Making a cornucopia."

"As a centerpiece?" she questioned.

"Yes." I nodded. "I need to grab the board to put down underneath so we can move it when we're done. It'll go on the table at the entry."

I left her to run to the storage area and search for the decorative rustic wood board. It was several feet long and a few feet wide—perfect for a large display. Macy stepped back as I pushed through the kitchen doors.

"Let me get this stuff out of the way." She rushed to make room for the board on the table, moving everything off to the side.

"Perfect." I nodded my approval and straightened my toque. "I think we're ready to get started. Do you need to put on lipstick or anything?"

"Ha. Ha." She rolled her eyes at my playful joke. "I think people will survive my naked lips."

"Fuck, Macy, don't say things like that." I bit my bottom lip and tried to quell my thoughts about both sets of her lips. "I'll get banned if I go on a live video with a hard-on."

She giggled and looked down, licking her lips when she saw the telltale bulge. I adjusted my chef's jacket, hoping to hide the evidence of my arousal until it went down—something that could take a while with Macy around.

I cleared my throat and turned to the rest of the staff. "Hats on, please. Live video in progress."

Black ball caps topped heads, and the conversation quieted enough that nobody on the video would make out precisely what the rest of the staff was saying. That was probably best, given that my line cooks and dishwasher could put sailors to shame with their swearing and inappropriate jokes. They'd gotten a bit better since Macy started, but they'd never wholly change their nature, and I wouldn't want them to. The kitchen had life because of the variety of personalities working within it.

I watched Macy zone out for a minute, her eyes searching around the kitchen as she silently counted something on her fingers.

"Why do you do that?" I asked when she turned to face the camera.

She looked perplexed. "Do what?"

"You always count something before we shoot video," I pointed out.

"Oh, that." Macy's eyes dropped to the ground, and she fidgeted. "It helps with anxiety. I'm uncomfortable knowing thousands of people are watching my every move."

"People love you." I reached out and brushed my fingers over her palm, feeling how soft she was. I could tell it took a lot for her to share something so personal, and I wanted her to know I accepted it as part of who she was. "But I'm glad you have something to help when needed."

She gave me a brief nod and pulled her shoulders back, taking deep breaths as I started the video and waited for viewers to filter in.

"Welcome back for another episode of *Mofongo Musing*s!" I waved at the camera. "Instead of our usual food segment, Macy will help me put together our fall centerpiece. Everybody welcome Macy."

Comments scrolled on the screen. My viewers loved Macy, and I was pretty sure they were growing on her.

"Remember, no online dating for my lovely sous chef, so you can cut that out." I chuckled at the inevitable questions about her relationship status. "Plus, nobody wants to be used for their culinary skills."

"That's right," Macy spoke up. "I expect any partner to cook just as much as I do."

We exchanged a secret look; then I focused on the task at hand. "I'm going to show you how easy it is to put together something beautiful, impressive, and festive for the Thanksgiving holiday."

I started by explaining where to find the cornucopia horn and a website for making one out of paper mache if they were crafty. By the time we began arranging things inside, Macy was conversing with me like she'd forgotten about the audience. She was charming them all if the comments rolling in were any indication.

"I like to alternate the colors," she said, pointing to the various gourds. "But not so much that people can search out a pattern."

I grinned as I read the comments scrolling by. "Have you seen what they're asking?"

"No, why?" Macy leaned forward and squinted as she tried to keep up with the comments.

"They want to know what your social media is."

"I don't have one for business," she admitted to the camera. "Sorry, friends."

I kept reading, watching her fan club expand before my eyes. "They want you to start an account and think I should help you. *The Sensible Chef.*"

"I can't tell whether or not that's flattering," she murmured as she placed more greenery. Though she seemed unsure, I caught her lips tipping up at the corners. She liked the attention.

"Yeah, what does that mean?" I feigned offense. "Are you saying I'm not sensible?"

Their protestations rushed in as people tried to reassure Macy that they loved her. I saw her blush as I read off the compliments. My social media was transforming into a Macy fan account, and I loved it. She deserved every bit of their praise.

***

"Great dinner service tonight, crew," I praised as I shut the oven off. "You handled it like pros, even with the birthday party."

"At least they tipped well," Leo called out from the other side of the kitchen. "Though maybe you should make it a mandatory twenty percent gratuity if they get that drunk. I thought I was going to have to take barf buckets to the table."

I cringed at the thought. "I'll take that under advisement. For now, be glad we survived. They raved about your service."

"Yeah, because I gave them complimentary *empanadas* to help them sober up at the end," she said with a laugh.

"Take a few home for yourself," I suggested. Leo nearly ran herself ragged, trying to keep up with the party of fifteen intoxicated adults. "I'll wrap some up for the others, too. Give me a few minutes to clean up, and I'll have *coquito* for everybody."

"Thanks, Chef!" Leo called out as she headed back to the front of the house.

"I can whip it up if you want, Chef," Macy volunteered as she passed by with clean sheet pans.

"Are you done?" I asked, not wanting to pile more work on her plate.

She nodded. "Yeah, I'm just helping Pedro."

Of course, she was helping our dishwasher. Macy didn't leave people to work alone if it could be done faster with a partner.

"If you get to it before me, that's fine." I went back to clearing and sanitizing my prep area, getting everything put away for the days we'd be closed. Seeing it all done on a Sunday night was satisfying, knowing that I had just enough of a break that I'd be itching to get back into the kitchen Wednesday morning.

I took my notebooks back to my office, shut down my computer, and then changed out of my uniform. There was no reason to stand on formality at the end of the day if we were having a drink and heading out. I didn't have the energy to head to the bar with the staff after closing.

When I returned to the kitchen, Macy had a pitcher of *coquito* ready to go and poured it into little disposable cups so Pedro wouldn't have more work. She nodded in my direction when I thanked her and murmured something about changing since she'd gotten sprayed with water in the dish room.

I sipped on *coquito* and conversed with my staff members until they filtered out, and Macy strolled back into the kitchen in her street clothes. I handed her a cup of *coquito*.

"Thanks," she said, pressing the cup to her lips and sipping. "This is perfect."

"Don't thank me," I teased. "You made it."

"I'm getting good at this," she boasted. "Careful, or I might put you out of a job. First your followers, now your customers."

I laughed at her light mood. "I'm not too worried. I'll take a break and let you try working as a head chef while I work under you."

"Hmm," Macy murmured, her eyes wide. "Under me, huh?"

My blood heated at her insinuation. "Any time you want it, all you have to do is ask, *ariete*."

"Is there any more booze?" Leo asked as she pushed her way into the kitchen, hair in disarray. I understood why when Hector followed close behind.

"Here." Macy handed them cups and looked at the last bit in the pitcher before shrugging and pouring it into her cup. "Might as well."

"I'm so proud of you." Leo beamed. "Give me a few minutes, and I'll be ready to go, okay?"

"I can give you a ride home," I offered, addressing Macy. I wanted to be with her as long as possible, and I hoped she might invite me in one night when she was ready.

"We accept," Leo answered for them as she pulled Hector back out of the kitchen. She called over her shoulder, "See you in ten."

"I guess you're my ride, then." Macy grinned at her friend's antics, finished the rest of her drink, then washed the pitcher herself and put it away.

"You know," I nudged her with my hip when she returned. "We have a few minutes until Leo is ready, and everybody else is gone. Maybe we should step out back."

"I like how your mind works." She bit her lip. "I'll grab my things and meet you there."

As soon as she left the kitchen, I flipped off the lights and raced to my office, pulling my coat on, shoving my wallet and phone into my pockets, and grabbing my keys. I didn't want to waste a single minute with Macy.

I made it outside before her, standing behind the door and grabbing her from behind when she walked into the chilly night air.

"Gotcha," I growled against her ear.

She squealed, then melted against me. "You scared me."

"Sorry," I whispered, running my lips down her sensitive neck. "I'll make up for it."

I pressed her against the wall and gently took her lips with mine, savoring each brush of our mouths. She smelled of coconut and sugar, and I couldn't resist running my tongue along her lower lip to see if any drops of *coquito* were left.

"Open for me," I murmured against her mouth. Macy parted her lips and let me inside, and my hands began to wander over her body.

She let me unzip her coat, and I pressed my body close, slipping my hand under her sweater and feeling the skin of her stomach. She was like silk, warm and soft. I lapped at her mouth and cupped her breast in my palm, finding the hardened bud of her nipple through her bra and rolling it between my fingers.

"Matteo," Macy whimpered.

"Too much?" I asked, releasing her nipple and drawing slow circles on her stomach.

She shook her head. "No, feels good."

"Good," I repeated, kissing up her neck. Her other nipple was just as hard when I palmed her breast, and my cock throbbed against the zipper of my jeans as I toyed with the little peak.

With my foot, I nudged Macy's legs further apart and bent my knees to grind my erection against her center.

"Don't stop," Macy begged, moving her hips against me.

"Never," I growled, claiming her lips again.

Nothing could tear me away from the woman in my arms.

Except the door swinging open and nearly hitting us. I shielded Macy's body with mine and tugged her sweater into place as Leo and Hector walked past.

"Goodnight, Chef," Hector called before heading off the lot, leaving the three of us.

"Come on," Leo motioned toward the truck. "Time to stop sucking face and take us home."

"Leo," Macy groaned, pressing a hand to her lips and hurrying after her friend.

I leaned my forehead against the cold stone, willing my erection to go away. Not a chance in hell was I getting into the truck with Leo so she could make comments about plantains.

Satisfied I was flaccid enough to avoid garnering attention, I sighed and pulled out my keys. I'd be spending some quality time with my hand in the shower when I got home, but I doubted that would douse the fire Macy had lit within me.

Chapter Eighteen

T UESDAYS, WE CLEANED TOILETS. Rather, Leo and I cleaned
the entire house on Tuesdays after relaxing for most of
Monday. That's why I was kneeling on the floor in front of the
downstairs bathroom, scrubbing the base of the white porcelain.
Unlike some houses with single people, we kept things relatively
clean, a necessity when we both worked long hours at the restaurant.

"Oh, you're going to love me!" Leo exclaimed as she leaned against
the doorframe. She wore torn dark wash denim and a loose black
t-shirt that had seen bleach splashes and better days. Her lopsided
messy bun wobbled as she spoke, dark tendrils of escaped hair
floating around her face.

I sat up. "I already love you, but tell me what's going on."

"I have put on my super sleuth hat and found your no good, dirty,
rotten ex," she said triumphantly.

"You found Ethan?"

"Do you have another sad excuse for a man you're divorcing?" she asked with an eye roll.

I pushed myself off the floor and grabbed the cleaner and paper towels. "No, I'm just surprised you could locate him."

"Well, you shouldn't doubt me," Leo said with feigned offense.

"I don't doubt you," I explained, trying to wrap my head around the new information. "I didn't ask you to find him. How did you find him, anyway?"

"I checked the location tags on Aaron's photos, then started looking locally for men named Ethan or something similar." She paused, momentarily distracted by a hangnail.

"And?" I prompted, pulling her out of her fixation.

"Oh, yeah, he was going by Nathan Hart." She made a disgusted sound. "Just as unoriginal as he was in the sack."

"I'd rather not think of that, thanks," I said drily. "So we've got a name and a city?"

"I wouldn't leave you with that." Leo turned her phone screen toward me. "I have his fucking address. Can you smell the alimony yet?"

Ethan's address. I'd be able to finalize the divorce sooner if we could show we served him papers. It was like I could see the jailer opening the cell door and outside light poured into my place of relational confinement.

"This is amazing, Leo!" I grabbed my friend and hugged her fiercely, showing my gratitude.

"I know, I'm amazing."

I let that go, hugging her a moment longer and planting a peck on her cheek. "Send me that address, will you? I'm going to email my lawyer right now. Hopefully, this gets things done more quickly."

"Not so fast." She held up a hand and arched her brow. "We haven't discussed payment."

"Oh, sorry." I paused. "I didn't realize you'd spent money on the search. What do I owe you?"

"I didn't spend money," she admitted. "But my time is worth something, too."

"Of course."

"You can pay me back by dating Matteo," she said smugly.

"Leo, we've talked about this," I sighed. "First, he hasn't officially asked me out on a date. Second, I'm not sure I'm ready for that."

"Someday, you'll have to stop letting what Ethan said and did rule your life." She stomped her foot petulantly. "It's not fair that he gets to move on and find happiness when you're still miserable."

I frowned. "I'm not miserable."

Leo gave me a pointed look. "You're not blissfully happy."

"Few people are," I said flatly, tugging my grey leggings up my waist and toying with the hem of my black tank top.

"Regular happy, then," she compromised. "You're not even as happy as the people around you."

"I'm happy." I listed it out for her. "I'm happy living with you and working at *El Corazón Borikén*."

"Two things in your life make you happy?" she asked drolly. "That's not good enough for me. I think Matteo will make you happy. He brings out a side of you I haven't seen since you were fifteen, and you smile when he's around. *Really* smile. None of that smiling while you're really dying inside shit."

I hate that she had me pegged so well. "Maybe I could say yes if he asked me on a date."

"That's all I'm asking!" Leo hugged me. "Just give yourself the opportunity to be happy."

"Fine." I wasn't sure a man could ever make me happy in the long run, but I'd spent a year trying to find happiness on my own. It hadn't been a failure. My therapist was happy that I enjoyed walking around Portland and working. Not everybody had a million habits on the side. "Can I have the address now?"

"Oh, yeah." Leo waved a hand dismissively in the air as she walked away. "I sent it to your email before I told you about it."

"You're a conniving bitch. Do you know that?" I called after her.

She laughed in response. "Proud of it!"

"But I love you for it," I added affectionately.

I put the cleaning supplies away, grabbed my phone, opened my email app, copied the address Leo sent, and then pasted it into an email to my lawyer. I would have to pay her more, but moving the divorce along faster would be worth it. Working at the restaurant on a salary allowed me to put more money into monthly savings. Once the mess with Ethan was over, I could pay what I owed the lawyer and start over, free from the weight he'd tied around my left ring finger.

The line from my wedding band was long gone, but I rubbed my thumb over the spot where there used to be a lighter ring of skin on my finger. For months, I'd stared at that fucking strip of skin and longed for Ethan's return. Sometimes it disgusted me to remember how weak I'd been, how desperate I'd been for him to love me as I thought I'd loved him. And I had loved him, but I'd given more love than he'd had to offer, and that only ate away at me in our toxic relationship. It wasn't always yelling and hitting that made a relationship dysfunctional, but careless words, actions, and an unwillingness to communicate or be truthful. It all led to our downfall.

Was I ready to be rid of Ethan, finally? Yeah, I thought I was. Whether that meant moving on alone and living with myself or facing a future with Matteo, I wanted the weight of my past gone.

***

"Okay, don't move. Focus on my hair. Smile." Amaia spouted off directions as she snapped photos of me wearing my chef's uniform in the kitchen at *El Corazón Borikén*. "No, not that smile. Try to look natural."

"Nothing about this feels natural," I grumbled, looking at where my arms crossed over my chest, and I held a whisk in one hand.

"Don't worry, it looks fine," she assured me.

Amaia had a side business as a family photographer, and when word of my budding social media career spread around the kitchen, she'd insisted on taking photos for me. Sometimes I hated that the restaurant staff functioned as a very well-informed gossip mill. In this case, free headshots were a perk to not having privacy. It was a wonder nobody had figured out whatever was happening between Matteo and me.

"What if I just cook something and you take pictures when you see an opportunity?" I suggested.

Amaia nodded, her pink curls bobbing. "Yeah, we could do that. What do you want to make? I can help prep."

"How about *mofongo*?" I smirked. "It can be a nod to Chef and his fault in all this."

"Come on now," Matteo called out from the other side of the kitchen, pretending to be hurt.

"I like that." Amaia grinned. "You want to get in on the photo, Chef?"

Matteo shook his head. "Nah, I'm good over here. You already roped me into the live. Wouldn't want it all to go to my head."

"I'm not sure anything could make that ego of yours bigger," I said playfully as Amaia walked away to put her camera in its case.

I washed my hands and grabbed a plantain, slicing it and letting it soak in salty water while I grabbed a pan and set it on the stove, pouring oil in to heat.

"I can tell you something you can make bigger," Matteo whispered suggestively as he passed behind me.

"Behave," I warned.

"I'm an angel." He circled his finger over his head. "You want the *pilon*?"

"Yeah, thanks."

After I drained the plantains and dried them, I carefully dropped the slices in to fry. Matteo set the mortar and pestle at my station, and Amaia worked on the garlic while I watched the plantains, flipping them halfway through the cooking time. My stomach growled as the aroma permeated the kitchen.

"Did you eat breakfast?" Matteo asked, nodding at my stomach.

"I had a protein drink," I answered.

He shook his head in disappointment. "You must eat, *ariete*. You're going to be on your feet all day. I'm going to make *empanadas*, and you'll eat."

"Are you channeling your *Abuelita* right now?" I teased.

Matteo chuckled. "She was a wise woman, and nobody ever went hungry when she cooked. She would demand that I feed you."

"Fine, I will eat *empanadas*," I conceded. "But why don't we just make them on the live and knock out both tasks?"

"Then you'll eat the *mofongo* when you're finished," he insisted.

"Deal."

"I'm going to sauté up some shrimp for the plating," Matteo said, heading to the walk-in and leaving no room for my objection. It wasn't a bad idea.

I pulled the fried plantain slices from the oil and let them drain for a minute before adding them to the garlic, *sazon*, and other spices in the *pilon* and grinding everything up. I'd certainly built arm strength working with the stone mortar and pestle for the last couple of months. Amaia sprinkled some *chicharrones* into the mortar, and I mixed the bits of fried pork in with the other ingredients until I reached the right consistency.

"Here." Amaia set a couple of *mofongo* molds on the table, and I grabbed a spatula to pack the plantains into the little metal cups.

Leo burst into the kitchen, a large bag in hand, and I nearly dropped one of the *mofongo* molds. "I'm here! So sorry I slept in, but I wouldn't miss your international debut for the world!"

"What have you brought us?" Matteo asked, craning his head in her direction as he tossed the seasoned shrimp into a pan.

"Makeup for Macy." Leo opened the bag so he could see what had to be everything we both owned. "But I can do your makeup, too."

Matteo's face scrunched up. "Yeah, no thanks. I'm good au naturale."

"I bet you are," Leo said suggestively.

I shot her a glare, pursing my lips and raising my brows in silent communication to get her to shut up. "I did my makeup before I left this morning."

"Oh, I know," she said sympathetically. "That's why I'm here to help."

"Hey!"

"It's not that you did a poor job," Leo continued, ignoring my outburst. "It could be better, and I want you to look spectacular for your first time hosting a live video."

There was no getting out of it, so I gave in. I knew they were all just trying to calm my nerves since I was anxious about being the focus of a video instead of just occasionally throwing out commentary. "You've got five minutes. All this food is going to get cold."

"Have Matteo put it under the warming lights," she said dismissively. "If you want hot food, you'd better hurry and follow me."

"Can you handle that?" I asked Matteo, unwilling to pile things on him if he didn't want to do it.

"Keep the food warm," he repeated. "I'll make sure it's still safe to eat when you return. You promised to feed yourself. Or I can do it if you'd like."

I smiled at his offer. "I think I can get a fork from plate to mouth."

He chuckled as I rushed off after Leo. She sat me on a folding chair in the back room, and I figured it was best to stay silent as she worked so she didn't go off on a tangent. I was trying to get everything done before the rest of the staff arrived for the day.

I couldn't stay silent when she produced a set of fake lashes. "What do you think you're doing with those?"

"Saving you from having to wear mascara, so there's no chance of it dripping down your face when you sweat," she supplied as she put a thin line of adhesive on the lash and carefully waved it in the air.

My eyes closed reflexively as her fingers approached. "I hate that you have a point. Will I be able to get it off later?"

"Yeah, sure." I opened one eye as she applied the lashes to the other. She bit her lip in concentration. "I'll help you remove it. There. Look in the mirror."

"I'd better not look like I'm going to a rave."

"I wouldn't do that to you," Leo promised as she led me to the mirror on the wall. "See?"

"Okay, this is good." I looked at my reflection. The makeup looked natural, but a little liner and the lashes made my eyes look bigger, and she'd put more color on my cheeks and lips.

She nudged my shoulder with hers. "Remember me when you're famous."

"Like I could ever forget you," I scoffed playfully. "You're the gum on my shoes."

"Damn straight." She patted me on the head, smoothing my hair back. "Now go crush it. I believe in you."

Tears stung the back of my eyes, and I fanned myself, refusing to cry. "Thanks. Love you."

"Love you more." Leo made the shape of a heart and pulsed it against her chest.

I pulled myself together and returned to the kitchen, quickly plating the mofongo and garnishing it for photos. My smiles came more easily, and it didn't take long for Amaia to get what she needed.

"Perfect," she declared, and I made quick work of the food on my plate.

Leo clapped her hands in the background, and Matteo leaned against the counter, watching my every move, a heated look in his eyes. A lock of hair fell onto his forehead, and my fingers itched to reach out and touch it. I might not survive the video if he kept that up.

"Okay, let's get the *empanadas* done." I smoothed my jacket nervously and ran my tongue over my teeth to ensure no food lingered. At least the audience couldn't smell the shrimp on my breath.

"The first batch is in the oven, so we can show the finished product without you having to kill time on video," Matteo said. "I also set up the recording stuff. I thought that might be helpful."

"Thank you," I said gratefully. I wanted to keep my first video shorter and wouldn't turn down the help.

He helped me get my phone set up, and Amaia set up the ingredients we'd need while Leo handed me a shot of Don Q, reminding me it was five o'clock somewhere. I took the shot and a few deep breaths, then pressed the Live button. Viewers filtered in, and I turned to Matteo, surprised at the quickly rising number.

"I don't even have that many followers yet," I whispered.

He shrugged, his chef's coat pulling taut against his muscular shoulders. "I might have shared it with my followers."

There wasn't time to say anything else. I launched into the spiel I'd rehearsed for my first video, which sounded very similar to how Matteo spoke to his audience. With my own twist, of course. I wasn't as naturally funny, so I tried to be congenial.

The audience interacted as Matteo and I cooked, and they praised our finished product when I produced the pre-cooked *empanadas*.

I smiled at the camera. "Now for the taste test. You go first, Matteo."

He took a bite, and I turned slightly so the viewers couldn't see me lightly scratching an itch by my eye. Matteo closed his eyes and made a satisfied noise, and I took a bite of my chicken *empanada*, but something furry tickled my tongue.

"What the—"

I pulled an eyelash from my mouth and realized what had happened. Mortified, I turned to Matteo, holding the lash between my fingers. His eyes widened, and he tried but failed to hide his laughter. I could hear Leo and Amaia giggling in the background.

Matteo gagged, and I rolled my eyes. "Come on; I know they aren't that bad."

He shook his head, and I watched as he brought his hands to his neck in the universal sign of choking. *Oh, shit.*

"Matteo!" I rushed to his side, slapping his back hard because there was no way I could get the leverage for the Heimlich. After several hard hits, a piece of chicken flew from his mouth, and he gasped, coughing as he sucked in air. "Are you okay?"

"I am now," he said breathlessly. "Thanks to you. I'll never complain about how hard you hit again."

It was then that I realized the live video feed was still running, and I froze. *Fuck.* This was a disaster.

"And that's why kitchen safety is so important!" I blurted to the camera as if somebody else had inhabited my body. "Always know what to do in an emergency, whether it be a kitchen fire, injury, or somebody who cooks and eats for a living choking on their own creations."

I watched the laughing emojis flood in and realized hundreds of people had just watched my live video crash and burn. It was time to end it before I cried. Leo was hovering just off camera, concern in her eyes.

Plastering a wide smile on my face, I held up an *empanada* in salute. "And that's it for today, friends! Go forth and food!"

I tapped the end button and slumped, dropping my head to the table and groaning.

Leo rubbed my back and took my phone out of the holder. "It wasn't that bad, Macy."

"I almost ate my eyelash!" I whined. "Matteo almost died! And—*go forth and food*—what the hell was I thinking?"

"I thought it was cute," Matteo pitched in, his palm resting low on my back.

"I'll never be able to show my face in public again," I lamented. "I'm deleting the account."

"You're not deleting the account," Leo and Matteo said simultaneously.

My face burned, and I gave in to the tears and sobbed on the cold metal surface under me while my best friend and would-be lover tried to soothe me. Just when I thought life was looking up, I dug another hole to climb out of.

Chapter Nineteen

"**H**AVE YOU SEEN THE video?" Julian asked when I answered his call.

"Yep," I said. "It's hit a million views in less than a week."

"Does Macy know yet?" he asked.

I leaned against the balcony door of my apartment and ignored the chill in the air while I watched the morning sun glisten on the river in the distance. "I don't think so. Leo said she won't even look at the account."

"Odds she'll take it well?"

I thought about that for a moment. "Not great, considering she sobbed for ten minutes and swore off social media forever. Leo has been running the accounts without Macy. I wish you could see how the staff keeps secretly taking photos and videos of Macy while she works. It's like mission impossible in my kitchen."

Julian chuckled. "I love it. Remember to tell her that all publicity is good publicity."

"Yeah, that didn't fly when I tried it." I rubbed my hand across the back of my neck. "She said something along the lines of serial killers get life in prison when they get publicity."

"Seriously? That's a little dramatic."

I bristled, driven to defend Macy. "She was upset."

"Relax, I'm not mocking her," Julian said to pacify me. "It happens to the best of us."

"Yeah, Luna told me all about how dramatic you got when you accused her of corporate espionage back when you were dating."

"Not my finest moment," he admitted before changing the subject. "When will you bring her around to meet the family?"

"I haven't even had a real date with her yet." Not that I didn't want to ask Macy out, but we'd both been busy, and a part of me wanted to make her desperate before I finally popped the question. The dinner question, that is.

"You should know that the girls told Bella about Macy," he warned. "She's coming for Thanksgiving, and Viola says she's pretty set on meeting Macy."

I groaned. Bella could be a little much sometimes. "Can you hold her off?"

"Probably not," Julian admitted. "Your best bet is to get a few dates under your belt, then invite her to Thanksgiving."

"And if she says no?"

"Then expect Bella to arrange a *chance* meeting," he advised.

"Time to stop procrastinating, then," I mused. Maybe it was the push I needed. "Macy isn't used to family affairs. From what I've gathered, her family wasn't close growing up, and her ex-husband wasn't the caring type."

"Yeah, he sounds like a real gem, gallivanting around with a mistress." Anger suffused Julian's words, and I felt the same. I was a natural pacifist, but I wouldn't mind meeting Ethan in a dark alley.

I glanced at the time on the stove and wrapped up the conversation. "If I'm going to stop by the store and grab celebratory champagne before breaking the news to Macy, I need to head out now."

"Good luck, man." Julian's tone said he meant it as a brother teasing brother, with a hint of sincerity underneath.

"Thanks, I'm going to need it."

I ended the call, grabbed my things, took the elevator down to my truck, and then dropped by the store to get some nice bottles of champagne—no ten-dollar bottles for Macy. I would spoil her as I was able.

When I arrived at *El Corazón Borikén*, Macy was already in the kitchen. I snuck a couple of buckets of ice to keep the champagne chilled and caught the others as they filtered in to give them a heads-up.

Amaia helped me make chicken empanadas for the day while Macy prepped the line with Ian. She was completely unsuspecting, and I had second thoughts until Leo waltzed through the door and touched a finger to her nose in secretive solidarity. I gave her a nod and snuck out to grab the champagne.

When I returned, Macy was chatting with Leo, and the other staff members found reasons to be present. Several had their phones out to record what was about to happen.

"Macy, come here, please," I said, setting the champagne down on my prep area and working to remove the metal cage from the first bottle.

"What's going on?" she asked, standing by my side. The confusion on her face was adorable, and I wanted to reach out and brush a tendril of blonde hair behind her ear, but I held back.

"We're here to celebrate," I began. Macy looked at Leo, who was bouncing with a broad grin. "Your first video went viral!"

"What?" Macy asked as the rest of the staff cheered and clapped.

Leo patted her arm. "Sorry, but I didn't delete it. People love it."

The cork popped free from the champagne bottle, and I poured bubbly into the restaurant's champagne flutes, handing the first one to Macy. I took the last one when everybody had a glass and raised it. "To Macy, the hottest new chef on social media!"

"To Macy!" the others cheered.

I leaned close to her ear. "Congratulations, *ariete*. You're a hit. I'm so proud of you."

"Thanks." Macy flushed crimson, still in shock at the news. She looked from me to Leo. "People liked it?"

"They loved it," I assured her. "They love all your posts."

"What do you mean?" She asked quizzically.

Leo looked uncertain. "We've been posting pictures and captions for you. I couldn't let you give up."

Instead of reacting angrily, Macy pulled Leo into a one-armed hug, conscious of where the glasses were. "You're the most amazing friend I could ever ask for."

"I know," Leo whispered. She blinked back moisture before facing Macy again and could see how deep their bond went. Suddenly, Leo's approval meant even more to me.

Macy let out a choked laugh. "What am I supposed to do now?"

"Be your fabulous self and pose for photos," Leo said. "Maybe do some more videos where Matteo doesn't try to off himself and your food isn't winking at the audience."

They dissolved into giggles, and I chuckled with them. If there was one thing I knew, it was how to integrate food and social media. "Maybe hold up that glass and thank your viewers."

"That's a great idea," Leo said enthusiastically, pulling out her phone.

Macy dabbed at her eyes and held up her glass. Leo hit the record button, and Macy expressed her thanks. I listened but didn't hear a word, so caught up in the joy that made her eyes twinkle and her face glow.

***

There was a tap on my office door Sunday night after closing, and I looked up to find Macy standing in the doorway in a pair of dark jeans and a pale pink t-shirt. "Chef?"

"What's up?" I asked, closing my laptop and leaning back in my chair.

"I was wondering if you might give me a ride home?" she asked nervously. "Leo went home with Hector. I can take the MAX if you don't want to."

"No, of course, I'll give you a ride," I said. I hated that she even felt it necessary to ask. "Go grab your bag. And Macy, call me Matteo, especially after hours."

"Thanks, Matteo," she said, turning and slipping out of my office.

I looked down at my unbuttoned jacket and uniform pants and decided to change. I shrugged out of my white coat and pulled my undershirt over my head, tossing them in the hamper I kept in the corner. The restaurant had a washing machine to wash all the linens, which made it easy for me to leave my uniforms at work. After toeing my black clogs off, I unfastened my pants, letting them drop from my hips to the floor and feeling the cool air against my bare legs.

"Oh, sorry!" Macy stood inside my office, covering her eyes with her hand. I could feel my dick twitch with anticipation.

"Macy." My voice came out gruff with desire. "I don't mind."

She slowly parted her fingers, then let her hands slip from her face entirely. I turned and tossed my pants to the hamper, giving her a nice view of my ass, then flexed my muscles as she watched. When I turned around, heat suffused her eyes.

"Like what you see?" I asked.

My cock tented my black boxer briefs as Macy licked her lips hungrily. "Uh-huh."

"Close the door behind you and flip the lock."

"Everybody else is gone," she whispered, but did as I asked.

"Come here, *ariete*."

Macy dropped her bag by the door and walked slowly to me, stopping a couple of feet away.

I held her hands in mine, drawing her closer and kissing the back of each. "Do you want to touch me?"

"Yes," she breathed.

I placed her hands on my chest. "Then touch me."

Her fingertips were like live wires, sending sparks across my body as she trailed them down my heated skin. I sighed and rested my hands on her hips, content to let her explore. She stopped at the waistband of my boxer briefs, but her eyes remained focused where my cock pressed prominently against the fabric.

She looked up at me with those wide blue eyes, and I was lost in her. She traced the elastic at the waistband, and her nail grazed my skin, making my abs flex. "May I?"

"Please," I nearly croaked, desperate to feel her palm against my cock again. Her small stroked over my length, and I leaned my forehead against hers, watching as she gripped me firmly. "*Fuck*. Kiss me, Macy."

I brushed my hand over her cheek and tilted her chin up, pressing my mouth to hers as she tortured me by stroking me through my boxer briefs. Unable to keep still, I thrust against her palm and savored how my entire body felt afire with need for the woman before me. I devoured her, tasting and moving my tongue against hers in the same rhythm as my hips until the sensations overwhelmed me. I needed more.

"Let me touch you?" I asked, praying to everything good in the world that Macy wouldn't deny me. I'd stop if she were uncomfortable, but I wouldn't like it.

"Yes."

That single word released a tide of emotion, passion, and purpose. I stroked my hand down the side of her neck and her torso until I found the hem of her t-shirt. My dark eyes met her blue as I asked silently. She nodded, and I lifted her shirt over her head.

"You're beautiful." I brushed the back of my fingers over the swells of her pale breasts, leaning down to kiss her soft flesh. The tip of my cock wept precum, but I ignored my desire. I wanted to see the pleasure on Macy's face.

To my astonishment, my formerly shy, hesitant, Macy reached behind her, unhooked the tan bra, and let it slip down her arms until she could set it on my desk. Her rosy nipples mesmerized me as they hardened into little buds.

"Matteo," she whispered. I hadn't realized I'd been staring with my mouth hanging open, but she giggled as I shook my head and shut my mouth.

"They're better than I dreamed," I proclaimed, palming her breasts and squeezing until she leaned back against my desk. My lips lowered to first one peak, then the other, licking and sucking until the skin puckered, and Macy moaned. I tested her, grazing my teeth lightly over her nipples. She whimpered in response, and I smiled.

Macy stiffened when I reached down to unbutton her pants, and I stopped. "Is this okay?"

"I'm not ready for sex," she told me.

"That's okay," I assured her. "I just want to touch you."

"I just spent ten hours in the kitchen," she said nervously.

I understood what she was getting at, and I didn't give a fuck, but I understood her reticence and didn't want to make her uncomfortable. "I'll use my hand, then. Sound good?"

She nodded. "Yeah."

I unfastened her jeans and pushed them and her underwear over her hips and down her thighs enough that I could comfortably fit my hand between them. Her skin was even softer there, and I stroked, feeling her clit through her outer lips and pressing there until Macy asked for more.

"Matteo, please."

"Tell me what you want, *ariete*," I said, leaning forward and sucking on her bottom lip.

She blinked and bit the lip I'd just sucked. "I want your fingers inside me."

Eager to please, I parted the sensitive skin with my fingers and found Macy hot and soaked. "Oh, fuck, you're wet for me. Amazing."

She huffed out a throaty laugh. "You must be doing something right, then."

"I hope so." I took her lips again as I pressed a finger inside her tight channel, feeling the muscular ridges tighten around me as I slowly worked the digit in and out of her heat. When I slid another finger in and found Macy's clit with the heel of my hand, she jumped. "Okay?"

"Yeah," she panted, rolling her hips harder against my hand and kissing me hard. "Feels so good."

"Ride my hand, Macy," I growled, feeling her drip around me. "I want to feel you come all over my fingers."

"Harder," she begged, wrapping her arms around my neck and nipping at my bottom lip.

I almost blew in my boxer briefs. She was more responsive than I could have asked for. I shifted the angle of my hand, pressing harder against that soft, spongy place inside her. It was good that everybody else was gone because Macy cried out as her orgasm washed over her. I swallowed the sound with a kiss and held her to me as I worked her through it, gentling my movements as she came down from her peak.

"That was incredible," she said breathlessly.

"*You* are incredible," I returned, slipping my hand from between her legs and holding up my wet fingers. I slipped them into my mouth and sucked, my eyes rolling back as her flavor exploded on my tongue. Sweet, tangy, and rich, I could sate myself on her at every meal.

When I'd had my fill, I speared my other hand through Macy's hair and claimed her mouth, thrusting my tongue against hers so she could taste the gift she'd given me. She didn't protest.

After a minute, I pulled back and watched as some of the lustful haze cleared from Macy's eyes. She pulled her underwear and pants up, buttoning and zipping her jeans before reaching behind her to put her bra back on.

I wasn't sure what she needed, so I grabbed my jeans and t-shirt from my locker and dressed, wrestling my hard dick into the confines of my jeans so I could get them buttoned.

"Are you okay?" Macy asked, motioning downward. "I didn't take care of you."

"I'm great, really." I stepped forward and helped her pull her shirt over her head. "I didn't go into this expecting you to reciprocate. Getting to pleasure you was more than enough for tonight."

"I guess you should probably take me home now," she said reluctantly. It thrilled me she didn't want to leave me, but I knew I couldn't keep her at the restaurant all night, even if I didn't want her to go.

"I don't want this to end," I admitted, "but it's been a long week, and you're not ready for more."

Macy nodded and walked to the door, pulling her coat on and slinging her bag over her shoulder. "Thank you."

"Thank *you*," I returned. "That took something for you to trust me, and I'm so glad you did."

I held the door for her and set the alarm as we left the building.

"Will you go out with me tomorrow?" I asked impulsively as the door closed. It was long past time to shoot my shot. "On a real date?"

Macy offered me a soft smile. "Yeah, I'd like that."

I grinned broadly, taking her hand in mine as we headed to my truck and whatever the future held.

Chapter Twenty

I HAD A SENSE of déjà vu as Leo stood with me in front of my closet, pondering what I should wear for my date with Matteo.

"My palms are sweating," I lamented, rubbing them on my bare thighs. That didn't help.

Leo looked over at me. "There's nothing to be nervous about. You've worked together for months, you've spent the night at his house, he's given you an orgasm, and he's seen you naked."

"Mostly naked," I amended.

"Fine, *mostly* naked." Leo rolled her eyes. "He didn't have any complaints. You've got nothing to worry about on this date."

"What if I say something stupid?" I ran my hand down my face, then remembered I was already wearing makeup. I ran to my bedroom to mirror, sighing in relief when everything still looked fine. "What if I choke on my food?"

"I think that's Matteo's wheelhouse," she joked. "The dude smelled your morning breath and still pursued you, Macy. Give him a little credit for not being a total ass."

She was right. I needed to get over myself and ignore the voice—that sounded a lot like Ethan's—telling me no man would ever truly want me. "He's a good guy."

"Yeah, he is," Leo agreed. "I'm a little jealous. I mean, I'm not attracted to him, but I envy that you found a good person."

"Now I feel bad." I wanted my friend to find somebody special. Leo deserved all the good in the world. She was the best of people.

"Oh, shut up," she snapped playfully. "No man has put me through the shit Ethan put you through. Plus, I'm way too wild for somebody like Matteo. If I'm a firecracker, I'll need to find a nuclear missile to handle me."

I laughed and perused the selection in my closet, finally pulling out a curve-hugging dress in a deep rose color. "What do you think of this?"

"That's perfect," Leo declared. "Wear those black booties and your leather jacket."

"I can do that." I slipped the dress over my head and smoothed it down my hips, satisfied with my reflection in the mirror. Matteo had never seen me in anything other than my chef's uniform or jeans. I hoped I wasn't going too far with the dress.

Leo handed me the black shoes while I pulled on pantyhose, hoping they would offer a little additional warmth on the crisp November night. The low-heeled boots made my legs and ass look better when I turned in front of the mirror.

The doorbell rang, and Leo did a little dance. "He's here! You get your jacket on. I'll answer the door."

She was off like a shot before I could protest, but I didn't trust her not to say something that would embarrass me in front of Matteo. I ripped my leather jacket off its hanger and quickly pulled it on, checking my hair one last time to ensure the soft waves had held up after curling it. Happy with how I looked, I hurried to the front door, slowing down on the last few steps when I could see Matteo's black boots and jeans.

"And what are your intentions with Macy?" Leo asked, just as I came into view.

"Hey." Matteo's face lit up as noticed me, and I felt even more beautiful with how he looked at me like I was art and a meal.

"Hi," I said shyly. Where had my confidence gone? My hands shook with nerves, and I was sure he could feel it as he helped me off the last step. Fuck, my palms were sweating again. He didn't drop my hand, though.

"I guess your intentions can wait for later," Leo said begrudgingly. "Macy doesn't have a curfew, so feel free to keep her out all night. I've got your number if she lets her phone die again."

"Leo," I hissed at her. "I think we've got it."

I picked up my purse, and Leo's eyes when wide before she ran up the stairs, yelling back, "Wait a minute!"

Matteo drew me into a hug, and I got a whiff of his forest scent with just a hint of cilantro and lime. "What's she doing?"

"I have no idea," I said against his dark green shirt, careful not to let any of my makeup rub off.

I heard Leo's footsteps before she nearly tripped down the last steps. Matteo reached out his arm to steady her, and she looked at him with wide eyes. "Oh, you're strong."

"Thanks," he chuckled.

I looked down and realized what she was holding. "Leo!"

"What?" She shrugged innocently and began shoving condoms into my purse. "Can't be too careful."

"Fair enough," Matteo agreed with a grin.

Then Leo went too far. "Macy isn't on birth control, and we all know you're hot for each other. No breeding her tonight."

"I'm joining a convent," I moaned, leaning against the wall with my eyes closed, hoping I was having a bad dream.

"Not with his dick on the menu, you aren't," Leo added. "Sorry to objectify you, Matteo."

"No offense taken," he answered, chest rumbling with humor.

I peeked at them through one eye and found them both trying to hide smiles. "You're both terrible."

"I mean, you can try joining a convent," Matteo said, lifting a hand. "But I'll do my damndest to make you reconsider."

Leo slapped him on the back. "Good man."

"Can we just go, please?" I begged, clasping my hands together in front of me. Matteo took pity on me and opened the door, ushering me in front of him.

"Have fun!" Leo called out behind us. "Love you!"

I held my hands in a heart over my head as Matteo opened the passenger door of his truck, and he waved back at Leo.

"She's a good friend," he observed.

"The best," I agreed. "But she's also single-handedly responsible for the most humiliating moments of my life. And she just added another to the list."

***

Dinner at the Brazilian restaurant was terrific, with the servers bringing meat on big sticks and carving it right at our table. It was immediately apparent that somebody at the restaurant knew who Matteo was because a complimentary bottle of wine appeared at the table not five minutes after we arrived.

I was nearly stuffed, and the conversation was winding down as we perused the dessert menu.

"What's that tattoo on your forearm, anyway?" I asked when I glimpsed the edge of it peeking out from under his long-sleeved shirt. I'd seen it nearly every day but hadn't gotten a close enough look.

Matteo pushed his sleeve up his arm and set his forearm on the table. "It's a rosary made of *gandules* and cilantro."

"That's inventive." I stroked a finger across the little green pigeon peas and down to where the cilantro leaves created a makeshift cross on his hand.

"I didn't want the typical chef's knife on my forearm," Matteo said with a laugh. "Do you have any tattoos?"

"I have two," I admitted, reluctant to elaborate. They weren't as impressive as his.

"What? Where?" he asked, wiggling his eyebrows.

"I have a little heart and script that says be true." I hoped he wouldn't ask the meaning behind them because the first resulted from naïve and childish love, and the latter resulted from the heartbreak that followed that love. "You'll have to find them later, I guess."

"I'm looking forward to it." Matteo took my hand and rubbed his thumb over my palm suggestively. Why was his thumb so damn sexy?

I sipped on my wine, unsure how far I wanted to take that kind of banter. My traitorous brain made me blurt out, "I'm still not ready for sex."

"Okay," Matteo answered slowly.

"I'm sorry." I finished my wine and poured more into my glass. "I know that Leo made a show with the condoms and cautions, but I don't just jump into bed on the first date."

"Macy." Matteo wrapped his hand around the wine glass after I chugged it down, setting it out of my reach. "I'm okay with that. I've told you already that I won't pressure you into anything. Suppose you want to kiss me, great. I'm all for it if you want to touch or please me. If you let me make you come until your knees are too weak to stand, even better. But if you want to sit on my couch and watch a movie, maybe fall asleep—that's a perfect night in my book, too. It's about me getting to spend time with you."

Why did he always have to say the perfect thing? I wasn't used to men who listened and respected my boundaries. Why couldn't I have found Matteo instead of Ethan, married him instead of my ex? We'd probably have a bunch of little chef children by now.

"Macy?" Matteo looked concerned.

"I'm good," I choked out. "You're just so *nice*."

"That's a good thing, I hope," he said cautiously, running a hand across his jaw.

I nodded. "It's the best. You're the best, and I appreciate everything you just said."

"Good." He picked up the dessert menu. "Have you decided what looks enticing?"

You, I wanted to say. I glanced down at the menu and perused the dessert selection. None of it stood out to me. "Honestly? I can make most of it at home, and I have a hard time eating dessert at restaurants for that reason."

Matteo's shoulders relaxed, and he grinned. "I'm so glad I'm not the only one."

"Really?" I asked skeptically. I couldn't tell if he was just being nice.

"Totally." He signaled to the server and handed them his card. "What do you say we head back to my place and make our own dessert?"

"I like the sound of that." I couldn't keep track of everything Matteo said that marked every box for the perfect man. He was creating boxes I didn't know I needed to check.

When we walked out of the restaurant, it was pouring rain outside. Matteo stopped me. "You wait here. I'll get the truck and pick you up at the curb."

"That's okay," I assured him. "I don't mind a little rain. I grew up in Oregon, remember?"

"If you're sure," he said reluctantly.

I nodded. "I am. You ready to run?"

When he smiled, I tugged his hand and pulled him out into the cold shower, hurrying down the block to the nearest parking garage. I couldn't help the happy laughter that burst from me, and Matteo joined in, squeezing my hand and tugging me to a stop in the middle of the sidewalk. Before I could ask what he was doing, he pulled me close and framed my face with his hands, kissing me right there in the pouring rain.

The biting cold couldn't reach me through the heat Matteo's kiss spread through my body. I stroked his rain-streaked cheek with my fingers, sipping the last taste of the wine from his lips. My head felt light, but it wasn't from the alcohol. Matteo was my high.

I was panting when he finally pulled away, my mouth open and my lips tingling. He said nothing; he just licked his lips, took my hand in his, and pulled me to the parking garage, where he helped me into the truck and headed back to his apartment.

"Any ideas what you'd like for dessert?" Matteo asked, as we ascended to his floor in the elevator.

I shrugged. "I don't know what all you have."

"Do you like chocolate?"

I arched a brow at him. "Does it rain in Oregon?"

He chuckled. "We could make truffles."

"Sold," I declared, rapping my knuckles on the elevator wall.

We arrived at his floor, and Matteo let us into the apartment. I took off my coat and shoes, but realized I was pretty well soaked from our brief stop in the rain. I rubbed my arms brusquely, trying to warm up.

"You're cold," Matteo observed, removing his coat and bending to untie his boots. "We could take a hot shower."

I gave him the side-eye. "I'm not sure being naked together is the best option after I've had wine."

"Then come with me; you can borrow my clothes." I followed Matteo across the apartment to his bedroom, where he pulled out two pairs of grey sweatpants and a couple of black t-shirts. "Here, these should work."

I didn't want to be rude and tell him he might be a smaller size than me, so I took the clothes. "Thanks."

"You can use the bathroom to change if you want." He pointed across the room. "I'll change here."

I trotted to the bathroom and locked the door behind me, even though I didn't think Matteo would walk in. I wanted privacy in case his clothes were too small for my figure. He was tall and slim, and I was short and—not. I stripped out of my dress and hose, pulling the sweats on and rolling the waistband several times because they were too long. The t-shirt was snug, but at least my boobs looked good.

When I emerged after folding my clothes and leaving them on the edge of the bathroom counter, Matteo wasn't in his room. I found him in the kitchen, already scalding cream on the stove, while he chopped up a bar of chocolate.

"Couldn't wait to start, huh?" I asked, coming up behind him and wrapping my arms around his waist as I peered around him.

He lifted his arm so I could stand at his side. "I figured there was no sense wasting time. Do you want to pick out a movie?"

"Sure. Any preference?" I found a remote on the coffee table and scrolled through his Netflix account. Cooking shows, action movies, and—"Romantic comedies?"

"Yeah, guilty pleasure. Pick one of those."

I giggled and found something that looked promising about people in the wine industry. It wasn't about food, but it was close enough to what we did that we'd probably know a thing or two.

Matteo was stirring the cream into the chocolate when I returned to the kitchen, my feet cold on the hard floors. Once the mixture came together, he handed me the spoon to lick and covered the bowl with plastic wrap before putting it in the refrigerator to set.

"Save some for me," he joked as I cleaned the spatula. He leaned down and licked the other side, our mouths meeting at the end, where we shared a chocolatey kiss and laughed. "Okay, more wine?"

"Sounds good."

We settled on the couch and shared the bottle of wine, rolling the truffles when the ganache had firmed up enough, then coating them in cocoa powder. It was simple yet decadent. Matteo put the truffles in a small bowl and took them back to the couch so we could feed each other. *Feed each other.* Who was this man?

Popping the truffle bites into each other's mouths turned into nipping and sucking chocolate from fingertips, which turned into me climbing onto Matteo's lap and making out with him for half the movie. I could kiss him all night.

I was still hungry for him after we took a break to drink water and start a new movie. Feeling bold, I slid from the plush couch to the rug on the floor, running my hands up his thighs.

"*Mmm,* what are you doing, *ariete*?" Matteo asked through half-lidded eyes.

"I thought I'd have another dessert." I palmed his erection through the grey sweats. When I tugged at the elastic waistband, he lifted his hips so I could drag the sweats and his green boxer briefs down his hips. "You like to match, huh?"

"Pure coincidence, I assure you," he said gruffly as his cock bobbed free of its fabric constraints.

He was thick and long, the veins prominent along the underside. I fisted him, stroking up, then down so I could take the head into my mouth. He was salty but smelled clean, like whatever soap Matteo must have used when he showered. I savored the feel of his smooth flesh against my tongue, toying with the little ridge at the base of the head and making him twitch in my mouth.

"Macy." Matteo's hand threaded through my hair. "That feels so good. Fuck, your mouth."

He didn't finish because I lowered, taking as much as I could fit into my mouth until the head of his dick met my throat. I kept myself from gagging, but I was a little out of practice. Hopefully, it was like riding a bike. My fist closed around his base, and I worked it in rhythm with my mouth until Matteo couldn't form words, only moans of pleasure.

I loved having the ability to make his fingers tremble in my hair as he got close. I reached my other hand to cup his balls, tugging lightly.

"Macy, you'll make me come," he warned in a strangled voice, pulling my hair with his fist.

Instead of stopping, I ignored him, intent on seeing the act through to the end. His cock swelled in my mouth, and I sucked harder, rolling his balls until his hot come filled my mouth.

"*Macy!*" The sound of my name on his lips as I swallowed his release made wetness pool between my thighs. I stroked him a couple more times, keeping the suction as I released his cock from my mouth with a *pop*.

"*Fuck,*" Matteo moaned breathlessly. "That mouth is dangerous."

I giggled and lapped at his tip one last time, making his softening cock pulse. Matteo ran a hand down his face and pulled his clothing back into place.

"You liked it?" I asked coyly, but secretly I needed to hear his praise.

"So much." Matteo nodded, gripped my arms, and pulled me up, tossing me onto the couch like I weighed nothing. "My turn."

I squealed as he tore my sweats off and my panties down my legs, baring me completely. There was no time to object demurely; the mild-mannered chef turned into a ravenous animal, diving between my spread thighs and parting my labia so he could lick up my slit and suck my clit.

"*Oh, fuck,*" I whimpered as he thrust two fingers into my weeping center. I was already close to coming because sucking his cock had turned me on.

"Give it to me," Matteo demanded, finding my g-spot and making my legs shake around his head. "I love how you taste. Come on my face, *ariete.*"

"More," I begged, so close to my release.

He added a twisting motion to his fingers, and I was lost. My orgasm crashed into me fast and hard, my muscles clamping down on Matteo's fingers and hips bucking against his face. It was wanton, but so fucking fantastic. Even better than the night before and so far above what my toys could do because he was warm and *real*.

Matteo slowly withdrew his fingers, licking them clean and laying his head on my lower abdomen, breathing hard. I should have gotten up and gone home, but I was boneless. Instead, I stroked his soft dark hair. When his breathing grew slow and steady, signaling his slumber, I gave in, too.

Chapter Twenty-One

MACY'S LASHES FLUTTERED AGAINST her cheeks as she slept next to me. She'd agreed to spend the night after work last night, and I'd held her in my arms all night. I was floating on the high of our new relationship, which had fallen into a routine after our first date the week prior. Macy met me for coffee some mornings, and we stole whatever moments possible at work. It might not have been very professional, but I couldn't get enough of her.

"Good morning," Macy said sleepily as she peered at me through slitted eyes.

"Good morning, gorgeous." I kissed her on the forehead and stroked her back. If there was something better than touching her first thing in the morning, I didn't know what it was.

She'd brought plaid flannel pajamas to wear, even though I'd volunteered my clothing, claiming it would be easier to *sleep* if we wore pajamas. I found it adorable how upfront she was regarding her boundaries. Any man who thought sex was more important than a genuine relationship with a woman had it all wrong. Self-control wasn't difficult if it meant I spent more time in Macy's presence.

I'd fallen hard for her, but I'd take any bumps or bruises along the way because she'd be standing at the finish line with open arms. As if some invisible force connected our thoughts, Macy rolled out of bed and stretched, spreading her arms wide. I couldn't help that my cock hardened at the side of her full breasts thrust out. My mouth watered with the memories of sucking her dusky rose nipples last night.

"We don't have time for any of that," she admonished like she'd read my thoughts.

I tried for an innocent expression. "I don't know what you're talking about."

"Sure you don't." She lifted a brow, clearly not buying it. "So you aren't thinking about dragging me back to bed and missing our coffee date?"

"I plead the fifth." I chuckled and climbed out of bed, and nodded toward the bathroom. "Come shower with me. We've got enough time. I promise to behave myself and only make you come once."

Macy whacked me on the arm playfully. "You're insatiable."

"Agreed. I'll never get enough of you." I pulled my toothbrush from the bathroom cabinet drawer and squeezed toothpaste onto it before passing it to Macy. We brushed our teeth, and I made an excuse to leave the bathroom so she could take care of business; then, she thoughtfully did the same for me. It was like we were in sync, perfectly compatible.

"I suppose we can shower together," she conceded, as I let the shower water warm up.

I held my hand out to help her step under the hot spray. "Ladies first."

"I love that you've made that phrase a goal in your life." Macy bit her lip, and her sly smile had me clambering into the shower after her.

"It's an essential motto," I agreed, pulling her back to my chest and wrapping an arm around her waist, swaying gently until she relaxed against me, our wet bodies sliding against each other.

"Matteo," she breathed.

I whispered against her ear, "Come on, *ariete*. Let's get washed, and I'll take you for coffee."

"Caffeine is always a wonderful reward." She grinned. "Now, pass me the shampoo, so we aren't late."

I watched as she washed and realized I wanted to see her like that every day. Macy belonged in my life, belonged with me. I was about to put her to the test with my Monday coffee date with the Rivera brothers. She'd met Julian and Gabriel, but Xander could be gruff and offputting.

"Hey." I pulled Macy in for a kiss. "I've got a question for you."

"Yeah?" Macy kissed me again and sucked her lower lip into her mouth.

"Would you come to Thanksgiving with me?"

"Oh." She paused, and I grew wary that she would reject me. "I usually spend Thanksgiving with Leo's family, but I'd like to spend the day with you."

I chuckled nervously. "I'm not sure if that's you accepting my offer or turning me down."

"I'm accepting," she said with a nod, and my heart soared.

"Thank you." I kissed her again and reluctantly let her go because the brothers would immediately know why we were late.

***

"Are you sure I look okay?" Macy asked for the sixth time as she paused to check out her reflection in a shop window.

"You look amazing," I assured her. She'd donned a long navy cardigan over a white shirt and wore jeans that had me drooling over her ass. I resisted the urge to reach out and slide my hand under the sweater so I could palm her plump backside.

"I'm nervous," she admitted, clasping her hands together so tightly her knuckles turned white.

I covered her hands with mine and gently pried them apart, kissing her cold knuckles until the color returned. "They're my brothers. They'll treat you like family because you're mine."

"Matteo." The vulnerability on Macy's face tugged at my heart. "I've never had a family like that."

I couldn't imagine the pain she held within, the girl who was forgotten by her parents and the woman rejected by the man who had vowed to love and cherish her for life. Softly, I cupped her cheek and brushed my thumb along her jaw. "Then it's long past time I introduce you to mine. I'm good at sharing."

She offered me a watery smile and nodded. "Sounds good."

I kissed her because I didn't think she'd like the more emotional offering I wanted to give her. What had been a niggling at the back of my mind was now a constant companion on my shoulder, calling out that I loved Macy.

I took her hand and led her down the sidewalk to the coffee shop, inhaling the nutty coffee smell when we entered the warm atmosphere. The staff waved and called their greeting, and Macy smiled, seemingly more comfortable than she had been outside.

"Do you want your usual?" I asked. "Or should we re-enact our first meeting?"

"I think it's safer for everyone if I stick with the iced coffee," she said drily.

After I placed our order, we waited a minute to collect the cups, then moved to the back of the shop, where the three Rivera brothers already sat on the couch and chairs, imposing in their fancy suits. They all stood as we approached.

"I thought I told you not to scare her," I chastised, pointing to their attire. Plus, they made me look bad in my worn jeans and grey hoodie under my leather jacket.

"It didn't make sense to dress down when we have to be at the office in a couple of hours," Xander offered, ever the practical one of the group. "Besides, if I'd gone casual, Viola would have asked why, and I don't lie to my wife. She would have insisted on coming with me, and she would have told Luna and Jane. We would have had a full house, which would have been more intimidating than a damn suit."

"It's fine," Macy said, tugging on my hand. "I've seen people in suits before."

"Macy, it's good to see you again." Julian offered his hand and shook Macy's. The brothers waited for Macy to have a seat before they followed.

"Olivia will be disappointed she missed out on talking to the *real lady chef*," Gabriel added.

"It's nice to see you again," Macy answered. "I would have enjoyed seeing your daughter, too."

Xander looked at me, and I introduced him. "Macy, this is Xander. He's the oldest brother and can be crotchety, so don't take him seriously."

"Hey," Xander protested.

I ignored him. "Xander, this is Macy, the woman you've heard so much about because Julian and Gabriel gossip like *tias*."

Macy hid a giggle behind her hand and took a sip of coffee. "It's very nice to meet you."

"It's my pleasure." Xander's faint accent thickened as he put on the charm and leaned forward, shaking Macy's outstretched hand. "You make Matteo happy."

Macy blushed furiously. The simple words held weight coming from Xander since he wasn't known for *sentimental drivel*, as he liked to call it.

Xander gave Macy a moment and turned to me. "Did you ask her about Thanksgiving?"

"She agreed to come," I told him.

"Perfect," he answered. "Viola said to tell you to show up by one. Dinner will be later, but you know how the wives are."

"Oh, dinner is at your place?" Macy asked, shooting me a questioning look. In my haste to ask her, I'd forgotten to tell her I spent Thanksgiving with the entire Rivera family.

"It's big enough for everybody," Xander explained. "My parents are flying in, and my sister Isabella will come down from Seattle with her husband."

"That sounds like a full house." Macy blanched. I took her free hand in mine before she could fidget nervously again.

"It's a bit loud but fun," I tried to reassure her.

"And Matteo's toughest food critic will be there." Gabriel laughed. "Our mother might be the only person telling him the food doesn't live up to her cooking."

"Really?" Macy asked. She didn't enjoy telling the restaurant kitchen staff they needed to make a dish again. I couldn't imagine what she'd think of Maria Rivera's unsolicited culinary opinions.

"Last year, she told Matteo that he over-salted the chicken," Julian recalled with a smile.

Macy turned to me. "What did you do?"

"I didn't have to do anything." I chuckled as I remembered the scene. "Xander's wife had enough of her attitude and stood up, stabbed the chicken thigh with the serving fork, and told Maria she would wash the extra salt off."

"You should have seen *Mamá's* face." Gabriel's chest shook with laughter. "Viola marched into the kitchen, ran the chicken under the water, then patted it dry with a paper towel and plopped it back on our mother's plate."

"She couldn't refuse to eat it, then," Xander added, smiling and shaking his head.

Macy's palm covered her mouth, muffling her response. "Oh, my goodness."

"At least eating damp chicken kept her humble long enough that she forgot to tell me I put too much cinnamon in the *coquito*," I pointed out.

"But your *coquito* is perfect!" Macy exclaimed.

"Very little is perfect for our mother," Gabriel said in a monotone.

"And she'll be at Thanksgiving," Macy stated nervously.

"You don't have anything to worry about," Julian assured her. "You aren't a son who can let her down. We'll have your back and make sure she behaves."

"Thank you," Macy murmured. I couldn't decipher her expression, but she squeezed my hand firmly.

Gabriel leaned toward Macy. "I hope you aren't reconsidering."

"If she can survive Matteo in the kitchen, she can handle *Mamá*," Xander said confidently. He was making an effort to be accepting of Macy.

"I won't reconsider," Macy assured them.

"I hope you make something," Julian said. "Everybody brings a dish."

"Absolutely." Macy was confident about her culinary abilities. "Is there anything I should avoid? Or something everybody loves?"

"I'm sure we'll enjoy whatever you choose." Julian smiled. "Your dinner at *El Corazón Borikén* was fantastic. Luna and I are looking forward to trying your food again."

"Maybe you and Matteo could cook together," Gabriel suggested in a not-so-subtle attempt to get us to spend more time together.

I interrupted him before he could say anything that would embarrass me. "I'm sure we'll work it out."

"So, tell me how you all met," Macy said to the brothers, settling back to sip her coffee as they launched into their versions of our friendship.

Watching her smile and laugh with my closest friends made that voice in my head chant louder. I even let the brothers embellish their stories because it meant seeing how much Macy belonged with me.

***

Macy pushed the kitchen doors open and strode through. "I've got everything set up, I think."

"Great. We've got a few minutes before kids start showing up." I was hosting the Thanksgiving community cooking class, and Macy agreed to help without hesitation when I asked her over the weekend. We worked together seamlessly. It was the chemistry I'd always wanted from a sous chef, where we could anticipate what the other needed.

I loved that our chemistry flowed into our budding relationship. Though was it still budding? I'd known there was something special about Macy the first time I saw her in the coffee shop. Fate deserved credit for bringing her back into my life in such a perfect way. Sometimes I wondered if *Abuelita* was somewhere above, orchestrating everything because if anybody had the *huevos* to pull strings, it was my grandmother.

"They're here!" Macy called out as she stood on tiptoe to peer through the window in the kitchen door.

I pushed the door open and held it for her. "Showtime."

Macy was much more comfortable this time, moving around and chatting with students as they made their pie crust and pumpkin pie filling. Even Sam looked up to talk to her, forgetting about using her hair as a veil. If I didn't trust my feelings, I could rely on the judgment of children who had experienced horrors no child should know about. They liked Macy.

When we got to the end of the class, I had her make a big batch of whipped cream, and the children took turns piping a swirl onto their pies.

I held up the piping bag with the leftover whipped cream. "Okay, everybody, open your mouths!"

"What are you doing?" Macy asked, confused.

"A right of passage in childhood," I responded with a grin. I walked down each row, depositing a dollop of the whipped cream into each open mouth as the kids giggled happily.

When I reached the end, I turned toward the adults in the back of the room. "Any grown-ups want in on this?"

A few took me up on it, and the kids erupted into even more laughter. I thanked everybody for coming, and Macy helped the kids carefully wrap up their pies for the trip home. As they all left, we stood together by the door, then turned to survey the room.

"This shouldn't take long to clean up," she observed, pushing tables back into position. "It's brilliant of you to make them wash their dishes."

I shrugged. "It's a good habit to develop. My Abuelita wouldn't let me go to bed until the dishes were washed and put away."

"Smart woman. I figured you'd learned it in culinary school."

"Well, I still had to wash my dishes there, too." I grabbed the piping bag of whipped cream. "Open your mouth."

"I'm good."

"Come on, you have to try it," I cajoled.

Macy shook her head but parted her lips. I piped the whipped cream until it overflowed her mouth, then kissed the excess away as she giggled.

"You know, I've eaten whipped cream straight from the can before," she said when I released her lips.

I gave her a nod as we returned to the kitchen. I set the mixing bowl in the sink and popped the piping tip out of the bag of whipped cream so I could wash it. "Yeah, but it's more fun this way."

Macy took the bag from me and disposed of it while I finished the dishes. When I turned from the sink, she was leaning against the prep table, staring at me thoughtfully.

"I have more fun with you than anybody else," Macy admitted, turning serious.

I reached out and wiped away a rogue drop of whipped cream. "More fun than you have with Leo?"

"It's different," she said. "With you, my heart feels full. It's like you fill a space nobody has fit into before."

"I feel the same," I shared, my heart swelling at her words. She wasn't the most expressive person, so I listened carefully when she shared her feelings. "And I like how you fit so perfectly."

Macy bit her lip, and I saw the moment she questioned sharing such an intimate thing with me. I needed to change the subject before she closed her heart off again.

"Pie!" I exclaimed, clapping my hands. "I've still got the one I made. Why don't we split it before I take you home?"

She laughed and removed her apron. "Okay, but I don't think I can eat that much."

"I'll send the rest home for you and Leo to eat later."

"She'd love that. Pumpkin pie is her favorite," Macy said. "She'll ask me to make it in the middle of summer."

"I like her style." I chuckled. "It's my favorite, too. Every Thanksgiving and Christmas, *Abuelita* would make a kitchen full of pumpkin pies for the dinners her church gave out. We baked all day, singing and dancing to Christmas music in the kitchen. Those were some of the best times."

"I love that," Macy said wistfully.

"It wasn't very traditional since lots of people would rather eat *tembleque*, but it was our thing." I took a deep breath and let the memories come. "When I think of it, I can still smell the spices on her when she'd hug me at the end of the day and tell me I'd done well."

"I wish I could have met her."

"*Abuelita* would have liked you," I said, cupping Macy's cheek. "She always said I'd find the perfect woman to stand by my side, one who would share my passions and complete me. She was right, because you are all those things and more."

Chapter Twenty-Two

I T WAS NO SURPRISE that I lost the impromptu pumpkin carving competition with Matteo, but my payment had come due in the form of cooking dinner for him at my place. He had no idea what he was getting into because Leo had prepared a single-spaced, bulleted list of questions for him, and no amount of begging or threatening could convince her to abandon her pursuit of answers.

Clams simmered in white wine butter sauce on the stove, and I was boiling water for pasta in a large pot. The chicken breasts were already done and staying warm in the oven until I could put everything together. I made lemon bars for dessert, figuring Matteo might appreciate something simple.

I popped open a bottle of white wine and poured a generous amount into my glass, figuring it couldn't hurt to lubricate a little if I was about to sit through the most awkward dinner in history. There was a tap at the door, and I chugged the contents of my glass, wondering if a heart could explode from stress because mine was pounding at a harrowing rate.

I paused to check my reflection in the entry mirror, smoothing my flowy blue cropped shirt and tugging the waistband of my jeans up to cover my belly. Then I rushed to the door, hoping Leo hadn't heard Matteo knock, and opened it as quietly as possible. Ushering him inside, I leaned close and whispered, "I'm so sorry for everything you're about to endure."

"Is that Matty I hear?" Leo yelled excitedly from her bedroom upstairs. Matteo cringed at the nickname. I'd never heard anybody shorten his name like that. Leave it to Leo.

"There's still time to back out," I said ominously. "Run and save yourself."

"I'm sure it's not that bad," Matteo said with a laugh. He leaned down and kissed me, but I pushed him away before he could use any tongue, hoping it would make him listen.

"And I can guarantee it *is*," I fired back, just as Leo thundered down the stairs. It was amazing how much noise she could make for such a small person. I patted my hand against his black shirt, allowing myself to feel those taut pecs for a moment before backing away. "*Too late*. Best of luck, and I'll make sure to notify your next of kin."

She flung her arms wide when she jumped down to the entry. "Welcome to our humble home."

"I've been inside before," Matteo reminded her, shrugging out of his leather jacket. When he turned away, I tilted my head and admired his ass for a second, blushing when he caught me looking and winked.

"Not long enough to be considered a guest," Leo determined. "Stepping inside to pick Macy up or to make out when you drop her off doesn't count."

Matteo's face reddened. He'd learn that there was no use trying to hide things from Leo. That is, if he survived the evening with us.

"Let me pour you a glass of wine," I offered, grabbing his arm and dragging him to the kitchen, where I'd set the glasses on the counter.

I poured wine into his glass and Leo's, then poured myself another glass, which I immediately started drinking.

"Thanks," Matteo said, sipping his wine as he leaned against the counter. "Something smells amazing. What's for dinner?"

I opened my mouth to tell him, but Leo beat me to it. "Macy's specialty. Clams in white wine and butter, and chicken with fettuccini in a lemon basil cream sauce."

"That sounds delicious." Matteo smiled at me, and I nodded as I sipped on my wine. "Are the clams done?"

"Oh, yes!" I set my wine down and pulled three bowls from the cabinet. Leo handed me a large spoon, and I piled the clams into the bowls, topping them with the broth and a few slices of toasted baguette.

We slurped the clams and their liquid from the open shells, and Matteo nodded his approval. "So good. Did you put a little lemon in there, too?"

"Yeah, just a squeeze," I confirmed. My theme through the dishes was lemon because it was so versatile.

"Good choice." He ate another clam and followed it with a bite of bread dipped in the broth.

The water in the pot was boiling, so I added a generous amount of salt and my homemade fettuccine while I found the strainer and got it set up in the sink. In a large skillet, I melted butter, added garlic and spices, then cream and a splash of wine.

When the pasta was ready, I drained it and dropped it into the sauce, adding a spray of lemon and tossing it all together in the pan. Leo set out three plates while I pulled the chicken out of the oven, and I plated everything, not worrying too much about the presentation because Matteo was never that formal when I went to his apartment.

I took the plates to the table and found Matteo washing my dishes when I returned. "You don't have to do that. You're a guest."

"You do dishes at my place," he pointed out as he scrubbed the pasta pot.

"Yeah, because I'm trying to be polite."

Matteo lifted his brows and pointed to the dishes in the sink. "Same."

"Fine, but let Leo do the rest," I said. "That's how we divide the labor. She who cooks doesn't touch the dishes."

"Makes sense."

"It's worth it if she cooks," Leo added, doing a chef's kiss.

Matteo chuckled and set the pot on the drainboard. "I can see why."

"Shall we sit?" I held my hand out toward the small dining table and snagged my wine glass from the counter, finishing the last of it.

"I'll grab the bottles," Leo offered, taking two bottles in one hand and her glass in the other, then settling at the head of the table. That left Matteo and me sitting across from each other, which suited me fine.

I felt warm and relaxed as we dug into the chicken and pasta.

"*Mm.*" Matteo pointed his fork at the pasta. "I'm going to need the recipe for this."

"I'll text it to you later," I promised. "More wine?"

"Just a little." Matteo held up his hand to stop my pour when he had enough.

I gave Leo a splash more and filled my glass again. She was busy snapping photos of the food for my social media account. If I ever made it big, I'd hire her to do my social media full-time. I'd never have anything to post if it weren't for her.

When we reached the end of the meal, I breathed a sigh of relief as I sat back and sipped my wine, listening to Matteo recount a story about the time he and Gabriel Rivera went clubbing in Miami. So far, Leo had behaved herself. Maybe she would forget the list.

"So, does he remember doing body shots with Jane?" I asked.

"No, and I haven't had the heart to tell him." Matteo laughed. "I didn't even realize she was the same girl when I first met her until Gabriel told me about their one-night stand."

"It's funny how fate works things out." It was romantic in a way that their one-night stand led to Olivia and a happy marriage. Things didn't work out like that for everybody. The alcohol made me feel melancholy as I thought about my broken marriage.

"Okay, Matteo." Leo's tone made my stomach drop. She pulled her list of questions out of the pocket of her jeans. So much for her forgetting. My mind raced as I tried to figure out how to get out of the impending questions. I drew a blank.

"You're not the head chef in this house. And per the laws of best friendship, it is my sworn duty to give you the third degree and make sure you're good enough for Macy." Leo glared at him. "I mean, you're not, and you never will be. But we'll see how close you come."

I poured myself another glass of wine and took a gulp. Matteo looked at me, and I mouthed, *I warned you.*

"I'll admit that I wouldn't consider myself good enough for Macy," Matteo said with a straight face. He was so wrong. He was so much more than enough for me.

"Good. How much money do you make?"

"Leo," I hissed, nearly choking on my wine. Finances were one thing you were never supposed to bring up in polite company.

"What? I want to know if he can afford to support you in the lifestyle you deserve."

"I make enough to keep us both comfortable, even without Macy's income from the restaurant," Matteo supplied.

"Do you have a college degree?" Leo held up a hand to stop Matteo as he was about to answer. "And I don't mean a cooking college—a real degree."

"No," Matteo said, folding his hands on the table. "I went to culinary school and started working in restaurants, then eventually opened *El Corazòn Borikén.*"

Leo tapped her chin with her finger. "Hmm, interesting."

"Neither of us has college degrees," I pointed out, then turned to Matteo. "I really don't care about that kind of thing."

Leo plowed right on. "Do you currently, or have you ever, had any sexually transmitted infections?"

Maybe I could fake food poisoning. Probably not; we'd all eaten the same thing.

"No, and I've been tested. I've only had one partner in the last year." Matteo looked pointedly at me, and I blushed. I hadn't asked about past partners, but he gave me that anyway, letting me know we were on the same page. It made me want to leap across the table and hug him.

"Are you or have you ever been married?" Leo pointed to her left ring finger for emphasis.

I drank more wine.

"No, never been married," Matteo answered, the corner of his mouth twitching with amusement. At least he was a good sport about it.

"Do you intend to marry Macy for citizenship?"

I choked on my wine, and Leo smacked me on the back until I could catch my breath. I did my best to shoot daggers at her through my eyes. We were going to have a serious chat later about boundaries.

"Uh," Matteo's lips pressed into a flat line, and I swear he took three long breaths. "Puerto Ricans *are* US citizens. Because Puerto Rico is a US territory."

"Oh, of course." Leo turned to me, her eyes wide, and mouthed *oops*. "I knew that. Just making sure you did, too."

Matteo wasn't convinced. "Yeah, sure. How many more questions are on that list?"

"A few," Leo answered vaguely. "How many children do you currently have?"

"None."

The wine was going to my head, and the room blurred at the edges. Great, Matteo would see me smashed on top of everything else.

Leo made a clicking noise with her tongue. "Is there a problem with the baby batter?"

Fuck my life. I was about to walk out the door and flag down a ride for anywhere but here.

Matteo leaned back in his chair and crossed his arms. "I couldn't say."

"Never tried putting a bun in the oven?" My best friend was shameless.

My soon-to-be ex-boyfriend shook his head. "Uh, no."

"Do you have a breeding kink? Am I going to get to spoil a whole brood of nieces and nephews?"

"You don't have to answer that," I blurted, covering my face with my palm. *Had I slurred? Hmm, how much wine had I consumed?*

"I have no current plans to impregnate Macy," Matteo explained. "Any future children would be a decision made by the both of us."

"We haven't even fucked," I said absently. "I don't think we have to worry about spawn."

"Don't call my future niece or nephew spawn," Leo snapped.

I narrowed my eyes at her. "You're kidding, right?"

"If you'd like, I can prepare you a list of appropriate alternatives," she supplied.

How was this my reality? "Anything would be better than the list you're currently reading. Maybe you should go work on the names *right now*."

"The names can wait." She looked down at the paper she held. "You gave me an idea for another question."

"Disregard whatever you heard, then," I begged.

"You haven't had sex," Leo stated. I laid my head on the table and groaned. "Is that because Matty here has issues with *rigidity*?"

Matteo's jaw dropped at that, but he recovered quickly. "No problems there, either. I'm very attracted to Macy. I also happen to believe in respect and consent. Something you might revisit after this conversation."

I lifted my head at his words. Leo froze, and the room went silent as she assessed Matteo. I held my palm to my mouth, worried I might vomit.

"You're right," Leo finally said softly. "I apologize. I only want the best for Macy, and I think you might be that man."

"Thank you. I appreciate that," Matteo said in return. I looked between them as they reached a silent truce.

"Anybody want dessert?" I definitely slurred that time. When I tried to stand, my legs refused to move in sync, and I plopped back into my seat indelicately.

"Why don't I get the lemon bars?" Leo offered, rushing off to the fridge and pulling the pan out. She brought dessert plates with lemon bars to the table.

Matteo watched me miss as I tried to stab one of the two lemon bars floating in my vision with a fork. "I didn't need two."

"I only gave you one," Leo giggled. "Oh, this should be fun. Have you ever seen Macy drunk?"

Matteo shook his head. "I think maybe we should make some coffee."

"Yes, coffee," I mumbled, finally getting a bite of the lemon bar on my fork.

Soon, the smell of coffee filled the air, and somebody set a mug in front of me prepared the way I liked it.

"Drink," Matteo ordered. When had he gotten so close? "You need something to counteract all that alcohol in your system."

"You're so pretty. And you smell good," I said as I stared into his deep brown eyes. I had to squint to get my eyes to focus. Suddenly, I needed him to understand that I wasn't to blame for Leo's questioning. As far as I was concerned, he was perfect. "I know you don't have any erectile issues. I'll tell Leo that later. You were *very* erect when I—"

"I think it's time for me to go home." Matteo chuckled. "Can I help you up to bed before I go?"

"Carry me?" I raised my arms and wiggled my fingers, waiting for Matteo.

He helped me stand, but didn't lift me into his arms. "How about I help you walk? I'm not sure that narrow stairwell is big enough to carry you safely, and I don't want to hurt you."

"You're so silver—shower—*chivalrous*."

"You tuck her in," Leo said from behind Matteo. "I'll get the electrolyte drink and ibuprofen."

I heard Matteo agree before he wrapped a muscular arm around me and helped me shuffle across the house to the stairs. Without his help, I would have had to crawl up the hard stairs. He was practically carrying me up them, anyway.

"Which room?" He asked, pausing at the top of the stairs.

I pointed to the end of the hall. "That one."

Matteo found my room and flipped the light on so he could lead me to my bed. He brushed his fingers along the hem of my shirt. "Can I help you get changed?"

I began to giggle uncontrollably. "Yeah, baby, strip me bare."

"As much as I would love to spend time like that, I think you're about two minutes from passing out cold."

"Nah, I'm *soo* awake!" I insisted as he pulled my shirt over my head and unfastened my jeans, laying me down so he could tug them off my legs. "Did you know that I've never tried anal?"

"I'll file that information away for later." He chuckled and walked away, looking through my dresser drawers and returning with the ugliest granny nightgown I owned.

"Oh, you'll never want to fuck me if you see me in that."

"Macy." Matteo leaned over and helped me sit up so he could remove my bra and slip the nightgown over my head before pulling the covers back to tuck me into bed. He cupped my jaw in his hand and kissed me gently. "One day, when you're ready—and *sober*—I will fuck you in this very nightgown to prove how much I want you."

"I'm more likable when I'm drunk," I whispered as my eyelids grew heavy and fell closed, sleep pulling me under. "Everybody says so."

"Well, not me." Matteo brushed kisses over my closed eyes. His voice faded. "I love you just as you are."

Chapter Twenty-Three

I LIVED FOR THE end of the work week at *El Corazón Borikén* because that meant Macy spent the night. Since the restaurant was closed for Thanksgiving, she'd stayed overnight Wednesday so we could get up and prep food for the Rivera's gathering. I watched as she lined up recipes and began fishing through my pantry and refrigerator for ingredients. We'd shopped late after work for a few last-minute ingredients, but the store shelves were sparse because of the holiday. In the end, we managed to find everything we needed, but not enough to plan to make items twice if something went wrong.

"Matteo, where did you put the butter?" Macy called from where she was looking in the fridge.

She wore one of her oversized night shirts that barely covered her ass when she bent over. I had a perfect view of her thick thighs and the bottom curve of her butt. My cock hardened in my grey sweatpants. I hadn't bothered with a shirt because I didn't think we'd start cooking at seven in the morning.

"It's on the counter by the stove," I supplied.

Macy found it where I'd indicated and put it with the other ingredients. "Thanks. Are you ready to get started?"

"I thought we might have breakfast first," I suggested. "Maybe take a shower."

Macy stood with her hands on her hips and head cocked to the side. "I'll shower when we finish cooking since we'll probably end up coated in sugar and butter."

"Fair enough," I conceded. I turned toward my bedroom and looked over my shoulder, where I caught Macy biting her bottom lip as she watched my ass. "I'll grab a shirt. What do you want to get started on first?"

"Hmm?" Macy's eyes shot up to mine when she realized I'd caught her. She blushed adorably. "Oh, I thought maybe we'd do the personal pumpkin pies first so that they can cool."

"Sounds good," I called from the bedroom as I grabbed a black t-shirt from my closet and pulled it over my head. Macy already had things lined up in recipe order when I emerged. "Why don't I make us breakfast while you get started?"

"I like that idea." She grinned and looked me up and down.

"If you look at me like that, I won't be cooking," I promised sensually. "I'll feed you my cock until you're so full of my come you can't do anything but lay boneless as I eat my fill of you."

"Matteo," she warned breathlessly, her eyes darkening. "Why do you always say things like that when we don't have the time?"

"Because you look at me with desire in your eyes, and my self-control has never been tested so often." I pinned her against the counter and stroked a hand over her cheek, down her throat, and over her turgid nipples. Macy lifted her head, and I caressed her lips with mine before pulling away and taking a shaky breath. "Say the word, and I'll tell Xander we won't make it. I'll spend the day feeding you and fucking you with my fingers and tongue."

"As amazing as that sounds, I would hate to let your family down."

There she went again, burrowing further into my heart with her consideration for those I loved. I wondered if she'd yet realized that she was among those I cared most about. When I'd put her to bed after our dinner date, I'd thoughtlessly expressed my love when she was too inebriated to remember. Now, every time I wanted to tell her I loved her, my nerves got the better of me.

"You're perfect," I said instead, mentally kicking myself for being a coward. "Do you want pancakes?"

Macy nodded. "I will never turn down pancakes."

"I don't do dick shapes, but I'd be willing to replicate your boobs."

"No thanks, I think I'm good with regular circles." She shook her head, but I caught her smile as she turned away.

I pulled a bowl out of the cabinet and measured pancake ingredients while Macy did the same with her recipe for personal pumpkin pies. My thoughts wandered as we cooked in pleasant silence, neither requiring constant conversation—just each other's company. I would be happy to have that kind of connection for the rest of my life.

It might take some time for Macy to be open to another chance at forever, but I was willing to be patient. No woman had put the thoughts of marriage and family into my head like Macy. I dreamed of our future together—spending our days at *El Corazòn Borikén* and nights entangled in the sheets. Little blue-eyed blonde girls making costumes out of bedding and boys with endless energy running through the kitchen as we made Sunday brunch together.

Had I done an internet search to find the acceptable time to wait to propose to a woman who's just been through a divorce? Perhaps. Then I realized it didn't matter. All I needed to know was whether Macy could see a future with me.

I piled pancakes onto plates and wiped the pan free of little brown batter particles. It didn't take long to scramble eggs and pluck some cotton candy grapes from their stems to eat on the side. While Macy wrapped her pie dough in plastic to rest, I set our breakfast at the dining table.

"Coffee, milk, or juice?" I asked as I folded napkins and placed forks and knives next to our plates.

"Coffee," Macy answered without hesitation. "All the coffee."

I popped pods into the machine and found two mugs. Macy washed her hands and sat at the table when the coffee was made. I added creamer to our cups and sat at the end of the table, handing Macy her coffee.

She breathed it in and sighed. "This is just what I needed."

"You say that, but you haven't tried the pancakes yet," I quipped, cutting into my stack and mopping up extra melted butter and syrup before shoving the bite into my mouth. People often thought that chefs always ate fancy food, but I loved simple meals. It was more important that food evoked pleasant feelings than looked amazing.

Macy hummed her approval of breakfast. "Okay, they're a tie with the coffee. Nothing can oust caffeine from first place in my book."

"Understandable." I lifted my fork in victory. "I'll take it."

"How long will it take to make the other foods?" Macy asked between bites.

"The *mofongo* stuffing takes about thirty minutes to crisp in the oven after it's mashed, and the *amarillos* only take like ten minutes." I glanced over at her. "Have you not made them at the restaurant yet?"

"No, I haven't made many of the desserts aside from *empanadas*," she answered, popping a grape into her mouth and savoring the candy-like taste.

I'd been so wrapped up in my attraction to Macy that I'd neglected part of her training as my sous chef. "Well, we'll have to change that. You should be able to make the entire menu."

"I'm a quick study." When she glanced downward, I envisioned her on her knees, showing me just how much of an expert she'd become when it came to my cock. It was a wonder I could function at all with how much my thoughts wandered when she was near.

"If you can make *mofongo*, you can make *amarillos*."

I stood and picked up my empty plate, taking it to the sink and rinsing it before placing it in the dishwasher. Macy followed close behind. We washed our hands, and I turned on a holiday music station—because I wasn't a Scrooge who saved holiday music for after Thanksgiving. I helped Macy roll out the portioned pie dough and fill the tiny pie tins, swaying my hips to the pop-rock Christmas music.

"Dance with me, *ariete*." Macy giggled as I pulled her to me, our floured hands sending off a cloud of white particles as we moved. I hummed, then sang dramatically, "All I want for Christmas is *you*!"

I spun her in a circle and let her go as the song ended so we could fill the pie crusts and get them in the oven. While they cooked, we made *mofongo* and prepped the stuffing for the oven, the trays waiting for the pies to finish.

"Now, we make the dessert?" Macy asked, holding up the bunch of ripe plantains. We'd used the green plantains to make the *mofongo*.

I nodded and pulled a container of cinnamon spice sugar from the pantry before turning the burner on to reheat the oil. "Go ahead and slice the plantains on the diagonal, less than an inch thick. Careful not to smash them because they're soft."

"Like this?" Macy sliced them perfectly, of course.

"Great." I nodded and poured some of the cinnamon sugar into a baking dish. "This is to coat the fried plantains after. You'll get the spiced sugar, the caramelization on the plantain, and the soft, sweet inside."

"I can't wait." Macy stuck her clean finger in the sugar concoction and brought it to her lips, licking it off slowly. My dick felt it as surely as if her tongue were tracing my flesh. She shot me a sultry look that said she knew exactly what she'd done. "Close your mouth, Matteo."

My teeth clicked as I snapped my jaw shut. "You saucy little chef. I should bend you over the counter and spank you for tempting me."

"Have I been bad?" Macy asked coquettishly, wiggling her ass at me.

I grabbed those gorgeous round globes and squeezed, biting her neck gently. "So bad... but such a good girl for being so perfectly tempting."

"*Mmm*," Macy moaned, arching back against me.

"The oil is ready," I said huskily.

"What?" she asked, pulling away and turning to look at me, perplexed.

"For the *amarillos*," I clarified, determined to control myself—and avoid a grease fire in my kitchen.

"Oh, right." She smoothed her hands down her shirt. "I just fry them?"

"Until they're dark golden brown," I added.

Macy carefully placed the plantain slices in the oil, and we made small talk while waiting for them to finish. I could still see her nipples projecting through the thin sleep shirt, a beacon to my dick that I tried to block out of my head.

Five batches. Multiply that by about ten minutes per batch, and that's how long it took to get through cooking with Macy while my cock stood rigid and aching in my sweats. An hour where Macy kept stealing glances and blushing, but I couldn't do anything because safety came first. There was no throwing caution to the wind with hot oil on the stove.

I waited as she pulled the last of the fried plantain from the pan, drained them before coating them in the sugar mixture, and set them on a wire rack. The knob clicked loudly in the kitchen as I flipped it off and moved the pan to the back of the stove. My kitchen timer disrupted the quiet with its obnoxious beeping, but I breathed a silent sigh of relief that the *mofongo* stuffing was done.

"Here." Macy handed me the hot pads, and I pulled the pan from the oven, setting it on the only empty area of the kitchen counter to cool before we wrapped everything up.

"Why don't we make some whipped cream?" I suggested. My voice sounded strained, and Macy paused for a moment but retrieved the heavy cream from the refrigerator.

"How much?" she asked, holding the container of cream up.

"Lots," I answered, finding the powdered sugar in the pantry while Macy started frothing the cream in the mixer.

The kitchen smelled like we'd prepared a feast between the savory scent of garlic and spices in the *mofongo* dressing and the sweeter spices in the pumpkin pies and *amarillos*. I measured the powdered sugar by sight, pouring it into the mixture as the cream stiffened.

Macy smelled like my toothpaste, the cologne on my shirt, and that expensive perfume she still wore. I wanted to lick her. Instead, I plucked one of the warm *amarillos* from the wire rack and brought it to her mouth. "Open. Take a bite."

Her lips closed around the sweet, fried plantain, and her eyelids fluttered shut as she chewed, the mixer whirring as background music. "Oh, that's so good. I could eat those for breakfast every day."

"Sometimes we have them on the buffet line." I popped the other half of the *amarillo* into my mouth and chewed slowly as the flavors infiltrated my tastebuds. "If you like them, I'll make them every weekend."

Macy shut off the mixture and grabbed a spoon, dipping it into the whipped cream and pulling it out to ensure it had stiff peaks. She licked the piece of silverware clean. "You don't have to do that."

"I know." I nodded. "But I want to make you happy."

"You do," Macy acknowledged. "So happy."

I closed the distance between us and dropped the mixer bowl, yanking the beater free and swiping the whipped cream from it. "Happy, hmm?"

"Yes," she whispered as I traced her lips with the sweet cream before devouring her.

Macy tasted better than any specialty desserts I knew how to make. She was sweeter than sugar, more decadent than the darkest chocolate. I could stay full off of her love and affection.

I grabbed the hem of her shirt, whisking it over her head and letting it fall to the floor as I took in Macy's gorgeous, nude body. She didn't wear panties to bed, so she was bare for my perusal.

"Matteo," she panted.

"Cross your arms above your head," I demanded, gathering more whipped cream on my fingers. When she complied, I traced the whipped cream over her nipples and wrote *I*, traced a heart, followed by *U*, on her abdomen. She couldn't make out what it was from where she looked down.

I tossed the mixer attachment in the sink and dropped to my knees in front of Macy, slowly licking my way through the sweet, fluffy cream on her soft stomach. She relaxed against the wall as I sucked one of her perfectly peaked nipples into my mouth, grazing my teeth lightly over her flesh to make her whimper and squirm. Her noises spurred me until both her nipples were reddened, and my little marks peppered her breasts.

"Matteo, please," she panted, trying to tug me up.

"Tell me what you need, *ariete*," I rasped, pushing myself to my feet and ignoring how my stiff knees protested.

"I want to feel you." She pawed at my shirt, working her hands under the fabric and pressing her nails into my chest.

"Then feel me." I practically tore my shirt off, eager to give in to Macy's demands. She swiped her finger through some whipped cream on the side of the bowl and leaned forward, mimicking what I'd done, and traced my nipple with her tongue. "Fuck, Macy."

"You like that?" she asked, repeating the attention on the other nipple.

"Yes," I groaned. "Don't—"

My phone rang where I'd set it on the counter, interrupting our interlude. I silently cursed whoever was calling. "Give me just a second."

Xander's name flashed across my screen. "Yeah?"

"*Mamá* would like to know if you can bring extra *sazon* with you," Xander said, not bothering with pleasantries.

"How the hell did you run out?" I asked. "Are you even Puerto Rican?"

"Don't ask. It involved Viola's attempts at making her contribution to the meal."

"I can bring mine," I said. "It might be faster if you ran to the store, though."

"And leave *Mamá* alone with Viola?" He chuckled. "A very hormonal, pregnant Viola? Not a chance in hell am I leaving them alone."

I sighed. "Yeah, understandable. I'll bring the *sazon*."

"Great." Xander cleared his throat. "Can you have it here in an hour?"

"An hour!" I ran a hand through my hair. "We haven't wrapped the food up or showered yet."

"You had a guest last night, huh?" he teased. "Fine, two hours. We'll see you then."

"See you then," I said grudgingly, ending the call.

"Is something wrong?" Macy asked, holding her shirt to her chest.

"Xander is cockblocking me," I grumbled. "He needs *sazon* and doesn't want to go to the store, so we need to get showered and head over early."

"Oh." She bit her lip and lowered her gaze. "That's fine. We'll have more time later."

"Yeah. Later." I didn't bother telling her how exhausting a Rivera family holiday could be. "Just do me one favor, okay?"

"Sure, what?"

"If you feel stressed, come talk to me." I took her hand and led her to the bathroom, starting the shower and stripping so we could climb in. "Don't resort to chugging bottles of wine."

Chapter Twenty-Four

MATTEO'S FAMILY WAS BOISTEROUS, welcoming, and overwhelming at the same time. He'd stayed by my side since we arrived, holding my hand and squeezing it in his larger palm often. The wine flowed freely, but I'd been careful about my consumption. It was bad enough that Matteo had seen me lose control; I didn't need all the billionaires to see it, too.

How did that much wealth even happen in one family? I'd searched for the last name online and found plenty of articles about Julian's company, Atabey Industries, one of the biggest and best marketing agencies worldwide. Gabriel and Xander both worked for the company; Gabriel was the COO, and Xander was a corporate lawyer.

Their wives were more normal. I'd already met Julian's wife, Luna. Jane, Gabriel's wife, was more reserved and spent much of her time chasing her daughters across the house. They looked just like her, with their dark hair. Xander's wife, Viola, was the opposite of the others and her husband. For as much as he was grumpy, she was sunny and sassy. Her bright red waves haloed her head in wild disarray, but she had impeccable taste in clothing, dressed in style with her maternity outfit. She was very obviously pregnant and close to her due date.

The only daughter in the Rivera family, Bella, happened to be best friends with Viola—they were even pregnant at the same time. There was no doubting her relation to the brothers based on looks. She was quick-witted and vivacious, but once in a while, she faded to the side with her husband, Chase, to recharge. The couple had fallen in love after thinking they hated each other for years since Chase had been friends with the brothers and considered Bella off-limits. Eventually, they couldn't deny their attraction and embraced it instead.

Their father, Marcos, mostly sat in an oversized chair in the living room, drinking beers and watching sports, occasionally commenting on the game to his sons. Maria was as daunting as she'd sounded in stories, so I tried to steer clear of the family matriarch as much as possible. After two hours of preparation, the table was finally set, and Maria shooed everybody from the living room to the massive dining area.

"Matteo, you take your *friend* and sit there," Maria directed with her forefinger, pointing at the seat she wanted us to take. The woman was a tiny powerhouse, taking over whatever task struck her fancy.

Matteo held my chair out, and I sat, taking his hand again as soon as he took his seat next to me. I looked around and felt under-dressed in my jeans and sweater when the rest of the women were wearing dresses. The men no doubt wore designer labels, while Matteo sat next to me in well-worn black jeans and that green shirt I loved. Leaning close, I whispered, "I don't know that I've ever seen so much food for one family."

"You haven't been around for Christmas," he said with a laugh. "Try to envision mountains of pastries and enough *coquito* to inebriate the entire neighborhood."

"And you thought a bottle of wine was excessive," I said flatly.

"There might not be quite so much this year with the pregnant mothers," he said thoughtfully as he watched Julian strap his son, Adrian, into a high chair for dinner.

The room fell silent for the first time since we'd arrived, and Marcos spoke the blessing over the meal. Then everybody crossed themselves, and I did my best to imitate them to be polite. It could have been a picture in a family magazine with everybody sitting around the table together, smiling and passing plates to be filled with food.

Matteo took my plate, and a couple of minutes later, it was returned to me piled with *pernil*, turkey, *mofongo* stuffing, *arroz con gandules*, *tostones*, potato salad, and a plethora of other samples. There was no way I would have room for the other food on the table. I got to work on what I was given, listening to the siblings banter back and forth.

"So, Matteo," Maria interrupted Julian, who was talking about a new marketing strategy for *El Corazón Borikén*. "You've brought a friend."

"Yes, *Mamá*," he responded with a gulp. He took a sip of his wine, and I wondered whether I would have to cut him off after she finished talking.

"You're a chef?" she addressed me.

I glanced at Matteo, and he offered me a small smile. "Yes, I work with Matteo."

"Good," Maria said decidedly. "Then you know how to cook and take care of a man. Of a family."

"I know how to cook," I said noncommittally.

She eyed Matteo. "You know where to send the wedding invitation."

I choked on a *gandule*, and Matteo patted my back while I reached for my water, chugging the entire glass. The others hid smiles behind their hands or pretended not to see what was happening. They didn't seem shocked, and I suspected it wasn't the first time Maria had been so forward.

"We're not there just yet," Matteo said diplomatically, squeezing my thigh under the table.

"You will be," Maria declared, pointing to her temple. "I know these things."

"*Mamá*," Julian said in warning.

She rolled her eyes at her son. "I do. Look at the rest of you. Settled down, having families."

"It's a wonder, after all your meddling." Gabriel chuckled.

"And I was right." She pinned Matteo and me with her stare. "There is always room for more *nietos*. Yours will fit right in."

Matteo's throat worked as he nodded without a word. It must mean a lot for his friends' mother to tell him she would be the grandmother to his children, given the relationship he had with his own *Abuelita*.

It made me think of Leo in a new light. Sure, she could be wildly embarrassing, but she was the best person in my life until Matteo came along. Ours was the kind of friendship that lasted for a lifetime and beyond. I could see her and Maria sharing many similarities. I hoped they would get to meet eventually.

The meal soon wound down, and the children grew tired and cranky after dessert. Julian, Gabriel, and their wives took the children home to bed. Viola napped on Xander's shoulder as he held their daughter Carolina, who watched a children's show on the tv. Calm kids superseded sports in importance. By the fire, Bella reclined in a chair, and Chase sat on the floor in front of her, massaging her feet while they whispered.

I looked around and realized that as dysfunctional as the large family could seem, they all held abundant love for each other. It was everything I'd always dreamed of, and my biggest regret in choosing the wrong man to marry. I could have had a family by now if Ethan hadn't been a selfish prick.

Shaking the regret from my mind, I resumed wiping down the counters in the kitchen. Matteo and I had volunteered our services as dishwashers, letting those who had prepared the bulk of the meal rest and recover. Even Maria eventually acquiesced and sat next to her husband on the couch, his hand resting on her knee as they made faces at Carolina to entertain her.

"You're very fortunate to have a family like this," I murmured to Matteo when he put the last dish away and stood at my side.

He looked around the room and nodded, placing a hand on the small of my back. "I'm thankful for them every day."

"Good," I whispered, emotion catching in my throat.

He leaned down and kissed the sensitive skin below my ear. "I'm thankful for you, too, Macy."

"Thanks for not letting a little hot coffee scare you away," I returned, dabbing my eyes with the paper towel I held.

"Nothing could keep me from you." He tugged me to my side. "I'd like to keep you forever if you'd allow."

I tilted my head to look at him and found his expression void of humor. He was serious about wanting me around. If I hadn't loved him before, my feelings for him would have been sealed at that moment. "Yeah. I'd like that."

Matteo kissed me softly and rubbed my back in slow circles. Nothing inappropriate for the family gathering, just enough to share that special moment.

"Would you like to come back to my place tonight?" he asked, the vulnerability in his eyes touching.

"Take me to your home, Matteo."

***

I was a nervous wreck, but I did my best to hide it. Matteo seemed utterly oblivious, pouring glasses of *coquito* and heating some leftover *amarillos* to eat while we watched a Christmas movie. The man was serious about his cheesy romantic comedy movies. While I hadn't ever been one to watch that kind of thing, I couldn't deny that they left me feeling lighter.

I hadn't told Matteo I was ready to see how our next step would look. I curled my toes into the couch, where they were tucked under my nightgown. Matteo seemed to find them just as sexy as lingerie.

He sat down next to me and handed me a glass, setting the plate of food on his lap. "Did you pick something to watch?"

"Yeah, it's about a woman who has to return home for the reading of her estranged aunt's will, and she reconnects with a childhood love." The last part left a bitter taste in my mouth, given my past, but it was obvious from the start that the man the female main character was dating in the big city was the jerk. I felt for her.

Matteo's arm draped over my shoulders, pulling me closer. "How's the *coquito*?"

"You were generous with the rum," I said. "This is my second glass, and I'm feeling the buzz."

"I might have added more rum when we got back," he admitted. "I thought you might need it after today."

"I loved today," I rushed, not wanting him to think it had been too much for me. "You've got something really special there."

"You can have that too, you know." Matteo held my hand in his and stroked his thumb over my knuckles. "They'd love to be your family."

"But will they let Leo tag along?" I asked, unable to handle the emotion I felt.

"She'd fit in just as well as you," he assured me. "Viola and Bella would love her. They'd probably drag her out dancing with them if they were a few years younger."

"Leo would love that. I'm not the best dancer."

His eyes raked down my body, and I felt suddenly warm. "I think you move well with me."

"That's different," I told him. "I just move like you move."

Matteo took my glass and set it with his on the table next to the plate of food, then tugged me so I was straddling his lap, my nightgown riding up my thighs. He pressed his lips to mine, one hand wrapped around the back of my neck and the other guiding me to roll my hips against him.

My core throbbed, already anticipating the release he would give me. Tonight, I wanted more. "Matteo, take me to bed."

"You don't like it here?" he asked, confused. "You're tired?"

"No," I giggled, running a hand down his chest. "I just think sex might not be that comfortable on the couch."

"Sex?" It was like the word took a moment to click in his brain. His eyes widened, and his mouth fell open. "You and me?"

"Well, there's no other man," I retorted.

Matteo's face broke into a broad grin, and he stood abruptly, steadying me with his arms around my waist. "Do you remember what I promised you?"

I wracked my brain, trying to remember a specific promise. "Sorry. Should I?"

"When I took you to bed that night you were smashed, you hated that I picked this nightgown from your dresser." He fingered the bow holding the low neckline closed, then slowly pulled on the ribbon. "I told you that one day when you were ready, I would fuck you in this nightgown to prove how much I want you."

"Oh." The word was barely a whisper from my lips as Matteo leaned down and kissed the swells of my breasts.

"I guess tonight is the night," he said with a smile.

I squealed as he picked me up suddenly and carried me quickly to his room, shouldering the door open to make enough room for us and placing me gently in the center of his bed. I'd never seen a person strip as quickly as he did, tugging his shirt off before kicking his sweats and boxer briefs to the floor. Then he was on me in a flash, naked and sliding between my thighs while I still wore my nightgown.

"I feel overdressed," I quipped as he kissed my neck, working his way down to my chest.

He grinned deviously. "You're perfectly attired."

I gasped as he sucked my nipple into his mouth through the thin cotton fabric, using his teeth to pinch the hardened flesh in a way that sent electricity down to my clit. I bucked against him, but he stilled me with a hand on my hips. He kissed down my belly and inhaled between my legs as his hands found the hem of my nightgown and slowly pushed it up. I lifted my butt off the bed so he could move it above my hips.

"I love that you don't wear underwear to bed," Matteo said, stroking over the smooth skin there. He gazed at me adoringly as he parted my folds and pressed his thumb against my clit. I bit my lip and relaxed into the bed, content to let him play.

I spread my legs further as he pressed two fingers into my already wet pussy, sliding them in and out slowly at first, then faster as he pressed against my front wall. I could feel myself dripping onto him as he got me close.

"Are you going to come for me, Macy?" Matteo asked, his voice strained.

I nodded and shifted my hips against his hand. "*Mmm*, yes."

As if my verbal acquiescence was all my body was waiting for, the wave that had been rushing in crested in my orgasm, and wave after wave of ecstasy poured over my body. Matteo's fingers worked me through it, then he laid between my spread thighs and kissed my clit, barely brushing his lips across the most sensitive part of me until I wanted more and shifted against his mouth, trying to get him to use more pressure.

He chuckled and swiped his tongue from my opening to my clit. "Patience, *ariete*."

"I need more. Please," I begged. "We've waited. I don't want to wait anymore, Matteo."

"You're sure?" he asked, a hint of doubt in his voice.

"More than sure," I said immediately. "I won't have second thoughts or regrets. I want to be with you. Feel you in me."

"As long as you don't make a pancake in the shape of it and rip it apart," he said, making me laugh. Matteo swooped down, taking my lips in a hard kiss, his tongue plundering my mouth with everything unspoken between us. His voice was raspy when he spoke. "Thank you."

His hard cock pressed against my thigh, and I shifted to rub my leg against it while I twined my tongue with his. He moaned and pulled away, stroking his rigid length as he walked to the nightstand and opened the drawer, pulling out a strip of condoms and tearing one off before tossing the rest on the bed.

I raised my brows at him. "Ambitious, are we?"

"Mise en place," Matteo quipped, making me laugh. He rolled the condom down his length, and I sat up to remove my nightgown. "Don't. I promised to fuck you in it, and fuck you, I will. Lay down, Macy. Legs spread. Show me that pretty pussy."

He lowered himself over me, dragging the tip of his dick through my labia. I was suddenly nervous because I'd only been in that position with one other man in my life. "Do you have lube?"

"Am I hurting you?" Matteo asked, going still.

"No," I said, feeling awful that I was about to mention my past. "But it usually hurts because I'm not wet enough, and you're—well, you're big."

"Macy, if you were any wetter, I'd slide right off you," he reassured me. He shifted and thrust two fingers inside me, moving quickly and making me moan in response. "See? I promise to go slow. I won't hurt you. You were made to fit me inside you."

"Okay."

He notched himself at my opening, and his length slipped inside inch by inch, stretching my long-unused muscles. I held on to Matteo's shoulders, my nails digging into his flesh as I breathed and tried to relax. His forest scent surrounded me. *Matteo was filling me.*

He leaned down and kissed me, sliding all the way in when I sighed into his mouth. "See? It fits just fine. Does it hurt?"

"No," I breathed. I rolled my hips against him and felt an electrical current shoot through my body when the head of his cock dragged against my g-spot. "Feels full. *Good.* So good."

"I'm glad." Matteo withdrew until only the tip was inside, then thrust his hips forward again, setting a leisurely pace until I couldn't take it anymore.

"I need you to move faster," I panted, snaking my hands down his body to grasp his hips and make him move more quickly. "And harder."

He smiled down at me and braced his forearms on either side of my head, threading his fingers through my hair. "I can do that. Rub your clit. I want to watch as you come around me."

I'd never done that during sex, but the promise of another orgasm—this time with Matteo filling me—set me in motion. I circled my clit as he snapped his hips forward, the bed moving with the force of his thrusts. Our bodies slid against each other, and our heavy breathing filled the air. I whimpered as my inner muscles tightened, creating even more friction.

"I'm close," I moaned and closed my eyes when Matteo changed the angle of his thrusts, so he was hitting my g-spot relentlessly. Rational thought abandoned me, along with any worries and self-conscious thoughts. All I could do was feel how perfectly we fit together, like our souls were in sync.

"Open your eyes, *ariete*," Matteo demanded. "Eyes on me when you come on my cock."

I focused on his dark gaze, parted lips, and the low sounds of pleasure he was making. His thrusts became erratic, and I recognized the signs that he was close, too. My muscles fluttered with the first contractions of my release.

"*Fuck*," he groaned and thrust deep, holding himself inside and making me cry out his name as he spilled into the condom. He murmured Spanish in my ear, and though I didn't know the language, it sounded like love.

My muscles spasmed until my legs ached, and I went limp. Matteo stroked my hair, kissed my cheeks, and then took my lips again. His following words were soft but sure. "I love you, Macy."

"I love you, too," I whispered, wrapping my arms around his neck and bringing him flush against my body. "So much."

Chapter Twenty-Five

FUCK, MACY WAS TRYING to suck my soul from my body through my cock. We'd gotten up early, had coffee, then decided to nap until we had to go to work. She was spending more nights at my house than at her own now that we were an official couple in love.

I'd awoken later to her head bobbing on my length beneath the covers like a fantasy come to life. She was the most perfect woman in the world and was all mine. I stroked her head, threading my fingers through her sleep-mussed hair.

"That's a good girl," I praised as she pumped my shaft in sync with what her mouth was doing. "Take me down your throat. *Yes*, just like that. So fucking *good*."

I didn't even know what I was saying, English turning to Spanish as I praised Macy's efforts and spoke of my love for her. She was a generous lover and paid attention to detail, so she knew exactly when to tug on my balls to send me over the edge, which she was about to do.

"Wait." I pulled her off my cock.

She looked at me in confusion. "Did I do something wrong?"

"Yes," I responded, pulling her to me for a kiss and tasting my precum on her lips. "You're not riding my face. Turn around."

Macy smirked at me but obeyed, and I propped myself up with pillows so I could reach her sweet pussy while she sucked me off. I swatted her ass, watching it jiggle, before diving between her legs. "Fuck, you taste amazing."

She responded by deepthroating my cock, her saliva dripping down my shaft to my balls as she worked me. I momentarily forgot what I was doing, but quickly resumed with a growl. I thrust my tongue into her pussy, pulsing and licking to draw more of that wetness out. My left hand steadied her hip and held her to me while I found her clit with the other, circling and tapping it to tease her, getting her close to the edge but not allowing her over.

"Matteo," Macy whined as she popped free of my cock.

I swatted her again. "I'll let you come when I'm shooting down your throat, *ariete*."

She dove down again, and I sucked at her opening, feeling the muscles flutter against my mouth and around my tongue. I didn't say anything when her rhythm faltered because it meant I was doing something right. Instead, I doubled my efforts, feeling the base of my cock flex and tingle. I could get off just by getting Macy off.

When she tugged on my balls, I lost it, groaning against her pussy as I filled her mouth, and she swallowed greedily just before I moved my mouth and shoved three fingers inside her, knowing the sensation would overwhelm her and throw her over the edge.

"*Matteo!*" Macy cried out, releasing my cock as she came.

I had to catch her and gently turn her to the side before laying next to her, our feet at the head of the bed.

"Good morning again, *ariete*," I crooned, wiping a bit of saliva from the corner of her mouth. Her lips were red and puffy, and I couldn't resist tasting them.

"Mmm," Macy purred. "I think I'm going to need second breakfast after that."

"Coffee doesn't count as first breakfast," I pointed out. "But I'm happy to make you whatever you want."

"Do you still have leftover *empanada* dough?" she asked.

"Sure do." I stroked my fingers over her cheek. "Do you want savory or sweet?"

"How about both?" she suggested. "I'll help you make them."

I stretched and rolled off the bed, looking down and admiring how Macy was sprawled out on my covers. She belonged there. "I can handle it. Why don't you shower while I make them?"

"You don't want to shower with me?" Macy sounded offended.

"It's not that I don't want to shower with you," I explained. "We have to be at the restaurant in a couple of hours, and it wouldn't do for both the head chef and sous chef to be late. I know if I step in that shower with you, we'll be doing a hell of a lot more than getting clean."

"Fair enough," Macy conceded, raising her arms above her head.

It was too much for my lust-addled brain. I snagged a condom from the nightstand and made a show of leaping onto the bed, set on ravaging my beautiful girlfriend so I could watch her walk funny all day.

***

"It's not funny," Macy hissed when I chuckled as she stretched her sore legs again.

"I didn't say it was," I replied innocently.

"You're laughing," she pointed out.

I shot her a wicked grin. "I'm not laughing at you. I'm chuckling to myself for fucking you so hard you could barely stand for an hour after, and you have to lean up against the wall as often as possible."

"Fuck you," she whisper-yelled, rubbing her thighs again.

"I don't think you're in any condition to make offers like that."

"Ugh!" Macy threw her hands up in the air. "You know what I mean."

I rubbed my jaw. "I'm not sure I do. Maybe we can discuss it at my place after work."

She flipped me off and walked away, busying herself with dinner orders. I followed, brushing up against her when I could, just to hear her gasp at my touch. I loved cooking with her, but I couldn't wait to take her home and hold her in my arms all night.

The next hour passed in a blur, dinners going out as fast as we could plate them. I twisted the cap off a water bottle and handed it to Macy, who chugged it down. She nodded. "Thanks. I should really be taking vitamins, too. I don't want to catch Leo's cold."

"No problem," I said, drinking my water. Leo had been out of work for two days with something like the flu. "How is she doing today?"

"She texted and told me her fever broke, so I think she's on the mend," Macy replied.

"That's great. Tell her I hope she feels better soon. We need her sass back here." I tossed the empty bottles into the recycling bin and washed my hands, ready to finish up the next two hours until closing.

"Hey, Chef," Santiago, one of our servers, called out as he entered the kitchen. "One of the guests asked to speak to the chef. He said Macy, but I think he might be confused about which of you is the head chef since he mentioned the celebrity chef."

"It could be either one of them," Diego yelled across the kitchen. "Macy's videos are nearly as popular as Chef's."

"Have you heard what they're calling you?" Pedro asked. "The hottest celebrity chef duo in a decade. I don't know who the last was, but I guess you're it now."

Macy shook her head. "You're kidding."

"Cross my heart!" Pedro made the motion over the left side of his chest.

She turned to me, brows raised. "Have you heard of this?"

"Yeah," I admitted. "If you ever looked at your social media, you would know about it, too."

"Leo is still doing all that." She shrugged. "Speaking of the account, I'm supposed to take pictures with some food tonight since Leo can't do it. She says we're running out of content because she's sick, and I'm inept at social media. She's not wrong."

I covered my laugh by clearing my throat. "I'll help you take some later."

"Thanks." Macy tried to see out to the front of the house through the window in the kitchen door. "I bet that person isn't even here to talk to me."

"He did use your name," Santiago repeated with a shrug. Macy scrunched up her nose. She was happier in the kitchen, with as little interaction with customers as possible, though she came across as likable when she talked to them.

"It's okay," I said. "I'll go out with you; that way, whichever person he wants to talk to is there."

"I guess that works," she said with a sigh. I grabbed my hat and handed Macy her skullcap so we'd look more presentable. Macy even smoothed her hair down.

"Come on." I placed a hand on her lower back and held the kitchen door open.

She stopped on the other side of the door, wringing her hands nervously as the dining room din reached our ears. "Why don't you go first? That way, if they only want to see you, I can slip back into the kitchen."

"Sure, I can do that."

Santiago passed us, carrying a tray of food, and nodded across the dining room. "Table twelve."

I led the way, weaving around tables and greeting guests as we walked through the area. When I looked back, Macy smiled politely at people, and several people recognized her from the videos. As we approached the table in question, I saw the back of a blonde man dressed in a black suit. He was alone in the booth, which means he likely had reservations because the usual practice was to put single diners at a table for two unless they insisted otherwise. We allowed those making reservations to choose the type of seating they wanted online.

I stopped next to the man's table, placing a hand on the back of the booth where he sat. "Good evening, sir. How is everything?"

"Oh, hi." The man turned to me, his features ruddy but chiseled like he was pushing his jaw forward. "I thought I asked to see—*Macy!*"

The man's face lit up as Macy walked around me. She paled, and her mouth dropped open. "Ethan?"

"Yeah, baby, it's me," he said with too much enthusiasm.

My stomach dropped. Ethan, the ex-husband, Ethan? He'd walked out on Macy over a year ago now, and she supposedly hadn't heard from him at all. She only knew what he'd been up to because of that photo Leo had found online.

"Wh–where have you been?" Macy forced out, her hands balled into fists at her sides, knuckles white. I bristled, ready to toss the man out of my restaurant.

"I just got back into town and couldn't wait to see you!" He glanced around, where others were beginning to take notice. "I got your little care package and thought maybe we should discuss it together."

"My *care package?*" she looked perplexed for a moment, but then her brows shot up, and she leaned forward, tapping the table to emphasize her words. "Do you mean the *divorce* papers my lawyer sent you?"

He grinned like nothing was amiss. "Yeah, I received the paperwork and came straight home to help out."

"Look, I don't know what you're trying to—"

"I had to see you. I've missed you so much, baby." Ethan stood, bumping me out of the way and wedging his way between Macy and me. He was shorter but carried more muscular bulk. "I know

I've been an ass, but you know I love you. I couldn't stay away any longer."

"I wasn't the one who left," Macy said numbly.

"I know I've made mistakes. I wasn't myself, but I'm going to do better now." He pulled something out of his pocket, and I heard the ladies gasp as he opened the black velvet box to reveal a giant diamond ring. "Please, Macy, I'm begging for your forgiveness. Come home to me."

"I don't understand what's happening," she said in a monotone. I was at a loss for what to do. I couldn't just throw a customer out and make a scene, and Macy didn't seem to be kicking him out.

"I'm making a grand gesture, baby." Ethan reached for Macy's hand and slipped the rock onto her ring finger. I couldn't tell if her lips were trembling with fear or whether she was overcome by emotion at Ethan's non-apology. The rest of the nearby diners bought it. They had cameras out, and they were snapping photos when they could like it was a proposal. Come to think of it, short of Ethan getting on his knees to declare his love, it looked an awful lot like a proposal.

"I–I don't know what to say," Macy stuttered, staring at the ring where Ethan still held her hand in his.

"I know you must be speechless," he said dramatically. The snake. It was clear he was only performing for the benefit of the general public. If he cared at all for Macy, he would have contacted her privately.

Ethan wrapped her up in a tight hug and whispered into her ear, "I'll call you tomorrow. Answer your phone. We have a lot to discuss."

Then, he actually bowed—the idiot—and threw down a hundred-dollar bill before walking out of the restaurant. Macy still stood with a shell-shocked look on her face.

I tapped her on the shoulder and turned her back toward the kitchen. "Let's get to the back, okay?"

"Yeah, sure," Macy murmured, walking robotically to the back. "What just happened?"

"I don't know." I shrugged. "You'll have to tell me. I gather that was the MIA husband?"

"Oh, this is so fucking messed up," she snapped suddenly, her entire body shuddering. "I feel sick. I need to get some air."

"I'll come with you," I offered.

She held up a hand—the one that now sported a ring from her husband. "No, I need to be alone right now."

Maybe I should have gone after Macy, so she wasn't alone. Perhaps I should have kicked her husband out of my restaurant before he could proclaim his love to my girl. I could have done any number of things differently, but I didn't. I stood there in the kitchen and watched life as I knew it crumble at my feet.

Chapter Twenty-Six

"Y OU CAN'T BE SERIOUS," Leo croaked when I came down the stairs dressed for coffee with Ethan.

"He wants to meet," I explained for the hundredth time. "It's just coffee. I'm not planning to move back in with him or anything."

She shoved the blankets off her lap and stood with her hands on her hips. The effect was somewhat less intimidating since she wore bubblegum pink pajamas. "Yeah, not yet. He's going to use that slimy charm to mess with your head and make you think you were the problem in the marriage. You weren't. It was all his fault."

"I won't let him do that," I said firmly. "I've been through a year of therapy, and I know better now."

"Did you tell your therapist about this meeting?"

"Well, no," I hedged. "I've only known about Ethan being back for like two days. He called yesterday."

Leo scrubbed her hands down her face. "I should have made you change your number when he left."

"I needed a way for him to contact me for the divorce," I countered. "And now he has. I'll go see what he wants and hopefully get some answers."

"What more can he say that his actions haven't screamed?" Leo argued. "The man left you to spend a year on vacation with his mistress!"

I cringed at her blunt words but didn't feel the devastation I always expected when thinking of Ethan's extramarital affair. "I just want closure."

Leo sighed and dropped her hands to her sides in surrender. "I can't blame you for that. I want to punch Ethan in his stupid face for hurting you."

"And I want you to stay out of jail." I hugged her tightly. "Thanks for having my back, though."

"Side note." Leo's expression turned thoughtful. "Do you know if he has life insurance? You might get more from that than alimony."

"I don't know, and I don't want to end up on a true crime podcast, so please shift your thoughts to something less murderous."

She took a few deep breaths for show. "Have you talked to Matteo yet?"

"We've texted." I hadn't been in any condition to go home with him after seeing Ethan. I barely remembered the rest of my shift at the restaurant. With Ethan's very public display, word made it back to the kitchen staff before I returned to the kitchen. They'd sent me curious and pitying looks, which only made me feel worse.

"I think this might be the kind of thing you need to talk about in person," she reprimanded. "If you're meeting with Ethan, you can take time to see Matteo outside of work. He must be pretty confused right now."

"I tried to explain that I didn't know Ethan was coming back to town," I said defensively. "There wasn't anything else to say because I don't know anything else. That's why I'm meeting with him. And I'll be late if I don't get going right now."

Leo took my hands and held my arms out as she took me in from head to toe. "You look amazing. Make him regret everything."

I grinned at her and headed toward the door, slipping my leather jacket over my gold sweater. I'd paired it with jeans and black booties. Classy, but without too much effort. "I plan to."

Leo stood at the door as I left and called out behind me, "If you're not back in two hours, I'm calling with an emergency!"

I waved and made the short trek to transit. The coffee shop was only one stop down the MAX line, but far enough that Ethan wouldn't guess which direction I'd come from. I didn't want him to know where I was staying, and the girls at the coffee shop knew me well enough that I'd feel comfortable asking them for help if Ethan got weird.

My palms started sweating as I approached the shop, and I smoothed them on my pants before opening the door. Today, the warmth and scent of coffee offered no comfort. I felt like I was walking into the unknown, and though I was in control of whether I stayed, I had no way of controlling what Ethan would say. My mind raced with all the worst thoughts I'd dwelled on for months.

I ordered my regular iced coffee and glanced around the place while I waited. Ethan hadn't arrived yet, so I took my coffee and found a table for two. I didn't want to sit on the more comfortable couches and chairs in the back, or he might think I was prepared to stay a while. No, I'd be out of there as quickly as possible so that I could enjoy my day off.

"Macy, is that you?"

I turned my head and froze. Of all the inconvenient times to run into people I knew, this might have been the worst. Viola and Bella stopped before me, drinks in hand and their pregnant bellies protruding in their oversized sweaters.

"Hey," I greeted them weakly, hoping my mouth curved into a smile instead of a grimace.

"Have you recovered yet?" Viola asked, smirking. I frowned, trying to figure out what she was talking about. "From Thanksgiving."

"Oh, yeah," I said with a wave of my hand. "It wasn't bad at all."

"Good." Bella nodded at me with a smile. "I hope you'll come back for Christmas, then."

Viola elbowed her friend. "Don't go scaring her off."

"I'd like to think I have more staying power than that." I huffed out a laugh. "Very little scares me after some chefs I've worked under."

Bella narrowed her eyes. "Matteo had better not be included in that. I'll send Chase to straighten him out if he's anything less than a gentleman."

I shook my head. "No, nothing like that. Matteo is great."

"Where is he this morning?" Viola asked, looking around as if he might appear.

"Probably at home." I shrugged. "I haven't seen him since work yesterday, and we were pretty busy, so there wasn't much time to talk."

"You didn't stay the night last night?" Viola raised a brow.

And that was the downside of having a large family who talked. "Does everybody know our business?"

"Honestly?" Bella asked and waited for my nod. "Yeah. Eventually. That's why I know Matteo would never be caught away from you if he didn't have to be. Did you have a fight or something?"

"No, nothing like that," I insisted. I felt my lip quiver, the stress of everything catching up to me. "It's my ex."

"There you are!" Ethan had fucking horrible timing approaching right now. He held a coffee cup, which probably had twelve ingredients if he held to his pretentious standards. Of course, he looked perfect in his expensive suit, his blonde hair styled without a strand out of place. Even his stubble was probably intentional and fashionable.

He leaned down to kiss me on the cheek, but I recoiled, narrowly avoiding his lips. His cloying cologne smelled like rich trash, and I'd bet money he picked it for the high cost without considering the quality. Bella and Viola looked on with shocked expressions, and I tried to apologize with my eyes. They would probably rush out the door and call Matteo.

"Who are your friends?" Ethan asked, pointing at the women. He didn't even bother trying to hide his perusal, but when he put on that smile he used when talking to prospective clients, I knew he'd noticed they wore designer brands. His blue eyes flashed with greed when he held out his hand. "I'm Ethan, Macy's husband."

"Soon-to-be ex-husband," I murmured, and he glared at me before smoothing his features.

Bella narrowed her eyes at Ethan, then shot me a glance, one that every girl who's ever had a man harassing her can decipher—she was offering me an escape. Did I want to ditch Ethan? Kind of, but I wanted an explanation more. I made a face that told her I might need an outlet later.

"We'll be right over there when you're done so we can go over those custom clothing orders," Bella said clearly, shooting a look at Ethan.

"Oh, I didn't realize you'd double booked," he said disapprovingly—the ass.

I rolled my eyes and didn't bother trying to hide my exasperation. "Well, I didn't plan on your return, and I have a life."

He took the seat across from me, and Bella and Viola reluctantly walked to the back of the coffee shop where I'd sat with Matteo and the Rivera brothers. I'd rather listen to Maria Rivera tell me I was getting old and needed to have Matteo's babies than sit and deal with Ethan.

"So what is it you want, exactly?" I asked, sipping on my coffee.

Ethan used that fake smile on me. Didn't he realize I knew whatever came out of his mouth next would be an act?

"I want another chance," he said, mouth down-turned and eyes widened slightly, so he looked remorseful.

"Why do you deserve one?"

"I don't, Macy." He ran a hand through his hair. "And I realize that. I'm not coming back thinking I can just move back in, and we'll go back to life as normal. I want to earn my place with you."

My jaw dropped. "Have you tried going back to the house? Do you not even know we lost it?"

"What?" Ethan sounded genuinely shocked. "You didn't pay the mortgage?"

"With what money?" The pitch of my voice raised. "You drained our accounts! I had nothing!"

He closed his mouth with a snap. "Didn't you get a job? You were always resourceful."

"Of course, I got a job. I got three jobs, but it wasn't enough to cover the car and mortgage and your other debts. I couldn't sell the house because your name is on it. The cars were repossessed because you were still paying for them, and I couldn't cover the bills."

"You lost the house and the cars?" I caught a flicker of annoyance on his face. "What's left?"

"There's nothing." I held my arms out to the side, hands palms up. "I don't have the fancy degree. You could afford your degree because *I* was the one waitressing."

He tipped his head. "I hear you're quite the celebrity chef now. That must make some money."

I laughed outright at his assumption. "I don't make anything off those accounts. They're just for fun."

"Well, I'm glad you've found a way to amuse yourself while I've been gone," he said flatly.

"Amuse myself?" My eyes widened. "Do you think I was *amused* when a tow truck showed up and hauled our cars off? That I laughed when the bank took the home back? Or maybe you think I danced merrily through the streets while I searched for jobs and got turned down repeatedly."

"Macy, quiet down." Ethan glanced around. "You're causing a scene."

"I don't think you get to tell me when I get to be quiet or loud—whether I'm wired or calm. I did everything for myself while you were gone. You aren't going to come back and think you're in charge."

"I said I was sorry," he cajoled.

"Then you should realize that saying sorry isn't the same as making up for everything you've done."

Ethan looked down into his coffee, his thumb brushing over the edge of the cup. "I know, but I'm willing to do whatever it takes. Just—please—don't give up on me yet."

The nerve of the man, thinking a few apologies and sad faces would sway me. "You were the one who gave up on me over a year ago. I waited for you for months. Even when I lost everything, I hoped you would come back and save me. I prayed that I'd wake up and find it was all a nightmare. But it was my gut-wrenching reality, and I was almost free of all those feelings of rejection—almost free of you."

"I understand why you're so upset. I do." Ethan laid his hand over mine on the table and held me tight enough that I couldn't pull away. "And I know I don't have a right to ask for anything with all I've done, but I'm just asking for a little time."

"The last court date is in two weeks," I reminded him. "My lawyer says the judge will finalize the divorce."

"Please, can we put it off?" Ethan practically begged, and I thought I caught a hint of desperation in his voice. "If we can't work things out, we can always get another date."

I paused, wondering if it would be so bad to wait another month or more when I'd already waited an entire year. Could I find it in myself to listen to Ethan and give him a fair chance? Maybe, but he'd lost the privilege of influencing my decisions.

"I'm not going to change the court date, and if you get a lawyer and try to put it off, I'll take you for whatever you're worth in those Caribbean bank accounts," I told him.

Ethan paled and stuttered. He didn't think I knew where he'd been.

"I'm not like you, so I'll give you two weeks. I can tell you now that I doubt anything you say will sway me from my path. You asked for this meeting, but other than repeating your apology, I haven't heard any of the explanations you promised. Your time is up for today."

"Dinner, then," he blurted, rubbing the stubble on his jaw. "Let me take you out next week."

"Fine. Until next week."

I stood and walked away without another word, dropping into a chair where Bella and Viola sat. My hands trembled, and my stomach threatened to return the coffee I'd just consumed.

"Are you okay?" Bella asked, reaching out and hesitantly patting my arm.

"Yeah," I sighed. "I'll be fine."

"I gather that was the husband who pulled the disappearing act?" Viola surmised, sipping on what looked like tea.

I nodded. "That would be him. This is all a mess. Why did he have to come back now?"

Bella stiffened. "Is he bothering you? My husband helps solve *problems* for people—if you need help. He especially likes dealing with assholes like that."

"You sound like Leo. She offered the same, but in a more permanent way." I laughed ruefully. "Thanks for your offer, but I'm so close to the end. The divorce is supposed to finalize by the end of the year, and then his attempts to change my mind will stop."

Bella looked dubious. "If he doesn't fade into the background, please let me know. No woman should have to deal with an obsessive man."

Viola shot Bella an understanding glance before turning to me. "Why has he come back now?"

"I have no idea," I admitted. "Leo found his address last month, and my lawyer had divorce papers served in the Caribbean. I guess when he got them, he decided to come back and try to save the marriage."

"Ha," Viola barked out. "More like he saw the amount of alimony he'd be paying and decided it would be cheaper to stay married."

I froze as the possibility washed over me. Why hadn't I considered that before? "The money."

"Sorry," Viola rushed. "I didn't mean to upset you."

"No, you didn't." I waved her off. "That makes a lot of sense. He didn't even know I'd lost everything. The jerk thought I'd get a job and cover the bills myself. I guess he thought everything would be the same now that he's back."

"Maybe your friend Leo has the right idea," Bella murmured into her cup.

Viola tittered at her friend's dark humor. "Well, I hope you're not falling for that horrible show he just put on."

"No, but I told him I'd go to dinner with him."

Their faces fell, and Bella looked at me with something akin to judgment in her eyes. Her jaw clenched. "What about Matteo?"

"I love him," I whispered. "But I've known Ethan since we were kids, and I guess I just want to make sure I'm making the right decision. I want to hear him tell me why he left me, and I want a real apology."

"You know you may never get that." I didn't reply to Viola.

Bella held my gaze. "Don't hurt him, Macy. He's my brother, and besides my blood and Chase, he's the best man I know."

"I hope I don't," I answered, biting my lip. Only, I was a liar. I knew Matteo was already hurt that I'd met with Ethan, and I suspected we were about to have our first disagreement when I told him I was going to have dinner with my estranged husband.

The thought of disappointing Matteo sent tiny barbs of ice into my heart.

Chapter Twenty-Seven

Gingerbread and sugar scented the air in *El Corazón Borikèn*, but it all held a bitter edge with the situation regarding Ethan looming over my relationship with Macy. I wanted to believe that he wasn't a threat, but the man was her legal spouse. Even if he'd fucked her over, she'd loved him a lot longer than she'd loved me.

It hurt to watch her interact with the children and consider that all those future scenarios I'd spent the last month dreaming up might not be possible. She knelt by Sam, helping cut peppermint patties for roof tiles. The little girl had taken to her quickly when it had taken me six months before she'd speak more than a few words during a class. She beamed at Macy, and they giggled together.

"Chef, I can't get the roof to stay on!"

I saw Jacob trying desperately to hold his gingerbread house together. Holding back a smile, I hurried over and lifted the crumbling pieces from the walls. "Why don't we get you a couple of new pieces? I think these were defective. Where's the inspector when you need him?"

Jacob smiled when I brought him two pieces of gingerbread that didn't have warped areas making them more vulnerable to collapse. I showed him how to pipe the correct amount of icing glue onto the frame so it would hold and not slide right off. It would be nice if the houses made it home with the kids.

"Perfect," I encouraged him when the gingerbread stayed put. "Now you can put things on top—carefully."

"Thanks, chef!"

I walked around the room as the kids affixed liberal amounts of candy to their gingerbread houses. It was like a competition to see who could empty their candy bowls and take as much candy home as possible. I should have put a disclaimer on the class application that we were not responsible for candy comas resulting from the activities.

As Macy helped the kids put pre-made popsicle stick frames around the gingerbread houses, I stopped at the front table to look at Macy's contribution. She was more creative than she gave herself credit for. A candy cane picket fence surrounded her gingerbread house, and she'd piped shingles on the roof. Little icing hedges framed the door, and she'd dusted her board with powdered sugar after smoothing a layer of icing as a base. Bits of snow gathered on the rooftop, and icicles hung from the eaves. It was an idyllic Christmas cottage.

"This is amazing," I told her when she stopped by my side.

She offered me one of those smiles I loved, open and expressive. "Thanks. One day I want to find a little cottage with snow and spend a weekend just disconnecting and reading by the fire."

"That sounds like a good time," I agreed. I wanted to tell her I'd take her, but a commotion at the front door interrupted me.

Ethan pushed through the families, an obscenely enormous bouquet in his hands. He nodded at the people who got hit by the floral atrocity. "So sorry. Couldn't see where I was going."

Macy sucked in a breath, and her face went pale. I barely caught her whispering, "*Shit*."

"He can't be here, Macy," I said low enough that nobody else could hear. "This is still my place of business, and right now, we're not open to the public."

"I didn't invite him," she explained quietly. "I don't know why he's here."

"I'm going to guess he's trying to woo you," I said flatly. "But it looks like he stole flowers from a funeral."

"Macy!" Ethan exclaimed when he spotted her. The remaining families looked on with interest as he thrust the flowers into her arms. "I brought you a gift."

"Are these white lilies?" she asked, trying to keep a straight face.

"Yeah, I thought they represented you well," he said proudly. "You're so pure and sweet."

"Ah," she shot me a glance, and I lifted my brows. "How thoughtful."

Ethan preened at her words, even though she was being polite because she *was* sweet underneath her prickly exterior. "You deserve them."

"I suppose they're à propos in a way," she mused. "You did rip my heart out when you left."

I covered a laugh with a cough at her dry humor, but Ethan looked confused. "I don't know how many times you want me to tell you I'm sorry for hurting you."

I turned and imitated a popular video online to myself. "It'll *never* be enough."

"Ethan, this is where I work," Macy began. "You cannot just walk in whenever the mood strikes."

"Chef Macy!" Sam ran up with her finished gingerbread house. "How does it look?"

"Wonderful!" Macy turned to the little girl and applauded her efforts. "I bet you'll be a famous pastry chef one day, making beautiful creations in a fancy restaurant."

"It's a cookie with some icing and chocolate stuck on it," Ethan said under his breath, unimpressed. "Hardly anything to be proud of."

Macy's expression turned thunderous. "Ethan! That was completely uncalled for. Does it make you feel good to bully a child?"

Sam stepped up to Ethan and fisted her hands on her hips, defiant. "I don't like you. Your smile is too perfect."

"I paid a lot for this smile," Ethan said, taking offense.

"You can paint poop any color you like, but it will still be poop," the little girl retorted. "You're just hiding the ugly underneath."

Macy laughed as she wrapped the gingerbread house, but quickly stared Ethan down as she silently dared him to say more. He seemed to realize there was still an audience and wisely kept his mouth shut. I was ready to walk him out back and have a few words with him.

Sam took the gingerbread house from Macy, but before she could go, Macy leaned down and whispered, "Never let anybody tell you that you can't do what you dream of doing."

"Same to you, Chef." Sam wrapped an arm around Macy's waist and gave her a quick hug before pulling the hair back over her face to cover her scars. "Merry Christmas!"

"Merry Christmas, Sam," Macy returned, her eyes misting. Her face hardened when she saw Ethan tapping his fingers against his leg. Were his fingers manicured? Everything about the man was fucking perfect.

"You always had a thing for kids," he said disdainfully.

"And you promised me a family you never intended to have," she shot back.

Ethan looked down his nose at her. "Your attitude has changed since I've been gone. Probably Leo's influence."

"I think it's time for you to leave," I interjected, afraid I wouldn't have the patience to deal with the man without breaking his nose.

"How did you know I was here, anyway?" Macy asked suspiciously.

Ethan shrugged. "You never got rid of your phone. I just checked its location."

Macy's jaw dropped. "You've been stalking me?"

"I can't stalk my wife," Ethan said flippantly. "I just wanted to make a grand gesture. I didn't think it would be a problem."

"If you knew me at all, you would know that this isn't the kind of grand gesture I appreciate," Macy hissed.

Even though he looked genuinely bewildered, I couldn't feel bad for the man. "I always used to bring you flowers. You loved it."

"I like flowers," Macy confirmed. "I hate public attention. And you brought me funeral flowers, Ethan."

"I'm trying here," he stressed.

I felt like I was watching a live soap opera and desperately wanted the director to end the scene. I turned to my—what was she now, anyway? Girlfriend? Employee? "Macy."

"I know. I'm sorry," she apologized. "Ethan, you need to leave."

"I'll see you next week, then," he said dejectedly, looking like a pouting trust fund baby in his expensive suit.

"Sure," Macy said with a dismissive wave.

Ethan turned to leave, and Macy whirled away, stomping back to the kitchen. I followed, unsure of what to say. She swung the door so hard it nearly hit me in the face on the rebound. That was a new one for her.

"That man!" she huffed and chucked the flowers into the nearest trash can. "Who the hell does he think he is, waltzing into my life whenever it suits him?"

"I don't know," I said mildly. "It seems like he thinks he's your husband."

Macy's shoulders slumped, and she untied her apron, wringing the fabric in her hands. "I'm sorry about that. I would have stopped him if I'd known he would pull that stunt."

"It's okay." It wasn't, but Macy had enough on her plate for now. "Are you ready to head home?"

"Yeah, but could you take me back to my place, please?"

It was like she'd dumped ice water over my head. Ethan was coming between us, even if Macy didn't see it. She was too involved to realize she'd been pushing me away.

"Sure." I nodded and got to work cleaning the last of the things from the class. I couldn't help but fear that the death knells of our relationship sounded with every passing day.

***

I stared into my coffee cup as I waited for Macy to arrive at our usual coffee shop. When I tried calling her, the number said it had been disconnected. It was unlikely she would ghost me completely, but everything lately had been so uncertain that I felt anxious. As a result, I'd made a decision I wondered if I would later regret.

"Hey," Macy said as she approached with her iced coffee. She looked perfect in those jeans that made her ass look incredible and a red sweater with her leather jacket on top. She'd stuffed her hat and gloves into her purse, and her hair was slightly static. "Your text was ominous. Is everything okay?"

"I don't know," I countered. "Is it? You disconnected your phone."

She pulled her phone from her pocket as she sat down. "I got a new phone because Ethan could track the old phone. I'm sorry, I should have texted you the number."

"That might have been helpful." I felt like a heel for the way I was talking to Macy.

"I'm here now," she said tiredly. There were dark circles under her eyes that indicated she was losing sleep. "What did you want to talk about?"

I took a deep breath and a fortifying gulp of hot coffee. "I want to talk about us."

"Okay," she said hesitantly, drawing the word out. "Anything in particular?"

242

"Let's not play games, Macy," I said shortly. "Things have been strained since Ethan came back to town."

She took a sip of coffee and nodded. "I agree. He's brought a lot of stress into both of our lives, and I'm sorry for that."

"I understand it's not your fault." I reached out and rubbed her thigh soothingly. "I care about you, but I have to think about the restaurant."

"I know," she sighed. "It will all be over in a couple of weeks."

"Will it?" I asked, skeptical that it would be so easy. "That assumes Ethan won't do or say something to convince you to stick it out with him."

"Matteo, it's not like that." Macy leaned forward and took my hand. I looked down at how her little fingers wrapped around my larger palm, wanting nothing more than to take her in my arms and whisk her back to my apartment so I could lock her away until all the drama passed. If I could keep her away from Ethan, things would be fine.

But that wasn't the kind of man I was. I couldn't live with myself if I knew I was the reason she still wondered, *what if*? She needed to make those decisions on her own without my influence.

"I will never approve of how Ethan betrayed you and everything he put you through," I began. "But I see the question in your eyes when Ethan is around. I feel how cold my sheets are at night because you're not lying beside me. There's a distance between us, and it's not anything I can fix."

Macy's lower lip trembled, and she bit down on it. "I don't want to feel this way. All I wanted was closure, but I still don't have it, and I don't know if I ever will. Ethan says he'll explain everything at dinner next week, but I don't know if I can trust anything he says. I don't want to be married anymore...."

She trailed off, and I finished the sentence for her. "But you have a history with him, and you feel it deserves your attention until it's officially over."

"Yes," she agreed. "I hate that I'm hurting you, Matteo. I never intended for any of this to happen. If it makes things easier, I'll take a leave of absence from the restaurant until this is all over. The last thing I want is for my presence to cause you pain."

"Macy." I stopped her. "You don't need to take a leave. That's your income, and you've earned your spot there. No matter what happens or how I feel, I will not take your livelihood from you. That would make me no different from Ethan, and I am *not* that man."

"You could *never* be like him," she insisted, squeezing my hand.

I gripped her fingers, then pulled away. Everything in my soul screamed at me not to say the words on the tip of my tongue, but I knew they were necessary. "You need to decide where your feelings lie, whether that's reconciling with Ethan or needing more time to process the end of your marriage. I won't stand in the way of that. I've made arrangements to visit the L.A. location of *El Corazón Borikén*."

"Please, don't leave," she begged, a tear slipping from the corner of her eye.

My voice cracked as I spoke. "Please don't ask me to stay. I can't stand by and watch, wondering who you will choose in the end. I love you, and right now, I'm not sure how I'll cope with losing you, but what I want more than anything is for you to find happiness because you deserve it, Macy."

"I love you, too."

I stood and leaned down to brush the tears from her face, then inhaled her floral perfume as I let my lips linger against her cheek in what might have been our last kiss. "Take what you want, *ariete*. The world is yours."

My heart cried out in agony, making every breath burn as I walked away from the woman I loved.

Chapter Twenty-Eight

I STARED AT MY reflection in the mirror, noting the dark circles under my eyes. Matteo had been gone for a week, and it was like he had taken a piece of me with him. He'd been my living infusion of joy and happiness, but a dark cloud had settled over my mind in his absence.

"You can still back out, you know," Leo suggested as she leaned against my door frame. She wore an old band t-shirt and plaid pajama shorts, with fuzzy bear's paw slippers that squeaked when she walked.

"I'm more determined than ever to see this through," I said through gritted teeth. "I know you mean well, but please stop trying to talk me out of the things I've already decided."

"Sorry." She came up behind me, wrapped her arms around my waist, and rested her chin on my shoulder. "I just want you to know that you don't have to give in to Ethan pressuring you to have dinner with him. I'm a text away. You send me the words, and I'll run into that restaurant covered in blood, screaming to get you out."

I laughed, shaking my head at Leo's antics. "Fake blood, I hope."

"Needs must," she answered with an arched brow. "It would be the performance of the year."

"I believe it." I sighed and patted her hands where they crossed my stomach. "One week."

"One week," Leo parroted. "How do you feel about that?"

"My stomach is in knots," I admitted. "There's this harsh sense of reality that an entire season of my life will be over, and it's odd to think that I'll have lost a decade for nothing."

"Don't think of it like that." Leo's hair tickled my ear. "You grew as a person because of everything you lived through. Sometimes life throws shit at us, so we learn. I mean, look at you."

I did, staring myself down in the mirror. My mood colored my opinion of myself. "I see an average woman. Average size, average height, average beauty."

"We need to get you glasses, then." Leo squeezed me and withdrew, making her fingers into circles and putting them in front of my eyes. "Your vision is fucked up. I see resilience, determination, success, beauty, and heart. You're the best friend I could ask for, and I'm proud to live life with you, my platonic life partner."

"You're going to make me cry." I choked up and blinked rapidly, fanning my eyes and hoping the tears welling wouldn't destroy my makeup.

Leo grinned. "What kind of best friend would I be if I didn't give you the feels now and again?"

"One who understands that I don't like emotions," I said with a watery laugh.

"That's exactly why you need to feel them sometimes," she pointed out. "And I'll always give you a safe space for that."

I nodded, afraid I'd burst into tears if I kept talking. Leo scratched my back soothingly with her nails. "You know, if you're worried I won't make it to the restaurant in time to save you, I could put a blood packet in your purse, and you can pretend to bleed internally or something."

"Where do you even get a blood packet?" I asked, incredulous. She never ceased to freak me out and amaze me.

"Anywhere that sells costume props," she said with a shrug. "Anyway, I'll put it in there just in case. But be careful when you reach for your phone and keep your keys away. It's not a good look to have blood dripping out of your purse. Trust me."

I was too afraid to ask how she had firsthand knowledge of that particular faux pas.

"Bloody emergency escape aside, does this say, 'you gave up the best thing you ever had when you left me,' or should I change?" I stared at the low-cut neckline of my black bodycon dress. I wanted to look fabulous without looking like I'd made the effort, so I curled my hair into loose waves and kept my eye makeup light so my eyes would pop. My leather jacket and black boots completed the look.

"Almost." Leo darted out of my room, and there was a crash before she returned with a slight limp.

"Are you okay?" I asked, concerned.

"Yeah, I forgot that I was reorganizing my bookshelves, and I may have knocked three piles of special edition hardbacks over in my haste," she explained. Then, she held up a bright red tube. "But I found the best lipstick ever. So it was worth it."

I took the offered lipstick and swiped it across my lips. "Okay, you were right. It's incredible."

I knew Ethan was weak for a red lip. It was probably why his little assistant caught his eye.

"He's going to take one look at you and suffer all night with an erection," Leo said confidently. "Should we bet he tries to take you home?"

"I'm definitely not going home with him." If there was one thing the time away from Matteo had taught me, it was that I missed him far more than I wanted to be around Ethan. I wouldn't see Ethan after dinner unless he showed up at court next week.

"Good. I'll give you three hours," Leo said sternly, mimicking her dad's voice. "If you haven't texted me to let me know you're on the way home, I'm bringing the bloodbath."

"Fair enough." There was no way I would be late. I grabbed my purse and wrapped my scarf around my neck, covering half my face. I didn't want to mess up my hair. The scarf and gloves would have to keep me warm as I walked to and from transit.

"Love you more than dick," Leo said, hugging me before playfully shoving me out the door. "Go stomp on his heart a little."

I laughed as I walked away, silently rehearsing what I wanted to say as I traveled to the upscale Italian restaurant. I stood outside the building, looking through the windows at the tables covered in pure white tablecloths and set with expensive place settings and candle centerpieces. Ethan would pick something like that. I loved making Italian food at home but rarely went to Italian restaurants because they reminded me of when I worked in one.

Taking a deep breath, I stepped through the door and breathed in the familiar scents of basil and oregano as I greeted the hostess. I shoved my gloves into my pockets before she hung my coat with my scarf. She showed me to the table where Ethan already sat, looking every bit as perfect as always in a navy suit with a blue striped tie. The asshole didn't even stand when I approached; he just looked up from his menu and raked his eyes down my body.

"I see you're still eating well." He shook his head disapprovingly. "I'll have to get you a gym membership."

"Eating is a basic necessity for *life*, Ethan," I said caustically. My therapist helped me realize my body issues started after I began dating Ethan in high school. Even after a year of therapy, I still had self-deprecating thoughts about my body. "I walk all the time. I don't need a gym membership. There's nothing wrong with how I look."

He flagged the server down and ordered for both of us without asking me what I wanted. And he ordered me a salad with grilled chicken. Oh, hell no. I decided right then that I wouldn't be staying for the meal.

"I found a condo in the recently updated downtown area," Ethan explained. "I figure we can go back there after dinner so you can check it out."

Yeah, right. He might mock my body, but the look in his eyes said he'd be all too willing to grunt as he thrust between my thighs and came before getting me off. *I don't think so.*

"We'll see how dinner goes," I said instead. "There's no sense in skirting around the issue. Tell me why you left."

Ethan leaned back in his chair and unbuttoned his suit jacket. "My therapist says I was having a midlife crisis."

"You're not even thirty," I pointed out. "When did you get a therapist?"

"Oh, you know, recently." He waved his hand at the answer like he wanted to push it aside. The man was lying through his teeth. I'd bet a year's salary that he'd never set foot in a therapist's office.

"I'm so proud of you for taking that step," I forced out. "I already know you went to the Caribbean."

"Yeah, I gave everything up and lived like a local. Life and *home* had gotten too stressful, and I kind of snapped and just took off. Traded corporate America for a simple life," Ethan effused. I caught him drumming his fingers impatiently on his thigh under the table.

I crossed my arms. "Yet you're back and looking every bit the executive."

"You know, money only goes so far." That was the real kicker. He'd blown through everything and came home expecting to live off what he thought I'd have.

"So you're broke."

I knew that would get him. Ethan scowled at me. "It'll only take a few clients to fill the bank account. More than you can say about your little job at the restaurant."

Ethan couldn't bait me into fighting with him. I wouldn't ever get answers from him. He was determined to gaslight me until he wormed his way back into my life. I couldn't believe I'd ever loved him.

I grabbed my purse and stood abruptly. "I just remembered I have to be somewhere else."

"What?" Ethan asked, agitated that I would consider leaving him there. "Where could you possibly need to be?"

"Anywhere but here with you," I snapped, flipping my hair over my shoulder. "You haven't changed one bit, and I don't know why I thought maybe you'd become a decent person in the last year."

"Macy, don't be stupid." He smacked his palm against the table. "Sit down and behave like an adult."

Anger heated my face. "I'll see you in court next week, Ethan."

I spun on my heels and walked away from Ethan with my head held high. There was nothing he could offer me anymore.

***

"Macy!" Leo rushed into my room Tuesday evening. "Get dressed!"

"Why? What's going on?" I asked, putting my e-reader down where I'd been huddled under my covers, getting lost in a book.

"I may or may not have been stalking Ethan a tiny bit," she admitted, wringing her hands.

It took a moment for her words to register. "What? Why? I told you I'm done with him."

"I know." Leo paced back and forth. "But he's slimy, and I was afraid he would do something to ruin it all."

I sat up, nervous. "And did he?"

"Not that I found."

I breathed a sigh of relief. "So, what's the big deal?"

"Something is hinky about the condo he's staying at," she explained. "Like he's hiding something. And since we're not doing anything else tonight, I figured we'd have a little adventure."

"I don't want to go look in Ethan's window as he jacks off," I said flatly.

"Oh, come on," Leo whined. "It'll be like when we stalked Jake McAlister and found out he was dating Emmie Larkin *and* Jade Johnson."

I giggled at the mention of our former classmate. "I still think it's funny Jade made a career out of her fans website. It's like her parents paved the way for her pornstar status."

"Yeah, hilarious. Focus." She snapped her fingers. "And find something black to wear because I've already ordered the Uber."

"Seriously? I was comfortable." I hauled myself out of bed anyway, pulling on a pair of black thermal leggings, a black long-sleeved shirt, and my leather jacket. There was no way I was sneaking around Portland in heels, so I slipped my sneakers on and tied them just as our ride arrived. "You owe me hot coffee after this."

"Deal." Leo led the way to the car, and I climbed in next to her.

We watched the city pass by until we entered an affluent and trendy neighborhood.

"Well, this is nice," I observed.

"Yeah, it's got to cost money." Leo agreed. "I don't think he's as broke as he led you to believe."

She might be on to something. We stood in the shadows outside Ethan's building, waiting for something to happen. Ten minutes turned to thirty, then an entire hour before my thermal leggings couldn't compete with the chill in the air.

"How long do you plan on standing out here?"

"I hadn't thought that far ahead." Leo rubbed her gloved hands together and jogged in place.

I looked around the quiet neighborhood. Nobody was out on the street late. "Somebody is going to call the cops on us."

"Do you still have that blood packet?"

"Leo, I am not going to pretend to have internal bleeding!" I whisper-yelled at her.

"Fine, I'll pretend I got my period or I'm free bleeding or something. That'll freak them out."

"Maybe we just don't stand outside all night and freak the residents out," I offered.

"Oh, shit!" Leo slapped her hand over her mouth. "Hide!"

She shoved me between two cars, and I whacked my knee on a bumper, muffling my swearing with my sleeve.

"What the fuck was that for?" I hissed at her.

"Shh!" She held a finger to her lips and opened her eyes wide.

"I thought we were going to a club after dinner," a woman whined down the sidewalk.

"It's Tuesday. The club was closed," came Ethan's voice. I perked up, leaning over next to Leo as I tried to see who Ethan was with. I might be done with the man, but that didn't mean I couldn't be pissed that he was with another woman.

"I think it's the blonde from the beach photo," Leo whispered, pulling her phone out and zooming in to take pictures.

I squinted as they came into view, confirming it was the woman from the Caribbean, then pulled out my phone and started recording. I'd thought of a way to ensure Ethan cooperated, and I wasn't above a bit of blackmail to make it work.

"I promise, as soon as I can figure out how to transfer the money back from the offshore accounts without getting hit with taxes, you will have every luxury," Ethan said to her.

"What about your wife?" the blonde asked. "Won't she notice all the money?"

"Macy knows nothing about money. I've convinced her I spent everything over the last year. She won't go snooping," Ethan assured her.

My body shook with rage at the way he spoke about me. I kept recording until they started making out, and Ethan pulled the woman through the lobby doors. A minute later, a light flipped on in a condo on the second floor, and Leo and I scurried around the car to avoid being noticed when Ethan stood shirtless at the window.

"Holy fuck," Leo breathed. "That man is an ass's asshole."

"I can't believe it," I said numbly. "I just thought he didn't love me. He hates me."

"He probably can't love anybody but himself," Leo concluded, pulling me to stand with her. We walked to the end of the block, and Leo ordered another Uber.

I played the video back. The street lights made it easy to see who was speaking, and Ethan's voice was clear on the recording. I grinned at Leo when the video ended and sent a copy to my email and her phone for good measure.

"Why are you so happy?" she asked dubiously.

I laughed, not caring who heard. "Because I'm about to be free."

Chapter Twenty-Nine

THE CHEF'S TABLE AT the L.A. location of *El Corazón Borikén* was booked every night of my visit. I spooned *arroz con gandules* onto plates next to *pernil*, then added *amarillos* because my diners loved them. I had the pleasure of serving Ana, one of my customers from the original location in Miami. Her husband Nolan booked her dinner at my table every night I was in town. She swore she never tired of my cooking because it reminded her of home, and she didn't have to prepare it.

"This looks amazing," Ana gushed when I set the plates in front of them. She leaned down and closed her eyes, holding her dark wavy hair back and breathing deeply. "There's nothing else like it."

"Are you sure I can't convince you to move down here?" Nolan asked, only half-joking. His light blonde hair and icy eyes made for an imposing presence when paired with his expensive navy suit. He ran the rival company to Julian's, and they had their own history, but since Luna was a friend of Nolan's, the two had put most of their differences behind them.

He ate, but his attention remained on his wife and the pleasure she took in her meal. I slipped away to prepare an extra lunch for them to take home because I knew Nolan would request it at the end of the meal. Last night, he'd offered to pay for me to move to L.A. and become a personal chef for his wife. I'd seriously consider the offer if things didn't work out with Macy. The restaurants would run fine without me for a bit.

Nolan leaned close to his wife and whispered something that made her blush as he stroked the back of her neck with his fingertips, playing with the delicate gold chain that hung there. I smiled to myself at the man's dedication. I hadn't known him before he was married, but I'd heard from Julian that he'd been a real asshole. You'd never know looking at him now. I guess love could really transform a person.

After I boxed the food up, I poured glasses of *coquito* and generous slices of *flancocho*. The dessert, a combination of flan and chocolate cake, was always on the menu in L.A. and Miami, but it hadn't taken off in the northern locations. People were missing out.

Ana clapped her hands when I presented them with the dessert. "Come on, Matteo, sit with us for a minute."

I didn't bother arguing with her. She'd hound me until I caved. I took a seat, leaning back and relaxing for a minute. I watched them eat their dessert and chuckled. "Are you sure you're not feeding two yet?"

"If I say yes, can I get another slice?" Ana asked slyly.

"You can have another slice either way," I said, motioning to the server on standby for the table. He brought another piece for both of my diners.

Ana finished the first piece and dove into the second. "Not pregnant. Never going to happen. I'm very happy being the only girl in Nolan's life."

Her husband smiled at her indulgently. "And you're more than enough for me."

"Hey! Be nice." Ana whacked him playfully on the arm before focusing on me again. "How about you? Anybody special in your life?"

"That depends on whether you've spoken to Bella recently," I said cautiously.

"I talked to her this morning," Ana answered with a grin.

I shook my head ruefully. "Then I suspect I don't need to tell you a thing because she's likely spilled the *gandules* all over already."

"Tell me about Macy," Ana said wistfully, resting her chin on her hand. "It sounds like a match made in culinary heaven, from what Bella said. I love a good love story."

"She's my sous chef," I said carefully. Fuck it; I might as well tell her. I launched into the story about how Macy and I met, then told Ana how amazing she was with the kids in my community classes and how she'd mastered all my recipes in no time.

"So you've met your soulmate," Ana concluded, her blue eyes sparkling.

"I hope so." I nodded. "She's got some personal things to work out, but I hope to know more by Christmas."

"By this time next year, you're going to be wearing a baby on your back in the kitchen," she predicted.

Nolan rolled his eyes and shot me a sympathetic look. "Ana, not everybody wants a big family. Riveras just breed like rabbits."

Ah, there was that hint of rivalry.

"I'm going to tell Bella you compared her to a rabbit," she threatened lightly. "Then you can deal with Chase. And when he calls to yell at you, convince him to bring Bella down one last time before she has the baby. Remind him you have an on-call doctor if she goes into labor while she's here."

"She'd better not go into labor in my house." Nolan looked a little green at the prospect of a home birth in his mansion.

"Anyway, I know Matteo wants babies," Ana explained to her husband. "Isn't that right?"

"I would like to have a family one day," I confirmed. "But I'm not sure about starting quite as soon as you hope. We're kind of on a break right now."

Ana sighed dramatically, and Nolan shot her a questioning look. She tipped her head to the side. "So, did you do something wrong?"

"What? No."

Nolan flattened his lips and looked at me sympathetically, but didn't attempt to step in and save me from Ana's questions.

"In my experience, men can be dense." She looked pointedly at her husband, and Nolan shrugged. "Was it a miscommunication?"

"No, there was plenty of communication." I briefly explained the situation with Macy's husband.

"Oh, well, that's a shame," she said dejectedly. "But I'm sure once everything is settled, things will pick back up for the two of you."

"I hope so," I admitted.

"You could always ask her to marry you," Ana suggested. "That's a good way to tell what direction she sees the relationship heading."

"Did you miss the part about her divorce still pending?" I asked, lifting my brows.

She waved dismissively. "By the time you go home, it will be over and done. Just make the proposal romantic. Women love a sappy proposal."

"Do you think my proposal was *sappy*?" Nolan asked with a cold edge to his voice.

Ana giggled. "No, I think your proposal was perfect, and I wouldn't have it any other way."

"Which one? You made me ask twice."

"You didn't even ask the first time. You just put the ring on my finger and declared us engaged.," she admonished. "Just take the compliment."

Nolan scratched his chin thoughtfully. "If you propose, make sure you actually say the words."

"Thanks, I'll try to remember that," I said dryly.

The conversation devolved from there, and when Ana yawned, Nolan stood and told her it was time to head home. I handed them their food, and Nolan left the staff a few hundred dollars' cash on the table. I enjoyed working in L.A., but my heart was still in Portland with Macy.

***

I woke to my alarm on Monday morning and stumbled out of bed, determined to caffeinate until I could see straight. I'd usually go for a run and then meet the Riveras at the coffee shop, but I didn't feel much like running this morning. The last time I felt so down was when *Abuelita* died, which bothered me since Macy was very much alive.

I tried to focus on the good that had come out of our relationship, but none of it seemed to matter if everything was temporary. My fingers itched to pick up the phone and call her, but I'd told myself I would give Macy all the space she needed to process the overwhelming amount of shit happening in her life. Had I made a mistake?

Regret was a sharp blade to my heart, but deep down, I knew Macy wouldn't be the only one with unanswered questions if I hadn't given her space. I would have wondered whether she was only staying with me because she felt guilty. So, as much as our distance ate at me, it was necessary.

I turned the shower on and stepped under the scalding water, bracing my hand on the white subway tiles and staring at the water as it swirled around the drain like thoughts of Macy swirled around my head. I could see how she smiled at me in the morning with her lips pressed together, afraid of opening her mouth before she brushed her teeth, how her blonde hair fanned over my pillow, and how she purred when I raked my fingertips through her hair and massaged her scalp.

My cock hardened, and I fisted my length, pumping slowly, trying to mimic how she touched me. The veins stood out prominently over my darkened flesh. I never told her, but her hands were always cold when she started, and I missed that. I knew how to get myself off, but Macy's touch reached deep inside and dragged some fundamental element of my being out, melding us on a deeper level than simple lust.

Her touch was a language of love, each stroke unspoken words with meaning I instinctively understood. It was the same when I touched her, our bodies dancing together as humanity had from its inception. Pressure built at the base of my cock, and I closed my eyes, drawing upon memories of Macy on her knees before me, the corners of her mouth tugging up in a smile as she kept me on the edge before sucking me down. My other hand moved downward, and I leaned my forehead against the shower wall, squeezing my balls and sending my release spurting from the tip of my dick down the drain.

I was going to call her.

No. I shouldn't. I needed to get to the restaurant and distract myself. I washed quickly and climbed out of the shower, drying off and styling my hair before pulling on my uniform pants and a plain white t-shirt. My phone rang as I shoved my feet into socks, and I looked over to see Xander's name on the screen. I cringed because Xander never called to chat.

I reached for my phone and swiped my thumb across the screen, answering and tapping to activate the speaker phone. "Hey, man. What's up?"

"I've been appointed the family liaison," he said gruffly. He was using his professional voice, which set me on edge. "The *collective* would like to know what the hell you're doing down in L.A. when Christmas is less than two weeks away."

"I'm checking in on the restaurant," I lied. Technically, it wasn't a big lie since I was working at *El Corazón Borikén.*

"You haven't traveled to the other locations in six months," he observed.

Of course, they'd choose the lawyer for this cross-examination. "Right, so it was about time I checked on things."

He grunted, and I heard Viola murmuring something in the background. "The *collective* would like to know whether you'll be coming home for Christmas and New Year."

"I'll fly in the day before Christmas," I explained. "Depending on things, I might visit the other restaurants after the New Year."

There was a commotion on the other end of the line, and I heard Xander growl something about a spanking before Viola's breathless voice filtered down the line. "You have to come back. She's not going back to her husband."

"Good morning, Vi," I greeted her, ignoring her comment. "How's my niece or nephew?"

"Kicking up a storm and taking up the space my lungs and bladder used to occupy," she quipped back. "Now, about Macy. I ran into her at the coffee shop again."

"How is she?" I asked before I thought better of it.

"A wreck, obviously," Viola said. "I guess she had some disaster with that asshole ex, but after a few choice words, she sounded completely certain that the marriage would be dissolved next week. So you need to come home."

I sighed, running a hand through my hair, thoughtlessly mussing it. "I told her I was going to give her space. I'll come back when I said."

There was more bickering, and I heard Viola huff, then her voice from further away like she was leaving, as Xander chuckled before taking the phone back. "She invited Macy to Christmas. And our New Year's celebration."

"Of course she did." It was just like Viola to reach out and interfere when she thought it was for a good cause.

"I just thought you might like a heads up about what you're returning to."

"I appreciate it," I said gratefully.

"I've got to get to the office." Xander cleared his throat. "I'll see you at Christmas. Pull your head out of your ass before then."

The line went dead, and I stared at my phone for a moment. It could be fate telling me that my feelings were valid and reciprocated. My fingers tapped open the messages from Macy and hovered over the keys.

Good morning, ariete.

Too casual.

I miss you. Hope you're not burning down the restaurant.

No.

Ultimately, I couldn't bring myself to send anything, and my last message sat in the draft window as I pocketed my phone.

I love you.

Chapter Thirty

A FINE DUSTING OF snow coated the sidewalk outside the courthouse as I approached to meet my lawyer and see the judge for the divorce finalization. I'd waited for this day to arrive, and my heart raced with anticipation of the taste of freedom—from my past, Ethan, and the limbo I'd been living in for more than a year. I was ready to move forward with my life.

My breath plumed out in a white cloud as I inhaled deeply, then opened the door and searched for the correct room on the board in front of the elevator bank. As I stepped onto the elevator, I pulled my leather gloves off and tucked them into the pocket of my navy wool peacoat. On the off-chance Ethan decided to show up today, I'd donned clothes from my past—a white blouse and navy pencil skirt—so I wouldn't look out of place next to his high-end style. My navy heels clicked on the floor as I went down the hall after exiting the elevator.

My lawyer, Marylin, stood outside the room. "Macy, nice to see you again. Why don't we go inside? We're first up this morning."

I trailed behind her into the nearly empty courtroom. It looked so different from on tv, more like a converted conference room than a courtroom. Just the knowledge that it was a place where law and order were upheld had my palms sweating, and I hadn't even done anything wrong. And yes, I was also that person who slowed down if they saw a cop car, regardless of whether I was going the speed limit. I was an excellent rule follower.

Not five minutes later, Ethan walked in with a lawyer dressed just as well as him. They looked like they'd coordinated their black suits and green ties. He was clean-shaven now, with no hint of that stylish stubble he's sported for dinner on his chiseled jaw. As conventionally attractive as Ethan was, the arrogance that dripped from his posture and the disdain that coated his features made him repulsive to me.

He smirked at me from across the aisle, offering a cocky head nod when I glanced over. The man was so sure he'd get out of paying me anything. I'd glanced over the response his lawyer drafted and the outright lies he'd told about having to support me. Little did he realize I'd kept impeccable financial records. He used to mock me for scanning checks and receipts into my budgeting app. It all came in handy because my lawyer's staff had added up exactly how much I'd paid for Ethan's education and our bills over the years.

Out of the corner of my eye, I saw Leo slip into the back row. When Ethan turned, she flipped him the bird and made a threatening gesture that the deputy by the door missed. Ethan's eyes widened, then narrowed in haughty disdain.

The deputy announced the judge, and we stood as she took her seat and brought the court to order. She went over the details of my petition, including the spousal support, division of assets and debt, and my request to change back to my maiden surname. I carefully schooled my face as she read through Ethan's response and the lies.

"Mr. Smith," the judge addressed Ethan's lawyer. "You must know your client's information varies greatly from every bit of physical evidence provided by Mrs. Hart. This court does not appreciate your response, which amounts to little more than carefully worded obfuscation and thinly veiled lies."

I hated hearing my married name, but it was worth watching Ethan's lawyer blunder his way through his response to the judge. She had no patience for his excuses and attempts to buy them more time.

"I am not inclined to rule in your client's favor based on the evidence. He shirked his responsibilities and left Mrs. Hart to deal with the financial and emotional fallout. Based on the hidden bank accounts revealed in discovery and the video evidence provided by Mrs. Hart's counsel, I'm ready to read my ruling if you have nothing else to say for the record."

Ethan leaned toward his counsel and whispered angrily, but his lawyer shrugged in response. As much as I would have liked to blackmail Ethan, I followed my moral compass and reached out to Bella for her husband Chase's help. His team dug up more carefully covered dirt and reached out to some of their government contacts about Ethan's questionable activities. I turned the video evidence of Ethan's tax evasion over to my lawyer to present to the court. From what I could hear across the aisle, Ethan hadn't taken his lawyer seriously when they received a copy. He believed himself untouchable. Vindication was sweet.

"Mrs. Seth," the judge addressed my lawyer. "I'm ruling in favor of everything you submitted on behalf of Mrs. Hart."

I felt my breath catch as she read off the long list of requests and awarded me all three forms of spousal support Marylin requested based on my financial contribution throughout the marriage. She also saddled Ethan with all of our debt. Everything had been in his name.

Marylin handed me a tissue when I lost my composure as the judge granted my name change and completed her judgment of the dissolution of my marriage.

"Good luck, Ms. Davis," she said, using my maiden name. I hiccoughed my thanks, and she turned to Ethan. "Mr. Hart, there's an agent outside who would like to speak with you."

The judge punctuated her final decree with the gavel, and the air rushed from my lungs as the weight of my dissolved marriage lifted from my shoulders. I braced my hands against the table and lowered my head, feeling lightheaded when I stood. My lawyer patted me on the back and congratulated me.

Leo squealed quietly and rushed forward, wrapping me in a tight hug and rocking back and forth. "You did it! I've got champagne in the fridge at home. I'm going to buy you breakfast, brunch, or lunch—whatever the hell you want—and we'll drink for the rest of the day."

I couldn't help but laugh through my tears of relief. She tugged my hand and took me to wait for a copy of my divorce decree. Ethan stood outside with his lawyer as a man in a suit, wearing a badge, spoke to him. I couldn't muster a fuck to give that he was reaping what he sowed.

Once I received the decree, I held the envelope close to my chest as we left the building. "Is it weird that I want to frame this like a diploma? Proof that I survived all the shit Ethan put me through. It's really over now, isn't it?"

"Yeah, it is. I'll buy you the frame." Leo laughed and held the door for me, stopping outside and looking up. "It's snowing."

So it was. I spun in a circle, arms outstretched and tongue out to catch the fat snowflakes floating down from the sky. Leo and I laughed like children, and I felt genuine joy. The future was looking up.

***

Leo stayed true to her word. She took me shopping and bought me a pair of skin-tight vegan leather pants to celebrate. When we returned home, she opened bottle after bottle of champagne and ordered food so we could sit around and talk about all the possibilities for life now that I was unencumbered by Ethan. I'd managed to crawl up the stairs to bed and collapse into a dreamless state of unconsciousness for the first time in weeks. It had been worth it to have that emotional release. This morning I'd awoken with a wicked hangover and a healthy amount of hope.

Leo made strong coffee and handed me under-eye gels to help combat all the swelling my sobbing caused before she headed home to spend the holiday with her family. I'd moved slowly, eating a bit of toast until my stomach was steady enough for scrambled eggs.

My morning passed quickly, watching holiday movies with all the curtains pulled and the Christmas lights turned on. I napped in the early afternoon, then decided to be more productive by showering. I stood naked and stared at myself in the mirror, wondering if I looked as different as I felt. Since I was alone in the house, I didn't bother getting dressed until I'd styled my hair and applied makeup.

When I squeezed my hips into the pants and found a festive red sweater to pair with it, I didn't even need Leo to tell me how hot I looked. I borrowed her red lipstick and smiled, doing a little dance and pouring myself a shot of whiskey, then another. I needed the liquid courage because I was about to take what I wanted.

After donning my outerwear and grabbing my purse, I hopped on transit and headed to Matteo's apartment building, texting Luna for the code to the elevator when I arrived. She was in on my little plan, and it was a wonder she hadn't blabbed to all the other women in the family.

I took a deep breath as I stepped off the elevator onto Matteo's floor and approached his door, decorated with a wreath gifted to him by the parents of one of the kids that attended his culinary class. I didn't hesitate to reach out and rap out a pattern with my knuckles.

It took a minute, but finally, the lock turned, and the door swung open, revealing Matteo in a black long-sleeved shirt and jeans, his hair mussed like he'd been running his fingers through it and eyes tired. I wondered if he'd had as much trouble sleeping as I had without his presence.

He looked surprised to see me. "Hey."

"Hi, I thought I'd come and introduce myself," I said, holding out my divorce decree. I felt a twinge of uncertainty as I continued. "I'm Macy Davis. Newly legally single, but hopefully still taken."

Matteo grinned and pulled me to his chest, embracing me tightly. I burrowed my cold nose against him, breathed in his woodsy scent, then pressed my ear to his chest to listen to his voice rumble as he spoke. "It's nice to meet you, Macy Davis. I feel like we've known each other forever."

Warmth flooded my body at his words, and my breath hitched. "Me, too. And hopefully forevermore. You offered me a life with you before. If the offer is still good, I'm here to take you up on that."

"It never expires." He released me and took my hand, dragging me into his apartment as I shoved the divorce decree back into my purse. "I was making dinner. Are you hungry?"

"I could eat." I nodded and sniffed the air. "Chicken? Is that a Christmas Eve tradition?"

"It's easy," he countered. "I figured I'd eat light since I'll gain ten pounds at Xander's place tomorrow."

"Right." I remembered what he'd said about the dinner there. "The famous Rivera family Christmas feast. I snagged myself an invitation to that, you know. I might need a plus one."

"That's convenient." He pulled my hips to his and lowered to kiss me.

I'd missed the feel of Matteo's lips against mine. I stood on tiptoe, sliding my fingers around his neck and holding him to me, savoring the taste of his tongue on mine. Reluctantly, I let him go when the oven timer went off.

He pulled what looked like half a pot pie out, set it on the stove to cool, and then turned to me with heated eyes. His gaze raked down my body. "How hungry are you?"

"Very, but not for the pot pie," I answered. "I think it'll take a while to cool, don't you?"

"Absolutely." Matteo was on me in a flash, devouring my lips and leading me backward across the apartment until we reached the bedroom. He lifted me and wrapped my legs around his waist. I held on tightly as he carried me to the bed and lowered his body over mine. "Fuck, I've missed you so much."

I looked into his eyes. "I've missed you too, and I'm so sorry for everything."

He pressed a finger to my lips. "Don't apologize. I don't fault you. I'm just happy you're here now."

I felt the evidence of his desire press against my mound and shifted my hips against him, making his eyes drift closed and his mouth open with a sigh. I needed to be closer to him. "It's been too long. Make love to me, Matteo. Please?"

Chapter Thirty-One

MY DECISION TO SKIP the Rivera's Christmas Eve dinner was reinforced as Macy ground her hips against mine. I braced my forearms on either side of her head and sipped at her lips, momentarily content with kissing her.

Soon enough, I explored her body as if for the first time again, slowly stripping her out of her sweater and finding a hot little black lace bra underneath. "One day, I want to see you walk around here wearing only this bra and these pants. Maybe some black heels. *Fuck*, you're sexy."

Macy giggled and shimmied her shoulders, making those bountiful breasts bounce enticingly. She didn't have to ask twice. I reached behind her and unclasped the bra, drawing it down her arms and flinging it haphazardly across the room in the direction the sweater had gone. When I bent, Macy pressed my face between her breasts, and I was in heaven. I could have breathed in her floral scent all day while my head was pillowed between those two plump globes.

Shifting slightly, I flicked her nipple with my tongue and sucked the little peak into my mouth. She gyrated under me as I lavished attention on her nipples, then kissed my way down to the waist of her tight leather-like pants. I peeled them down her legs, leaving her black lace thong in place, then kissed my way back up to her mound, nipping lightly and pulling her underwear, so it created friction against her clit.

"Matteo," she panted. "Stop stalling."

"I'm not stalling," I said, running my fingers down the lace. "I'm taking my time with you so I can remember everything about the moment you were mine alone."

"I've been yours," she insisted.

"I know, but it's a possessive male thing." I shrugged and pulled the thong to the side, skimming my fingers over her opening and spreading her fluids up to dampen her clit. "You're so fucking wet for me. I love it. I can't wait to feel you soak my cock when I'm deep in your tight pussy."

"Please," she begged, trying to pull me closer. Her face was beautifully flushed, and my kisses left her lips swollen. "I promise we can do it all night if you move faster *now*."

I chuckled, enjoying tormenting her with pleasure. "Oh, we'll do it all night. But I'm a starving man, and I want to feast now."

I used my teeth to pull her underwear off, inhaling before shooting them across the room like a slingshot and making Macy laugh. That laughter turned strangled as I dove between her legs, sucking and nibbling, then parting her lips to taste her arousal. I groaned, forgetting for a moment that I wanted to go slow, and thrust my tongue into her pussy, pulsing and curling it to lap up every bit I could get.

"Your taste. I can't get enough of you, Macy."

"I promise you can have me for one meal a day," she giggled. "If you keep doing that, I'll even cook you a meal with food every day."

"Hmm," I hummed against her, making her buck her hips when my lips latched onto her clit and sucked it until it was hard under my tongue. I flicked it rapidly and slid two fingers into her center, twisting and reaching that place that made her shriek. "That's it. Tell me how much you love my fingers in your pussy, Macy."

"*So much*," she moaned, threading her fingers through my hair, her nails raking across my scalp and making my cock threaten to burst through the zipper of my jeans. "*Oh, fuck*, Matteo. Don't stop. I'll come."

I sucked her clit harder and moved my fingers firmly enough against her g-spot that my wrist ached until she clenched, her orgasm making her muscles ripple around my fingers. "That's it, *ariete*. Come all over my fingers."

In a flash, I'd withdrawn my fingers and frantically stripped out of my clothes, snagging a condom from the nightstand and rolling it down my length. Macy wrapped her arms around me as I filled her in one smooth glide.

"Oh," she moaned, her muscles still fluttering. "Don't hold back."

"You want to take all of my thick cock, Macy?" I thrust in hard, making her cry out. The sensation of her hot channel enveloping me was nearly overwhelming. I wasn't going to last long. "Feel that? I can feel the back of you against the head of my cock. You're gripping me so hard."

She flexed her muscles in response, and I almost fell on her. "Can you feel that?"

"Yeah," I gasped as she did it again. Her pussy was magic. That had to be it. "Feels so fucking good."

I shifted, kneeling with my back to the headboard. Macy climbed on top, and I held my dick as she lowered herself over it. "I'm so deep in you. One day, I'm going to fill your sweet pussy with all of my hot come."

"Fuck," Macy whispered, grinding against me. "Say it again."

I grabbed her hips and slammed her down on my length. "I'm going to pump you so full of my come that it drips down your thighs, and I'll make you walk around in nothing but one of my shirts so I can use my fingers to shove it back inside you, make you keep it there like a good girl."

Macy cried out as another orgasm made her collapse against me. I took control, thrusting up into her until I found my release. I wrapped my arms around her and held her like that, keeping her as close to me as possible.

"I never want to let you go," I whispered against her hair.

"Then don't," she breathed against my neck and pressed little kisses against my sensitive skin. "Keep me."

***

Macy and I walked hand-in-hand through Xander's door, only to be greeted by boisterous cheers from everybody inside. I'd sent a warning text ahead of our arrival and specifically asked them not to make a big deal of Macy's presence, but what was family if they didn't completely disregard your wishes occasionally so they could celebrate?

"Matteo! Macy!" Viola waddled forward as fast as her burgeoning belly would allow, hugging us both from the side. "We missed you last night, but I'm so glad you could make it today!"

"I wouldn't have missed it for anything," Macy said in return. "I've heard all about your Christmas traditions."

"It's a bit much," Bella said from my other side. "But I can promise you won't leave hungry or sober."

Macy giggled, and the women pulled her away from me to the kitchen, where they were all cooking together. They were bringing her right into the fold as one of their own.

"I see you worked things out," Xander said with a nod as I kicked my shoes off in the entry.

"Yeah. Things are good now."

"Well, then, let's celebrate." He led the way to the living room, where the other men were sitting, and handed me a beer. It was barely noon, but Christmas day was filled with various food and alcohol. If Bella and Viola weren't pregnant, they'd be making mimosas for the wives.

The smells of the holidays permeated every inch of Xander's expansive home. Everybody snacked on *quesitos*, *tostones*, and my contribution—*coquito* empanadas. The sweet cream inside tasted just like the drink but without the alcohol.

Gabriel's daughter flitted around wearing her birthday crown and waving a fairy wand, telling everybody she was sharing her birthday as a Christmas gift. Macy knelt for the little girl so she could dub her the *big chef birthday girl*. I could see her doing the same for our daughter one day. Julian's son Adrian climbed onto my lap and offered me a partially gnawed *quesito*. "Want some *Tio* 'Teo?"

"No, thanks, little man. I'm waiting for all the food the girls are making."

"Mama makes 'roz con 'dules," he explained earnestly. He already displayed some of his father's personality traits.

"I bet hers is the best," I said, brushing crumbs from my dark green dress shirt.

Adrian nodded. "Uh-huh."

And just like that, he was off again, distracted by what his cousins were doing with blocks by the fire.

"It looks good on you," Chase spoke up from the chair next to me, pointing to the kids. "You'll make a good father."

"Which one of them paid you to say that?" I asked with a laugh.

"My wife," he admitted readily. "But I'm an excellent judge of people, and I agree. Same for Macy as a mother."

"She wants kids," I said absentmindedly.

"Yeah." Chase nodded. "I give it a month before the girls give her baby fever. Something about newborns flips a switch. And then we get that."

He pointed to Bella and Viola, who had her hand pressed against Bella's stomach.

"Sit, sit!" Maria Rivera called out, bustling through the living room and using a kitchen towel to whack all the men with frightening accuracy. It didn't take long for us to sit around the table and listen to Marcos say the blessing.

"Here we go again," Macy muttered as I handed her a plate piled high with food. "I shouldn't have eaten breakfast. Or dinner last night."

"I think we burned off those calories," I whispered. "But I'd be happy to help later if you'd like."

"You're going to have to roll me out of here at the end of the day," she said as she shoveled a bite of *mofongo* into her mouth.

I grinned. "I can roll you onto our bed later."

Macy sipped on her red wine. "Deal."

For once, Maria didn't set out to embarrass anybody during the meal. Instead, she told stories of Christmases in Puerto Rico because some of the women hadn't visited yet. Macy leaned forward with a serene smile, absorbing every word. I would take her to my country one day to experience everything firsthand.

After the meal, we gathered on the massive couches in the living room, pulling additional seating from the area by the fire. The kids played and eventually napped, and the adults played board games. I quickly learned that Macy was competitive.

"Take that!" she exclaimed as she jumped four of my pieces on the checkerboard. "I win again!"

I froze, trying to process what had happened. "You never mentioned you've played before."

"So you thought I was an easy mark?" She asked, arching a brow. "Leo and I used to sleep over at each other's houses most weekends. We've played games all day on more Saturdays than I could count. My Uno game is unmatched."

I chuckled and reset the checkerboard for the next players. "I'll remember to avoid that one, then."

"I want you on my team when we play charades," Viola called out. "Only winners allowed."

"You created a monster," I accused Xander. "Why did you let her play?"

"She's more persuasive than you," he said, reaching out and pulling his wife onto his lap.

I shook my head. There was no way I was competing with that.

Macy stood and stretched, her sweater pulling taut across her chest and drawing my eyes to my favorite pillows. She pointed toward the kitchen. "I'm going to go grab a snack. Want anything while I'm up?"

You, I thought. "Thanks, but I'm good."

I watched her walk off and pushed myself off the floor. My knees popped, reminding me I wasn't as young as I once was.

Bella approached and handed me a small piece of greenery. "I had Chase get what you asked for."

"Thanks."

She patted my cheek and gave me a peck. "Good luck."

I took the mistletoe and followed Macy as the others quietly watched. I watched as she took the *mofongo* out of the microwave, testing the temperature with her finger. She nodded, pulled a fork out of the drawer, then turned and saw me standing there.

"Oh! Did you want some?" she asked, pointing to the plate. "I can heat more, or we can share."

"I'd like to share," I said with a smile, and she turned back to grab another fork. I took a step closer and held the mistletoe above her head.

Macy looked up and giggled. "Mistletoe?"

"'Tis the season," I said with a shrug. "Share those lips with me."

She closed her eyes and tilted her head. As I kissed her softly, I pulled the little black box from my pocket. When she opened her eyes, I held the ring out and set the mistletoe on the counter.

"This seems fitting." I pointed to the *mofongo* and the sprig of greenery. "Mistletoe and *mofongo*. Hope and home."

Macy's eyes misted when she realized what was happening. "*Matteo*."

I wanted to remember exactly how she breathed my name.

"You're mine, Macy Davis," I began. Everything I'd rehearsed flew out of my mind, and it left me with whatever my heart wanted to speak. "You asked me to keep you. The months we've known each other have felt like a lifetime."

"Well, that's not what a girl wants to hear," she said wryly.

I tried to recover. "I mean that in the best way. It feels like I've known you forever. We're in sync with everything we do. I love that grumpy face you make."

"Hey!" she crossed her arms and frowned.

"Yeah, that one right there."

The corners of her mouth turned up in a smile, and her blue eyes sparkled.

"And I love that I can turn that frown upside down." I continued, getting down on one knee and wishing I'd chosen to propose on carpet or grass as the tile made my knees ache. "I know my timing is probably off, and this isn't a romantic setting, but *Abuelita* always said the heart knows what it wants, and my heart wants you, Macy. I think yours wants me, too. Will you marry me?"

"Yes, Matteo." Macy nodded. "*Yes*, I'll marry you. My heart is yours as much as yours is mine."

I slipped the modest diamond ring onto her finger. It fit perfectly. "It was my grandmother's."

"I love it," she choked out. "I'm going to cry now. I hate crying."

"It's okay to cry," I whispered, grasping the back of her neck and pulling her to me for a kiss. I tasted the joy in her tears and felt my own trickle down to mingle with hers where our lips met. *So that was what it's like to taste forever.*

Somebody sighed behind us, and I reluctantly pulled away, using my sleeve to dab away Macy's tears before mopping up mine. I sniffed and turned to face my found family, holding Macy's hand up. "She said yes!"

Their collective cheer was deafening, but Macy and I laughed. Phone cameras flashed, and we posed for photos before Maria pushed through the crowd. She grasped Macy's hands and kissed her on each cheek. "Welcome to my family, Macy. *Mi hija*."

Chapter Thirty-Two

"I'M GOING TO VOMIT." I slapped a hand over my mouth and breathed slowly through my nose. Leo rubbed my back in small circles.

"I have mints!" Viola called from across the room, holding up candies in green and yellow wrappers. "I also have ginger candies, though that might make for a less than lovely first kiss."

"But he might give her a fun nickname like *gingersnap*," Leo quipped.

Nope, that wouldn't do. I pointed to the green candies, and Viola handed me a few. I unwrapped one and popped it in my mouth, the relief almost immediate.

"He already has a name for her," Bella said. "Though, I don't understand it."

"Wait, do you know what he calls me?" I blurted out, momentarily distracted from my roiling stomach. "He's never told me."

Bella laughed. "He's probably afraid you'll smack him."

"He gave me the name after I nearly broke his nose," I admitted reluctantly. "He has a habit of waiting until he's nearly touching me to let me know how close he is, and it's a reflex."

The women around me laughed, and Bella clapped. "I love it. Never apologize. It makes much more sense now since he's calling you a ram. Maybe a battering ram?"

"Seriously?" I flushed with embarrassment, and another wave of nausea hit. "Ugh."

"Are you pregnant?" Viola asked. The entire room fell silent, and four Rivera women and Leo stared at me expectantly.

"No, not a chance."

Jane spoke up from where she sat. "Are you sure? Sometimes it's hard to tell, especially if you've been under a lot of stress."

"Yeah, I'm sure."

"Have you taken a test?" Bella asked, unwrapping another mint for me. I popped it in my mouth.

"No, I haven't because I'm not pregnant." They still looked skeptical. "Look, I've had my period since Thanksgiving. We didn't do it again until Christmas Eve, and we've always used protection, so the nausea isn't from pregnancy. It's getting worse the longer you look at me like that, though."

"Sorry." Viola backed away. "We just like babies."

"I still think he's going to breed you," Leo said indelicately.

I dropped my face to my palm out of embarrassment—partly because of Leo and partly because I liked the idea. "Don't start taking bets on nieces and nephews yet."

Leo grinned. "With the size of your family, we'd have a whole underground betting ring."

"Why have we not thought of this already?" Bella asked the others. "Next baby, we're taking bets."

"Call me when that happens," Leo said, poking her in the shoulder. "I've got some ideas for how you can team up and beat those boys."

"It had better not involve fake blood," I warned. Leo just smirked at me and motioned locking her lips and throwing the key away.

"How are you feeling?" Viola asked, handing me another candy. I took that one, too, figuring it couldn't hurt to keep a baseline of mint to stave off the nerves.

"Better, thanks."

"Okay, let's get you into your dress, then." She and Leo held up my simple white gown, and I stepped into it, letting them preen over me.

It was a long-sleeved mermaid-style creation that dipped low in the front and back, hugged my curves, and sparkled in the light. A New Year's Eve wedding allowed me to add a little flash. Matteo's tux was black and sparkly to match.

I checked myself out in the floor-length mirror and was shocked by my reflection. My curves were killer, and my hair was curled into waves, teased for volume, and pinned back on one side in an old Hollywood style.

"I've never worn anything so beautiful," I breathed. I'd been young and poor for my first wedding, so I bought a bargain prom dress and did the alterations myself. It had been pretty enough, but it didn't compare to what I wore now. Bella insisted on making my gown on short notice once she heard what I envisioned, and I was so grateful because she'd blown us away with the finished product. I ran my hand carefully down the sleek fabric. "This is incredible, Bella. Thank you."

"Don't mention it." She waved her hand in the air. "I knew it would be perfect for you."

They wore silver sequined gowns of their choice since it was nearly impossible to find bridesmaid dresses on short notice. I hadn't seen what the Rivera men were wearing, but they probably all owned black tuxes, given the events they attended for work.

There was a tap on the door, and Claudia, Xander's housekeeper, popped her head into the bedroom we were using to get dressed. "Is everybody ready? The priest has arrived."

The women all looked at me, and my stomach lurched again. I thought of Matteo, and calm washed over me. "I'm ready."

I slipped into my white sequined heels and stood, walking carefully, so I didn't trip on the short train. The others descended before me when we reached the top of the stairs. Nobody could see me until I came around the bottom of the staircase, so I paused and took deep breaths, finding things to count.

My mind kept choosing Matteo. His scent. What I imagined he'd look like in his tuxedo. The sound of his heartbeats when I lay my head on his chest. The feel of his kitchen scars. How his lips tasted. I took a deep breath and turned the corner, my eyes finding him immediately.

The living room had been transformed; all the furniture was removed, and the tree re-decorated in white and silver. The entire room looked like a winter dream, with flocked garland and matching décor. You'd never know it had been decorated for Christmas only days before.

Soft instrumental music played, and Marcos took my arm, leading me down the aisle. My parents hadn't cared enough to come. They were still angry that I'd divorced Ethan—the hypocrites—but I was done trying to please everybody but me. Matteo made me happy and loved me as I deserved.

Even now, his eyes shone with pride, love, and adoration as I approached. I barely heard the priest's words to Marcos as he gave me away in place of my father. The Rivera family was my family.

"You look beautiful," Matteo whispered as he took my hands in his. "I'm the most fortunate man in the world."

"And I'm the luckiest woman to have a man like you," I whispered back.

The priest began the ceremony, and we repeated traditional vows. When we were pronounced man and wife, Matteo pointed up. Above us, mistletoe hung, waiting for us to seal our vows with our first kiss as a married couple.

"Hope and home," Matteo whispered, carefully working his hand under my hair.

"Hope and home," I repeated.

Our lips met softly, sensually, laden with the promise of a future life lived with love and happiness. When we pulled apart, I held Matteo's gaze, and we stood transfixed by each other for a moment before somebody in our small audience applauded. Leo handed me my white roses and mistletoe bouquet, and we posed for pictures Xander and Viola gifted us.

I couldn't taper my smile and wouldn't have wanted to. They were our first photos as a family, and I would cherish them forever. Maria fussed over everybody and insisted on adding three additional poses, but we made it through.

After, we ate finger foods because I'd insisted we keep the wedding small. We'd have to return for the Rivera New Year's Day celebration the following afternoon. By eight, Matteo led me to his truck under a shower of white biodegradable confetti. We returned to our apartment before the ball dropped in Times Square. He picked me up and carried me over the threshold, tickling my sides and making me giggle before he set me down inside.

"Do you need anything?" Matteo asked as he untied his dress shoes and removed his tuxedo jacket. He was far more comfortable in a chef's uniform than in a fancy suit.

"Just you," I replied, stroking my hand down his white shirt. I unbuttoned it, exposing the tattoos scrawled across his skin and kissing my way down until I reached the last button. I didn't even pause, just quickly unbuckled his belt and released his throbbing erection into my hand.

"*Macy.*"

I could listen to Matteo say my name forever. I took the head of his cock into my mouth, licking and sucking, paying attention to the sensitive ridge around the edge. He groaned, and I pulled him deeper, letting him graze the back of my throat before pulling away and sucking harder.

"Fuck," he swore through clenched teeth. "You have no idea how hot it is to watch you take my cock between your red lips. I hope you stain my dick because I want to look down and see your marks in the morning."

I worked him faster, tugging his tuxedo pants down his thighs further so I could cup his balls. He jumped, then moaned. I could tell he was close when his cock swelled in my mouth, and he tried to buck his hips.

"Macy, I'm going to come." Matteo groaned when I pulled gently on his balls, rolling and tugging as I hollowed my mouth around his cock until my jaw ached. "Yeah, like that. *Ohh*, yes. You going to swallow my come like my good girl?"

"*Mmm*," I answered, nodding around his length, redoubling my efforts. I tasted the first salty spurts of his release on my tongue and held his hips close, so his come shot down my throat, and he could feel me swallow around the head of his cock.

When Matteo's knees buckled, and he pulled my hair to stay upright, I released him with a pop, a string of mixed come and saliva stringing from the tip of his cock to my lips.

"I don't know what I ever did to deserve you, but I'm never letting you go," he said, pulling me to my feet and kissing his release from my lips. "I love the taste of me on your tongue."

"Want to taste something else now?" I asked suggestively, swaying my hips.

"You will *never* have to beg me to lick your sweet pussy," Matteo said, palming my mound. When I laughed, he continued. "I'm serious, Macy. Never be afraid to ask me to touch you, taste you, fuck you. There is no other woman in this universe—only you."

"Thank you," I whispered, my voice raspy from taking his cock down my throat. I couldn't take the emotion that threatened to drown me, as grateful as I was for his words. Words I didn't even know I needed to hear. "I think I'd like to eat something else off you."

"Oh, you would, would you?" Matteo smirked and touched his finger to the tip of my nose. "I have something on hand, just in case."

He jogged the short distance to the refrigerator and pulled out a metal canister, waving it in the air.

"Is that homemade whipped cream?" I asked, impressed.

"Sure is," he said with a grin. "We can have food fun on demand. I even snagged a pack of wipes from Xander to be safe."

I paused, startled. "You told Xander you needed sex wipes?"

"Not in so many words." Matteo shrugged dismissively. "It's not like they don't know we're going to have sex."

"Logically, I know that," I said. "But another part of me doesn't want people to know what we do in our private lives."

"You haven't talked to Bella enough yet, then," Matteo said with a cryptic laugh.

I fisted my hands on my hips. I hated being left out of the loop after all of the lies I'd endured in the past decade. "What is that supposed to mean?"

"Her husband, Chase, owns kink clubs."

"What?" The word came out high-pitched and squeaky with my surprise. I cleared my throat. "Really?"

"Yeah, it's not a secret," Matteo said dismissively. "I'm sure you'll hear about it, eventually."

"Wait." I held up a hand. "Do you go to these clubs?"

Matteo laughed until he had to brace his hands on his knees. "No, *ariete*, I'd much prefer to keep you to myself at home."

"Battering ram, *hmm*?"

Matteo froze with the whipped cream in hand. "Who told you?"

"Bella," I answered smugly.

"Fuck, it's starting already," he lamented with a hand over his face, slipping into Spanish.

"You didn't expect to bring me into the family and not have me acclimate fully, did you?"

"I might have hoped it would take more than a couple of weeks," Matteo admitted, closing the distance between us and grasping my chin. "But I wouldn't have it any other way."

He kissed me hard and ushered me to the bedroom, where he pulled the package of wipes from the nightstand and tossed them onto the bed. "I want to fuck you in this dress. It's the polar opposite of that nightgown. Turn around."

I faced Matteo and the sensual energy surrounding him. He stood in front of me silently and used his thumb to coax my mouth open. "I want to fill all your holes, *ariete*."

He tipped the whipped cream canister and sprayed it into my mouth. "Swallow for me, now."

I obeyed, and he stroked his fingers down my throat in time with my movements, gently circling his hand around my neck. I grabbed the back of his neck and pulled his mouth to mine, sharing the lingering sweetness on my tongue with him. We made out for several moments before Matteo pulled away, panting.

"You know, I tried to figure out how to make *mofongo* work in the bedroom."

"You didn't," I laughed.

Matteo looked sheepish. "I did, but it wasn't sexy. We'll stick with the whipped cream and avoid crumbs in bed."

He rubbed my ass and spun me around, bending me over the mattress. I heard him set the canister down on the nightstand and crack open a bottle of water, swishing it in his mouth before he returned and slowly worked the skirt of my dress above my hips.

"Well, isn't this a treat," he declared, fingering the white lace thong I wore underneath before peeling it down my legs. "It's only going to get in my way."

He knelt behind me and tongued my center, making me moan as my legs weakened. The gentle brush of his fingers across the backs of my thighs made me tremble uncontrollably. I laid my head on the covers and closed my eyes, letting the sensation take over. I whimpered when Matteo pulled away, just as I was on the edge of my orgasm.

"Spread your legs for me. I need to be inside you, Macy."

I widened my stance, and he dragged the tip of his cock through my folds, nudging my clit repeatedly. "Take me, Matteo. Make me yours and fill me with your come."

He froze with his dick at my entrance. "Are you sure?"

"Yes," I panted. "Please."

"Fuck, I love you," he groaned as he pressed his hips forward, his length filling and stretching me.

"I love you, too." I wiggled my hips, and his fingers dug into my flesh, holding me against him. "Give it all to me."

Passion replaced words; our mutual cries of pleasure were the only language we needed to speak as we joined as husband and wife. I slipped my hand between my legs and found my clit, applying pressure in time with Matteo's thrusts.

He leaned over my back and growled in my ear, "Come with me, *wife*."

I shattered, spasming around his cock and pulling him into ecstasy with me, feeling the hot pulse of his release. He kissed me on the back of my head and withdrew, wiping me tenderly before helping me undress and walk to the bathroom.

When I wobbled on the way out, Matteo was there to catch me and carry me to the bed. "Are you okay?"

"I'm amazing," I replied, looking up at him. The furrow in his brow smoothed, and he held my hand, kissing my ring finger where his mother's and Abuelita's rings nested together. He wore his father's ring. Representation of the love of generations past as we paved a future together.

I must have drifted off because a loud pop jerked me from my slumber, and I sat straight up in bed in time for Matteo to thrust a champagne flute into my hand before pouring a flute for himself. He stood in nothing but boxer briefs, and I patted the covers next to me as I sat against the headboard, my naked breasts on display.

"Are you ready to count down to midnight?" He asked in a tired voice, taking a lazy perusal of my body and smiling.

"Did you sit up just to ring in the New Year with me?" I mumbled, taking a sip of champagne.

"I did," he admitted, climbing into bed beside me. There was a countdown on the TV on the wall. "I didn't want to miss our first moments together in the new year."

I snuggled close to him, pulling the navy covers up around us. Instead of counting, we gazed into each other's eyes, connecting in a way I would never experience with another person.

"Happy New Year, Macy," Matteo whispered at the stroke of midnight, kissing me deeply, putting all of his feelings for me into mere seconds of contact.

I lifted my glass, and he mimicked me. "Happy New Year, Matteo. To forevermore."

"Forevermore, *ariete*."

Acknowledgements

This book was absolute chaos from my brain, and it almost didn't happen because I was on a tight deadline and life kept happening. You can all thank my husband (and I thank you, too) that this book exists because one day he told me he believed I could do it, so I did. This was my first attempt at a romantic comedy, but I knew that it was perfect for Matteo and Macy's story, and I hope you loved it as much as I enjoyed writing it.

Sarah Crisp—you took Matteo and Macy from my head and made beautiful artwork that I stared at for hours as I wrote because it really allowed me (and the readers) to connect with the characters. Thank you for your talent.

Thank you Alphas and Betas. You were troopers as you powered through this manuscript and waited (sometimes impatiently) for me to add more chapters every day. I'm glad you all forgave me for what I put Matteo through in the end.

Each and every ARC reader who managed to fit this into your holiday schedule—you're all rockstars and I appreciate you so much!

My Heathens. My girls. My friends. I spent an amazing weekend with you all where I couldn't write, and I'm sure you all wondered how I ever managed to publish a book. I returned home recharged from my time with you, and as a result of your constant encouragement, I pumped out something like 3/4 of this book in a week. Murs—your peanut butter yogurt dip became my go-to snack for the duration of this book, and it's now a staple in my house.

Thank you to all of you who have been excited about the books that I write, and those who take the time out of your lives to read what my mind creates, even if it's not dark romance. I am so grateful for all of you.

Julian

"*MIERDA!*"

This was a disaster of epic proportions. I repositioned myself on the plush black leather seat of the town car transporting me to my hotel and watched the skyscrapers slowly pass outside my window. Downtown Chicago was a dreary grey in late October, and the air had a chill I could feel in my bones.

I sighed and re-read the email from Tori, my executive assistant. *Preterm labor.* We were on our final day in Denver for a visit to the Colorado Atabey Industries division when she started to have pains. At 30 weeks pregnant, I wasn't taking any chances and made her go straight to the hospital. I nearly panicked when they whisked her

290

away to Labor & Delivery and wouldn't let me stay with her. Making the call to her husband, Rick tore at my insides, and I put him on the next available flight out of Portland.

I spent hours sitting in the waiting room, helpless. I paced and made calls, clearing my schedule for the day. I wasn't about to leave the woman who had become such a good friend over the five years she had been my right hand. Tori managed to text me a couple of times, but I didn't understand the terms, though I was sure she was trying to reassure me. *Contractions. Terbutaline. Admitting for the night.* I knew next to nothing about pregnancy, but I did know they wouldn't keep her if it wasn't serious.

They finally let me see her after I'd driven the nurse at the desk nearly insane with my constant requests for updates HIPAA privacy policies wouldn't let them give me. She looked tired but normal and reassured me that the doctors had everything under control; the baby was fine, and there was nothing I could do. Then, because I wouldn't take no for an answer, she sent me to the cafeteria to get her a chocolate shake. Rick arrived shortly after, and I left to give them some space.

Unfortunately, I couldn't get out of the conference I was speaking at in Chicago, so I reluctantly left her in Denver while I worried throughout the entire flight back East. On some level, I knew things weren't fine, but I denied those thoughts and hoped she would catch up in a couple of days. The email in front of me confirmed my fears. She was cautiously flying back to Portland, where doctors would put her on strict bed rest for the remainder of her pregnancy.

I ran my hand down my face, loosening my silk tie and undoing the top button of my crisp white cotton shirt. It was too early for alcohol, but I needed a drink. I could do nothing except ensure Tori continued to get full pay and search for a replacement. This was not what I had anticipated. I took several deep breaths, scrolled through my phone contacts to my brother Gabriel's number, and swiped right to dial.

"Hey, Jules, what's up?" he answered on the second ring. His voice was light, overly enthusiastic, considering I had informed him of Tori's trip to the hospital.

"*Estamos jodidos,*" I replied gruffly. I didn't need to be placated. "Tori has been sent home on bed rest, and she won't be back."

"That moves our timeline up," Gabriel replied, his tone turning serious. "She's okay? The baby?"

"She says they're both fine, and he's just as active as ever in there. Apparently too active," I explained.

Gabriel chuckled. "Of course, he's Rick's son."

He wasn't wrong. Tori's husband was in fitness, and even when he was still, it seemed like he was moving. I wasn't sure how the woman kept up with him while also running my life.

"Do you have a shortlist for her replacement?" I redirected, keeping him on topic. My brother was brilliant but had a tendency to distract easily. "I need somebody ASAP. I've got this week booked in Chicago and Minneapolis, but I'll need somebody by next week."

Gabriel was more than reliable. As the Chief Operating Officer of Atabey Industries, he ran the day-to-day operations while I primarily traveled and showed my face wherever necessary. Where people seemed afraid of me, his jovial personality had people jumping to do whatever he asked. He'd always been like that as the youngest of the three of us brothers. A people pleaser, he understood how others worked and used it to his advantage.

"I do." Gabriel let out a frustrated breath, shuffling something at his desk. "I don't know how I'm going to get somebody trained in time for that. Don't expect perfection."

His warning had me running my hand through my hair, mussing the dark, styled waves. I reminded myself that this was an inevitable outcome; it had just come to pass sooner than expected. Tori was always going to leave when the baby arrived, preferring to find a less demanding job so she wouldn't miss his formative years.

"Just get it done. I'll work with whatever you can give me by the time I return. Tori will get you the training materials she's been assembling, and you've got access to my calendar. If the prospects are as good as your headhunter has promised, we shouldn't have a problem." I sounded more confident than I felt. Tori was the first truly competent assistant I'd had in a decade, and I had little faith anyone could adequately replace her.

"I'm on it. I'll start making calls for final interviews now. I'll have somebody in the office by next week to train." His no-nonsense response gave me some relief from the overwhelming stress.

"*Gracias*. I'm pulling up to the hotel, so I'll leave you to it. Have Shannon handle my calls until things get worked out." I looked out the window at the familiar stonework and blue awnings of the Waldorf Astoria.

"On it, bro." I heard Gabriel say before I tapped the screen to end the call.

I was ready to get to my room and settle in. I intentionally arrived a day before the conference, and I was glad Tori had put a "day of rest," as she called it, into my itinerary. I was going to need it to catch up and get things in order. Then I was going to take advantage of the jetted tub and an excellent blue-label scotch.

Deep breaths. *It would work out*; I tried again to convince myself. It didn't help much.

The Frayed Edge

Chase

PARTIES WEREN'T REALLY MY kind of scene. I stood at the back of the reception hall, taking in all the merriment of my friend Julian's wedding to his assistant, Luna. I liked to maintain that I played a pivotal role in their relationship because Julian had been an ass, firing Luna and accusing her of corporate espionage before I stepped in and discovered the truth. Now they were lost in wedded bliss, Julian twirling Luna around the dance floor without a care in the world.

I couldn't help but smile at their happiness, though I could never see myself giving in to matrimony; I enjoyed bachelorhood too much. It was much easier to travel for my job without a wife and kids sitting at home waiting for me. As a corporate fixer, I spent my time cleaning up messes for rich people, which paid very well.

My years in counterintelligence gave me the know-how and the connections to run a very successful business, ferreting out information and covering things up when needed. I'd assembled my team carefully, each one with military experience and just jaded enough to understand that life, in general, was morally grey. We did some things that were definitely unlawful, but I tried my damnedest never to involve or harm an innocent person in the cleaning process.

Raucous laughter drew my attention to the far side of the Victorian-style hall, one with white walls, pillars, and scenes of near debauchery in the wallpaper. I wondered who thought that type of decor was a good idea for weddings, but I supposed the night usually ended in a fairly compromising position for many. The source of the laughter was Julian's little sister, Isabella. She stood with her brothers' significant others, including the bride, motioning as she told some kind of story that made them all double over with laughter.

Isabella grated on my nerves and always had. I wasn't sure whether it was her carefree, nearly flippant attitude or whether our personalities just didn't mesh. She'd always seemed relatively immature to me, but she'd only been just over 18 when I met her for the first time. Barely a woman. Over the years, she'd grown into a beauty that even I couldn't deny.

Her black hair was a wild mane of curls surrounding a face with soft angles and striking hazel eyes that seemed to vary between shades of gold and green. Her tan skin hinted at her Puerto Rican heritage but was unique enough to leave people wondering about her origins. With her exotic looks, she was popular as a model and social media figure; the last I'd heard, she had dipped her toes into the world of fashion design, as well.

She'd worn a red lace gown that dipped low enough to reveal a little cleavage but remained appropriate enough for their Catholic ceremony, tied at the waist with a white ribbon. All the bridesmaids had them on, but the style was particularly striking on Isabella. It was the inverse of the bride's gown and matched the plethora of white and red roses that filled the space. The little gaggle of women looked just like the colorful bouquets as they stood surrounding Luna in her white lace gown.

"What do you think?" The low voice that came from my left belonged to my friend Xander, Julian's older brother. All three brothers owned Atabey Industries, and Xander was the head of the company's legal department. He also happened to be one of my few friends who knew I owned and operated a kink club on the side and moonlighted as a Dom.

"I think you're next." I chuckled, making a joke out of the obvious. His wedding was the following month, so I would fly back to Portland. It seemed like I visited the city all too often, even though I lived just north in Seattle.

"I can't wait." He gave me a rare smile, his stern features lighting up as he spoke about his impending nuptials. "If I could, I would steal her away and make her mine today."

"That woman adores you and has been yours since the first time she stayed at your house." I watched as his fiancée Viola looked over and blushed when she caught Xander gazing at her intently. She was his 24/7 sub, and their dynamic was unique, both in its monogamy and permanency.

"You could have it too, you know." His ribbing didn't faze me. I'd long ago become immune to suggestions about my relationship status. "There's got to be a woman somewhere out there who can put up with all your bullshit."

"Doubtful." I laughed, sticking my hands in the pockets of my blue suit pants. "If such a woman existed, I would have met her by now."

"You never know. I didn't meet Viola until I was 40." Xander crossed his arms and stroked his beard thoughtfully as he watched Viola gyrate on the dance floor with the other women. His brothers were similarly attuned to their women from their various positions around the room. If ever there were just plain good men, it was the Rivera brothers.

"I guess fate has a couple of years left to impress me, then." I wasn't sure if Xander heard my retort because he was already striding over to where his fiancée was attempting some kind of hip-swiveling, ass-shaking dance with Isabella. I shook my head with disapproval, knowing it was likely Isabella who had put Viola up to it. It would be Viola who would have to pay the piper with her flesh later that night, though, if Xander's stormy expression before he'd turned to stalk toward her was any indication.

He pulled Viola into his arms and twirled her away, more gracefully than I would have expected from such a large man. He was close to my height, but his dark skin and brooding looks made him look more intimidating.

Having one less woman to influence, Isabella turned toward the bride, showing her the same questionable movements. With her husband occupied by his mother across the room, I felt the need to put a stop to the behavior. I found myself stalking toward the little group, knocking into a couple and briefly apologizing on the way.

I gave the ladies a disarming smile before grabbing Isabella by the arm, pulling her into an alcove, and releasing her. "What the hell is wrong with you?"

"Me?" She looked incredulous, eyes wide with outrage. "What the *fuck* is wrong with you, Chase?"

"Language, Isabella." I didn't enjoy hearing that word come out of her plump red lips.

"I'll give you language." She put her hands on her hips, hissing the words at me. "Fuck you, Chase."

She spun to leave the alcove, but I reached out and pulled her back. "I'm not letting you go out there and ruin your brother's wedding reception."

"What on earth are you talking about?" She looked genuinely confused at my accusation.

"I wish you could've seen yourself out there, how you moved on the dance floor. Making the others follow you- the bride, twerking at her own wedding. Really, Isabella?" I scoffed and touched the side of my head. "Do you think Julian wants all his friends, family, and business connections to see his wife shaking her ass like that? Do you think your *mother* wants to see that?"

"It wasn't that bad," Isabella insisted, and I realized her eyes were slightly unfocused because she was tipsy.

"How much have you had to drink, anyway?" I leaned in a little to see if I could smell the alcohol on her breath, but all I accomplished was getting a whiff of her floral perfume.

"Not *that* much." She rolled her eyes at me, making my frustration greater. "I'm perfectly able to interact in public."

"You'll forgive me if I don't believe you after what I just witnessed out there." She did not appreciate my sarcasm, as evidenced by the angry flush creeping up Isabella's neck.

"Two glasses of wine. That's all I've had, okay?" She shrugged dejectedly. "I was just trying to have a little fun. It's over now, though; you've killed it."

I almost felt bad—almost. Isabella needed to learn to curb her behavior and feel out her environment when it came down to it, so she acted appropriately. She couldn't rely on her popularity to be forgiven for every mistake she made.

"Bella!" Luna beckoned from somewhere nearby. Before I could say anything else, Bella glared at me and gave an angry little huff before darting out of the alcove.

"Over here!" She called out. I peered around the pillar to see her waving her arm so Luna could find her.

"There you are! It's time for the bouquet toss!" Luna waved her little bouquet, executing a quick bow. "Come get in the group of ladies!"

When she turned and Isabella followed, I stepped out of my hiding place to watch the fiasco that was sure to ensue. I'd seen a few bouquet tosses before, and they usually dissolved into some kind of fight over the flowers for who would get the coveted spot of the next to be wed. I didn't understand why anybody thought that was a worthwhile endeavor.

Strolling to the refreshment area, I stopped and ladled some punch into a cup, sipping on the fruity spiked concoction as the single women assembled into a brightly colored bunch of flowy tulle and lace. It was like watching a train wreck- I didn't want to look, but I couldn't bring myself to walk away as Luna stood with her back turned at the other end of the room and tossed the bouquet of roses backward over her head.

Red and white petals sailed through the air as the women below elbowed and shoved each other, vying for the honor of catching the bouquet. One woman stepped on another's dress, and soon many of them had collapsed into a heap, leaving the flowers to fall squarely in Isabella's arms, where she stood separately at the back of the group. The look of absolute horror on her face as she stared at the bouquet like it was a rabid animal about to attack made me laugh outright.

Her brother's new wife ran over and wrapped her in a celebratory hug, holding up the arm in which Isabella held the bouquet like she was a fight champion. "Bella's the next to be wed!"

Better her than me, I thought to myself.

***

That night I found myself unable to sleep, which wasn't an unknown phenomenon. The air conditioning wasn't made to combat August heat in an otherwise temperate climate. I climbed out of my bed in the guest wing of Xander's house and pulled a pair of shorts on before heading to the kitchen for a late-night snack. Having stayed with my friend countless times, I felt just as at home in the large house as I was in my apartment. As I passed the living room, I heard glass breaking in the kitchen and a muffled curse. I rounded the corner to find Isabella bending down in a skimpy little tank top and shorts, wobbling as she reached to pick up the pieces of the glass she dropped.

"Ow, fuck!" She cursed when one of the shards sliced her finger, and I couldn't stand back and watch. I flipped on the light and carefully stepped around the glass until I reached her side, where I pulled her up and carried her across the kitchen and away from the hazard.

"You really should be more careful, Isabella." She squinted, trying to focus on my face, and I could smell the alcohol on her breath now. Clearly, the two glasses of wine had only been the start of her night. She smelled like she'd bathed in wine and whiskey, and the swaying of her body supported my assumption. "And maybe drink a little less."

"You again?" Isabella said accusingly, finally glaring in my direction. "Do you just follow me around and wait for me to mess up so you can get on my case about it?"

"No, you seem to do well enough in the disaster department on your own," I poked back at her. She shook her hand, and I looked down to see blood dripping onto the tile floor. "You're hurt."

"No shit, Sherlock." Her abrasiveness added to my frustration, and I reached for her hand, gripping her harder when she tried to pull away.

"Just let me help you," I cajoled, putting her hand under the faucet in the sink and turning the cool water on to wash her cut so I could get a better look. "There's no need for you to be prickly all the time."

"Around you, there is," she replied absently, hissing as I added a little soap and gently washed her cut. "That hurts!"

After poking and prodding at her finger, I rinsed it again and turned the water off, grabbing a paper towel and wrapping it tightly around the bleeding digit. "It doesn't look like there's any glass in there, and it's not deep or wide enough to need stitches. Just keep the pressure on it for a few minutes, and you should be fine."

"Thank you, *Doctor* Chase." Isabella rolled her eyes and cradled her hand to her chest as I tiptoed around the glass and opened the cleaning cabinet, pulling out a broom and dustpan to take care of the mess she'd made. It wasn't the first time I'd cleaned up rather than left a mess for Xander's housekeeper, Claudia. "You don't have to do that. Just give me a minute, and I'll be fine."

"I'm not willing to risk you hurting yourself more in your current state." Ignoring her protests, I swept the entire kitchen, gathering all the glass in the dustpan and tossing it in the trash bin. I would have vacuumed just to be thorough, but it was after midnight, and I didn't want to wake anybody.

After putting the cleaning supplies back in their place, I reached into the refrigerator and grabbed a couple of water bottles, twisting the top off of one and handing it to Isabella. She took it from me and drank. My eyes were drawn to her slender neck and the way it rippled as she swallowed the water. Against my wishes, my cock began to swell in my shorts, and I turned, removing the cap from my own bottle of water and drinking the entire thing, hoping the frigid liquid would shrink my dick down.

When I regained control over myself, I tossed the water bottle in the recycling and looked back to see Isabella removing the paper towel and checking out the cut, which looked mostly sealed. Just for good measure, I sorted through the cabinets until I found a first aid kit, pulling a band-aid out and motioning for her to give me her hand.

"This should help protect it while it heals." I wrapped the bandage around her finger carefully, covering the cut to keep it clean.

"Thanks," Isabella murmured, using her other hand to cover a yawn. She was tired and tipping to one side.

"Come on, Bella," I coaxed, turning her and placing a steadying hand on her back as I directed her toward the staircase. "Let's get you back upstairs."

Bella wobbled her way up the staircase, and I helped steady her the rest of the way down the hall to the guest wing, stopping in front of her door. She just leaned against the wall, so I turned the knob and wrapped an arm around her waist, guiding her back to bed and holding her there while I flipped the plush white comforter down. She practically fell onto the sheets when I let her go, so I helped arrange her in the bed in what I thought would be a more comfortable position and tucked her in.

"Chase?" Bella's quiet voice called out in the dark room.

"Yeah?" I stopped at the foot of the bed, looking at where she lay huddled in the covers.

"Don't tell anybody, okay?" She sounded tired, vulnerable, and something about her tone tugged at a place inside that I didn't realize still existed.

"Of course. Get some sleep." I patted her feet through the covers and turned to leave the room.

"Goodnight, Chase," came Bella's breathy reply just before I heard a soft snore.

"Goodnight." I closed the door softly behind me and headed back to my room, not hungry anymore. I wondered what made the vivacious, smart-mouthed woman so concerned about people seeing the side of her that wasn't perfect.

Books By Lyra Blake

The Rivera Brothers
Julian
Gabriel
Xander

The Edge Series
The Frayed Edge
Over The Edge
The Darkest Edge
Crave The Edge

The Saucy Chef Series
Mistletoe and Mofongo

Neretti Mafia
Of Grief And Gratitude – Coming Soon

About The Author

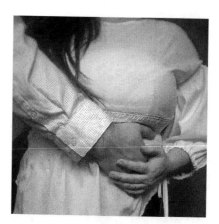

For legal purposes, I must disclose that this bio is being transcribed as Lyra is a little... tied up... doing research for her next novel.

Lyra Blake hails from the PacNW, keeping it weird with her sarcastic wit and gutter mind. She is fueled by caffeine and whiskey—with a dash of chocolate thrown in for good measure. When she's not writing, you can find her spending time with her husband, children, dogs, and cats. You'd never know her if you passed her on the street, but that's just how she rolls.